THE TAILS OF LITTLE FLOWER

LAURA NAPOLI

The Tails of Little Flower

This is a work of fiction. All the characters and events portrayed in this book are fictional, and any resemblance to real people or incidents is purely coincidental.

Cover art by Jessie Marony

https://jessiemarony.com

Images used under license from Shutterstock.com.

First Edition, 2022

Second Edition, 2025

Ebook ISBN: 979-8-9884636-9-6

Print ISBN: 979-8-9884636-8-9

Heating Cats Pawblishing, LLC

https://heatingcats.com

DEDICATION

This book is dedicated to everyone who has ever felt like they never quite fit in. In this grand universe, there is only one of you. Embrace your uniqueness.

A special thanks goes out to everyone who has had to put up with me talking incessantly about my book as this 'tail' was born. Especially those who have taken the time to read through multiple iterations. To my mother, who has read this story nearly as many times as I have, yes, there are changes. Sorry, you're going to have to read it again. But I promise, this time I'm done. Maybe...

With all my love, this story could not have happened without you.

IMPORTANT IN-FUR-MATION

Parents: This series is intended for adult and mature young adult readers due to scenes with both sex and violence. If you're unsure whether this book is suitable for your child, I recommend reading it yourself first.

Detailed trigger warnings and other in-fur-mation can be found on my website at https://heatingcats.com

To my fans: from the bottom of my heart, I thank you! I would love to hear from you. Please consider leaving a review or sending me a message, even if you threw my book in the freezer until the characters learned to calm down. (Yes, that's happened.)

CONTENTS

THE AGENCY

1

JERAN: FIRST CONTACT

Councilor Jeran Chenzira sat anxiously, waiting with the rest of the two thousand members of the Full Council, as they watched the long-range transmission that was displayed on the massive monitors surrounding the council chamber. Their joint delegation had left nearly two months prior, and now finally approached the source of the signal that the Ship's Guild had intercepted nearly a year before. While they'd been unable to decipher the signal, they were clearly not of natural origin, and they were all hoping they'd find another friendly sentient species. It was all Jer could do to maintain the calm demeanor expected of a councilor or keep his tail from twitching in both excitement and nervousness.

The five massive interplanetary ships, containing representatives from all five planets, had spent most of those two long months circling around so that they made their final approach from a direction that did not lead back to any of their home worlds. War might not have existed for millennia, but they weren't taking any chances.

The ships had been built specifically for this mission and were designed to support long-term habitation and observation. If they did find another sentient species, they knew it would take close to a year to determine if it would be safe for them to interact.

Each ship was equipped with the most advanced long-range sensors and medical technology they'd ever created, including stasis chambers for every crew member, which also doubled as escape pods in the event of an emergency, and the same defensive technology used by the Water Sprites to ward off the massive predators on their home world.

Every volunteer member of the five ships knew that this might be a one-way mission. Should the inhabitants of that distant world prove to be a threat, they were prepared to destroy their ships, rather than give a potential enemy information on where their planets were located.

Quiet murmurs ran through the council chamber as they watched the crews of those distant ships make their final approach. Unlike a normal session, the floor had been closed off to outside visitors. And, while the press was in attendance and the session recorded, as was the law, they were not allowed to broadcast until they knew just what they'd found. By unanimous decision, the Council did not want to cause a panic in the general population if it turned out the inhabitants were, in fact, dangerous.

"Ma'am, we have visuals on the planet," a voice said on the monitor.

The Council quieted instantly.

"Long-range scans show one moon and what appears to be a large field of artificial satellites and debris surrounding the planet. Initial estimates show the planet orbits its sun just over three times per standard year, with its day being slightly under half a standard day. Gravitational pull is slightly less than Flyer's, but not enough to be noticeable. I'm also picking up similar signals to the one we intercepted, on multiple frequencies, coming from both the planet's surface and many of the objects surrounding it. Most appear to be retransmitting those signals back down to the planet, but a few are pointed outwards."

"Excellent. Display on screen. Ships, adjust speed and course to maintain this distance," the Senior Ship Master commanded. She was both the commander of her own ship and the Senior in charge of the mission.

"Yes, ma'am," came the immediate reply.

The image on the screen, now several hours old, due to the vast distance and the amount of time it took for the transmission to be relayed back to Jeran's home world, switched to show a tiny blue and white dot, surrounded by a haze of satellites. The image slowly expanded as the ships slowed and adjusted their orbits, eventually taking up the whole screen.

"Are you able to intercept one of those signals?" the Ship Master asked.

"Yes, ma'am," the first voice replied.

"Good. Send that information back to the techs and see if they have any luck translating it. I want a better understanding of the people on this planet before we announce ourselves."

"Ma'am, I'm detecting heat signatures on one of the satellites surrounding the planet," another voice called out.

"On screen."

The image shifted and zoomed in to reveal an odd sprawling structure with seven small heat signatures moving around within. From what Jer could tell, based on the information that displayed on the monitor, the creatures were not much bigger than his young grand cubs.

"So, we have confirmation that they've left their planet, not just placed objects in orbit?" the Ship Master asked.

"Confirmed. I'm picking up indications of an atmosphere similar to that on the planet. Initial analysis indicates that it should be reasonably safe for us to breathe for short visits, but I am picking up high levels of carbon dioxide, methane, nitrous oxide, and a list of other contaminants that will probably make us uncomfortable or sick with any extended exposure," came another voice. "It's also making it hard to get a clear picture of the surface."

"Huh," the Ship Master said, pausing to consider that information. "Pass those scans along to the Healers. Have them confirm that it's safe for us to land, and find out how long it will take to adjust the masks to filter out those contaminants. Have the long-range sensors found anything on the other planets yet? I want to know how far they've explored."

"Yes ma'am, I have confirmation on the fourth planet. No signs of life yet, but I am picking up several drones that are transmitting back to the third," came yet another voice. The image on front changed to show a small robotic drone slowly making its way across the sands of the fourth planet.

"Confirmation on the moon as well," came another voice. "The moon appears to be tidally locked, and I've found what appear to be several artificial structures on the side facing the planet, but no heat signatures." The image changed again to rotate through several scenes.

"Go back to that last one," the Ship Master ordered.

The image flicked back to show a craft or structure of some sort, and what looked like tracks leading away from it.

"Are those tracks from a drone or a creature?" she asked.

"It's not regular enough to be a drone. Based on the gravitational pull of the moon, the computers say that there's a ninety-three percent chance of it being from the same creatures on that orbital station."

"So, we have the strong possibility that they've landed on their moon, not just sent drones. That's encouraging. Do we have visuals on the surface of the planet yet?"

"Negative. I'm still trying to filter out the interference from their atmosphere," the prior voice responded. "I should have something in a few minutes."

Suddenly, an alarm blared on one of the side monitors.

"Report!" the Ship Master bellowed.

"Ma'am." There was the sound of a deep intake of breath before the speaker continued in a voice shaking with emotion. "Ma'am, I have a rather large asteroid on long-range scanners. The computers are warning of a potential impact with the planet."

Councilors around Jer gasped, and his own tail poofed out in instant fear for the inhabitants of that distant world. Even the five members of the normally stoic Senior Council looked worried.

"On screen," the Ship Master commanded.

The image in front shifted away from the planet and zoomed in to show the slowly tumbling asteroid. It looked deceptively small on the screen, but the readouts showed just how massive it was. This was no mere asteroid. *This* was a planet destroyer.

"Display projected course," the Ship Master ordered.

The image changed again to show the planet, asteroid, and the asteroid's projected path, along with a color-coded degree of error. When the screen changed again, there was no denying the unavoidable truth. The asteroid was going to hit, and there would be devastating consequences.

"How long before impact?" the Ship Master asked, her voice steady but soft and tinged with sorrow.

"Twenty-three minutes and fourteen seconds," came the reply a few moments later.

"Probability of survival after impact?" she asked.

The councilors all held their breath while they waited for the answer. It was so quiet in the council chamber that you could have heard a whisker twitch.

"Assuming a direct impact, the probability of immediate survival is .0001 percent on the far side of the planet. Long-term survivability is essentially none," the tech replied.

"Plot an intercept course with the planet, emergency jump. In five minutes, I want to know if there's any way we can deflect or destroy that asteroid, and if not, if a rescue mission is possible. I want to know how long it will take to get to the planet, how long we'll have to perform a rescue mission, and the areas with the greatest probability for survivors."

The edges of the screen shifted and blurred as the ship shifted into jump. The Council broke into an immediate uproar, all protocol ignored as questions were shouted across the floor.

Jeran sat and thought frantically as many of his colleagues argued, tails lashing, and in many cases, like his, sticking straight out in fear. Even the Diggers, a species not normally known for their emotional responses, were reacting, and he saw that several were struggling with their instinctive response to curl up and hide in their shells. Most of the Water Sprites were tinged in white, including Senior Councilor Clear Seas, although he quickly regained control of his emotions.

"What are we going to do with the survivors?" yelled a councilor.

"How are we going to keep everyone else safe? We don't know what kind of pathogens they carry," yelled another.

"What about the first contact protocols?"

"There isn't time to worry about protocols, you idiot!" someone shouted back.

"QUIET!" Senior Councilor Tabor roared.

The room fell silent immediately, as they all turned their attention to her.

"I want everyone to sit down and shut up. We don't even know if anything will be left for us to rescue. Let's wait for the Ship Master's report. We'll worry about what to do when, and *if*, they actually manage to pull off a rescue. It will take more than three days at maximum emergency jump to make it back here, giving us time to prepare for the casualties."

Grumbles came from the Council, but everyone sat down and waited as ordered. It was one of the longest five minutes of Jer's life.

"Report! Can we deflect or destroy the asteroid?" the Ship Master asked, exactly five minutes later.

The side displays now showed the Ship Masters of the four other ships, while the main screen remained focused on the asteroid and its projected trajectory. A countdown to impact flashed in the lower corner. Every second ticked a deep gouge on Jer's soul, and he knew he'd never see a timer the same way again.

"Negative. Even at emergency jump, we won't make it in time," one of the pilots replied.

"Is there a possibility of a rescue mission?" she asked next.

"Yes, ma'am. The current models project that the asteroid will hit here, just offshore of this southern continent. Based on the size of the asteroid, we project the likeliest place for survivors to be on the other side of the planet here."

The main screen changed to show several highlighted locations.

"These four zones are the areas least likely to be impacted by the crossing shock waves. The chance of survival is minimal, but not zero. These two zones are also possible, but they appear to be in major cities. While we might be able to rescue more individuals there, the damage incurred by the shockwaves would make rescue significantly more challenging and dangerous, as it would increase the risk of retaliation. If the inhabitants believe we are the cause of their planet's destruction, they might fight back, and we have no idea what kind of weapons they might have. This northern zone, here, is the only one we think will be safe for the Water Sprites to exit their craft due to the protection of the glaciers, which will both provide protection from falling debris and keep the nearby waters cool enough."

"How much time will we have once we arrive?" the Ship Master asked next.

"Two to four hours, depending on location. By the time we arrive, the asteroid will have already hit, and the first of the shockwaves will have made its way around the planet. Our shields should be able to withstand reentry, but it'll be a very bumpy ride. The biggest problem we're going to have is falling ash and debris thrown up into the atmosphere by the impact, and any volcanic eruptions that are triggered afterwards. We should be able to deflect most of it, but anyone outside of the ships will be at considerable risk and will most likely have to be treated for smoke and ash inhalation, burns, and, quite likely, radiation poisoning by the time we're done, even with the masks. We project these two areas will likely be hit by a tsunami about two hours after we arrive, so the initial rescue should focus there and get out. We'll have another hour, maybe an hour and a half, before the temperature and radiation exposure will be lethal on land, at least for us. We have no idea what it will do to the local inhabitants. This location here, being both under ice and water, might have another hour, but exiting the planet will be far more challenging. At that point, the shields might not be able to deflect all of the ash and other objects thrown into orbit from the impact. After that, we expect the water temperature will be far too high for the Water Sprites to exit their ship safely."

"That doesn't leave us long to locate and rescue survivors," the Ship Master stated with a heavy sigh. "This will be an extremely risky mission. Do we have any objections to moving forward?" When none were raised, she nodded her respect and continued. "Good. I expect that communication will be difficult once we begin our descent. Ship Masters, I'll leave it up to you to decide when it's time to leave. Do *not* be heroes. Better to rescue those we can locate and rescue quickly and easily, than lose everyone by taking unnecessary risks. Make sure you do your best to gather flora as well as fauna, especially anything that appears to be a food source for the primary species. We'll need to know what these creatures eat."

"Yes, ma'am," came the simultaneous replies from the four other Ship Masters.

"Have we been able to break through the interference of their atmosphere to obtain visuals on the primary species yet?"

"Yes, ma'am. We believe it is this tiny biped here. They match the heat signature of those in the orbital station, and appear to be the primary inhabitants of the various cities." An image appeared showing a mostly furless creature with striped tan skin walking near a large body of water. Some sort of multi-colored garment appeared to be covering its head and lower torso.

"Good. Focus on this species, but rescue anything you can safely catch. We don't have time for first contact protocols, or to even try to convince them we're there to rescue them. Stun anything that moves. We'll deal with the consequences later. What of the creatures in the orbital station?"

"We believe they will survive the initial impact, since their station will be on the far side of the planet, but it will likely be hit by debris before we can rescue them. I'm not detecting shields of any kind, although there does appear to be a small escape pod. Chances are not good for their survival," the lead scientist stated.

"Understood. We'll focus on the planet's surface first. If they should survive in the orbital craft, we'll pick them up on our way out. Anything else we need to know?"

"No, ma'am."

"Good. Whatever happens, I'm proud of you, and it's been an honor serving with you all. May the Ancient Gods bring us luck!"

Senior Councilor Tabor lowered the volume on the monitors as the Ship Master prepared for the rescue. "At this point, they'll have already begun the rescue attempt. Let's assume that they're successful and that we will have badly injured casualties of many unknown species on our paws in approximately three days' time. Suggestions on where to care for them?"

Jeran hit the button on his desk that indicated his desire to speak.

"Councilor Chenzira. You were first. Go ahead," Tabor instructed.

Jeran stood, the mic on his desk already activated by the program used to control the session. "Ma'am. As many of you know, I am from the South District, a sparsely populated area due to the intense summer heat that turns the area into a desert for several months of the year. My partner, Master Healer Myra Chenzira, runs a small clinic about twenty-five leagues from our home. It's centrally located for the few dozen families in the immediate area, but nowhere near any major towns or cities. I recommend that we expand the clinic with quarantine habitats and bring the survivors there."

"What about any water species that are rescued? How are we going to care for them in the desert?" one of the other councilors asked out of turn. It was a valid question, so the Senior Councilor allowed it.

"The clinic sits above a large aquifer, so there should be plenty of water to support those species, and I imagine we should probably build holding tanks to keep the water species separate and away from our main water sources anyway," Jer replied. "We'll need to be careful of introducing what could become an invasive species to any environment. Plus, we don't even know if they will be able to survive in our oceans. If it's safe for the Water Sprites to exit, probably not. We may need to transport them to one of the other planets."

"Agreed," Tabor stated, flexing her whiskers forward in approval. "Does anyone have any objections to Councilor Chenzira's suggestion?"

Councilor Paxton Parner buzzed in. "I do. Why can't we keep them onboard the ships in orbit? Then there won't be any risk to our people?"

Tabor looked over at Parner with an expression that clearly indicated she thought he was stupid. It was all Jer could do to keep from bursting out laughing before the Senior Councilor recovered her composure and explained with the same exasperated tone of voice that one used with an unruly cub. "The ships do not have the resources or staff to care for mass casualties for any length of time. But you do bring up a good point. The crew of those ships should be quarantined as well. They can help care for the casualties once they arrive."

Tabor looked down at her control panel for the next person to speak.

"But why here and not one of the *other* worlds?" Parner asked again, out of turn this time.

"Because *our* world is the closest to theirs, and if any of them are going to survive, they will need care as soon as possible. Even at emergency jump, the delay in reaching another planet would be deadly," Tabor answered, frowning her displeasure at Parner for asking out of turn, then indicated that he should take his seat.

"Any other objections?" she asked. There were none. "Good. Mark your votes." When the votes were displayed, only Councilor Parner objected. "Councilor Chenzira, please contact your partner and begin arrangements for quarantine. Whatever she needs, this Council authorizes."

"Yes, ma'am," he replied. Raising the privacy shield around his desk, he placed the call to his partner while trying to figure out how under the three moons he was going to explain this to her.

"Hey Jer. What's up? I wasn't expecting to hear from you for at least another couple of hours. Did the first contact go well?" Myra asked when she came on the line.

"Not even remotely," he said, and then quickly filled her in on what was happening.

"Dark moons!" she said, putting a paw over her mouth in horror. "How can I help? I'm assuming that's why you called."

"I was hoping you would say that," he said with a wry smile.

"You were?" she asked, squinting at him with suspicion. "Why? What did you get me into, *this* time?"

"I sort of...well...I sort of volunteered your clinic to care for the casualties when they arrive," he explained, and braced for her reaction. She did not disappoint.

"You did what?!" she asked incredulously, blinking in shock at the absolute outrageousness of his actions. "Jer, how am *I* supposed to care for five ships' worth of some unknown species in my tiny clinic? There are only three healers here, and that's including myself, and the other two are only journeymen."

"I know that, Myra, but we needed an isolated location for quarantining the survivors, and well, I figured your clinic was about as remote as it gets on this planet. The Council has already authorized and prioritized anything and everything you need. You'll also have the crew of the five ships to help, as well as any volunteers, which I imagine there will be plenty of, once the word gets out."

Myra leaned back in her seat; her face devoid of all emotion.

"Speak to me, Myra," Jeran said, worried that she was mad at him. This was a massive undertaking that he'd volunteered her for, and she was far too good at hiding her emotions behind her healer's mask.

"I'm *thinking*. Give me a second," Myra snapped, pinning her ears back in annoyance at his interruption.

He wisely kept his mouth shut and let her think.

Finally, her ears flicked forward, and her attention returned to the screen. "Okay...I'll contact the Healers Guild and start implementing quarantine protocols. I'll need you to transfer the three patients I have here to Sand Dune for care, and someone is going to have to pick up Marsee from her classes at the Guild, since I imagine neither of us is going to make it home tonight. I'll need specifics, as soon as you have them, on the number of casualties, along with whatever medical scans they take. Oh, and I'll need to speak to the healers on board the ships as soon as it is even remotely possible. I'll call you back when I know more," she said, and hung up without saying goodbye.

He stared at his blank screen for several seconds, blinking at the abrupt ending to the call, and then smiled. His partner, and the love of his life, was the epitome of a true healer. She immediately focused on the needs of her patients, no matter how impossible the situation.

He texted Marsee, his youngest cub, asking her to see if she could beg a ride home from the neighbors, and possibly spend the night. Next, he called the Sand Dune Trauma Center to have transports sent out to Myra's clinic for patient pickup. He was transferred three times before he was finally able to speak to the Senior Healer and have the transports authorized. Once that was done, he placed a call to Command.

"We're a little busy here at the moment. This had better be an emergency," came the gruff reply on the screen.

Jeran flicked his ears back in surprise at the unexpectedly rude comment. He wasn't sure who he was speaking with, as the person was off-screen, but *no one* spoke that way to anyone on the Council, and whoever this was would have known full well who he was.

The scene on the screen in front of him was barely organized chaos. From the sounds of things, the ground crews supporting the five ships were scrambling to prepare and launch another rescue mission, in case any of the other ships were damaged during the rescue effort and unable to return.

On the off chance that this person hadn't actually looked to see who was calling before answering, Jer introduced himself. "It is. I'm Councilor Jeran Chenzira of the South District. The Council has chosen my partner's clinic as the landing site and quarantine location for the casualties. I'm calling to help coordinate those efforts."

Senior Commander Oscar Rynhold appeared on the screen moments later. As the Senior for the Ship's Guild, Rynhold was one of the few with the authority and rank to have spoken so harshly to a member of the Council. Even still, Rynhold shifted his posture to one of deference and respect.

"Forgiveness, Councilor. The last three calls I've had have all been from the press looking for information I don't have, or the time to tell them. Tell your partner, thank you." He leaned off-screen and bellowed. "Sampson!"

"Sir?" someone replied.

"Get over here!" Rynhold growled.

"Sir!"

A moment later, Sampson appeared. "Sampson, this is Councilor Chenzira. His partner is leading the quarantine effort. Whatever he or his partner says they need, make it happen."

"Yes, sir," Sampson replied.

Rynhold turned and left without a further word, bellowing commands to several others as he left.

"How can I help you, Councilor?" Sampson asked calmly.

Jeran blinked and refocused his attention back on Sampson. "I'm sending you my partner's contact information and the location of her clinic, which we've designated as the site for the quarantine facilities. She's requested whatever information you have on casualties as soon as you have it, and to be connected with the healers on board as soon as that's possible. She'll have more information and requests by now, I'm sure," he replied, and sent the information over.

"Understood. I'll contact her right away. Anything else?" Sampson asked.

"No. Thank you," Jer replied, and Sampson hung up just as quickly as Myra had.

Jeran lowered his privacy screen and refocused his attention on the main screens in the council chamber, only a matter of moments before the asteroid struck. A silent but massive explosion and plume of debris billowed out from the side of the planet, causing a visible shock wave that raced around the planet, destroying everything in its path.

The Council was silent as they bore witness to the annihilation of what was only the sixth known world in the universe with a potentially sentient species.

It was a sight he knew would haunt his dreams for the rest of his life.

2

JESSICA: WORLD'S END

essica O'Neil slammed her locker shut, following it up with a kick to the bottom of the ancient and dented door, as it never shut the first time. Today was no exception. It took her three tries to get it to shut enough to lock. With an exhausted yawn, she heaved her father's old army rucksack, practically overflowing with textbooks and art supplies, onto her shoulder and started slowly trudging her weary way up to her first class of the day.

She was positively dreading the next hour and the Spanish test that awaited her, and she hadn't slept well the night before because of it. The hall was crowded with her classmates, and she had to weave her way around clumps of people chatting and milling about in their small cliques.

"Jess! Wait up!"

She turned to see her best friend running down the hall to catch up with her. Susie's pigtails bounced as she ran. Jessica grinned when she saw her friend's outfit for the day. As she often did, Susie was wearing a goth-style outfit, loosely based on her favorite television show, NCIS, and her signature black army boots. Her friend was ridiculously smart and had already started taking several classes at the local community college, as it was her dream to go into forensic sciences when she graduated, just like her favorite character on that show.

It amazed Jessica every day that someone as smart and as popular as Susie was her best friend. If she were being honest with herself, Susie was her *only* friend.

Several years before, Jessica's family had moved back to the small, podunk town in the middle of absolutely nowhere, where her father had grown up. She loathed it here. The nearest art store was an hour's drive away, which she could never get her parents to make, and everyone thought she was weird; everyone, that is, except for Susie.

Susie had latched onto her on Jessica's first day of school, when she found Jessica sitting alone in the otherwise packed cafeteria, and decreed then and there that they were now best friends. Jessica had snorted and muttered something about not realizing she'd ended up in Green Gables, which had made Susie roar with laughter, and they'd spent the rest of their brief lunch discussing their favorite TV shows and movies. True to her word, they'd been best friends ever since.

They couldn't have been bigger opposites either, but somehow that just worked. Susie was an extrovert to Jessica's introverted nature. Susie could learn anything with little effort, while Jessica struggled with all of her classes except for art. Susie could make even the strangest clothing choices look like the latest fashion, while her style, or lack thereof, was third-hand, hand-me-down farm clothes that were always too big, stained, patched, or worn out, and did nothing to help with the short, flat, boyish frame that Jessica felt she'd been cursed with.

Her family had little extra to spare on the latest clothing styles, and most of what she owned came from her older male cousins. This added to the effect that made her classmates think she was weird. She couldn't even work to raise extra money, because her parents expected her to work in the family bakery after school.

Thankfully, Susie shared everything with her and had even helped to dye her hair the week before, as there was no way she could ever hope to afford a professional hair coloring.

That they shared the same first period was the only thing that made her Spanish class even remotely bearable, or school, or life, for that matter. They were required to take two years of a foreign language to graduate, and she had made the horrible mistake of picking Spanish, as she planned to return to the city after she graduated and had been somewhat fluent before, or so she'd thought. She'd barely passed the first year and, in all honesty, she would have failed if it hadn't been for Susie's infinite patience and tutoring.

"So, did you ask your dad if you could come to the fair with us this weekend?" Susie asked when she finally made her way through the crowd and caught up with her.

Jessica rolled her eyes in annoyance. "Yeah. He said *'maybe'*."

"Maybe?! What kind of answer is that?" Susie asked, incredulously.

"He said it all depends on whether or not Grampa Ben and Uncle James need our help with the apple harvest this weekend, *and* whether or not I do well on the Spanish test today. He says I have to at least get a B, which means I have a better chance of waking up on the moon tomorrow. I'll be surprised if I even pass," Jessica replied woefully.

"Ugh! That's totally unfair! He knows how hard you've been studying. That should count for *something* at least," Susie commiserated. Her friend had been over every night for the past week, trying to help her prepare.

"You'd think, but you know I don't do well with tests, no matter how hard I study," Jessica replied.

She worked her way past a large group of cheerleaders who were taking up most of the hall while they practiced for the upcoming homecoming game. *They're far too preppy and bouncy for this early in the morning,* Jessica thought as she squeezed past and tried to stifle another yawn, failing miserably.

"I don't get it. You're amazing when we study together," her friend said when she made it through the crowd as well.

"Yeah, if my grades were entirely based on class participation and verbal, I'd be fine. Tests, though, the words might as well be Klingon." Jessica frowned as she glanced at her watch. "Well, we'd better hurry or we're going to be late for class, and then I'll *never* stand a chance of passing. You know how Ms. Walters is when we're late."

They took off running down the long hallway and up the ancient and wooden flight of stairs to their second-floor classroom. "No running in the halls!" one of the teachers yelled as they flew past, but they only slowed until they were out of sight, then took off again, laughing.

The equally ancient bell began clanging the start of the school day just as they skidded into their classroom. Hurrying towards their customary place at the back of the room, Jessica slumped into her seat by the window and let her backpack hit the floor with a heavy thud.

Rubbing her ear as the bell continued to ring, Jessica muttered, "I'm pretty sure that bell is the reason my dad is deaf in one ear."

"What did you say? I can't hear you over the bell," Susie asked with an innocent expression, and cupped her ear.

"I *said*..." Jessica replied, and they both burst out laughing.

"Settle down, class," Ms. Walters ordered, once the bell finally stopped clanging, and they could actually hear again. "Now, are there any questions before I hand out the exam?"

"Can we have the answers?" piped up her classmate, Joey, causing the whole class to erupt into laughter.

"Um...let me think about that for a second." Her teacher paused dramatically, tapping her index finger on her lips as if actually thinking about it. "Hmm...No."

The class responded with a chorus of disappointed groans. Although no one actually expected her to say yes. *Miracles could happen,* Jessica supposed.

"Do bees have knees?" another one of her classmates called out, causing the class to erupt into laughter again.

"Not a clue, Mark. You'll have to ask your biology teacher. Any Spanish questions, pertaining to the material we've covered, the material on the exam, Kuzco's Spanish exam?" their teacher qualified. They'd watched the Spanish version of The Emperor's New Groove the first day of class as a refresher and had been referencing it ever since.

"Oh, you mean *that* exam?" the entire class said in unison, to which even their teacher chuckled. But when there weren't any actual Spanish questions, she walked over and picked up a massive stack of papers on her desk. Counting out a smaller stack, she handed it off to the person in the front of each row.

"You have the entire class to complete the test. If you have any *real* questions pertaining to the exam, raise your hand or come up to my desk."

Jessica took the thick stack of papers handed to her and double-checked to make sure that there was only one.

There is no way I am going to be able to get through all of this in an hour, and absolutely no way I'm going to the fair with Susie this weekend, she thought.

With a pained sigh, she put her name on the top and read the first question. Twenty minutes into the exam, she gave up. She'd barely made it through the second page when her test-taking anxiety, or whatever it was, kicked in, and she couldn't even see the words properly anymore. They just jumped around the page, not staying in focus, and the letters often flipped around on her. It happened every time, and no matter how hard she studied or what the topic was, she always struggled with the tests.

She'd tried talking to her parents about it, but they thought she was making excuses for her bad grades, since she had no problems reading for fun, and without their approval, she couldn't get tested for a learning disability. She'd tried several times anyway, and had spent countless hours doing her own research on the computers in the school library, trying to find a solution, but nothing she ever looked up fit quite right, and so far, nothing had ever really helped. Once or twice, she'd been able to get the teachers to read the tests to her, and those she'd had no problems with, but most wouldn't take the time without the proper diagnosis or the required paperwork.

She flipped the test over and started drawing to pass the time and calm her frustration. *Maybe if Ms. Walters likes my drawing, she'll feel pity for me, and not fail me completely,* she thought glumly.

She began to sketch a picture of her failing her exam, desk poised over a trap door, with Ms. Walters dressed as Kronk standing in front of a pair of levers.

Pull the lever, she thought, wishing it would be that easy to get out of failing her test.

A few minutes later, she had a rough sketch and glanced up to peer out the window for a moment as she considered what else to add to her drawing. It was a beautiful late September day, with the bluest of blue skies and sunny, with just a few fluffy white clouds off in the distance. The giant maple trees in front of the school were starting to turn, their green leaves accented with a smattering of oranges and red. Smiling at the beautiful scene, she returned to her sketch.

She loved to draw and wished everything came as easily to her as drawing did. Her dream was to illustrate children's books, but her father didn't think that would pay enough to live on, assuming she even found a job with her abysmal grades.

He wanted her to go into business school like he had, after he'd left the military, and she wasn't even going to think about how much she detested that idea. Still, no matter how much she argued with him, her father insisted that being her own boss was the only way she would make it in the world. If she wanted to do something related to art, he believed she should run an art gallery or store.

She swore under her breath as her pencil snapped and reached into her bag to grab her sharpener. She was digging through the large pocket where she usually kept it when she heard what sounded like a large truck using its air brakes. The vibration caused her pencil to roll off the desk and partly under the desk in front of her. She tried reaching for it with her foot, but it was too far away. So, she crawled under her desk to retrieve it, hoping that her teacher wouldn't assume she was cheating.

I'd do better if I did, Jessica thought with a snort.

"What the hell?!" she heard Susie exclaim.

Thoroughly shocked, because Susie never swore, and certainly not in the middle of an exam, Jessica looked up to see her friend staring out the window with a look of absolute horror on her face. That was the last thing Jessica saw as the world exploded around her.

Jessica woke slowly. A heavy weight on her back pressed her firmly to the ground, making it difficult for her to breathe. Her entire body throbbed in pain, especially her left arm and the side of her head, and her vision swam in and out of focus.

Blinking furiously, she was finally able to focus on what turned out to be a black boot in front of her. She attempted to sit up, but the dull throbbing pain in her arm exploded as she pushed up against the weight of whatever was on her back. Screaming, she collapsed back to the ground and lay there whimpering until the pain eased.

As she lay there panting, it slowly dawned on her that she couldn't hear anything but a high-pitched ringing noise, not even the sounds of her own screams. Freeing her uninjured hand from the rubble around her, she brought it up to her ear and felt something warm and sticky.

It took her several moments to refocus her vision on her hand and see that it was covered in a film of gray dust—all except for the globs of bright red on her fingertips. It took her several additional moments for her throbbing brain to realize that it was blood—her blood.

Whimpering in fear, she tried to sit up again, careful this time to only push with her good arm. The heavy object on her back shifted to the side, just enough to allow her to take a slightly deeper breath. Pushing again, with a scream she couldn't hear, the object slid off to one side, and she was finally able to sit up.

Pain radiated along her side with every gasping breath she tried to take, and her head spun, making it difficult to remain sitting up. Darkness clouded the edges of her vision and threatened to pull her under.

She focused on her breathing, trying to calm her panic and control the pain. Finally, when she was sure she wasn't going to pass out, she lifted her head and looked around her, but it took her a long time to make sense of what she saw.

Her school had been flattened, and it almost looked like it had been shoved over. The roof and most of the walls were gone, and it looked like her floor had collapsed onto the floor below, because she was now only a few feet above the ground and surrounded by crumbled brick, shattered glass, and the broken remains of the wooden window frame.

She turned to look behind her and found the mangled remains of her metal school desk, with a large pile of bricks next to it. As her vision slowly focused out past the school, she realized it wasn't just her school that had been destroyed. All of the nearby buildings and trees had been flattened as well.

What the hell indeed, she thought, remembering what Susie had said. "Susie!"

Struggling to her feet, she looked around in panic. "Susie, where are you?"

Not being able to hear her own voice, along with her inability to stay focused, gave everything an eerie, dreamlike quality. Only the throbbing, sickening pain told her she was awake.

Spotting the boot again, she started to dig with her uninjured hand. She wasn't sure how long it took for her to uncover her friend, but when she did, she howled in horror and grief at the extent of her friend's injuries.

Susie had been injured so badly that she barely recognized her friend. If it hadn't been for the outfit, she wouldn't have been sure it was Susie at all. Still, she checked desperately for a pulse. When she found none, she turned and stumbled away with a cry, tears streaming unchecked down her dust-covered and bloody face.

Somehow, she made it safely down the shifting rubble and out onto the street below. She started walking in a random direction, her mind completely lost in a daze of grief and pain. She paid no attention to where she was going until she tripped and fell hard over some debris.

The pain in her arm exploded as she tried to catch herself, and it pulled her out of her grief with a howl. She lay there rolling in the middle of the street, screaming for what felt like forever, before the agony subsided enough that she was able to, once again, struggle back to her feet.

Okay Jessica. What do we do now? she asked herself as she slowly spun, trying to figure out where she was.

Every building she could see had been leveled, and her small town looked completely unfamiliar. Most of the buildings were on fire, thick plumes of black smoke rising from the rubble. The streets were littered with debris, crushed and overturned cars, the crumbled remains of buildings, and a tangled mess of downed power lines and trees.

The pavement at her feet was ragged and torn. A piece of broken asphalt had tripped her up. As if to explain how that had occurred, the ground shook. She struggled to keep her balance as the earth bucked and heaved beneath her.

Did an earthquake really cause all this damage? she wondered. It didn't make sense. Earthquakes large enough to feel were uncommon in this part of the world, and even when they did occur, they rarely caused any damage. None of the videos she'd ever seen of earthquake damage even remotely came close to the devastation she was seeing before her.

No, something else must have happened, she decided.

Heavy, thick ash started falling silently from the sky, making her cough. She looked up at the now cloud-covered and darkening sky and frowned.

Volcano? she wondered, trying to remember if there were any in the area.

She pulled her shirt up over her nose and mouth to filter out the ash, not even noticing that her clothing was just as filthy. Nor did she notice as a piece of still-burning ember landed on her shoulder and burned her skin before fizzling out.

What happened? she wondered yet again, *a bomb?*

She'd seen footage of the Beirut explosion during her history class the year before, but this seemed so much bigger, and where was everyone? Surely, she couldn't be the only one left alive.

Who knows how much damage a modern nuclear weapon could do, or several, she thought, deciding that had to be what had happened. Nothing else seemed remotely big enough.

That decided, she struggled to figure out what to do next. When her eyes took in the downed and shredded trees in front of her, she realized that they had all fallen in the same direction.

Okay, so if they are all lying that way, then that must mean the blast, or whatever it was, came from the other way, which means I need to keep going this way if I'm going to find help.

She tried not to think about what had happened to her family. They would have been at work in her mother's bakery. If she was where she thought she was, that was in the direction the blast had come from.

Worrying won't help you now, Jessica, and if they're okay, they'll go in the same direction looking for you.

With that somewhat nebulous thought, she set off down the street, taking far more care now as she picked her way through the rubble.

She'd been walking for what felt like forever, but she'd barely made it a few blocks when she stopped to rest and pick out a safe path. There was so much debris to work around, and her vision continued to go in and out of focus. She'd thrown up twice from the pain in her head and arm, and that had caused her to whimper and gasp from the sharp throbbing pain in her side.

She was pretty sure she had a broken rib or three, along with her broken arm, and probably a concussion. The second time she'd thrown up, it had taken her several minutes to stand up again. She couldn't tell if the ground was shaking or if it was just her, and she couldn't feel her arm below her elbow or wiggle her fingers anymore, and that scared her more than she cared to admit, especially since it was her dominant hand. Path decided, she continued on.

When a large triangular shadow, obscured by the thick ash and smoke, slowly passed overhead, she stopped and waved, hoping it was someone looking for survivors. She couldn't tell what it was. It seemed far too big to be a helicopter, but it moved too slowly to be a plane. When she lost sight of it, she shrugged and kept shuffling forward. Whatever it was, it was heading in the same direction she was.

A few moments later, she realized she'd finally made it to the main intersection in town, obvious by the massive jumble of wires and traffic lights on the ground. There was only one set of lights in her rural town, so she at least knew where she was for sure now.

I never knew these things were so big, she thought, standing next to one that was nearly as tall as she was, and trying to catch her breath, which was becoming harder every minute, both from the smoke and ash, and from the sharp pain in her side.

She peered down the side streets, trying to see if there was an easier way to travel, but she couldn't see more than twenty feet past the intersection, in any direction. Ash and smoke completely obscured her view now, and everything had turned the same uniform shade of gray.

Wait! What is that? Is there something moving over there?

She squinted, trying to make out what it was, wondering if it was another survivor. As she stood there and watched, the shadow grew larger until suddenly running towards her was the biggest cat she'd ever seen, covered in tawny fur that was quickly turning gray with ash. Before she could even begin to figure out where to run, she watched in surprise as the cat suddenly stopped, stood on its back feet, and loomed above her.

How hard did you hit your head, Jessica? she thought, unable to process what she was seeing.

She stood there, mouth open in shock as it walked towards her on two feet, removed something from a harness it was wearing, and pointed it in her direction.

She had just enough time to think '*gun!*', spin around, and take one step in the opposite direction, before she felt something hit her in the back. Pain exploded through her, and she crumpled to the ground, darkness enveloping her before she had even finished falling.

3

JAMES: DRAGON FIRE

James woke secure in the arms of his partner, Benjamin Frank O'Neil, with the early morning sunlight streaming through the open window of their ancient farmhouse. The sun was reflecting off the water in the large crystal vase of flowers Ben had picked the day before. Gentle ripples of sunlight and rainbows danced on the walls, accompanied by the sway of the curtains in the light breeze coming through the open window. Wind chimes tinkled from the porch below, a gift from one of Ben's grandchildren. It looked to be an absolutely perfect morning. One of the few remaining before the cold of winter would set in.

He glanced over at the alarm clock on the bedside table and grinned. It had been a long time since they'd slept in this late. Neither of them had anywhere they needed to be this morning, and they'd been up late the night before, talking, among other things.

He was on a much-needed vacation from the stress of his veterinary practice, under the excuse that he was helping Ben with the fall harvest. But in reality, he was burnt out from close to forty years as a large animal vet, and he was seriously considering retiring and handing his practice off to one of his younger employees. He was getting too old to deal with his clients' unruly animals, and still had a large bruise from where he'd been kicked almost a month before. He'd been lucky and hadn't broken anything that time, but injuries took much longer to heal than they used to.

Ben was usually up early to feed the animals on their farm, and judging by the sounds coming from the direction of the barn, their old draft horse, Buster, was not particularly pleased by his late breakfast.

"I suppose I'd better go feed that old brute before he knocks the barn down," Ben said from behind him, but James didn't move.

James snuggled into Ben's strong arms and would have purred if he'd been a cat. Mornings like this were rare, and half the reason he wanted to quit. He didn't get to spend nearly enough time with his family. They lay there, content in each other's arms for several minutes before Ben sighed, kissed him, and climbed out of bed.

"You might be on vacation, but there's still work to be done. Come on," Ben said.

James chuckled and rolled over to look at his partner, arms laced behind his head. "Well, we could hire someone to come work on the farm so we could lie about all morning. Neither of us is getting any younger."

Ben snorted. "No point in paying someone else what we can do for free."

"You know, I'm half beginning to think you married me just for the free help and veterinary care," James said with a mock glare.

Ben chuckled. "The thought may have crossed my mind a time or two. However, you eat more than Buster, so economically it's a wash. Now come on. If you help me with the chores, there will be just enough time for you to take that naughty horse of mine out for a ride before we start picking."

James grinned wickedly. "Shall I grab the crop on the way back from the barn then? I didn't realize you were into that kind of thing."

Ben rolled his eyes, but they twinkled in amusement. "Well, you've never asked, but I was referring to Buster. The way he's kicking that stall down says I haven't been working him hard enough, and if Jessica's going to be up this weekend, you know she's going to want to go out on a trail ride. With that storm we had the other day, there's bound to be a tree or two down that we'll need to clear out before then."

"Uh huh, sure…" James replied. They'd just finished bringing in the last of the hay the day before, which meant their team of horses, Buster and Bonny, had been working hard for the past several days.

Grinning, he climbed out of bed anyway and found the clothes he'd hastily discarded the night before, deciding there was no point in putting on clean clothes if he was just going riding, and would shower when he returned instead, assuming Ben didn't put him right to work. It had been several weeks since he'd gone out for a trail ride, and that sounded like a perfect way to give himself some time to think.

Ben was already downstairs and cooking breakfast by the time he'd made use of the bathroom and located his missing sock, which had somehow managed to make its way halfway under the bed.

He snuck past Ben on his way to the cupboard and kissed him gently on the back of the neck, before grabbing dishes, which he set up on the island where they usually ate breakfast, and then dug through the fridge to grab something to drink. There was coffee brewing already, but James loathed the taste of it, unless it was buried under a ridiculous amount of cream and sugar, and usually avoided it unless he needed the caffeine. Grabbing a large glass of orange juice instead, he set that down on the table, along with the creamer Ben liked with his coffee.

He fixed up Ben's coffee the way he knew his partner preferred it and had that ready just as Ben finished cooking breakfast. Breakfast was always a large meal, and today was no different. Bacon, eggs, hash browns, and a bowl of fresh fruit topped with yogurt.

Far too often, he missed lunch as the demands of his profession meant he never knew when an emergency would come in. Then again, half the time he missed breakfast, lunch, and dinner when an emergency came in, too. That was the challenge of running his own clinic.

"I'm surprised you didn't go feed Buster first," James said as he sat down and dug into his meal.

"If I ran to feed him every time he got grumpy, I'd have an unruly horse on my hands," Ben replied. "Why do you think I keep you fed so well?"

"Well, you've certainly got me well trained," James said. "I haven't kicked anything in days."

"It's a work in progress," Ben said with a wicked grin.

Breakfast was far more leisurely than usual, outside of the banging and squealing that was coming from the barn, as Ben lingered over his coffee, long after they were both done with their breakfast.

"Your coffee okay?" James asked, not sure if he was stalling or not.

"Perfect," Ben replied. "As always. I'm just waiting for Buster to quit his temper tantrum." He paused, head cocked, listening, when things finally quieted. "Well, there's my cue." With a final long gulp, he finished his coffee and set the mug down on his empty plate.

James chuckled and began picking up the breakfast dishes while Ben made his way out to the barn to begin feeding the animals they had on the farm. The slam of the screen door as Ben left set off another loud chorus from the barn, this time from all the animals.

Theirs was a working farm, with most of the animals intended for harvest when they were big enough, although they had a flock of chickens for eggs, goats for making cheese and lawn care, half a dozen milking cows, the two horses that Ben used to farm and log with, a dog that was supposed to be for protection but ended up being anything but, and two very obnoxious geese, that they'd just ended up with, when one of their neighbors sold their farm and moved to Florida.

James had a sneaking suspicion the geese were going to end up as Thanksgiving and Christmas dinner. After being attacked one too many times, he was perfectly fine with that. They regularly joked that their neighbors had moved just to get away from the geese.

Once a massive dairy farm, Ben had decided he preferred working with the horses, as he'd learned from his father and grandfather. A good portion of their income now came from school field trips, tours, private lessons, and a growing interest in living with nature. Ben felt it was important to keep the knowledge of how they worked with draft animals alive.

In addition to the crops they grew to feed the animals, one corn field now always ended up being a maze for Halloween, and they made a lot of money on hayrides and their apple harvest every year.

They used wood for heat in the winter and for sugaring in the spring, as Ben insisted that wood-fired maple syrup was better than any other form. He honestly couldn't tell the difference, as he'd grown up in the south, but he was more than happy to have it with his meals, so he always agreed whenever the topic came up. They'd also converted one of the unused back pastures to solar. That had been far more lucrative than either of them had expected, and they were considering converting another field.

This weekend would be the first open pick for the apple harvest, so most of the rest of the week would be in preparation for that, including dragging the large cider press out of storage and setting it up, cutting the maze through the corn, and stocking the concession stand for those that didn't want to pick their own apples.

James made more than enough with his large animal practice to allow Ben to do whatever he wanted with the property. Farming made Ben happy, and the smaller farm was far more manageable in their old age.

That had been a big part of their lengthy discussion the night before, as they tried to determine if they were financially stable enough for him to retire and live solely off the income of the farm and savings.

Far too many of those Ben had grown up with had long since sold their farms, and James hadn't planned to retire for another five years. So it would be a big hit on their income. He wasn't sure he had it in him to make it that long. Stress was taking far too big of a toll on him, and his last physical hadn't been good. If he didn't change several things about his life, he was likely to have a heart attack before he could even retire.

By the time the dishes were washed and put away, Buster had been fed and was happily munching away in his stall. James helped with the rest of the animals, somehow managing not to get attacked by the geese for once, and by the time they were all fed and watered, Buster had finished his breakfast. Only a single piece of hay remained, sticking out of his now drooping lower lip.

"You know, I'm thinking we should get another horse so we can go riding together again," James said as he brought the giant Belgian draft horse clopping out of his stall and over to the cross ties to groom and saddle him. "Not that I'm complaining. Buster's the best horse I've ever ridden. I just miss going out on rides with you."

"I've been thinking about it too. The Johanssons down the road said they're thinking about selling their mare. She's quite a bit shorter than Buster, though, and if I get another horse, I'd like a matching team. Although finding a horse his size will be a challenge. Neither of these two is getting any younger either, but I'm not sure I have the energy to start from scratch again, nor do I really want to deal with someone else's problems."

"I have a few clients that might be interested in selling a team for the right price and to the right owner," James said. "Although a couple of good trail horses that were a few feet shorter might be nice, too."

Buster was one of the best horses James had ever worked with and certainly one of the best trail horses. He rarely spooked, and whenever he refused, it was usually for a good reason. But, he was nearly twenty hands high and as wide as a couch, which came with its own set of difficulties, the least of which was getting on.

Ben nodded and gave a noncommittal grunt of acknowledgement as he grabbed a brush to help him groom. Before long, the gentle giant was tacked up and ready to go.

James switched out of his muck boots and into his riding boots and grabbed his helmet as Ben held Buster for him, not that the horse would run off. He was too well trained for that. The draft horse was trying hard to grab Ben's hat, a favorite game of theirs, and one of the few antics Ben allowed the old horse to get away with, simply because it made the children who visited the farm laugh when it happened during the tours, which it inevitably did.

Taking the reins from Ben, James led the giant horse out into the yard and used the picnic table to climb on. It was barely tall enough.

"Where are you planning to ride today?" Ben asked, always cautious in case something happened.

"I think I'll take the loop past the cliffs today. I should be back in an hour or two."

Ben grinned as it was one of their favorite trails. "That should take the edge off him. Be careful, though. That path can get a little slick when it's been raining. I'll probably be in the orchard when you return. Do you have your phone?"

James nodded and tapped the chest pocket where he kept it. "Always," he replied, not the least bit concerned about Ben's protectiveness. Buster might be the best horse on the planet, but accidents did happen.

He nudged Buster into a walk, and the horse took off immediately, head up and ears forward as he examined the trail around them. He was pretty sure Buster enjoyed going out on trail as much as he did. There was never any hesitation, and there was often a bounce in the big horse's step. Granted, trail riding was probably much easier than the rest of the work Ben had him do most days.

The stress of his job vanished within moments, and he absently hummed out of tune as they walked down the long drive to the back pasture. It was an absolutely beautiful morning. The air was fresh and clean, but not cold. Just a hint of the coming winter laced the air. Leaves were turning and starting to fall, littering the trail with a multitude of colors. The sun streamed through the remaining leaves.

I could get used to doing this every morning, James thought. The best part was that the worst of the insects were gone this time of the year. About fifteen or twenty minutes out, they made it to the winding trail that led up the hill to the exposed rocky cliff wall, before it circled back down and around by the corn field they used for the maze.

Buster snorted, and he could feel the big horse's haunches collecting under him. This was where he often ran the horse, although he'd never tell Ben, even though he was sure Ben knew. The steep hill was wonderful for tiring the giant beast out, and the footing on this side was solid and clear.

Grinning, he leaned forward slightly.

That was all the signal Buster needed before taking off at a full gallop. This was one of the few horses James trusted to let loose like this, and he whooped with delight, urging the horse faster.

Buster stretched out and willingly obliged as they dodged the occasional tree branch along the way. His heavy feet pounded the earth in an almost primal rhythm, and James forgot about everything but the moment.

Heart beating fast, he focused hard on making the turns, dodging tree branches, and just staying on. When they safely made it to the top of the hill, James sat up and pulled back on the reins. Buster snorted and pranced a little bit, shaking his head, but willingly came back down to a walk, sides heaving with the effort he'd made.

"Good boy, Buster," James said, slapping the horse's now sweaty neck, and then wiped his hand on his already filthy jeans as they continued along the narrow path.

On one side, a rocky exposed cliff went up a good forty or fifty feet, and on the other, a steep embankment littered with trees and brush led down to a small stream at the bottom. He stopped just before the trail descended, checking it out.

Far steeper and rockier than the other side, it was significantly more dangerous. As Ben had mentioned, it had been raining, and there was less sun on this side, shaded as it was by the cliffs and the hill. Leaves covered the rocks, making it look slippery, and he considered turning around and going back.

This section was short, though, and the rest of the trail passed leisurely along the bank of the stream and led to a small pond where they often saw deer. It was one of his favorite areas to sit and think as he let Buster munch, another bad habit he'd never tell Ben about. The section closest to the cliff wall looked passable, so he started Buster slowly down the trail, trusting the horse to pick his own way.

They hadn't gone far when Buster snorted hard, head up, ears twitching, and began backing up.

"What is it, boy? Too slippery?" he asked.

Buster rarely refused, but this wasn't his normal refusal, and he'd rarely seen the horse this nervous before, which made him wonder if there was something ahead, like a bear or mountain lion, that he couldn't see.

James gave Buster his head to let him turn around. If Buster didn't feel the footing was safe, he wasn't going to push him, but kept pressure on the reins to keep him at a walk.

"Easy boy," James said, as Buster snorted again, loud and staccato against the quiet morning, then spooked with a slight jump, when off in the distance a flock of birds took to the sky. Moments later, the ground rumbled.

"Earthquake?" James thought, surprised. He knew some animals reacted to earthquakes before people felt them, but he'd never seen it for himself.

Practically before he could finish that thought, though, the ground below him heaved, sending rocks from the cliff wall crashing down.

Buster scrambled for footing and dodged the falling rocks with a scream, making it up to the flatter portion of the trail by the top of the hill. James held on with everything he had as the ground continued to shake and heave, and Buster threatened to take off.

A sound louder than anything he'd ever heard before roared past, followed by a gust of wind that toppled every tree around him in an instant. Only the cliff wall beside him saved him from the same fate. James struggled to keep Buster from bolting and held on for dear life as the horse began half rearing in fear.

He didn't blame him, though, as he was just as terrified.

"Easy boy," James called out, barely able to hear anything over the ringing in his ears, not expecting the horse to do so, but to his surprise, Buster calmed a bit.

James cautiously relaxed as he looked around him. Aftershocks continued to rumble underfoot. Buster pranced and side-stepped, but stayed where James told him. Granted, there really wasn't anywhere for them to go.

The trail on either side was now littered with down trees and large boulders that had fallen away from the cliff and somehow amazingly hadn't hit them. He was just about to climb off when another massive earthquake hit, and the ground under him fell away.

Buster tried to make a run for it, even though there was nowhere to run, but they were both tossed over and down the embankment. He had half a moment to think, '*this is really going to hurt*' before he hit.

———

HE HAD no idea how long he'd been unconscious, but when he finally woke up, the once blue sky had turned dark with clouds. To his immense surprise, he was reasonably intact, having landed mostly in a softer section of branches. He was sure he was covered in cuts and bruises, but everything appeared to work. His head throbbed, however, and his vision spun as he tried to sit up.

Unclipping his helmet and taking it off, he stared in shock at the crushed back of it where it had made contact with the trunk of the tree he'd landed on.

"Good thing I wore a helmet," he told himself, and felt the back of his head where a large knot was forming. He was having a hard time focusing, so he was pretty sure he had a concussion, but if he hadn't been wearing his helmet, he knew he'd be dead or very seriously injured.

When he was sick, a few moments later, he was sure it was a concussion. Once he stopped throwing up, he climbed carefully over the debris to check on Buster, who was lying on his side a dozen or so feet from him, struggling to get up, and screaming in pain.

The footing was an impossible jumble of rocks and trees, which made it even harder to navigate as he was seeing double, and it took him a long time to make it over to the horse.

"Easy boy," he called out again and again, as he climbed over the debris. When he arrived and pulled away a branch, he swore at what he found. Buster's front leg was badly broken. "Oh, Buster, I'm sorry," he said, swallowing hard as tears started streaming down his face.

He knew it was possible to treat a break like that, with a lot of effort, but there was no way he was going to be able to get Buster out of this mess to care for him, and that was assuming his vet clinic was even standing. As intense as the shock wave had been, he knew it had been no mere earthquake and figured it had either been a nuclear bomb or an asteroid that had hit. Neither one boded well for either of them.

He sat down next to the big horse's head, when the horse finally stopped struggling, and looked around at the devastation with a sigh, wondering how on Earth he was even going to make it back to the barn, and praying that Ben and the rest of his family were okay.

It would take him hours to make it through all the downed trees, and after climbing that short distance, he was pretty sure his ankle was either badly sprained or broken, too.

Buster lay his head on his lap with a pained groan, and James rubbed it, comforting the big horse and trying to figure out what to do. He didn't have any of the medicine he usually used to euthanize a horse. He didn't even have a knife with him, but there was no way he was going to leave Buster to suffer.

As he sat there, flakes of ash and cinder began falling from the sky, and he swore again. The few embers that landed near him fizzled out on the damp ground, but he knew if a forest fire started, he was as good as dead.

He finally remembered his phone and pulled it out. It was surprisingly undamaged, thanks to the heavy-duty case he had on it, but not surprisingly, there was no cell signal. He tried calling Ben anyway, and then tried calling 911, but nothing went through.

Sighing, he took a picture of Buster's badly broken leg to show Ben, assuming he was still alive, and considered what to use to put the horse out of his misery before attempting to make his way home.

Looking around, he examined the debris and saw a piece of sharp stone. Giving the horse another pat, he shifted out from under the big head and crawled his way over to examine it. The edge was sharp. He just hoped it was sharp enough to make it quick.

He made the mistake of standing up too quickly and promptly fell over, sick again. He wasn't sure how long he lay there, heaving and hoping his head would stop spinning, and watching the sky darken as more ash fell around him.

His head didn't clear, but he finally gathered enough strength to try standing up again anyway. If he didn't start moving soon, he'd never make it to safety. Carefully heaving his way back onto his feet, he turned back towards Buster and stood there in shock as four purple dragons flew over the remains of the cliff wall, straight towards him. He blinked hard, figuring he was hallucinating from the bump on his head. The four dragons solidified into two, then paused to hover above him.

"Well, this is certainly not the day I was expecting," he said to himself, moments before a blue orb flew towards him and struck him in the chest. He let out a gasp as searing pain rippled through him. His body seized, and it felt like his heart exploded inside him. The rock he was carrying toppled out of his hand moments before the rest of him followed.

4

MYRA: MASS CASUALTIES

*E*llie, I don't care what that pompous overgrown Guild Master says he can or can't deliver," Myra growled. "This isn't negotiable. I'm going to have thousands of badly wounded casualties, and an uncounted number of different plants and aquatic species to deal with. And that doesn't even begin to include the needs of five ships' worth of crew and nearly six hundred other healers and volunteers. I need those shields and isolation units here and up in two days. I can't give you more time than that. I just don't have it."

"Myra, be reasonable. How are we supposed to deliver everything you've requested to your remote location in two days?" the Senior Guild Master asked.

"I *am* being reasonable. I've given you Sampson's contact information. He'll coordinate transportation. You just have to have everything ready for pickup. This isn't just to care for the casualties. Without proper shields and quarantine habitats in place, our entire planet could be at risk from some unknown pathogen or virus that could kill us all. They arrive in two and a half days. We have no choice but to be ready."

"But Myra..."

"Don't you *dare*, 'But Myra,' me, Ellie. Are you the Senior Guild Master or not?" she growled, furious with her friend.

"Myra...," Ellie huffed.

"Are you the Senior Guild Master or not?" she repeated slowly and firmly, as if dealing with a patient in shock or an unruly apprentice.

Ellie just frowned at her, pursing her lips in frustration.

Myra sighed. "Ellie, you're my oldest and dearest friend. If *anyone* can do it, you can. You're the only one who can. I don't care what strings you have to pull or what you have to promise. The Senior Council has already authorized it. If you don't figure out a way to make it happen, I don't want to be you when the Senior Council finds out you've put the entire planet at risk. Two days," she said, and hung up before Ellie could reply with more excuses.

Before she could even take a full breath, there was a knock on her door. "Enter," she called out, trying hard to lock her emotions down. Her mask had been slipping far too much under the extreme pressure of coordinating the quarantine effort, and it was unbecoming of someone of her rank and experience to let her emotions slip, no matter how exhausted, overwhelmed, or terrified she might be.

Her protege, Journeyman Brice Morningstar, opened the door and leaned in. "We just had another shipment of food delivered, but the refrigeration units aren't online yet. What do you want us to do?"

Myra sighed at the four-hundredth problem she'd had to solve in the past hour. "How long before the units are working?" she asked.

"They're saying another five or six hours, at least. They're still laying the electrical grid," Brice replied.

"Are the delivery ships refrigerated?" she asked.

Brice flicked her whiskers forward, indicating yes.

"Good. Tell the pilots they're just going to have to wait. Better yet, wrangle them into setting up the shelters while they wait, and have them help unload any other deliveries that show up," Myra ordered.

"Will do. Any word on the shields and isolation units yet?" Brice asked.

"The Senior Guild Master is still working on it. We'll have the first shipment tomorrow around noon, but that only accounts for about five hundred units. If we have to, we'll put members of the same species in the same units until the others arrive, and pray they don't fight," she answered, trying hard to keep her frustration out of her voice.

"Are they even going to be up in time?" Brice asked, a hint of worry seeping around her protege's mask.

"They'll have to be. Won't they?" Myra replied, dismissing the question. "How many of the volunteers have arrived?"

"About three hundred so far, and I expect most of the rest will be here by tomorrow morning. Oh, and I just received word that the ships coming from the Water World with the tanks just left orbit. It'll take them another three and a half days to get here, so we'll have to keep the water species on board the Sprite's ship while we get the tanks set up," Brice replied.

"Well, we'll just have to make that work. If you wouldn't mind, let the other healers know there's going to be a meeting in half an hour out on the commons."

Brice nodded and left. A few seconds later, Myra's tablet dinged with an incoming call.

"Sampson!" she purred with delight when her new favorite person came on the line. She threw the call up on the big monitor on her wall. "Please, tell me you have some good news."

"Well, I just had a lovely call with the Senior Guild Master..." he said, with an innocent expression, although his eyes twinkled with amusement.

"Oh really? And what did *she* have to say?" Myra asked with a matching expression, propping her head on her paws as if she were a cub watching their favorite entertainment program.

"Only that another two thousand isolation units have been located, and could I pretty please send some ships to pick them up. I'll have them for you by tomorrow afternoon," he said.

Myra grinned at the news and sat up. "I knew she'd work something out. What about shelters for the volunteers? I've got close to three hundred healers sleeping in makeshift tents right now, and the rest will be here tomorrow morning."

"On their way as we speak, and the crews to set them up. They won't be fancy, but they'll be better and safer than tents," he said, then checked his information. "It looks like they should arrive in the next hour or so."

"Good enough for me. We can worry about comfort later. I hate to even ask about the shields?"

"Well, that's going to be a challenge. The size of the complex is our main issue. I can get you shields, but we don't have anything available that will cover a compound that big on short notice, but I have a plan."

"Oh?" she asked.

"We'll modify the ships' shields when they arrive. If we station each of the ships around the compound, we should be able to link them together to cover the entire complex at least for the short term. That'll give us enough time to work on more permanent shields, as well as installing the backup systems."

"It'll be far better than nothing. I'll take it," she said, relieved. "Thank you."

"Of course. I also have the latest transmission from the ships. It included the information you were asking for, regarding the latest scans of the survivors, injuries, and such. It should be on its way to you now."

A ding indicated the arrival of the information, and she picked up her tablet and quickly scanned through it. Much as she expected, broken bones, burns, smoke inhalation, and radiation poisoning were the most common and worst of the injuries.

"How long before I can talk with them directly?" she asked.

"They should be in range by tomorrow night, close enough to allow for near real-time communication. There'll still be about a fifteen-second delay, but that should be manageable. You've been given first priority."

Another ding announced the meeting invite with the direct contact information for the ship. "We'll be ready. Anything else for me?" she asked.

"That's all I had for this call. I'll have an ETA on the rest of your items in another hour or two," Sampson replied.

"Until then. Thank you again!" she said, and hung up.

After forwarding the information to the rest of the volunteers, she read through the more detailed report the Senior Healer on the ships had provided, and sighed.

Those poor creatures.

She prayed they'd survive the journey and that they'd be able to help them when they arrived. The healers on board the ships were all master level, but there just weren't enough of them to care for all of the survivors, and figure out how to treat them, even with every person on those ships trying to help. With an unknown species, normal treatments could be just as deadly as the injuries.

Tablet in hand, Myra made her way out to the Commons to instruct the newly arrived healers. When she arrived, the area outside of what used to be her clinic was packed with volunteers. She blinked in surprise at the transformation since she'd last been outside, only a few hours earlier.

Like most buildings in this part of the world, her small clinic was built inside of what used to be an ancient compound surrounding one of the massive bandala trees, which was the only source of water for months of the year. However, unlike her own personal home, this ancient compound had not weathered the test of time nearly as well.

The stone wall that surrounded the inner compound had crumbled centuries ago, leaving only a small knee-high wall, which she had slowly repaired over the decades she'd run the clinic. She'd added a pool and a small garden as well, nothing like the one she had back home, but it was enough to give the families of her patients a comfortable place to wait as their loved ones received care, and for those needing longer term care, a place to rest and recover should they need a break from their rooms.

Only a few of the buildings that had been part of the original compound had been salvageable when she'd finally decided on the location of her clinic. The surrounding community and Healer's Guild had helped her to repair and furnish the buildings that had become her clinic, the only one for nearly two hundred leagues in any direction. It had been her goal since she was a small cub, when her best friend had died after being stung by a sand spinner, and it had taken too long for her parents to make it to the Trauma Center in Sand Dune.

The rest of the ancient structure had crumbled into piles of stone, and she'd left it to help protect the inner compound from the larger predators. Those ancient stone piles had been cleared away, and brand new, if fairly utilitarian buildings now stood in their place, surrounding the ancient tree like spokes in a wheel.

The area had been swarmed with builders from all over the planet, and the habitats for the rescued creatures had gone up in a single day, although they'd yet to be furnished or outfitted with the static isolation chambers that were still on their way.

Additional buildings, including trauma bays where they would treat the refugees, offices, and storage facilities, were still being built. The bang of construction and the noise of the machines made her pin her ears back.

A veritable sea of multi-colored tents, where the healers would stay until their shelters arrived, was haphazardly packed into the area they were now calling the Commons.

She'd worried about what the loss of this clinic would mean for the surrounding community, but Healers had already informed her that they were planning to build and staff another one, which her other protege, Kelly, intended to run out of her home.

Kelly had just returned from maternity leave and decided that she couldn't spend the year of expected quarantine away from her cubs. Myra completely understood and sent her off with her blessing, and a promotion to Master, so she would have the rank and authority to run that clinic.

That had always been Kelly's goal anyway, and the Ancient Gods knew there weren't enough healers or clinics in this part of the world. Her other protege, Brice, had decided to stay and had been instrumental in setting up the new quarantine facilities, while Myra wrangled resources from stubborn Guild Masters.

She weaved her way through the sprawl of tents and Healers, greeting the few she knew personally. Not used to giving speeches, she took a deep breath before leaping up onto the wall so she could be seen and heard better.

"Can I have everyone's attention, please?" she yelled, and gave everyone a moment to crowd around and stop talking before continuing. The builders stopped what they were doing to listen as well. She nodded to them, relieved she wouldn't have to yell over the racket.

"Thank you all for volunteering your time to help with the rescue mission. You have all been selected from the list of volunteers because of your expertise and the recommendation of the Healers Guild, so I know you all understand the risks and commitment that this endeavor entails. If any of you are experiencing second thoughts and want to change your mind, change it now, no questions asked. I will completely understand, but once the ships arrive, you're stuck here with the rest of us, whether you like it or not. This is going to be a half a year to a year-long mission, if not longer, to care for the refugees and determine what risks of cross-contamination there might be between us, and find a cure before quarantine can be lifted."

She paused briefly to see if there was any reaction to that announcement, but there wasn't. She nodded her approval. Just about every healer here was a Master level healer, and they knew full well what they were signing up for when they'd volunteered. Only a few Journeymen had been accepted, and only because their Mentors had volunteered as well.

When no one left or spoke up, she continued. "I've just received the first batch of medical reports, which I've sent to everyone. I'm expecting around five hundred healers to show up once everyone is here. That means at least ten to fifteen patients for every healer. We have what appear to be thirty-seven land-based species, although only about fourteen are in large numbers, with the majority of the casualties being from what we believe is the sentient species of that world. They're still working through all of the water species and flora rescued. We were very lucky to find that fishing vessel and its nets, and they're still trying to identify all of the species since many appear very similar. Thankfully, most of those creatures do not appear to be injured. In order to avoid cross-contamination, we're setting up twenty separate pods."

She pointed to the building surrounding them. "Each pod will have its own environmental systems, volunteer housing units, cleaning and waste rooms, kitchens, storage units, patient isolation units or tanks, trauma beds, and offices. For the first month at least, no one will be allowed to leave their ward for any reason. If you are a family unit, I suggest making sure you are in the same ward. Put your preferences in by tonight, and we'll start assigning patients so you can be prepared when they arrive. If you have any questions or concerns about who you've been assigned with, or the patients you've been assigned to, I want to know immediately. Any questions?"

"Besides familiarizing ourselves with our patients, what can we do to help now?" someone in the crowd asked.

"That's an excellent question. Over the next two days, we will be receiving shipments from all five planets that will need to be unloaded, organized, and in many cases, assembled. Once you've been assigned to your pod, I want you to work together to make sure you have everything you think you're going to need when they arrive, and make sure it's unpacked and ready to go. Pick a representative for each pod. This will be the point person for your team responsible for coordinating with Healer Brice Morningstar. Do *not* contact her directly. Go through your point person."

"How are we feeding them?" the next person called out.

"Another excellent question. Right now, they are all sedated, with the worst of the injured placed in stasis. While we have no idea what they actually eat, we do have scans that show what's in their stomachs. We have scientists already working on determining what is safe for each species to eat and what their nutritional requirements are. Thankfully, they appear to be similar enough that there is a good chance we will be able to feed them with the same foods we eat, but we're going to have to watch carefully for signs of poisoning, allergic reactions, and malnutrition. That same similarity also means there's an increased risk of cross-contamination and infection."

"How are we going to care for the water species, and what about the Water Sprites? Where will they be staying?" someone called out.

"Tanks are being shipped to house the rescued water species. Until they arrive, they will remain onboard the Water Sprite's ship. Once the rescued creatures have been successfully transferred to the tanks, the Water Sprites will be placed in stasis while their ship is completely drained, cleaned, and refilled. At which point we will determine what to do next, whether that's build a habitat for them here, or send them home."

When there were no more questions, she sent them on their way and took a few moments to examine the changes around her before hopping down to deal with the next hundred challenges that were already waiting for her. Off in the distance, storm clouds were forming, signaling the end of high summer and the coming rains of spring. She usually looked forward to the rains, but this year she was hoping they'd hold off for just a few more days, long enough to get the shelters built and their patients transferred from the ships to their new habitats and treated.

TWO AND A HALF DAYS LATER, they were ready, just barely, for the ships when they arrived. The warning call came in from Sampson when they exited jump, only a few minutes before the ships landed, and they were all waiting by the entrances of their wards as the ships flew into view.

As they landed, sand billowed away from the engines in massive plumes of dust that practically hid the ships from view. They settled lightly on the five hastily built landing pads around the complex.

Techs were already waiting to hook up the cables that would run from each of the ships to link up their shields. Myra held her paw up to hold off the healers that were ready to swarm the ships, waiting until the moment she saw the haze of the static shield activate around the compound.

Myra gave the signal, and they all ran for the ships as the massive cargo doors slid open, and ramps began to extend. For better or worse, they were now in quarantine.

She stuck to Brice's side as they ran to find their first patient. The worst of the injured would remain in stasis until the rest were treated, and while Myra was not taking patients of her own, as she was officially in charge of the Agency, as the others were starting to call the facility, she intended to help Brice with the care of the fifteen that had been assigned to her.

Brice was still only a Journeyman and, while incredibly talented in her own right, did not have the decades of experience that Myra did. Granted, no one really knew what they were facing.

The healers on board the ships had been treating what they could with the help of the rest of the crew, but there were still hundreds who'd had only had the barest of care. It was hard enough just to keep them hydrated, and Myra prayed that the food supplements the scientist had replicated from their stomach contents would work to keep them alive until they could figure out what other foods were safe.

Myra made her way through the bay of strange creatures to the one she was looking for, 1A1, who they now believed was a small female cub of the sentient species. The cub would need multiple surgeries to repair several badly broken bones. She was the most critically injured of those who had not been placed into stasis, and who had not had more than basic triage by one of the healers onboard yet.

Crew, who Myra realized were mostly pilots and guards, were scattered about the bay, moving from one patient to another. Signs had been placed to help them find their patients. Hers, the first biped rescued, was by the far corner.

A guard, by the name of Avery Hunt, according to his badge, was by the cub's side when they approached, and he looked relieved to see them.

Myra briefly wondered if he was related to Kendra Hunt, the Senior Honor Guard, but she dismissed the thought to focus on her patient.

"Her condition began deteriorating rapidly after we exited jump, and she's having trouble breathing," Avery stated. That much was obvious as the tiny injured cub was visibly gasping for air, and Myra could hear the telltale rattle of a punctured lung.

She quickly scanned the cub as Avery continued with his update, confirmed the injury, then clipped her scanner back onto her harness and helped to transfer the poor injured thing onto the gurney they'd brought with them.

Brice unhooked the bag of fluids hanging from an improvised hook on the ship's wall, and they took off at a run back to the trauma bay they had already prepped.

As soon as the cub was transferred to the trauma bed, Myra began examining the far more detailed scans as they came in. The bed didn't know what to make of the cub and set off alarms and warnings all over the place.

Myra silenced them all and scanned the bracelet that was on the cub's wrist, bringing up the scan they'd taken when she'd first been brought on board the ship. She recalibrated the med scanner using that information as a baseline. They didn't have a healthy, uninjured individual to work from, but it gave her a way to see what had changed.

She began marking readings as normal for the species, or what she hoped was normal, and the AI in the trauma-bed began learning. As the ships' systems hooked up to the Agency's and other healers began doing the same, more of the alerts and warnings turned off, leaving her with what was still a very badly injured cub.

"Oxygen," Myra ordered, confirming the most critical need.

Brice grabbed the mask and placed it over the cub's mouth and nose, shaping it to fit the cub's tiny face.

As that stat began to rise, Myra moved on. The cub had a large crack on the side of her skull, just above her right ear, which was causing pressure to form on her brain, and three cracked and broken ribs, one of which had punctured her lung and caused it to collapse. Her arm had been shattered in six different locations, and she was dangerously close to losing that paw due to the lack of circulation.

She was also covered in cuts and bruises and had what looked like glass embedded in her skin.

She must have been near a window, Myra thought briefly.

The scanner flagged other anomalies, including smoke and ash inhalation, minor radiation poisoning, and other contaminants that Myra guessed were from inhaling toxic smoke from burning buildings.

She paused and frowned at the vastly different hormonal levels from the first scan, then dismissed them. Those were not critical and could wait, she hoped.

"Start cleaning her up and digging out the glass and other debris," she ordered Brice, who set to work immediately.

Myra began treating the pressure on the cub's skull and repairing the small bleeds, praying that she wasn't doing more harm than good, after deciding that was of higher priority as the cub still had one functioning lung. The crack on her skull was not at risk of breaking further, so she decided to let it heal naturally rather than using the bone knitter. The strange, mostly furless species had such a thin skull that she was worried that she'd slip and cause more damage to the brain underneath.

The small bleeds and pressure were quickly treated, thankfully responding normally to her care, so she moved on to the broken ribs. They had shifted out of place, so she made an incision to expose the broken bones and carefully pulled them back into position, then used the bone knitter to repair them.

The repair was fairly quick and easy, and thankfully, the bone knitter seemed to work just as well on them as it did on other species, even though the texture and shape of her bones were unlike anything she'd ever seen before.

That done, she repaired the damage to the lung and surrounding area, then drained the blood that had pooled around it. After checking the scanner for further signs of injury, she ran the suture wand over her incision.

When the wound was closed, she examined the scans again and frowned. The lung was not expanding like she expected it to. Examining the other still-working lung and the surrounding area for comparison, she grabbed another tool and pulled out the air that had been trapped when she closed up the wound.

This tool inserted a small tube into the cub's side where the air pocket was and provided gentle suction. When the air was out, and she saw signs that the lung was expanding, she removed the tube and sutured the small hole.

Brice covered both her incision and the tiny wound from the tube with bandage putty to keep the wound clean and allow it to heal better, then went back to the tedious task of picking out more glass and shrapnel, and washing the cub down to remove the blood and ash that covered her.

That left the mangled mess of her left arm to deal with. Using the cub's uninjured right arm as a guide, Myra began the delicate repairs to the damaged bone, muscle, tendons, arteries, and nerves.

She sighed with relief as blood flow was restored to the cub's paw, and several of the warnings turned off. She'd rather not have to try regrowing the paw if she didn't have to, as she had no idea how well that would work with this species. It took several hours to complete the surgery, but when she was done, she was pretty sure the cub would keep her paw.

Brice had finished digging the glass and debris out of the cub's front and sides and sutured several of the worst cuts. Myra examined her protege's work before casting the cub's arm, to give it stability while it healed. Together, they carefully rolled her over to begin pulling glass and debris out of her back and treating the cuts and bruises they found there. The poor cub was nothing but one giant bruise.

After another careful review of the cub's status, Myra gave her a breathing treatment to help clear out the rest of the damage to her lungs, treated her for the radiation poisoning, and injected her with the sensor that would allow them to monitor the cub's vitals safely from a distance.

They also gave her more fluids and a dose of the food supplement the scientists had come up with. While she waited for those treatments to complete, she reviewed and marked the hormonal changes for further review by the Healer's Guild, as they had no idea what was normal for a cub of this age, along with several other anomalies the scanners had picked up. Those, she decided, could all wait until the rest of the casualties were treated, as none appeared to be life-threatening. For all she knew, they could be normal readings.

When the cub's vitals improved and stabilized enough, Myra had Brice transfer the cub to her isolation chamber. She quickly cleaned down the trauma bed before making her way back to the ship to collect their next patient.

One down, fourteen to go, Myra thought, then did a quick calculation. If every patient took as long, it would be days before they were done. *Please let them make it,* she prayed, then stopped worrying. They would survive or they wouldn't. All she could do was try.

5

JESSICA: PATIENT

Mom? Dad? Where are you?"

Smoke, dust, and ash swirled around her, obscuring her sight. Vague shapes of ruined buildings came in and out of view.

"No!" she cried out in horror, as the air cleared briefly, long enough to reveal her parents lying sprawled in a heap, charred and burned almost beyond recognition, before the smoke obscured her vision once again.

She ran towards them only to be stopped as a giant cat appeared out of the gloom. Susie's mangled and half-eaten body hung from its mouth. She screamed and turned to run as it dropped Susie's body with a sickening thud and roared at her.

JESSICA WOKE WITH A JOLT, her heart racing in her chest as the fear of the nightmare slowly subsided.

Thank God, she thought. *It was only a nightmare.* But as her awareness slowly shifted from nightmare to reality, she began to wonder if she was still asleep.

She sat up and rubbed at her eyes, but that didn't change the sight in front of her, or rather, the complete lack of anything in front of her. She was alone in a large empty room, nearly as big as her classroom had been, and was sitting completely naked on a thick pad of some sort, covered only by a thin metallic-looking blanket.

The ceiling glowed with a soft light that made it difficult to tell where the corners of the uniform tan-colored room were. There were no windows, no switches, no decorations of any kind, and not a single door. She turned to look behind her, but found the same.

Where the hell am I, and where's the door? she wondered.

On her right arm, instead of the watch she usually wore, there was a silver bracelet with strange swirling symbols that meant nothing to her. On her other arm, a green mesh-like device went all the way from her wrist to over her shoulder. She could bend her elbow slightly and rotate her shoulder some, but the motion caused her arm to throb.

Is this some sort of cast? she wondered as she tugged at it, and found it stiff and unyielding.

It was then that her memories came flooding back to her: the explosion, her broken and useless arm, Susie's mangled body, climbing over debris on her way through town, and the massive feline that had taken her captive.

Fear and grief threatened to overwhelm her as she realized that her world must have been attacked and destroyed by those cat-like aliens. They had taken her captive, for who knew what reason, and taken her clothes and everything she'd had on her.

Probably to make it harder to escape, she thought.

She sat rocking for some time as her mind raced through all the possible implications before coming to the conclusion that she just didn't have enough information.

I need to figure out where I am, what they want with me, find some clothes, and then I need to figure out how to get out of here and find out if my family is still alive, she decided. How, though, was anyone's guess.

Struggling to her feet, she awkwardly wrapped the blanket around herself and held it pinned down by her broken arm, unable to make it stay in place, before staggering her way over to examine the walls.

Her head throbbed, and there was something very wrong with her balance. The room spun, and she nearly fell with every step. She was breathing hard and sweating by the time she made it to the nearest wall, just to keep from throwing up. She wasn't sure if she was feverish or if it was just really warm in the room, but her skin felt like it was on fire. She'd have left the blanket behind if she didn't feel so exposed without it.

Leaning heavily against the wall for both support and balance as she waited for the dizziness to pass, she found it both smooth and warm to the touch, and it gave off a slight static tingle, making the hair on her arm stand up. The wall was so smooth she couldn't even feel any imperfections, almost as if it wasn't even there, but she could clearly see and feel how solid it was.

She tried scratching it with her fingernails, but it didn't leave a mark, and the texture was so odd that her brain struggled to understand. It was like trying to scratch solid air. She hit it with her good arm, and much to her surprise, the wall gave, almost as if it were padded.

She hit it as hard as she could and then kicked it, but no matter how hard she struck, the wall just absorbed her impact, with no sound she could hear. After a few tries, she stopped, as the motion made her sick and the impact made her injured arm and side throb with pain.

Once the pain settled, she slowly walked around the room, keeping her hand pressed against the wall, both for balance and in the hopes that she might feel a seam where a door might be hidden, but she found nothing. It was just a large empty room with nothing in it but the mattress she'd been lying on and the blanket she currently had wrapped around her.

"Hello?" she called out, and then swore.

Her voice sounded muffled and distant, and it triggered the memory that her hearing had been damaged in the attack. She cautiously felt her ears.

At least they're still there, she thought. The whole right side of her face felt swollen and bruised, but without a mirror, she had no way to know how bad it really was. She prayed that she hadn't permanently lost her hearing.

I bet my eardrums were blown out during the explosion, and it will just take time to heal, she told herself, since she could hear a little better than she'd been able to after the attack, fervently hoping that it was the truth. The ringing had stopped at least, and she could hear her voice, if muffled.

"Hello? Is anyone out there?" she yelled, and banged on the wall again. "Hey! Let me out of here!"

Something tapped her on her shoulder. She spun around and immediately screamed, both from the surprise of something tapping her, in what had been a previously empty room, and instant fear at the sight that greeted her.

The sudden motion caused her already queasy head to keep spinning, and she almost fell again. Pressing her back up against the wall for support, she stared up at the terrifying, monstrous beast before her.

The feline was as tall as she remembered, if not taller, and seemed far more massive in the enclosed space. Its furry ears nearly touched the ceiling. If she had to guess, she'd say the creature was close to twenty feet tall. At a whopping four-foot-eight, she barely came up to its knees.

The alien's thick fur was a light cream color with a few small splotches of tan and brown. Unlike any cat she'd ever seen, this one was standing on two legs and holding a massive tray, easily the size of her dinner table. Slowly, the cat took several steps back and sat down.

Jessica stared at the creature, trying to determine its intentions. *They,* she chided herself, as the creature was clearly intelligent and not deserving of an 'it' pronoun, and she couldn't find anything to indicate sex or gender. They weren't wearing anything, like the strange harness the one that had captured her had been wearing, no clothing or jewelry, and if there was anything to denote their sex, it was completely covered by their long fur.

Be polite and follow instructions, Jessica, she told herself. *They could easily eat you if they wanted to, and you're far too injured and sick to even think about trying to escape right now.* The walk around the room had shown her that.

The massive feline slowly set the tray down on the floor and wrapped a long, fluffy tail around their feet. Sitting like that, the creature seemed far less intimidating and looked like nothing more than an overgrown house-sized cat.

Two beautiful, nearly glowing, turquoise eyes, almost the size of a softball, blinked slowly at her and waited to see what she would do. After a while, the cat opened their mouth and looked like they said something to her, but she couldn't hear anything.

Jessica slowly lifted her good hand and tapped her ear. "I'm sorry, I can't hear you," she said.

The creature in front of her tilted their head slightly, twitched their whiskers forward, and then made an obvious beckoning motion, before tapping the floor in front of them with a plate-sized polydactyl paw bigger than Jessica's head.

They made no other motion, just waited to see what she would do.

Absolutely terrified, but realizing that there was no way she could defend herself against this beast, she carefully shuffled forward, trying hard not to lose her balance without the wall to hold on to. If the creature really wanted to eat her, there wasn't a blasted thing she could do to stop them, so she might as well play along.

She'd almost made it to the spot indicated when the room spun wildly on her again, and she started to fall. Faster than she could see, the cat reached out and caught her, practically enveloping her with their massive paws, then held her gently until she regained her balance. Once the room stopped spinning, they slowly removed their paws as if making sure she wasn't going to fall again.

"Thank you," Jessica said, figuring if nothing else, she could try to be polite, even if they didn't understand her. Although she wasn't sure if she was thanking the big cat for catching her or for not eating her. *Both,* she decided.

The feline didn't respond, but when Jessica remained on her feet, they slowly reached down to the tray beside them.

Jessica followed the motion and took a closer look at the strange objects on the tray. She couldn't identify any of them. A few of the items looked like tools, or maybe computer equipment, while others looked like they might be containers. They were all clearly designed for the large creature's paws, though, as everything was enormous.

After picking up one of the objects, they pointed to Jessica's wrist and held their other paw out, palm up.

She could just see the tips of very sharp looking claws poking through the fur. Jessica held her breath and extended her shaking arm.

They carefully and gently grabbed her wrist and turned it over before applying the device to the back of the bracelet and the symbols that were written there. A blue light blinked on the part of the device that she could see. The creature looked at the device for a moment, then let go of her hand before setting the device back on the tray.

Hand still firmly attached to her body, Jessica began breathing again.

The alien cat picked up another device, and a blue laser beam fanned out this time.

She flinched as they pointed the beam at her, but when it didn't hurt, she relaxed.

"What is that? Are you a doctor?" Jessica asked as the alien focused the beam on the arm that had been badly broken.

The cat gave no indication that they'd heard her, but they gently turned her head so they could run the scanner along one ear and then the other. The creature's ears twitched when they looked at the device afterwards, but Jessica had no idea if that was good or bad.

"How bad are they?" she asked. "Can you fix them?"

No answer.

Jessica waved her arm to get the cat's attention and tapped her ear. "Can you fix my hearing?" she asked loudly and slowly, as if that would make any difference.

The cat looked at her, twitched their whiskers back, and set the device back on the tray.

"So, is that a 'no'?" she asked.

The cat looked at her but didn't answer. Then, slowly, with one massive claw, it reached out and tugged on the blanket Jessica had wrapped around herself.

It was all she could do to keep from running when she saw that claw, but there wasn't anywhere for her to run or hide in the empty room, and her body froze with fright. When she realized they were trying to take the blanket, she grabbed it close to her, holding on tightly, and shook her head.

The cat stopped tugging, retracted the claw, and pulled their paw away. They looked at her for a moment, furry head tilted, and then put their paw out in the same 'give me' motion from before.

Sighing, Jessica unhooked the blanket and handed it over, feeling very exposed, not that the flimsy blanket would have protected her at all.

They set the blanket down and stared at her for several long moments before motioning for her to turn around, or at least that's what she thought.

Having her back to the creature was terrifying. She started to shake and nearly screamed again when they lightly tapped her shoulder.

She looked back, and the creature motioned that she could turn around again. They had her stop so that her side was facing them and gently moved her arm out of the way, so that they could run the odd scanner over her ribs where the worst of the pain in her side was located.

She looked down to see that there was some sort of bandage along her side that she hadn't noticed before. She went to feel it with her good arm, but the cat grabbed her arm and stopped her, flicking her whiskers back, and held her arm out of the way.

She tried to pull her arm away, and to her surprise and relief, the cat let go.

Wrapping her arms around her naked chest instead, she stood there and watched as the cat ran the scanner over her side again, and then set it down before grabbing another odd device, and running that over the strange bandage.

Grabbing what looked like nothing more than a towel, they rubbed gently at her side, but the pressure hurt, and she hissed, shifting away.

Before she could so much as take a step, the cat reached out with their other paw, stopped her from moving, and continued rubbing, although not as hard as before.

When the feline set the towel back on the tray, it was covered in some sort of green goop, and when Jessica checked out her side, the odd bandage was gone, leaving behind several long, thin scars and an ugly purple bruise that ran almost the entire length of her side.

At this point, they let go of her, then reached down and flipped open a large square container and scooped a thick glob of a fluffy light-green substance out of it before pointing to Jessica's arm again.

When she gave the creature her arm, they took the cream and rubbed it gently into one of the nasty purple bruises there. Almost immediately, a cool tingle began to replace the burning ache. She was shocked at how quickly the pain went away.

That's one heck of a cream! she thought.

Surprising her yet again, they held the large container of cream out to her.

Jessica took it, sniffed it, catching a faint minty scent, and then rubbed some onto all of the bruises she could reach. She wasn't sure if it was okay to apply the cream through the mesh on her broken arm, but when she was done with all of the other spots she could reach, the creature took the container back, and carefully applied it through the mesh, and to the spots where she couldn't reach. When all of her cuts and bruises had been treated, the cat flipped the lid closed, set it down next to the tray, and handed her back her blanket.

Jessica took it and wrapped it around herself quickly, before they changed their mind, pulling it tight. The cat tilted their head again and made a face that Jessica couldn't decipher, and then picked up the first device again and did something on it. Suddenly, Jessica could feel a hum at her feet, and within moments her feet felt appreciably warmer.

"That's good. Thank you, but I'm not cold. Can I have my clothes back?" Jessica asked, but they ignored her and set the device back on the tray.

The next object the cat picked up turned out to be an oversized thermos. The cat unscrewed the top and poured what looked like water into it before handing the top to Jessica.

She took the large bowl-sized cup and sniffed it as well, not detecting any scent this time. She lifted the bowl to her mouth and took a tentative sip. The cat twitched its whiskers forward.

Approval? she wondered as she drank. It was water, or at least that's what it tasted like. Jessica realized just how thirsty she was and drank it all. When she was done, she handed the odd cup back to the creature, who screwed it back onto the enormous alien thermos, and set that down next to the container of the minty miracle goop.

Finally, they took the remaining large object on the tray and set it down next to the water, before opening the lid to reveal a dozen smaller containers, all neatly arranged inside. Each of the smaller containers had a different item in them, in fairly large quantities, with more of that strange writing on the top.

Food? she wondered.

The creature opened one of the smaller containers and handed a piece to her, but she had no idea what to make of it. She looked at it and shrugged. She wasn't going to eat something without being sure it was supposed to be food. It didn't really look or smell like anything she wanted to eat.

Realizing she must be confused or worried it was unsafe, the cat reached down and grabbed another piece, popped it in their own mouth, and started chewing. This action revealed very large canines that reminded her of a saber-toothed tiger, and made her swallow hard in fear.

The cat didn't seem to notice and made a motion towards her as if saying, 'go on.'

When in Rome, she thought, and took a bite of the strange substance and chewed. It was the most vile, disgusting thing she'd ever tasted, bitter and slimy, and it smelled like three-day-old gym socks. She gagged and spit it out, expecting the creature to be mad, but they just held their paw out for it. She handed the remains of the revolting thing back gratefully.

They removed the container it had come from and placed it and the spit-out remains on the tray before taking one more tilted look at her. After a moment, they flicked their whiskers at her again before picking up the tray and standing slowly.

Jessica scrambled away, as the cat took one slow step back, turned and walked right through the wall, leaving Jessica alone again, with nothing more than half a container of minty pain goop, a thermos of water, and several containers of some unknown revolting substances pretending to be food.

The moment the cat vanished, Jessica half ran, half stumbled over to the wall the cat had disappeared through, but it was just as solid as it had been when she'd examined it before.

How did they do that? she wondered, but at that point, all of the terror she'd reigned in through the encounter finally took its toll, and she started to shake violently. Her legs buckled, and she slid down the wall and sat there for a long time, shaking until the fear and adrenaline eventually wore off.

"Holy alien abduction, Batman," she whispered.

She had no idea why they were healing her, after destroying her home and killing everyone else, but for now, she'd thank her lucky stars that they were not actively trying to hurt her. They must want her alive for some reason, if they were feeding and healing her wounds, but the patience and kindness the cat had shown just didn't make sense after seeing the violence they were clearly capable of.

Maybe they see no reason to terrify me more since they could obviously kill me without even trying, she thought, as she carefully made her way back to the container of food and tried something else. She picked out a blue glob this time. It wasn't as bad. It smelled kind of lemony, but when she bit into it, it made her eyes pucker from how sour it was, but at least it didn't smell like it had spent three days decomposing in the bottom of a gym bag in the hot sun, like the first item had.

Deciding to wait to see if it presented any problems, realizing that she had no idea if any of this was actually safe for her to eat, and likely neither did they, if they were giving her options, she awkwardly poured herself another glass of water and drank it. Her head throbbed, and the room had started to spin again as she drank, so she grabbed the pain cream and stumbled back to her bed to lie down. After applying a generous glob to her head and sighing with the nearly instantaneous relief, she fell asleep.

She woke up some time later as another problem presented itself. She badly needed to use the bathroom, but there wasn't anywhere for her to go. She tried yelling and banging on the wall like before, but no one came this time. She managed to hold it for a while longer—how long, she didn't know—but there was nothing to give away any sense of time passing in the room.

When it got to the point where she couldn't wait any longer, she went to the corner as far away from her 'bed' as she could get. She winced as it splashed on some of the unhealed cuts on her leg, and it stung. She didn't even have anything to wipe herself with. She tried to tear a piece of fabric off her blanket, but it wouldn't rip, so she just drip-dried. Then, trying to ignore the smell, she dragged the large platter of food over by her bed and away from the mess.

After applying more of the pain goop to her stinging cuts and her arm, which had started throbbing when she'd tried to pick up the tray, she cautiously tried another piece of food. This one was almost as horrible as the first, and she spit it out immediately. She eventually found two other strange globs that were reasonably edible, took those containers out, leaving them by her bed, and dragged the putrid remainder over next to her mess.

Some unknown length of time later, the creature returned with another thermos of water and a tray of food, but stopped and sniffed as they entered. Their whiskers and nose twitched, and they turned and found the puddle in the corner. They set the tray down next to her bed, where she was still lying down, scanned her again with the blue laser, and after a few moments turned and left, only to return a few minutes later with various items to clean up her mess.

The cat sprayed the walls and floor with something that smelled faintly of antiseptic and wiped it all up with a thin towel that looked bigger than her blanket. When the mess was cleaned up, the cat walked over and touched a spot on the wall close to ten feet up, causing a panel in the floor to slide open.

They dumped the mess down the opening, which sucked the towel away, then pushed the button again to close the panel. The creature turned and tilted their furry head to look at her, before turning back to the wall and dragged their paw from the spot on the wall to one lower, about five feet down. Then they tapped the spot twice, causing the panel in the floor to open and close.

Did they just lower the switch down so I could reach it? That's some seriously cool tech, Jessica thought, and smiled her thanks.

The cat looked at her one more time, twitched their whiskers forward again, and left.

Jessica carefully walked over and peered closely at the wall, but she couldn't see anything different about that section of the wall than any other.

How did they know where to press? she wondered. Gently tapping what she thought was the same spot, she was rewarded when the panel opened. She peered down and found a large funnel that led to a tube about six inches in diameter. It only went down a foot or so before angling off towards the nearest wall. She placed her hand over the hole and felt a gentle suction.

She wondered if there were other hidden buttons and spent the next several hours methodically touching every section of the wall that she could reach. She found nothing. If they were there, they were too high for her to reach, like the first button had been. She tried jumping up once, but that made her so dizzy that she ended up throwing up in the hole.

The cat was back almost immediately, scanning her.

Jessica grabbed her head as she threw up again, and then collapsed to the side of the hole, eyes closed, trying to keep the world from spinning and her head from throbbing.

A few minutes later, they tapped her on the shoulder and she opened her eyes. They handed her a cup. Jessica didn't feel like drinking anything, but when she didn't take it, they physically sat her up and held it to her mouth, forcing her to drink.

Coughing and spluttering, she forced it down, and when done, they picked her up with ease and carried her back to her bed. To her relief, the dizziness faded somewhat, and she lay there watching as they picked up all of the food sources and carried them out. They returned a few minutes later with a different tray, scanned her again, twitched their whiskers, and left.

Eventually, the glowing ceiling dimmed, although more than enough light remained for her to see by. In the relative dark, she could almost make out a faint bluish white light from the spot on the wall that opened the newly christened Hole of Muck.

The only other light she could see was over by the section of wall the creature had exited through, but it was far too high for her to reach. Still, she crawled off her bed and stumbled over to the other light anyway. She tried balling up her blanket and tossing it, but it didn't activate the door. Disappointed, but not the least bit surprised, she used the Hole of Muck and staggered her way back to bed, where she fell into a deep and dreamless sleep.

She woke twice during the night, but since it was still dark and she felt horrible, she went back to sleep. The next morning, she woke as the room brightened once again. She carefully stretched, used the facilities, and waited. She was still very dizzy, but her head didn't hurt quite so bad, and she was shocked to see how much her cuts and bruises had healed overnight. While she waited, she applied more of the miracle cream to her injuries and sighed as the pain faded.

Before long, the creature returned with more food and water and went through the same process as the day before. This time, however, they motioned for her to tilt her head to the side and put something in her ears.

Whatever it was, it stung. Jessica flinched but didn't cry out, figuring that at least they were trying to help. They also pressed something against the side of her arm. She had no idea what they'd done as it left no mark, and she hadn't felt anything.

Once that was done, the creature left as quickly as they had come. This time, the food tray held more of the items she'd actually eaten before, plus a dozen strange new items. None of the foods she tried and spat out ever returned.

Are they trying to figure out what foods I can eat? Jessica wondered, surprised that they were even bothering to take her preferences into account.

She was able to add another item to the list of somewhat passable foods. *Nothing to write home about,* she thought, and then frowned. *Not that there was even a home left to write to.*

By the end of the day, her fear had turned into a deep melancholy. Jessica took her time trying the new foods, but that still left her with nothing to do but sit there or sleep. She was still quite dizzy, so she avoided walking as much as possible, although she thought it might be a little better since they put whatever it was in her ears.

As the night progressed, her broken arm began to throb even with the miracle cream, and she tossed and turned, trying to find a comfortable position on the thin mattress that was her bed, wishing she had a pillow or three.

Her hand felt stiff and numb. When she gave up trying to sleep and stumbled her way over to grab something to drink, she realized she couldn't make her hand work enough to unscrew the lid.

Worried now, she started yelling for help and held the thermos up, figuring that someone was watching her, since they'd come so quickly when she'd been sick before.

A few minutes later, the lights brightened. Her cat appeared and walked over to open the thermos.

Jessica set it down and shook her head hard, holding her injured arm up and pointing to it instead. In the light of the room, she could now see the telltale marks of an infection creeping out from under the same strange bandage that was under the cast, and it was so swollen that the skin of her arm was pressing hard up against the cast.

The cat sat and examined her arm, then left, returning moments later with the scanner. The cat's ears twitched as she examined the readings, and then, to Jessica's surprise, actually picked her up and carried her out of the room.

The cat walked right through the wall as if it wasn't even there and down a short hallway before passing through another wall and into a room that was clearly a hospital of some sort, as beds lined both sides of the room, separated by transparent walls.

Most of the beds had people in them, and teams of doctors working to repair injuries as bad, if not worse than hers had been, or at least that's what she thought was going on. She tried to see if she recognized anyone, but couldn't get a clear look with their faces covered by masks, and the large bodies of the cats in the way. At least she hoped they were doctors trying to save them, and not scientists dissecting them.

Her cat set her down gently on an open bed, and another cat appeared moments later. This one reminded her of a lioness, only their fur was longer and a beautiful, rich gold, except for where it darkened on their face and the tips of their ears, and faded to almost white under their chin and chest. Their eyes were a vibrant mix of yellow and green that sparkled in the bright lights of the operating room.

There was some sort of conversation between the two that she couldn't hear, as they both looked at the monitor that was above her bed.

She tried to see what they were looking at, but couldn't, as the gold cat placed a paw on her chest, holding her down, possibly thinking she was trying to get away.

Jessica stilled, and the cat took her paw away. Moments later, they began cutting away the cast on her arm, then carefully removed it.

She sighed in relief as the pain and pressure caused by the swelling of her arm against the cast was removed, although without the support of her cast, her arm now throbbed.

Setting the cast aside, the gold cat grabbed another tool and ran that over the strange bandage that turned it from white to green, and then carefully wiped it away, just as the other cat had done with the bandage on her side.

She hissed in pain but didn't pull her arm away.

The gold cat's ears twitched, and they looked over at her. Jessica wasn't sure, but it was almost as if the cat was surprised that she didn't pull away. Flicking an ear back, the cat went back to work.

When they turned away to grab something, Jessica lifted her head slightly to see the swollen and infected arm. A combination of jagged scars where her broken bones had once poked through, and a long, angry incision that went almost the entire length of her arm.

She quickly put her head back down when the gold cat turned back around. They flicked an ear back slightly and pressed something to her shoulder just above where the incision started. Almost immediately, her arm went numb.

The cream-colored cat that had carried her in held her arm down while the gold cat ran another tool along the incision, opening it back up. She turned her head to watch as blood and pus oozed out of the wound, but she didn't feel a thing.

Lightheaded and queasy from the sight, she swallowed hard and looked away. Suddenly, she found a mask being placed over her nose and mouth, and felt something pressed against her other arm. Moments later, she was asleep.

When she woke again, her arm was back in another cast, a mask was over her face, and an IV had been hooked up to her arm. She felt awful, queasy, and slightly delirious.

It took her a while to remember where she was, and that she had a raging infection in her arm, and judging from her cracked and parched lips, a very high fever. Before long, though, she slid back to sleep and drifted between nightmares and consciousness as the cats tried to save her life.

6

NAZARI: BROKEN HEARTS

*N*azari Jabri, the team leader of pod four, yawned as she left her room. She'd been up for three days straight, treating those patients who had been sedated and lying on the floor of the ship's cargo bays, assisting the other healers in her pod with their patients, as most of her patients were still in stasis.

They'd all crashed when the last surgery was complete, knowing those in stasis could wait, but she hadn't been able to sleep nearly long enough to recover. Her patients needed care and food. Stopping at the dispensary, she grabbed a stimulant, knowing it was going to be another long day, and snorted at the nearly empty box. They'd all been running on stimulants and would pay for it later, but there hadn't been any other choice.

Grabbing one, she sighed with relief as the fatigue retreated to more manageable levels and began restocking the dispensary and equipment room. They'd decimated their supplies, and the room was a mess. It took her nearly an hour to restock, clean up, and fire off a message to Brice, letting her know what they'd used so far.

She finished just as the first of the other healers in her pod started appearing, looking as exhausted as she felt, and heading straight for the box of stimulants.

That task done, she began preparing the morning meal for the patients in her care. She'd chosen to focus on the few pregnant animals rescued, as that best fit her experience and ended up with a mix of bipeds, what they were calling long-legged grazers, and two species that looked an awful lot like their own, although the adults were no bigger than their cubs.

Of the bipeds, there were four pregnant mothers, two in stasis, which was very concerning, as her own species did not do well with being in stasis when pregnant. She also had the youngest cub rescued, and one elderly male brought in with one of the long-legged grazers.

While not badly injured, he had suffered a heart attack from the stunner used on him and had been placed in stasis when initial triage had failed to restart it. Also in stasis were all of the long-legged grazers. Several, including one female that was pregnant with two cubs, had badly broken legs. The others hadn't been as badly injured but had started to have issues with being sedated shortly after they'd left the planet.

After preparing the first of her meals, she made her way to the larger of the two feline habitats and hit the switch so she could view inside. She found the creature pacing in her habitat, the sedative worn off. When it was on the other side of the habitat, she cautiously entered. It spun and immediately began growling, hackles raised.

"It's alright. I'm not going to hurt you," she said, and began purring, unsure if the creature that looked so much like her species purred as well, but hoping that it would recognize her lack of aggression.

She slowly set the tray of food down, and it hissed and spat at her, but didn't attack. She picked up her scanner and checked on the creature.

Her injuries are healing well, and everything looks good with her cubs, she thought as she examined the readings.

Her injuries had thankfully been fairly minor and easily treatable. The worst of which had been burns on her paws from stepping on hot embers from the falling ash. The nano treatment appeared to be working well enough, and while she'd like to give another treatment, she decided to wait until later, hoping that maybe she would be calmer with her next visit.

As the feline was acting now, she'd have to sedate her in order to treat her. Sliding the tray of food over, she sat and waited, wondering if she would eat or not, but after a few minutes, when feline continued to growl, Nazari stood and left to care for her other patients.

Her next patient, the smaller of the two feline mothers, looked to be no bigger than their own newborns, and Nazari found her curled up in a tiny ball under the blanket that had been left in her room. She scanned the creature through the blanket before carefully pulling it back, trying not to wake her. Her heart nearly broke at the sight, as she looked so much like how one of her daughters had looked when she'd been born.

Unable to resist herself, she started purring and gently reached down and stroked the tiny creature. It started purring in response, although higher-pitched than her own cubs, and stretched, rolling over, but seeing her, it bolted to its feet with a hiss, poofing out its back fur and tail adorably.

She chuckled and kept purring. To her surprise, it calmed and cautiously approached, her tiny nose sniffing furiously.

Nazari slowly held out a paw as she continued to purr.

The tiny feline sniffed at Nazari's paw and, to her utter shock, rubbed up against it and began purring again.

This will make things easier, Nazari thought.

After a moment, though, it turned its attention to the tray of food and sniffed at that instead, and to Nazari's relief, began eating.

Smiling, Nazari slowly stood and walked out.

Her next two patients were the two pregnant biped females in her care. They'd been terrified the night before when they'd come out of sedation, but they'd thankfully cooperated with her care and treatment of their injuries. This morning was no different, although they seemed a little less terrified.

Her final patient was the small biped cub. She hadn't interacted with him yet, as he'd been the last of her patients that she'd treated, being the least injured, only a few cuts and bruises. He'd miraculously been unhurt when he'd been buried by the rubble of the building he'd been in, but they'd lost two of the Digger guards trying to save him and his mother. The mother hadn't survived.

She watched him through the display and sighed.

He was sitting on his bed, sucking his thumb, and hiccuping, tears streaming down his tiny face.

She slowly entered, trying not to scare him, and sat down just inside the door, purring, as she set her tray down beside her.

She expected him to scream as the others had, or at the very least back away, but instead his tiny little face lit up and he ran over to her and buried himself in her fur, hugging her.

She reached down and carefully picked him up, and he snuggled into her arms, thumb back in his mouth, and within moments had fallen asleep. She sat there for far longer than she had time for, just holding him, her heart breaking with sympathy for the tiny cub.

Eventually, though, she carried him back to his bed and gently laid him down. She scanned him to confirm he was still healthy and covered him back up with the blanket. With a final look and a heavy sigh, she left. She had other patients to care for.

That evening, exhausted, she was just climbing into bed when her tablet alerted her of a potential problem in the cub's room. They had no idea what was normal for any of the species, so Nazari had set her tablet to alert her of any change.

His heart rate was up, and his oxygen level was down slightly. Neither was critical as far as they knew so far, so she pulled up the feed from his room to see what was going on.

He was crying again, this time, far more than the hiccups and tears from earlier, and his face showed he was scared.

Night terror? she wondered. She turned up the lights in the room, and he calmed somewhat, but he kept crying.

Yawning, she left her room and made her way over. The moment she entered his habitat, he ran over to her and she scooped him up and began purring. When he calmed, she tried to put him back on his bed, but he started screaming immediately and held tightly to her fur.

Sighing, knowing she was breaking all the rules, she lay down on the thin mattress and let him snuggle with her, hoping he would fall asleep quickly.

Thoroughly exhausted, she fell asleep before he did.

7

JESSICA: RESEARCH SUBJECT

Jessica woke to find herself back in her room, with a tray of food and water placed close to her bed. The cover of the strange thermos was already off, and water poured out for her.

She carefully sat up and drank until the cup was empty. As her queasiness and thirst faded, she examined her arm and flexed her hand, grateful to see it was working again.

Several days must have passed, she thought, as most of the small cuts and bruises on her body had disappeared, leaving only the one on her side, which was now a faded yellow and green instead of the angry blue and purple it had been before. Her arm was still in a cast, but it hurt far less than it had before. Out of all of her injuries, it was the knot on the side of her head that now hurt the worst. She unscrewed the cover on the pain cream and gently massaged some into the still tender lump.

That done, she laid back down, ignoring the food as she wasn't hungry and her stomach felt queasy. Moments later, she fell back to sleep. She must have slept through the return of the cat, as when she woke again, her cup had been refilled.

She drank again and, feeling a little less queasy than before, tried some of the food provided. She sampled each of the new items, only finding one that was even remotely edible. She forced it down, knowing she needed to eat, but it wasn't long before she was staggering over to the waste hole and throwing it back up.

The cream-colored cat was there moments later, scanning her and handing her another cup of water.

Jessica took it and drank, knowing that if she didn't, they'd just force her to drink it anyway. Like before, though, it calmed her stomach, and she wondered if there was something in the water.

They left, taking the tray with them, and returned a few minutes later with a new one. Hesitant now, she approached the tray, but the only items on it were ones she'd eaten before and had not had problems with. They were disgusting, but at least they didn't make her sick. She ate a few bites, then laid back down, and was soon fast asleep.

The next morning, she felt significantly better, and even her cream-colored fuzzy physician seemed pleased to see her sitting up and waiting for her. After a quick scan, they left, leaving her with her breakfast, which she picked at. Hours later, they returned with another tray of food and water, set it down, and then walked back out.

She was surprised at how disappointed she was that the creature didn't stay. At least the medical examinations helped to break up the day a bit. Sighing, she climbed out of her bed and walked over to the tray that had been placed in the middle of the room, rather than by her bed.

She wasn't really hungry, but it was something to do. However, this time there was a new object on the tray. Picking it up, she turned it over and over in her hands, trying to figure out what it was. It looked like nothing more than a wooden cube, maybe six inches long on each side. She gave it a shake and felt something rattle inside. She shook it again and was sure she could feel something moving around, although she still couldn't hear anything.

Dragging everything back to her bed, she leaned up against the wall, eating and fiddling with the box, turning it every which way, to see if she could find a seam, or something she could move.

It took her forever, but she finally found one tiny spot that pushed in slightly. This allowed another section to slide over. It took her most of the rest of the day to figure out how to open the box, and she cheered when the lid finally popped open.

There was a small pyramid-shaped object inside, about the size of a golf ball. Taking the object out, she set the box aside and examined the pyramid closely. It had rounded corners and iridescent sides that would sparkle when you turned it over, but she couldn't see any purpose to it.

Maybe it doesn't have any purpose besides being pretty, she thought, and absentmindedly gave it a toss in the air.

As she did, it lit up and sparkled a rainbow of colors on the wall as it went up and came back down. She put her hand out to catch it, but to her amazement, instead of landing in her hand, it slowed and stopped to hover a few inches above it, spinning slowly and lighting the room like a disco ball.

"Sweet!" she said and lifted her hand. The pyramid rose too, staying the same distance from her hand. She took her hand away, but rather than falling like she expected it to, it hovered in place. She then gave it a little push from the side, and she watched as it slowly floated across the room, right into the paws of the cat, who had appeared once again, completely unnoticed.

"What's up, Doc?" Jessica asked and waved. She wasn't sure, but she thought Doc looked pleased as they tossed the object back to her.

Jessica stopped it with her outstretched palm and grabbed it from both sides. It immediately stopped spinning and emitting light. When she looked back, Doc was already gone. A new tray of food and water was the only sign that they'd ever been there.

"So, it's a no to a game of fetch then?" she asked after the retreating cat, shrugged, and then proceeded to bounce the object off the walls for hours, for lack of anything better to do.

Jessica's days turned to one of absolute boredom as she healed. Doc would show up with meals three times a day and leave after briefly scanning her.

On what she thought was day six, since she'd returned from the other room, Doc carried in some sort of large canister with a nozzle on it, and made Jessica stand over the waste hole and began spraying her down with it. Whatever it was, it wasn't water and tasted horrible.

To her frustration, she wasn't even given a towel to dry off with. She tried asking for something to comb her hair out with, but Doc either didn't understand or refused, because a comb never showed up. Thankfully, her hair was fairly short, so she just did what she could to comb it out with her fingers.

Six days later, Doc appeared again with the canister, but before hosing her down, she took off Jessica's cast and bandage and examined the scar and bruising, which had healed considerably. Only faint lines showed where the wounds and incisions had been.

Doc tested her strength, comparing both arms and hands, before leading her over to the Hole of Muck and spraying her down again. A few moments later, the big cat returned with her meal and a squishy ball. Doc had her do a number of different exercises. The cat never spoke to her. They just motioned what they wanted, which Jessica copied.

She was bored, but they weren't hurting her, and the physical therapy gave her something to do. The ball was left behind, but every meal after for the next twelve days consisted of various exercises for her arm, most of which were range-of-motion related.

Twelve days later, they switched to strengthening exercises and left her with a large collection of oddly shaped magnetic building blocks and a stack of cards with different shapes and structures she could build with them.

She flipped through the stack of cards, wondering if they were testing her, as they got progressively more complex, or if they were just trying to keep her entertained while she healed.

After considering it for a few minutes, she shrugged. She was bored enough not to care and started work on the first one. She worked through the entire stack in a few days, and that was with taking long naps in between and purposely spacing them out between meals. In the event that they were testing her, she waited until after Doc had seen each structure before beginning the next.

Doc seemed pleased with both her recovery and her creations. When she finished with the last one, she made a house of cards with the stack and waited, wondering if they would bring a new stack.

Doc smiled at her stack, but that was it.

Shrugging, Jessica proceeded to make her own creations for lack of anything else to do. Then, when that became boring, she made towers out of them and used her drone and the squishy ball as a bowling ball to knock them down. After that, she made obstacles and tried to see if she could float the drone through without touching them.

After another twelve days of this, they provided her with a box full of randomly shaped plastic pieces. That turned out to be a three-dimensional puzzle that took her almost all of the next twelve days to complete.

At this point, she was pretty sure her intelligence was being tested, but it kept her busy while she was recovering. She was improving. Her arm was stronger, and the rest of her injuries had mostly healed up, all except for the lump on her head. She was still dizzy and had regular headaches, but they were bearable now.

When she finally completed the puzzle, she was actually fairly proud of herself and sat down next to it, waiting for Doc to come in.

Doc grinned when they entered with her meal and set it down next to her, then surprised her with the first show of affection she'd seen from the giant cat when they patted her briefly on her head.

Who's a good girl, Jessica? she thought, and grinned up at Doc. "Do I get a treat now?" she asked, resisting the urge to start begging like a dog.

Doc twitched an ear, grinned at her, and left.

"So no treat, then?" Jessica asked.

Shrugging, she examined the tray of food and tried one of the new items. It was actually halfway decent.

This is a change, she thought. She ate the entire container, wondering the whole time if it had been a reward for completing the puzzle.

8

MYRA: MEDICALLY NECESSARY INTERVENTION

Myra sat in her tiny office growling at her tablet as she read the official message that had just come in from Senior Councilor Tabor. When she was done, she placed a call to her partner.

Jer answered immediately. "I know, Myra. I'm sorry," he said, before she could even get a word out.

"Jeran Frederick Chenzira, this is unacceptable. I asked for an increase in my budget, and instead it's been slashed in half? How am I supposed to keep these species alive and thriving when you haven't provided me with more than enough of a budget to keep them fed? What happened to 'whatever she needs, this *Council* authorizes'? And what's with all of these extra restrictions you're placing on the healers? There's absolutely no reason for it. We haven't had so much as a cold, not since we figured out how to treat that infection the bipeds brought with them. We should be interacting with them more and trying to repopulate the species, not less, or at the very least trying to figure out how to communicate with them."

Jer frowned at the use of his full name, which she only used when she was really upset with him. "I know, Myra. Marcus and I both tried hard to convince the Council otherwise. Paxton and his crew feel pretty strongly about increased interaction until we can determine if there's anything else we need to worry about being able to treat. He claims he's worried that if we reintroduce them too soon, they'll get sick and we'll lose the species. And it's hard to justify wasting credit on *toys* when they already have so many."

"It's not a waste, Jeran," Myra snapped. "It's the only thing they have to do all day in those empty rooms, since the Council won't give us anything to furnish or decorate them with. And taking the Healer's time away from caring for the younger cubs? That's just cruel. Would you have left our cubs locked in a room alone for hours on end? They're a social species, I just know it, and cubs need a lot of interaction and play to develop properly, far more than the one toy a week that the Council had been sending. They should be placed in the care of another female, at the very least."

"I know, and I agree with you. The best I can do is try to get it on the docket for the Full Council meeting next month, but Tabor is in agreement with the others, so I doubt that it's going to happen. You could try sending letters to the other Seniors, or maybe reach out to Ellie and see if there is anything she can do on her end," Jer replied.

"Oh, trust me. *Everyone* is going to hear about this," Myra growled.

Jer flicked his ears back in surprise at the venom in her voice, and Myra pulled her emotions back under control.

"Sorry, Jer. I didn't mean to yell at you. I'm just frustrated."

"I know. I am, too. On the plus side, they agreed you can start interacting between pods again. That's a step forward at least."

Myra snorted. "We should have been able to do that a month ago. Still, it will be good to get outside again, if it ever stops raining." She leaned back in her chair with a sigh. "Jer, the scans are saying many of these creatures only live for a few years. If we don't start repopulating the species, we could lose them to old age before the tests are complete. As it is, we have no idea how many times they come into heat, and we could easily miss that opportunity."

"I know, Myra," Jer said with an equally heavy sigh. "But we may end up losing many of those species anyway, just because they don't have enough representatives. They were only rescued as a possible food source, not knowing what the bipeds ate, and they aren't even eating the ones we've tried to feed them."

"That's no reason to let a species go extinct," Myra growled, letting her displeasure out.

"I know, Myra," Jer repeated.

Myra pinned her ears and growled at him. "Saying I know doesn't help matters any."

"I know, Myra," Jer replied, his voice teasing this time, clearly hoping to lighten the mood. It didn't work. She continued to glare at him, and he sighed. "I don't know what else to do. I can't even get the Council to figure out what we're going to do with them, if we do manage to repopulate the various species, in the first place. None of the water species can even survive on our planet outside of the tanks they're in now, and none of the other planets have stepped up to take them yet."

She let out a snort and muttered under her breath.

"I didn't quite catch that," Jer said with a grin.

Myra knew full well he did and just rolled her eyes.

He stopped grinning and scratched at the back of his head. "There's something else I need to tell you."

"Now what?" Myra asked, frowning, worried about what other unnecessary restrictions the Council had placed on her.

"Marsee's switched guilds again. She moved over to the Writers Guild this time," Jer replied.

"Again?! She just earned her Journeyman's rank in the Artist Guild. What was her reasoning this time?" Myra asked, not expecting this change in the subject. Marsee hadn't said anything about wanting to switch guilds the last time she'd spoken to her.

"She went over to Marcus's last week when I was stuck late at a district meeting, and met a Flyer, who was there restoring a few old books Marcus had just purchased. Apparently, Marsee now wants to do *that* with the rest of her life. I caught her watching a Flyer language course in the family room the other night, so I'm not sure if it has anything to do with the books or the Flyer in particular, seeing as she's mentioned his musical voice several times now."

Myra raised a brow and considered. Cross-species partnerships happened, but they weren't all that common. That Marsee was showing an interest in anyone was even more unusual. The Flyers did have a very musical language that relied heavily on tone and pitch to convey meaning, and her older cubs were all musicians, a trait inherited from Myra's mother. But Marsee had never shown any musical inclinations, outside of listening to it, although they'd tried when she was younger.

Marsee had given up after a week, declaring that she couldn't stand the sound of her own bad performance enough to practice. Marsee's love for reading and books in general had been a passion of hers since before she could read, so it wasn't entirely surprising that she'd switch to a guild having something to do with that. She'd never done much writing before, outside of required school work, though.

Myra let out a thoroughly exasperated sigh, but shrugged. "Well, she's excelled in the other guilds, so I see no reason not to let her explore this one, and learning another language will serve her well if she *ever* moves away from home. You and I both know the language courses in the primary schools only cover the basics. Plus, if she's learning the other languages, she'll have to talk to someone to practice. Maybe we can convince her to go spend some time with your parents while I'm stuck here."

"That's not a bad idea. If nothing else, I'll probably have to drag her with me to the Full Council meeting, unless the neighbors will watch her. You don't think she'll leave home when she earns her adulthood?" Jer asked.

Myra snorted and rolled her eyes. "Only if she could move the tower with her, too. If she moves anywhere, it'll be right to Marcus's library."

Jer chuckled. "You're probably not wrong there. So, do you want me to package up some of the toys in the nursery and send those over?"

Myra nodded. "Jenny's cubs are getting too big for most of it. Send a few of the stuffies too. They're technically not allowed since they can't easily be sterilized, but the cubs will need something if the

Healers are pulled out of their rooms, and those at least haven't been around anyone in months."

"I heard nothing," Jer said, looking away with an innocent expression.

Mrya smiled in appreciation, knowing that they could both get in trouble if the Council found out. She was mad enough not to care.

"Maybe reach out to Jenny and the rest of the family, and see if they have anything they could spare. And ask Marsee if she'll make a few of those puzzle boxes that she did when she was younger. One of the cubs here loves them, but the ones we *were* getting from the Guild are getting too easy for her now. I'll pay for whatever material she needs out of my own credit. The more complicated, the better. I'll reach out to Ellie and see what else she can scrounge up. I imagine there must be a pile of rejected toys from some apprentice somewhere. Slightly damaged or used would be better than nothing, as long as it still works. And send me a list of the councilors who voted against this, if you wouldn't mind."

Jer nodded. It was public record, but he would do what he could to make Myra's life easier, even if all he could do was gather a list of names. "If you can convince Paxton, you'll stand a better chance with the rest. He's been the most vocal from day one."

"Thanks, Jer. I appreciate it," she replied. "And give Marsee a hug from me."

"Will do. Love you," he said, and hung up.

Myra growled at her blank tablet for several moments before forwarding the latest restrictions from the Council to the rest of the healers.

Brice appeared moments later. "You've got to be pulling my tail, Myra," she said, holding up her tablet.

"I wish I was," Myra replied, with barely controlled frustration.

"Those blithering, bumble crawlers. I'm half a mind to switch districts just to be able to vote Tabor out for this," Brice replied, then let out a derisive snort and stormed away.

Myra shook her head at her protege's retreating back, and considered doing the same, not that she thought it would do any good.

She'd just finished her objection to Senior Councilor Tabor when she received an urgent call from Nazari. She had the majority of the cubs in her pod, and her team would be the worst affected. Figuring it was about the Council's edicts, Myra sighed and answered. "I'm sorry, Nazari. I'm doing what I can."

Nazari blinked at her. "I'm guessing there's a message I haven't read yet and don't want to," she replied, then sighed at Myra's nod, but didn't wait for clarification. "I'm calling because 34 is in distress. It's been over an hour since her amniotic sac broke, but the birth canal still isn't dilated enough for the cub to come out."

Myra frowned. "Is the cub showing signs of distress?"

"Not yet," Nazari said, "But the mother is having strong contractions, about every twenty minutes."

"I'll be right over," Myra said, and hung up.

She stepped outside for the first time in just over two months and was immediately drenched. It was pouring so hard that even the static shields couldn't block it. She quickly ran over to pod four and shook her fur out.

Nazari was waiting for her with a curious frown and backed off before the spray of water could hit her.

"Before you ask, yes, I'm allowed. The Council lifted the quarantine between the pods today, but before you get too excited, it's the only good thing they did. Now tell me about 34."

Nazari pursed her lips at Myra's statement, but didn't comment. Instead, she turned and walked quickly back towards the trauma bay, giving her a full rundown on the way.

Nazari already had the scans up on one of the monitors, and Myra carefully examined them.

Nazari had been a Master Animal Healer for nearly as long as Myra had been in the Healer's Guild.

She had briefly mentored under Nazari to learn to care for the herds of Chenzies in her district, after their local animal healer had died. Myra had far more experience with childbirth, though, as she'd been responsible for a significantly greater area and population than Nazari.

She compared the first set of scans to the last one Nazari had taken and did some quick math. "If she continues to dilate at this rate, it's going to be at least another six or seven hours before she's ready to give birth. That would be far too long for any other species that I'm aware of, but it's not surprising that the amniotic sac broke based on the strength of these contractions. She must be in a lot of pain. Have you given her anything for it yet?"

"No, I've been keeping my distance. She's been showing signs of aggression for the past several days and not sleeping well," Nazari replied. "That's not uncommon when animals are close to giving birth."

Myra nodded as she continued to examine the scans. "I wasn't exactly all that fun to be around with my two litters either. Still, we have no idea what's normal for this species. We'll keep watch for the next hour and wait, as long as the cub doesn't show any signs of distress. I'd rather not operate if we don't have to. Do you think you can bring her here for observation without sedating her? I don't want to risk slowing things down further with a sedative."

"I can try," Nazari said and left, but returned a few minutes later without the biped.

Myra frowned at the look Nazari gave her. "What happened?"

"No luck. She refused to follow and then bit me when I tried to pick her up," Nazari replied, holding up her paw.

Myra pursed her lips and examined the other healer's wound. This was the second bite from a biped this week, and it worried her that they were starting to act with aggression. There were a few small bite marks, but nothing serious. Nazari's thick skin and fur mostly protected her, but a few teeth had broken through.

Nazari grabbed a jar of nano's and applied a liberal dose after Myra had finished examining it.

"Scan it hourly. If you start to feel sick at all, let me know immediately."

"So what are we going to do about 34?" Nazari asked as she put the jar of nanos away.

Myra shrugged. "If she won't leave her habitat, we'll just have to treat her there, unless something goes wrong. We'd have to sedate her then anyway."

Myra started putting together supplies they might need on a tray. When she was done, she followed the other healer out to the biped's room, while Nazari pushed one of the neonatal units.

The female was curled up on her bed in the corner of the room, grabbing the mattress tightly when they entered. Pain wracked the creature's face, and her bulging stomach rippled with the contraction she was having.

Myra remembered the pain of childbirth and winced in sympathy. *The poor creature must be terrified*, she thought.

"It's okay. We're just here to help," Myra said. She knew the female wouldn't understand but hoped her intentions would come across.

She sat some distance away. Nazari did as well, following her lead.

When the creature's contraction stopped, she sat up and backed herself further into the corner, wrapping her arms protectively around her belly. She positively reeked of fear.

They sat and waited for the biped to calm, and when she finally relaxed, they tried to move closer. The female started making high-pitched growling and hissing noises and making claw-like motions with her paws.

It was pretty clear that she didn't want them to come any closer, so they just sat and observed. Twenty minutes later or so, she had another contraction and gritted her teeth through the pain.

After an hour had passed, Myra compared the scans and confirmed that the birth canal was continuing to open at about the same rate. The cub remained stable, so they decided to continue waiting. Cutting the cub out would be far more dangerous to the female, and they honestly needed the information on what a natural birth looked like for the species, abnormal or otherwise.

Myra's own species only took about an hour per cub once contractions started, but hours passed as they waited, and with every one that did, Myra's worry increased, even though both the mother and cub remained stable.

The female stood and walked around the room several times,

bending over with each contraction as it occurred, but still she refused to allow them to approach.

After a few hours of this, Myra began to discuss with Nazari whether or not they should try to cut the cub out. They ultimately decided to wait, as the birth canal continued to expand. The cub was huge compared to the mother and would need a lot of room to come out.

The female finally let them approach when the contractions became too painful to keep her from screaming. Myra quickly gave her something for the pain. The mother collapsed in relief against her, and after that, didn't resist their treatments and examinations.

When the next contraction hit and the biped scrunched her face in pain again, Myra frowned in both sympathy and worry as the pain block didn't appear to be working. She had no idea if it was because of a species difference or if the pain was just that bad, and the female still wasn't ready to give birth even though she'd been in labor for hours.

How horrible, Myra thought, wondering if this was common for the species and praying that it wasn't.

Nazari left to bring food and water to her other wards, while Myra stayed with the mother and waited, lending a tail for support as the mother struggled to stand up and walk around the room again.

When a contraction hit, Myra winced, as the female crushed her tail from the pain and effort needed to stay on her feet. She was surprised at how strong the tiny creatures were, but didn't try to move her tail out of the way, and helped her back to the bed to lie down afterwards.

The poor creature collapsed, exhausted from a single trip around the room.

"It can't be much longer," Nazari said, examining the scans when she returned. "The opening is almost big enough now."

"I hope so. She's getting significantly weaker. She could barely make it around the room while you were gone. If the cub's not out in another half hour, we'll operate," Myra said.

As she did, though, another contraction rippled through the female, causing her to scream this time and bear down.

Myra pinned her ears back but let out the slightest sigh of relief. "Finally," Myra said, as the cub's head began to appear.

She clearly wasn't ready enough, though, as the skin tore around the opening, causing her to bleed, but there was little they could do to stop the bleeding until the cub was out.

The biped sagged as the contraction eased. Myra frowned and gave the female a little shove to wake her up again. The female scowled at her as she opened her eyes.

Myra tried to motion with her paws that the female needed to push and then had Nazari lift her up to allow gravity to assist. She was worried that the biped, as exhausted as she was, wouldn't have the strength to finish pushing the cub out.

This must have made sense because with the next contraction, she bore down with a scream that made Myra's heart whimper for the poor female, but it was enough to get the cub's head out.

She carefully supported the cub and applied gentle pressure as the female bore down again, and the cub was finally delivered. More fluid and blood began pouring out, though.

Nazari gently set the female down and quickly cut the umbilical cord, and then began the careful work of suturing the torn skin to stop the bleeding, while Myra began cleaning the cub and drying him off.

She set the tiny cub down in the neonatal unit, and the monitors on the bed activated and began warming the cub. The tiny little thing wiggled his paws in the air and made sucking motions with his mouth.

Myra worried that he wasn't getting enough oxygen, but the monitors said he was fine, as best they knew anyway. She decided it must be a nursing reflex and examined the cub's other reflexes, trying to get a sense of what was normal for a newborn.

The cub was the same dark brown color as his mother and had a tiny wisp of curly black fur on his head, but had light blue eyes instead of the brown ones his mother had.

The cubs of Myra's species didn't open their eyes until they were about a week old, and she worried that there might be a problem, as often occurred in her own species if the lids opened too soon. The scans said they were fine, though.

His neck was weak, but considering that his head was fairly out of proportion to the rest of his body, which seemed to be normal with younger cubs, she wasn't too worried. He didn't have all that much strength in his limbs either, but her own species took years to learn how to walk upright on two feet.

What he did have, though, was a very strong grip reflex, and Myra wondered what purpose that was for since the species didn't have all that much fur to hold on to. After recording her observations, she injected the chip so that they could monitor the cub's status outside of the unit and turned back to Nazari to see how she was doing with the mother.

The biped mother was passed out, sound asleep, thoroughly exhausted after her ordeal. She barely woke a few minutes later as another contraction hit and the placenta was ejected. She collapsed again afterwards, breathing hard.

Nazari quickly cleaned up the mess and placed it in one of the storage containers for further study and analysis by the scientists. By the time Nazari finished cleaning the mother, the biped was making a high-pitched chittering noise and making motions with her paws that looked like she was asking for the cub.

Myra carefully lifted him out of the unit and handed him over with a happy smile. He was tiny, but absolutely adorable, just like the rest of the species.

The new mother sighed with relief, holding her son tightly. When the biped's fear scent went away, Myra realized that she must have been afraid they were going to take the cub.

I wonder why she would think that, Myra thought, dismissing the idea as ridiculous. Still, she continued to smile at the new mother, wishing she knew how to tell her that she and her cub were safe and that the cub appeared to be healthy.

After helping Nazari clean up, followed by a quick shower, Myra collapsed gratefully into a chair in the common room, grinning at Nazari, who flopped into her own chair with an exhausted sigh.

"All I can say is right now I'm very glad I'm not a biped," Nazari said. "That took forever! I think if my own litter had taken that long to be born, I would have clawed both of my Healers and the next male that even glanced at me."

Myra chuckled and lifted her tail. "They have a surprisingly strong grip for such a tiny species, though. I'm pretty sure I'll have a bruise on my tail from how hard she was squeezing it."

"You'd have to be strong to survive that. Ancient Gods, Myra, she wasn't even big enough to give birth without damaging herself."

"She is one of the smaller adult females. I wonder if that had anything to do with it. Something to watch out for in the others," Myra replied. "Still, they both survived, and we have good news to report to the Council for a change."

"Did you see how terrified she was that we were going to take her cub from her?" Nazari asked.

Myra nodded sadly. "I didn't want to believe it, but I don't blame her one bit if that was what she was thinking. She has no idea what our intentions are, although I'd hoped she'd be more trusting of us by now."

"Would you be?" Nazari snorted.

"No, probably not," Myra replied. "And it's just going to get worse."

Myra explained what the Council decided, and Nazari let out a very colorful string of swear words, the likes of which she'd not heard in years. "What right do they have to dictate how we care for our patients?" Nazari asked when she finally stopped swearing.

Myra frowned. "Every right, unfortunately. They make the law, and their arguments aren't completely wrong, if ridiculously short-sighted. There's a risk that reintroduction would spread disease." Myra's voice dripped with disgust as she repeated the Council's words.

"What disease? We've cured everything we've found, and none of them have had so much as a sniffle for weeks. The only thing wrong is that they're losing weight, and that likely has more to do with missing nutrients from the foods we've found safe for them to eat than any illness."

"I know. How's your paw by the way?" Myra asked, realizing with a snort that she sounded just like Jeran at that moment.

"Honestly, I completely forgot about it," Nazari replied, and unclipped her scanner to check. "Outside of a little bruising, completely healed." She felt her paw, then shrugged. "Not enough to bother with another dose of nanos."

"Well, that's one less problem to deal with. Well, I suppose I should inform the Council of our good news and finish telling them what a wonderful job I think they're doing these days." Myra heaved herself out of her seat, to Nazari's snort of amusement.

"If you need help with that," Nazari said with an innocent expression, "I'm sure I could come up with a few choice words for you."

Myra laughed. "I'm sure you could, but I would like to avoid having the Guard show up at my office for treason."

Nazari nodded the point. "I guess that's why they made you Senior, not me. I'd likely throw my scanner at them."

"Please don't. I can't afford a new one right now. Check on the mother and cub every hour and let me know if there are any issues," Myra ordered, then left to return to her office.

The rain had calmed to a drizzle, and Myra took her time walking back. It felt so good to be outside again, even if she was getting wet.

An hour later, Nazari knocked on her door, looking concerned. "I'm worried. She's still bleeding. Will you come check on her?"

Myra nodded and followed Nazari back over, glad to see it had stopped raining. She took a deep breath of the cool night air and fluffed her fur up as she walked across to the other pod.

When they entered the isolation chamber, she noticed that the mother again hugged her cub tightly.

Myra smiled to try to put the mother at ease, not that it seemed to do any good. She squatted down to scan the female and check out the amount of blood on the towels they'd left behind. There was a lot, but not enough to be life-threatening, yet.

She frowned at her hand scanner. It wasn't as detailed as she would like, and she couldn't tell where the bleeding was coming from. "Grab a sedative. I want a better scan," Myra said.

Nazari left. As she did, Myra cleaned up the current mess and helped to put a new towel down on the bed. When Nazari returned with the sedative, the mother tried to scramble away as Nazari approached with the hypo, holding tightly to her cub and chittering loudly, but Myra caught her and held her while Nazari administered the sedative.

She caught the cub before he could fall, and Nazari gently took him from her and placed him in the neonatal bed, where he would be safe while they examined his mother.

She carried the mother out to the trauma bay and gently placed her on the bed. As she examined the scans, the mother had another minor contraction, and she frowned with worry.

The scans looked much like her species did after a failed heat, which often proved fatal for them because they lost too much blood in the process. The problem was they had no idea what was normal for a biped after they gave birth.

"Hook her up to an I.V. She's dehydrated," Myra said absently, as she continued to examine the scans and the bleeding that was still occurring. "The rest of her vitals appear to be stable. I think the blood is coming from this lining, as there's tissue and other fluids being ejected, not just blood. The other females don't have this, so it's possible this is a normal function of birth for them. I'm not seeing any other injuries that would account for it. Do we have any donors with her blood type?"

"No, she's unique," Nazari said, and examined Myra's findings and nodded her head in agreement. "She's still having minor contractions, so I agree this might be natural for their species, perhaps because she only had one cub?"

"I suppose that's possible, although as big as that cub is compared to his mother, I can't imagine they have more than one at a time. There just wouldn't be room," Myra replied. "That being said, she's not losing enough blood to be dangerous, yet." She set several alerts on the mother's vitals to track the issue. "We'll monitor for now. Make sure there are plenty of towels for her to use to clean herself up with."

Myra cleaned the mother up yet again, and Nazari carried her back. She watched as they left, praying to the Ancient Gods that this was normal for them and that the mother would survive, as they had no way to care for the cub if she didn't.

THE NEXT SEVERAL days were stressful for everyone as the mother continued to bleed, and they monitored the changes that were occurring in the mother's body. The biped didn't seem overly concerned about the bleeding, only annoyed at the mess, but Nazari made sure she had plenty of supplies to clean herself with and hosed both her and the bed down daily. It took days before the bleeding slowed and almost two weeks before it stopped completely.

Myra and a group of the other healers, including Brice and Nazari, were all examining the scans after the bleeding finally stopped. As she surmised, the uterine lining had been shed and was now back to the same levels they were seeing in the other female bipeds.

"That can't be normal, Myra," Brice said. "How could their species survive with a birth process that awful? That much bleeding would be sure to attract predators."

"I honestly don't know, but she survived, which is impressive, considering the ordeal she went through," Myra replied. "We'll know more when the other pregnant female gives birth."

Nazari frowned as she examined the scans, which showed various hormone changes over the past several weeks, both before and after the pregnancy. "102 started showing this hormone change about an hour ago. If that's an early indicator for labor, and it follows the same path, we should be seeing contractions starting soon, but I'm worried. Her cub isn't in the same position for birth." Nazari pulled up the other female's scans, and they conferred. "Positioned like this, the cub's never going to fit."

Myra frowned at the clearly breech birth. "The cub isn't as big as the other one, so we might have time, but I agree. Once it's clear she's in labor, I think we should plan on cutting the cub out instead."

They spent the next several hours discussing the best way to do so with the least amount of harm, then prepped the surgery. Nazari left to take another scan but returned shortly with the female already sedated.

"Her amniotic sac broke while I was in there," Nazari explained. "That must be common for them."

Myra nodded and began cleaning the incision site while Nazari hooked up the life support systems. When the biped was ready, Nazari began carefully operating. The animal healer had far more experience performing this operation on smaller creatures than Myra did, although they collaborated on every step of the process, checking and double-checking before every cut through the multiple layers needed to gain access to the cub.

Nazari was a skilled surgeon, though, and it didn't take long before the cub was safely out. Nazari handed the cub off to Brice to clean, while Myra continued to help with the surgery. After carefully removing the placenta, they discussed whether or not they should clean out the rest as well, but decided not to as they were worried it might cause more bleeding than what they'd seen with the other female.

It took far more time to repair the wound as they needed to pull up various other scans to confirm where everything should be, and triple-checked constantly to make sure everything was fully repaired, as they wanted this female to be able to have more cubs in the future, should she come into heat again.

Surgery complete, they checked on the cub, another male, whom Brice had already cleaned and placed in a neonatal unit. He appeared to be healthy as well, although quite a bit smaller than the first one had been. Both females had been rescued pregnant, so they had no idea if this cub was born prematurely or if the other cub had just been big.

Nazari indicated this female had been less aggressive, so Myra agreed to wake her in the trauma bay. She would feel a lot better if they could monitor her from here, as it would mean they could respond to complications quicker.

She woke confused and looked around in panic when she realized she wasn't in her isolation unit, but calmed when she recognized Nazari, and then frowned, remembering she'd been in labor and looked down at her belly.

Nazari carefully lifted the cub out of the unit and handed him over.

This mother didn't act nearly as possessive as the first, but she still looked at the cub with love and at them with concern.

Myra smiled, trying to calm the female.

They kept the mother under observation for the rest of the day. She slept through most of it and didn't resist their treatments, but when nothing but the expected bleeding occurred, Myra helped to move her back to her isolation unit.

Her heart broke at the heavy sigh and sagging shoulders the mother gave when they placed her back in her habitat. Myra didn't blame her one bit.

This is no place to raise a cub, Myra thought, her frustration carefully hidden behind her mask. Her letters to the Council had all gone unanswered. Only the Healers Guild had responded, and Witherspoon had sided with the Council.

After they left the habitat, Nazari turned to Myra with a frown. "It's not right, Myra."

"I know. I'm trying. Spend as much time as you can with her for observation. Until she stops bleeding, I can justify it as a medically necessary interaction."

Nazari snorted. "All interaction is medically necessary at this point," she said, then stormed away, tail lashing behind her.

Myra frowned but didn't disagree with the statement. She eventually returned to her office and sent out another dozen letters, deciding that she would keep doing so until someone changed their mind.

LATER THAT EVENING, Nazari left her office and snuck down to 84's room, as she'd been doing every night since the young cub had landed in her care. She didn't care what the Council said about it or what the consequences were if someone found out. Tabor was a fool.

She was not leaving a cub that young alone and isolated, and she had long since fallen in love with him. If the others of his species did not adopt him when they were finally released, she fully intended to.

What are they going to do anyway? Lock me up? I can't leave quarantine any more than he can, and if they do, I'll just move in with him.

She'd never been one to follow orders anyway, especially stupid ones. That's why she lived in a remote part of the world and worked with animals.

As always, when she entered 84's room, he came running over to her. She scooped him up into a hug and started purring. They played for a little while, and then she curled up on his thin mattress. Moments later, he snuggled down in her arms, safe and warm, as she purred them both to sleep.

9

JESSICA: EXHIBIT 1A1

The extraordinarily long days turned into weeks, which then turned into months, with very little to differentiate one day from the next.

Doc showed up three times a day with food and water, and every twelve days, they brought her a new toy, each one more complex than the next. It took months for the dizziness to pass.

When Jessica finally felt stable enough, she tried leaning her bed against the wall and climbing it, trying to reach the switch by the door, but the mattress was too flimsy to support her weight, and nothing she ever threw at the switch opened it.

It was some time before she realized that she hadn't had her period, but she was frankly a little relieved because she had no idea how to manage that in here. Bathing was out of the question since they only gave her enough water to drink, but every six days they sprayed her down again, which left her smelling better if not exactly feeling clean.

She'd never considered herself fat before, although she probably had a few extra pounds, but she was rapidly losing weight, and even though they gave her plenty to eat, she always felt hungry, like something she needed was missing. She found herself craving the sweets from her mother's bakery, and the thought of a bacon cheeseburger was enough to make her weep.

She figured that must be why her period had stopped. She remembered something from her health class stating that injury, illness, and lack of proper food could cause instability in her cycle. *Then again, maybe they did something to stop it. Who knows what they can do,* she thought. She just prayed she wasn't pregnant somehow, although she saw little evidence of that as the days, weeks, and months passed.

Still, outside of that one excursion to treat her infection, she never saw anyone but Doc, and never had more than brief interactions with them, once she'd healed up and no longer needed medical care.

Sadly, though, her hearing never returned. She could kind of hear herself talk, but it remained muffled and distant. After that first time, Doc never appeared to speak to her, and rarely responded when she talked to them, not unless she yelled and waved her arms. Outside of that one pat on the head, Doc never showed her affection again, although she did smile at whatever puzzle Jessica finished or solved.

She eventually adjusted to the quiet, although sometimes her brain would play tricks on her and she'd think she'd hear something. She dreamed about music all the time, and she hummed to herself even though she could barely hear it.

The puzzles and toys gave her something to do, but the isolation was wearing on her, and she started talking to herself just to have someone to talk to. Once the dizziness had finally passed, she tried exercising, but rather than making her stronger, it seemed to use up what little energy she had.

She wasn't sure if the gravity was stronger or if she was just so much weaker than she'd been before the attack. Eventually, she gave up and spent most of her day trying to sleep the boredom away, wondering if they were ever going to let her out of this room again, or if she was doomed to spend the rest of her life as a prisoner in some sort of alien zoo.

Sometimes she'd wake from her stupor long enough to count her toys, as it was the only measurement of the passage of time she had, but then the toys suddenly stopped appearing regularly, and after that, they only randomly brought her a new puzzle box. These always contained a small object as a prize for figuring them out, although none lit up and flew like her pyramid toy did.

Most were what looked like hand-carved wooden toys in the shape of strange animals, plants, and vehicles. They were incredibly well made, and some even had articulating joints.

She had no idea if she'd failed some test or if they thought she had enough toys to keep her entertained, but she had long since grown bored with all of them.

The last puzzle box they'd brought had taken her less than a minute to figure out, as it was similar to the others she had. She took the prize out, put it with her collection, and placed the box back on the tray, hoping that maybe Doc would bring her something different.

When Doc arrived with the next meal and found the toy untouched, she frowned and looked at Jessica, who purposely yawned, hoping Doc would understand. To her annoyance, Doc just took the toy off the tray and placed it on the new tray they'd brought.

Sighing, Jessica rolled over and didn't even bother to eat. She wasn't really hungry anymore. Eating was nothing more than a distraction from her endlessly boring days. When another puzzle box was brought some time later, she didn't even bother trying to open it.

Eventually, she stopped talking to herself and started having a hard time remembering how to think. She spent most of her time sleeping as her dreams were far more vivid and realistic than reality, and she often cried when she woke, finding herself back in her tan hell.

If she couldn't sleep, she'd get up and pace for hours or just stand, leaning against the invisible door, hoping that maybe she'd eventually fall through. Over time, her dreams turned to nightmares, and she woke screaming for hours, unsure if she was still dreaming.

Doc scared her often, appearing without sound or notice, and making her jump and scream every time. Eventually, Doc just started leaving the trays by the door if her back was turned, so as not to scare her. That was almost worse because she'd turn around to find the food, knowing it would be hours before she saw Doc again.

Screams were the only sound she made anymore, and then even that eventually stopped.

10

JERAN: ERRANT CUB

*J*eran disconnected from his latest council meeting and looked at the time with a grin. They'd finished hours earlier than expected. The next Full Council meeting was in a few days, and he'd been up to his neck in committee meetings preparing for it. He hadn't seen Marsee in almost a week and had only communicated via text, as he was up and gone long before she woke up, and she was usually in bed long before he returned home.

Deciding to surprise her and spend some time with her, he packed up, told Samantha he was done for the day, and left. He tossed his bag in his shuttle but decided to walk over to the Guild as it was a beautiful afternoon.

"Councilor, how can I help you?" the attendant at the front desk asked when he strode in.

"I'm here to pick up my daughter, Marsee," he said. "She should be in class."

The attendant pulled up her schedule and disappeared, returning not with Marsee, but with someone he didn't know.

"Councilor, my name is Gentry Fartooth. I'm Marsee's language instructor," he said.

Jeran nodded in greeting. "Is there a problem?"

"Possibly. Your daughter isn't here. She hasn't been for over a month," he replied.

"What?!" Jeran asked, thoroughly shocked and worried.

"She's fine," Gentry said, seeing his concern. "She's been attending classes remotely for the past month or so, saying that arranging transportation has been difficult, with you in the Council and her mother stuck at the Agency. I offered her a ride, but she declined. I figured if you were here, you didn't know, and I'd better come talk to you in person."

"No, I didn't," Jeran replied, dryly. "Marsee told me that she was getting a ride from the Manas, our nearest neighbor. Did something happen?"

"No. Not that I'm aware of anyway. Her work has been impeccable, one of the most gifted language students I've worked with in years, and from what I understand, her other instructors are just as happy with her. It's not too often we get someone with her gifts for both language and art, who wants to spend their days working on musty old books."

Jeran snorted. "Marsee would bury herself in musty old books if given half a chance. She inherited that from my grandfather. Getting her to leave my brother's public library is a challenge most days. Thank you for your time. I won't keep you any longer."

Gentry nodded and left.

Jeran watched him leave for a moment and then made his way back to his shuttle, worried about Marsee. It wasn't like her to lie, and he was worried that she'd had another flare-up of her hunting instinct. Marsee had struggled with her hunting instinct for far too long as a cub, and she was nearing adulthood, where a flare-up would have far more severe consequences, ones he did not want to think about.

Half an hour later, he was circling the compound to land in the shuttle bay, still unsure of what he was going to say to her. He tapped his claws on the armrest as the shuttle's autopilot brought him inside and landed.

With a sigh, he grabbed his bag and, after dropping it off in his office, made his way around the compound, figuring she'd either be in the family room, where the big monitor was, or in her workshop. He found her in her workshop, leaning over a book. The door was propped wide open to catch as much of the light afternoon breeze as possible.

He watched for several minutes before she looked up and startled at the sight of him.

"Hey, Papa. You're home early," she said with a grin.

"So, apparently, are you," he replied.

She shrugged. "Serin came home early."

He raised a brow. "Do you want to try that again? I stopped at the Guild before coming home and spoke to your language teacher. He tells me you haven't been to class in a month."

"Oh," she replied, ears and tail drooping, and looked away, but didn't say anything else.

"Did something happen?" he asked.

"No," she replied. "It's just easier here."

"How so?" he pressed, not liking that answer one bit.

Marsee still wouldn't make eye contact with him.

"Answer me," he demanded.

"I miss Mama," she said quietly, "and arranging rides all the time is difficult. I can focus better on my work here, and when it gets bad, I can study out in the garden and pretend she's just in another part."

He sighed. "I know, kitten. I miss her, too. But why didn't you tell me?"

"I didn't want you to worry about me," she replied.

He snorted. "I will always worry about you. That's my job. I was far more worried when your teacher said you weren't there, especially since I haven't seen you in person for a week."

"Sorry, Papa," Marsee replied.

He pursed his lips. "You're old enough to start making your own decisions. You'll be an adult in a few months. If you want to work from home, that's fine. Just tell me. You don't need to lie or try to protect me. If something's bothering you, talk to me. I know this is hard on you, and I'm not your mother, but I am a really good listener, at least I think I am, and I'll do my best to help."

"You're not mad at me?" she asked, looking up at him.

"Well, I'm a little annoyed. It's not like you to lie or keep secrets, and I'd like to think I've raised you better than that, but as long as you don't make a habit of it, I'll forgive you. Come here." He held out his arms for a hug, and she practically flew into his arms.

He held her until she pulled away, and shoved his feelings behind his mask. "But my forgiveness does not mean you are free from the consequences. You lied to your instructor and to me. I may be your father, but I am also a member of the Council. When you're an adult, those actions will have far more serious consequences. As it is, I could have your instructor demoted or removed from his guild for not reporting your absence, and if something *had* happened to you as a result, he could be found liable and executed, as could your mother and I for not ensuring you were properly supervised."

Her eyes widened in fear. "Please don't do anything to Master Fartooth, Papa. It was all my fault. I told him you knew."

He gave a single nod of acknowledgement. "I accept your desire to take full responsibility. For the crime of lying to a member of the Council about your whereabouts for the past month, I am grounding you for the same amount of time. Unless there is an emergency, you will be limited to the guild for travel. Your uncle's library and any other location will be off limits unless you have my permission. As I cannot supervise you while I am at the Full Council meeting, you will go to your sister's until I return, and you will not leave her sight or her home without her or one of your other siblings."

Her ears and tail drooped again as the realization that she wouldn't be going with him to Flyer hit. She'd been bouncy with excitement when he'd informed her. "What are you telling Grammy and Grampa?"

"The truth," he replied. "I know they were just as excited to see you, Kitten, and they will be disappointed, but your actions have consequences, even to those you don't intend to hurt. Trust me, I'm doing you a favor. My father is…stubborn to a fault. He makes your uncle look like a pushover."

Marsee's expression shifted to disbelief, but she didn't challenge his statement. "And Mama?"

He considered the question for a long moment before answering. "As long as you behave, I won't tell your mother. She has far too much to worry about right now. I'll tell her you decided to go to your sisters so you wouldn't miss any of your classes."

She sighed with relief. "Thank you, Papa."

"Now, why don't you show me what you're working on, and then I thought we'd do something fun for the evening."

"Like what?" she asked.

He grinned at her. "Well, since you're going to be an adult in a couple of months, I think it's far past time you learned how to play Rando-tat."

She grinned at him. "Really? I've always wanted to learn how to play, but Uncle Marcus won't teach me."

He looked at her with a glare and laughed. "You already know how to play, don't you?"

"Now, would I lie to you?" she asked, with an innocent grin.

"Yes," he replied, laughing as his tail curled in amusement. "You would."

11

MYRA: ISOLATION SICKNESS

Nearly six months had passed since the survivors of that distant world had arrived. Scientific research crews had jumped back to set up long range sensors to monitor the planet, on the off chance something should happen to emerge from the violent maelstrom of destruction left behind, not that they any clue as to how to safely rescue anything that did, as well as study the effects of a massive asteroid impact on a planet.

Other teams were working to identify and build technology to prevent the same disaster from happening to their own worlds. The Ship's Guild increased monitoring of foreign objects in their solar systems, as the population expressed their fears and concerns about the possibility of something like that happening on their planets as well. Three of the ships had left to assist with those efforts once the permanent shields were in place. The other two had chosen to remain behind to help with the more mundane tasks of running the compound, preparing food, storing supplies, and general maintenance.

Myra continued to try on a regular basis to get the Council and Healers Guild to allow them to begin reintroduction and repopulation, before the genetic tests were complete. They'd only given in on a few of the smaller creatures, where the scans showed incredibly short lifespans, and they'd lost members due to old age.

They'd lost several of the water species early on, unable to find a suitable food source for them or figure out how to clone single representatives before that representative died, although several of the other species were now thriving, and new tanks had been delivered to make room. Oddly, though, while they'd been the primary species found in one of the fishing nets they'd discovered, the bipeds refused to eat them when provided.

To everyone's surprise, they'd only lost two of the bipeds following the rescue, apparently due to heart attacks. Those were both still in stasis as they attempted to print new hearts for them and figure out how to keep them alive long enough to replace them.

While they'd managed to cure most of the injuries and illnesses the various creatures had brought with them, they still hadn't figured out what was causing the weight loss among the bipeds, which was extremely concerning. A few had lost nearly half their weight so far, even though they left a good portion of their food untouched most days.

As of yet, there hadn't been anything more than a sniffle from one of the gardeners, who had an allergic reaction to one of the plants, and that had been easily treated. Another plant had been found to cause a temporary narcotic reaction in the gardener who had handled it, and they were currently studying it for use in long-term pain management and depression, as the healer affected had reported feeling better than he'd ever felt before. Although there had also been an almost uncontrollable urge to roll in the plant, which had been very concerning, seeing as the urge to rub was an early warning sign when the females of her species went into heat.

There had been additional injuries to her healers as well. Dozens of her healers, in addition to Nazari, had been bitten, one had been impaled by barbs, and another had been kicked hard enough to come away with a broken bone. All of those wounds had thankfully healed fully without any complications.

The only long-term issue they'd found so far was the lingering odor of a tiny, noxious-smelling creature. They had tried for days to get the smell out of the fur of the poor healer that had been sprayed, and eventually the healer had given up and just shaved her fur off. They wore shields around that creature, and several of the more aggressive ones now.

The public was very interested in a few of the smaller species, as they looked like miniature versions of themselves and were absolutely adorable. This led many to speculate that this world had been their long-lost home world, but genetic analysis and the scans showed they were very different creatures, even if they happened to look the same.

Even still, the Ship's Guild searched their archives but found no reference to indicate they'd ever visited that planet before. It did make Myra wonder what the creatures they'd rescued thought of their similarity.

It also added to the debate on whether or not they'd actually rescued the sentient species, as the small creatures that looked like them made similar sounds to their own cubs before they learned to speak, while the bipeds did not, although several, like the pregnant female, occasionally made hissing and growling noises.

Myra had watched many of the camera feeds, especially the cub in her protege's care, and hadn't heard anything but the occasional squeak or cry when scared. They did use their paws often and seemed to respond to commands well, which left many wondering if they had a visual language like the Water Sprites. So far, none of the scientists had identified any sort of spoken language from the few sounds they'd heard. She knew many like 1A1 likely had hearing loss, but they didn't have the right equipment to treat it. It hadn't been approved yet, like so many other things.

After the initial arrival, triage, and the grueling rotation of surgeries that had been needed to repair the worst of the injuries, Myra had stepped back from the day-to-day care of the refugees, only stepping in when Brice or one of the other healers called for help, although she did spend much of her free time in the garden with the strange green plants.

The building that had once been her clinic had been converted into makeshift offices once the restrictions on travel between the pods had been lifted, and she'd moved back to her office there as it was more comfortable.

She now spent most of her day working with Sampson to coordinate supplies, providing updates to the Council and Healer's Guild, and trying to find solutions to the hundred and ten different problems that showed up every hour. But even with all of that, she was bored and lonely, and if she had to fill out another requisition form, she was going to scream.

Why does everything have to be reviewed by me? she thought, for the four-hundred and eighty-third time. *They're just going to deny it anyway.*

She'd much rather be working with the rescued creatures or in the garden, tending the plants, but someone had to make sure that the right supplies were ordered and showed up on time. Managing two healers and the small number of patients they'd had with the clinic had been cub's play compared to managing the hundreds of healers, volunteers, and the crews of the two remaining ships.

On top of all that, she missed her family fiercely and was very worried about her daughter. Marsee, already an introverted and shy cub, had drifted further into her isolation during her long absence, and she had just been informed that Marsee had stopped attending classes in person over two months before.

Both she and Jer had attempted to find out if something had happened, but Marsee was adamant that it was just easier than trying to arrange transportation all the time, with her there and her father at work. When she'd pressed Jer about why he hadn't informed her, Jer finally admitted that Marsee had claimed that it was because of how much she'd been missing her and found it easier to study in the garden. He hadn't wanted to cause her pain by the admission that they were missing her, or have her worry when there was nothing she could do.

Marsee had never been particularly social, but the last few months had seen her nearly as isolated as the strange creatures in Myra's care.

She sat in her office, head leaning on one paw, trying to focus on the report in front of her, but failing miserably as she worried about her family and the effects her long absence was having on them.

"Is everything okay?" Brice asked, gently tapping on the door at the same time.

"That depends. Is there any star fruit juice left?" she asked, trying to lighten the mood. The other healers didn't need her personal worries on top of their already challenging workload, and everyone was struggling with the isolation and separation from their families.

"Sadly, we are *all* out," Brice replied as she entered the office.

"Then no. We're officially doomed. Might as well pack up and go home," she joked with a half-smile and leaned back in her chair. "So, what brings you to my office this late at night? I'm assuming it's not a social call."

"It's not. I have a concern I wanted to bring up with you. I don't really have any proof, more of a gut feeling, and I wanted your take on it," Brice said, and then slid into a free chair.

"Well, your gut feelings usually have a way of being right. What's wrong?" Myra asked, leaning forward and giving her protege her full attention, excited to discuss anything that wasn't a requisition form.

"It's the bipeds. Something isn't right with them. They just don't seem as active as before, and I've confirmed with the other pods. They've all lost weight, most twenty-five percent or more since their arrival, and are eating less and less every day. They're losing interest in their toys. They don't react when we enter, and the littlest one in my care, 1A1, hasn't even looked at the last two enrichment toys we've provided. She just sleeps through most of the day now."

"I've already assigned three teams to try and figure out why they're losing so much weight," Myra replied.

"I know, but I think it might be more than just weight loss. If they were just missing something in their diet, I'd expect them to be hungry and eating more, not less. I'm starting to think they might be suffering from isolation sickness. I took a few scans of my patients and compared them to when they arrived, and I'm seeing a reduction in both brain size and activity during play, not just with them but in a few of the other species as well. In the long-legged grazers, for example, I'm seeing the same reduction in all but the one that gave birth shortly after arriving. Those two are doing fine. The biped cubs are the worst. Several scream for hours after their healers leave and have been throwing things at the walls. Others just sit there and stare as if we're not even there. Only Nazari's seems to be unaffected, but then he's the youngest we rescued, so he might not know any different."

Myra nodded. That fit with her observations. "It wouldn't surprise me at all, especially if they're a social species like we believe. I've been noticing issues with my own ability to focus, and I have people I can interact with and work to do, even if I do want to claw the next person to bring me another requisition form to review. What do you propose we do about it?"

As her mentor, Myra routinely questioned Brice on her treatment plans. This was no different, although frankly, Myra was at a loss for what to do with all the restrictions the Council had put in place over the past few months.

"If it is isolation sickness, then we need to start reintroducing members of the same species, maybe start moving forward with mating? If nothing else, we should start interacting with them more and try to communicate with them again. I wish we could take them out of their habitats, take them on a walk around the compound, or something. I'm getting sick of these barren walls, so I can just imagine how they must be feeling," Brice replied.

Myra sat back in her seat to think about what Brice had said. "There's absolutely no way the Council will let them out of their habitats. Tabor flat-out told me to stop sending requests to her because she's not budging until the genetic analysis is complete. It took months just to get her to budge on some of the smaller creatures, and that was only when we could prove the tests wouldn't be complete before they all died of old age. Paxton Parner and his crew refuse to budge on that, and he's managed to convince the majority, along with the rest of the Seniors, that we need to wait until we have a full genetic makeup of each species, as well as everything they brought with them. We can't risk getting them sick and losing members, any more than we can risk them getting us sick, or vice versa. We came close to losing too many of them before, as it is." Myra repeated the same excuses she'd been given a dozen times.

"But Myra…"

Myra held a paw up to stop her. "But if you can show that they are actually suffering from being isolated, we might have a better argument. Gather your research, and send it to me. If I can make a case that waiting for full results before reintroduction means we might miss out on the opportunity to save the species entirely, then we stand a better chance of convincing a majority of the Council to let us move forward. It's the only thing that's worked in the past."

"And if they won't budge?" Brice asked.

"I honestly don't know. I've tried reaching out to everyone I can think of, including the entire Full Council, members of the Healers Guild, and even the Press. For now, though, if you think there is an issue, then I can authorize more time spent in the habitats with each of them for medical evaluation. Spend some time with them, but no more than fifteen minutes a day to start, and I want to know if anyone gets so much as a sniffle. If we see improvements with that interaction, it'll go a long way towards proving this is isolation sickness. I don't doubt it in the least, but we'll need solid proof that we're going to lose the species in order to get the Council to change their minds."

"I can make that work. Thank you," Brice replied.

"Is there anything else?" Myra asked, a hint of her weariness seeping through.

"Yes. We're playing games in the common room tonight. Come join us. Those requisition forms can wait until morning, and I'd rather not get clawed when I bring you the stack I have waiting for you to sign," Brice replied, tail curled.

Myra's first instinct was to say no, but Brice was right. If games were good for their wards, they'd be good for her too, and right now she wanted nothing more than to forget about her responsibilities for an hour or two. Grabbing her tablet just in case there was an actual emergency, and not just another dozen requisition forms she needed to sign off on, she followed Brice out and shut the door behind her.

12

JESSICA: PRISONER

An eon passed, and nothing changed, until one day Doc arrived with her lunch but didn't leave right away. Usually, that meant it was time to hose her and the cell down, but they didn't show up with the usual equipment, and Jessica was pretty sure it wasn't the right day, although she could have easily lost track of the days.

She tried to remember how long it had been since her last shower, but the days ran into each other, and she gave up. Instead, she watched as they set the food down in the usual spot, backed off to the far wall, sat down, and stared at her, giving absolutely no indication of what they wanted from her.

Jessica walked over and checked out the tray. There was nothing different or unusual about what had been brought, just several of her favorites, if you could call any of them good enough to be her favorites. When Doc made no motions, just continued to sit there and watch, Jessica shrugged and picked up the tray and brought it back over to her bed to eat and stare back. After a few minutes, Doc stood and left.

Well, that was strange, her rusty brain managed to think. She spent the rest of the day trying to figure out what Doc was up to. It was more than she'd thought about anything in months. The next day it happened again, and again on the third.

No interactions, no commands, they just sat there and watched her eat. It was frankly a little unnerving. She eventually remembered that she could talk and tried speaking to them, but if they replied, she saw no indication of it, and she heard nothing in response. There were no noticeable side effects from her meals, so they hadn't been tampered with, at least as far as she could tell.

On the fourth day, she decided she'd had enough of them just sitting there staring at her, even if the company was welcome. "If you're going to sit there and watch me eat, you might as well join me," she told the feline, then picked up the tray and walked over to stand in front of them.

The creature did absolutely nothing as she approached, just sat there and watched. Setting the tray down in between them, she picked up two pieces and handed one to Doc.

Doc took it with a confused tilt of their head, so Jessica repeated the first day and tossed her piece back and chewed, then used the same go-on motion to indicate Doc should do the same. Doc's ears flicked back, but she ate the proffered piece.

Jessica grinned and took a few more bites, then, when Doc didn't make any further motion, she handed them another piece. This time, both their whiskers and ears flicked back, in what clearly looked like surprise.

"You didn't expect that, did you?" she asked.

After a few more bites, she offered again, but this time, Doc put up a paw to stop her, then stood and left.

I wonder what that meant? Did I offend them by not eating everything? She shrugged, picked up the remaining food, and brought it back to her bed to eat in comfort.

The next day, when Doc brought the meal, Jessica didn't get up from her bed; she just sat there. "What do you want from me?" she yelled out, but there was no reaction. A few minutes later, Doc left again. It was aggravating, and all she could think about for hours.

Jessica was bouncing the pyramid against the wall when Doc next came in and took their usual spot to observe. Then, on a whim, Jessica tossed the pyramid at Doc.

Surprisingly, Doc tossed it back.

Jessica pivoted to face the cat. Catching the pyramid, she tossed it back, bouncing it off a wall this time. Doc did the same. This continued for a few minutes, with her working out different angles to send the pyramid and Doc repeating them, until they caught it, set it down on the ground, and left.

It's the same amount of time every time, she realized, or at least that's what it felt like, since there weren't any clocks in the room to know for sure.

The visits continued for several days. She tried asking questions, but Doc never responded. She made motions with her hands, tried writing in the air, writing on the walls, not that it left a mark, but she was hoping to get something to draw with. She tried arranging her small collection of toys to say hello.

Doc stood and looked at them when Jessica motioned her over and pointed, but seemed baffled by what she was doing.

Then one day, Jessica got the nerve up to sit right next to the big cat and leaned in, needing the contact of another being and hoping that maybe if the strange cat began to care for her, they might let her out of her cell.

Doc wrapped her tail around her side and squeezed gently. It was all Jessica could do to keep from crying, but once the time was up, Doc stood and walked out.

She sat there and rocked for some time, hugging herself to remember the feeling for as long as possible and looking forward to the next day, hoping it would happen again, but the next day, Doc didn't stay. They just left the tray, frowned at her, and walked out.

The following day was the same. Jessica didn't know if she'd done something wrong by trying to interact with the cat or if Doc had gotten into trouble by reacting to her. She tried tossing the pyramid, but Doc just caught it, tossed it back, and made their way back out through the wall after setting down her meal.

Her anger and frustration grew until one day she couldn't take it anymore. In a fit of rage, she threw one of the puzzle boxes at Doc's retreating back.

Doc froze as it hit them squarely in the back of the head, and then turned to look at her in surprise. They glanced down at the shattered box on the floor, and then back up at her.

Jessica froze as well, just as shocked at her own audacity and the sudden fear of repercussions. She'd somehow forgotten how big they were and how easy it would be for them to hurt her in retaliation.

Doc simply let out a sigh, gave her what was clearly a disappointed look, reached down and scooped up the broken pieces of the puzzle box, and left.

Jessica sat there shaking for several minutes, waiting for some sort of punishment but nothing came. It was several days before she realized what her punishment was.

One day, Doc came in as normal and set the food down. There was another puzzle box on the tray, but instead of leaving her the toy, they picked up the puzzle box, showed it to her, gave her that same disappointed look, and turned and walked out with it instead.

"Like that, is it? If I don't play nice, I don't get new toys? Well fine, I don't want your toy anyway!" she yelled, and threw another one of her remaining toys at the door behind the frustrating, fuzz-brained, furry feline.

There was no response, and after a few moments, Jessica walked back over and slid down on her bed with a whimpered cry. "Please. Just let me out of here. I'll do whatever you want."

For the entire next week, Jessica made a point of ignoring her giant jailor whenever they entered. When she refused to leave her bed for the regular cleaning, Doc simply picked her up and physically moved her off of it as if she weighed nothing, cleaned the bed, sprayed her down, and left. At the end of the week, Doc showed up with the puzzle box again, but this time, left it.

Jessica made a point of not touching it, although she itched to. It was massive compared to the others, and she was practically sick with boredom.

When Doc came in with the next meal and saw the box hadn't

been touched, their ears and whiskers flicked back in surprise, but they did nothing. The box stayed there for the rest of the week, when a second one was placed next to it.

Jessica ignored them both.

Doc tried to push the boxes towards her a few days later.

Jessica hissed at her and turned her back, arms crossed. Later, in a fit of rage, she destroyed all of the other puzzle boxes that she'd already opened. It had been incredibly cathartic when she screamed, threw them at the walls, stomped on them, and broke them down into as many tiny pieces as she could.

When she was done and her rage had left her in an exhausted heap, she sat there panting and decided that if they weren't going to let her out, it was time for her to try escaping, not that she hadn't tried many times before.

There has to be a way through that door, she thought. After considering her options, she took the uneaten tray of food and brought it over to her pile of broken pieces. Setting the food aside, she took the two unopened boxes and placed them on the tray, surrounded them in a pile of broken pieces and all of her other toys, and deliberately placed the floating pyramid on top.

She smashed her food into a pulp and used it to draw a giant middle finger with the words 'F.U. CAT' in front of it. When she was done, she stood, examining her handiwork, and decided it needed a little garnish. So she dumped the rest of her mashed-up food on top of the broken pile of toys.

Satisfied with her artwork, she took her blanket and placed it on the floor in front of the door, hoping the cat would slip on it as they entered, and possibly leave the door open for her to pass through.

She waited, back up against the wall, for her captor to come through. As soon as they started walking through, Jessica tried to go through the wall, but it was just as solid as it ever was. She let out a string of curses, and then furious, stood defiantly in front of the door, blocking it so Doc couldn't leave, as if she had any chance of stopping the twenty-foot tall cat from doing whatever they damn well pleased.

Doc paused, after completely stepping over the blanket, and

looked down at it confused, then saw the pile of broken toys and must have realized that Jessica wasn't in front of them, turned around, and found her standing by the door, arms crossed and scowling.

When Doc stepped towards her, Jessica let out as ferocious a growl as she could muster, baring her teeth and flexing her fingers like claws. Doc froze, a look of ears-back astonishment on their face.

I wonder what I just said? Probably said their mother smelled of elderberries, Jessica thought. "Well, she does!" Jessica yelled, then added another hiss for good measure.

She was trying to keep from laughing in hysterics and fear at the ridiculousness of her behavior, but this captivity and solitude had to end. She honestly didn't care if they bit her head off at this point. At least it would be something new and different.

She deliberately pointed to herself and then hit the door as hard as she could with her fist. "Let me out of here!" she yelled.

Doc slowly put the tray they were holding down and sat like they had the first time, tail wrapped around their front paws.

Jessica pointed to Doc, to herself, then turned and hit the wall again, before turning back around and yelling, "I want you to let me out of here. Now!"

Doc's expression changed to one that could only be described as immense sadness, and her whiskers twitched back, in what she was pretty sure meant 'No'.

"Why won't you let me out of here? What do you want with me?" she yelled, but Doc just sat there.

Jessica's anger and frustration were boiling over, and she marched right up to Doc and stared the cat down—or up, rather, since they towered above her, hands balled into tight fists. Then, in a fit of rage, she kicked them as hard as she could in the shin.

Doc didn't so much as flinch, although her ears flattened and the tip of her tail twitched.

Jessica growled and hissed and kicked the cat again, but still there was no reaction. If anything, the cat's expression changed from annoyance to incredulity that something as tiny as her would even attempt attacking.

Glaring, she tried to stomp on their tail, but they flicked it out of the way before her foot landed.

"Like that is it!" Jessica yelled. "Fight me! Do something! I don't care. JUST LET ME OUT OF HERE!" She reached over and snatched some fur, yanking as hard as she could.

Doc's ears flicked back again, but other than that, she did nothing.

Jessica tried again, but this time, faster than she could blink, Doc scooped her up, pinned her arms to her sides, and carried her over to her bed, then ever so gently set her down, pressing, until Jessica sat, legs crossed.

She sat on the bed fuming at Doc, daring the giant cat to do something, anything. Doc eventually let go of her, turned, grabbed the tray of clearly unwanted and broken toys, and left.

She screamed her hate and demands for hours after Doc left. She screamed until she completely lost her voice, and hit and kicked at the door until she was exhausted, but Doc didn't return again until after she'd given up and flopped down back on her bed to cry.

The next several months were an absolute agony of boredom. Doc did not bring her any further toys or puzzle boxes, and she had nothing to do except try to figure out ways to escape.

She tried standing in front of the door again, but Doc just picked her up and moved her out of the way before leaving. She tried sitting against the door, hoping maybe she'd fall through when Doc entered, but somehow Doc knew she was there, and grabbed her and moved her out of the way before Jessica could react to the absence of the door. When she finally realized she had to be in physical contact with Doc to make the door work, she tried jumping on Doc as they left, but they always stopped, returned to the room, and peeled her off. She tried sneaking out as they entered or left, but they were ready for her every time, and stopped even entering with food unless she was away from the door.

Sometimes, she'd mash up her food again and purposely draw or write demands. But no matter what she did, the cat just came in, sighed at the mess, and cleaned it up. She tried one time to stop the cat, pointing at it to try to get them to pay attention and realize she wasn't just making a mess, but they just moved her aside and kept cleaning.

After that, she gave up and drifted back into the stupor she'd been in for months and did her best to sleep her days away when she could, or paced the room when it physically hurt to lie down any longer. She had absolutely no appetite anymore and just played with her food. What she didn't eat, she threw at the walls and ceiling. It gave her something different to look at, as it slowly slid down the strange walls, never leaving so much as a smear behind, and forced Doc to remain in the room for a few minutes longer each day to clean. It was company, of a sort.

Her depression and loneliness changed to where it was almost physically painful at times. Sometimes she would lean up against the door after the cat arrived, or purposely refuse to move on her bath day, just to feel the contact of another being for even a few brief moments.

One day, when her loneliness was particularly overwhelming, she tried walking over and hugging the cat.

Perhaps thinking she was trying to escape or attack again, they just peeled her off and carried her back to her bed before leaving.

Jessica rolled over and cried for hours after the rejection. After that, she never tried again and stopped acknowledging that Doc was even there.

13

MYRA: COUNCIL EXPERIMENT

Myra, I don't know what to do anymore. 1A1 won't even acknowledge my presence when I enter. I have to lift her off her bed to clean it. She's stopped eating, like the others, and has started throwing her food everywhere. She's lost another ten percent of her body weight in the last week alone, and none of the others are much better. We have to do something. I'm seriously ready to start breaking the Council's orders. To the moons and back with the consequences," Brice said, letting out all of her frustration in a growl.

"I don't know what to do, Brice. The Council has my paws tied. You know that," Myra stated, equally frustrated.

"That's not good enough! We were making progress with them until the Council, in their infinite stupidity, ordered us to stop, rather than seeing the harm they're doing by keeping them in isolation. Now I've got a full-blown riot on my paws. I've been kicked or had things thrown at my head so many times I've lost count. I've even been bitten twice. Moons, Myra, if the bites didn't cause any side effects or illness, they have to be safe for us to interact with more. If not us, then we have to start letting them interact with each other, or we're going to lose them and any chance we might have of building a friendship with them, if we haven't already."

"I know, Brice. We've been over this every day for months. I need ideas, not complaints. I'm worried about the cub, too. Give me something to work with," Myra replied.

"I just don't know. What I do know is that if we'd kept any one of our kind in the kind of isolation we're forcing on them, we'd go mad, and I'm pretty sure they're starting to too. We'd have been mad months ago. Keeping them locked up and separated for so long is cruel. Surely the Council has to see that? For moon's sake, why are they even having a say in the care of a patient? Shouldn't *we* be the ones to dictate their care? Can't the Healer's Guild do anything?"

"I've tried. All I get from both the Council and Healers is 'What we do here affects everyone on all the planets, not just a single patient.'" Myra sighed, as all of her efforts had failed.

"I know that...It's just...Oh, I don't know. Something *has* to change. To spend all this time trying to save them only to lose them to something as easily preventable as isolation sickness..." Brice stood and started pacing.

"You know, you might have had an idea in that rant of yours," Myra said eventually.

"What do you mean?" Brice asked, thinking furiously back over what she'd said, that she'd not said a million times already.

"The Council doesn't see what their edict is doing, and they need to. I have an idea, and I need to contact Jer. I'll come find you after if it works," Myra replied, dismissing Brice, who nodded and immediately left, shutting the door behind her on her way out.

"Hey, Myra! What's up? I wasn't expecting your call until tonight," Jer said when he answered her call.

"The situation with the bipeds is getting worse, Jer, and I have an idea on how we might be able to get it through to the rest of the Council."

"Oh?" Jer asked. "Do tell." Myra filled him in on her idea, and he agreed it sounded plausible. "It just so happens there's a meeting this afternoon. I'll put you on the docket."

"Thanks, Jer," she said, and hung up.

That afternoon, Jer conferenced her into the Council meeting, and she was given top billing. "Healer Chenzira, we've been informed that you wish to discuss something with the Council. Is there a problem at the Agency?" Senior Councilor Tabor asked.

"Yes, Councilor, there is. We have a situation here that I believe is directly related to the edicts of this Council, and I'm here to beg you to lift the restrictions this Council has placed on the Agency. If we don't, I fear we're going to lose the bipeds."

"What restrictions would those be, Healer Chenzira?" Tabor asked, although from her slightly annoyed tone, Myra could tell she already had an idea of what she was going to ask. It wasn't like she hadn't sent dozens of messages to everyone she could think of, trying to get those same restrictions lifted for the past several months, even if Tabor had ordered her to stop sending them to her after the fourth or fifth request.

"The Council's restriction regarding interactions between members of the same species," Myra replied. "It's been eight months since the ships landed, and in all that time, just about every land-based creature rescued has been held in what would be considered solitary confinement. Only a few have had interaction with their own kind, and those are the few that have given birth since arrival. Several species, including the bipeds, which we believe may be sentient, are now showing signs of an illness we call isolation sickness. In the bipeds' case, it's gone from a mild case to severe, and in some cases bordering on critical, especially with the cubs. More than half have become listless, some barely eating or drinking. On average, they've lost another fifteen percent of their body weight, and they were losing weight before they stopped eating. Others pace in their cells for hours on end. Many are starting to show signs of violence and are acting out in anger and rage, throwing themselves at the doors over and over again to the point where they are actually hurting themselves. They are destroying their toys and throwing their food at the walls. Our healers have been kicked, have had objects thrown at them, and dozens of our healers have been bitten. All of this because we've been ordered to remain out of the habitats unless medical care is required, and I'm here to tell you that medical care *is* required, and we are being prevented from giving it to them. What they need is to get out of their habitats and be allowed to interact with someone, preferably with others of their own species, but at the very least, we need to be able to spend more time with them, the cubs especially."

"We've been over this before, Healer Chenzira. We all voted last month that reintroduction and repopulation shouldn't occur until the results are in from the genetic analysis, since they are longer lived than the other species. Have those tests been completed?" Tabor asked wearily, clearly frustrated.

"No, ma'am. They have not. But I do not believe we have the time to wait for those tests to be completed. I'm not advocating leaving quarantine or even crossing pods. I'll lock down the pods again if that would ease the Council's concerns. I just want to start by pairing up members of the same species, within the same pod, and between members that the same healers are already treating. I've sent the Council a detailed plan of our reintroduction and repopulation plans in the past, and I assure you there's no more risk involved than having their healers go from one patient to the next," she replied.

"Councilor Surellis, you wish to speak?" Tabor asked.

"Yes, ma'am. At Councilor Chenzira's request, I've researched this particular illness. The symptoms mentioned by Healer Chenzira do match those as described in the medical journals. According to the journals, long-term isolation can lead to anxiety, depression, hallucinations, and various other forms of mental illness, and in critical conditions can and often do result in violence and the person attempting to take their own lives. I've also done further research, and assuming that the bipeds are determined to be sentient, we would be committing a serious crime against them by keeping them separated longer than absolutely necessary, as there is even mention of this illness in the Charter."

There was a murmur throughout the Council at this statement, and Tabor had to raise a paw for silence before nodding to Marcus to continue.

Marcus began reading. "Article one hundred and sixty-three, section four of the penal code. 'Forced solitary confinement for longer than two weeks is strictly forbidden, without direct medical recommendation for the prevention of the spread of a *known* communicable and deadly illness, due to the adverse reactions and severe mental hardship this incurs. Should any person be required to be kept in confinement for more than two weeks, for any reason other than an *existing* illness, a minimum of three hours of supervised outdoor activity is required as well as the supervised, in person contact with friends and/or family members of no less than one hour per day as requested by the accused and/or convicted. In the case of quarantine, the person should be provided with the means to communicate with others of their choice. At no time should any sentient member be prevented from contacting their legal representatives, for any reason.'"

"Since when are we giving animals legal representation?" Councilor Parner yelled out, interrupting Marcus.

"Order! Councilor Parner, you will remain quiet until you've been acknowledged by the Council," Tabor growled, in a barely controlled fury that made Myra jump.

Why is she so upset? Myra wondered. She'd watched enough of the recorded council meetings in her life to know that councilors speaking out of turn was fairly common, but she'd never seen Tabor react like *that* before. For that matter, she'd never seen any Senior Councilor react with that much emotion. Raise their voice, yes, but growl, never. Even the mild annoyance she'd shown towards Myra was unusual. No matter what they actually felt, they just didn't show it. Their mask was as solid as her healer's mask, and by the time they were appointed Senior Councilor, they would have had at least a hundred years to perfect it.

Marcus answered Councilor Parner's question anyway, seemingly unfazed by Parner or Tabor's outburst. "Since they've requested representation. Healer Chenzira shared with us a video of one of the bipeds, currently referred to as 1A1. You may remember her as she was the first biped rescued. With your permission, I would like to share this video with the Council."

"Granted," Tabor replied, mask back in place.

The main screen on the council floor changed to show the small biped who very clearly pointed to herself, then banged on the door before making a high-pitched chittering noise, one of the few sounds they'd observed from the creatures.

"It's clear to me that 1A1 is attempting to communicate with her healer," Councilor Surellis stated. "I would postulate that 1A1, barring any other translation, very clearly demanded to be let out of her cell. She also pointed to herself. The ability to communicate and awareness of oneself are two of the main criteria for sentience, and as such, I've agreed to take the case on behalf of 1A1 and demand her rights as a sentient being to time out of her cell and visitation with others of her kind."

"Councilor Parner, you wish to speak?" Tabor asked, with just the barest hint of warning in her voice.

"Yes, ma'am," he replied. "Whether or not this species is sentient is yet to be determined. Just because the creature can make a few simple gestures does not make it sentient. If Councilor Surellis wishes to take on the case of an animal, that is his choice. However, I fail to see how being stuck in a cell for another month or two would do the harm that's being suggested. I know many people choose not to leave their dwellings for longer periods of time." Parner's comments dripped with sarcasm and insult, which, to Myra's surprise, Tabor completely ignored.

"Healer Chenzira, can you elaborate?" Tabor asked instead.

"Yes, ma'am, but I can do better than that. I believe I can show you. I have a simple experiment that I would challenge the Council to try before making a decision on this matter."

"Continue," Tabor commanded with a curious tilt of her head.

"I propose that every member of the Council should spend just one day locked in a room of their choice. That room should have no more than what has been provided to the bipeds, a bed and a toy or puzzle. No technology, no books, no music, no window to the outside world, no tablets or other communication devices, no contact with anyone, including family, and see just how long it takes before boredom becomes uncomfortable or you before you decide to sleep rather than sit there and do nothing for hours on end. If what you are sentencing is not punishment, but a vacation, as Councilor Parner suggests, then this should be a welcome break. But if you find it at all uncomfortable and choose to leave before the day is up, I suggest you consider that when deciding if it's fair and just to do the same to a species that has no idea what is happening to it or why."

Murmurs rippled through the Council at Myra's words, and the Senior Councilor let them continue for a few minutes, as if judging the tone, before silencing them immediately with a raised paw.

"Healer Chenzira, your challenge and interpretation are just. This Council should at least be aware of what pain our edicts cause. As the need for forced isolation for any length of time is so rare, we do not have the experience to know the effects of our edict. I will grant your request. Following this meeting, every member who wishes to vote on removing the restrictions on reintroduction and repopulation placed on the Agency will lock themselves in their inner suite. This should adequately meet the grounds of Healer Chenzira's request, as the inner chambers are windowless and have adjoining waste rooms. Junior councilors will remove all items that could be seen as distractions, including tablets, voice-activated systems, and books. Any Councilor who leaves their room before a full day has passed will automatically be entered as a yes to allowing the healers to implement whatever policies they feel are best for their patients."

"You can't force us to do that!" someone yelled out.

"I can and I will," Tabor growled back. "If we are not willing to do what we force others to do, then we do not deserve to be on the Council. For that matter, if you choose not to try this little experiment, then I expect your resignation on my desk within the hour, because that tells me you are far more interested in your own comfort than the health and safety of the others you are sworn to protect. And furthermore, if you do not make it a minimum of six hours, I will consider that your resignation as well. You have one hour to prepare.

I'm calling this session ended. We will reconvene at this time tomorrow."

The Senior Councilor growled out her decision, then stood and left the chamber, her tail lashing in fury. The entire Council exploded in an uproar the moment she left the room.

Jer raised his brow and disconnected the call.

Myra sat staring at her monitor in shock for several minutes, trying to figure out why Tabor had been so angry. When she realized, Myra's paws started shaking. Between what she'd said and what Marcus had added, she'd essentially just gone before them and accused the entire Council of breaking the law. She hadn't even been aware that isolation sickness was mentioned in the Charter, or that it was against the law to isolate people for more than two weeks.

She thought back to her own training and tried to remember if it had ever been mentioned, then pulled up the training manuals from the Healer's Guild and read through everything listed about the illness. She sighed in relief, then copied the manual to her own tablet as evidence, in case the Senior Council tried to blame her for putting them in isolation in the first place. Jer had certainly never mentioned it, and she'd spoken at length with him about the conditions of the habitats in an attempt to do more to help them.

While she waited, she tried to figure out how to allow them to communicate with the others, with the edicts currently in place, assuming the Council didn't vote in their favor. The problem was that, with quarantine, nothing was allowed between rooms unless there was an emergency. Everything that left a room needed to be sanitized, and paper wouldn't survive the sanitation process. She didn't even know if they had a written language. They'd tried initially with one of the older bipeds and had only gotten a page full of looping scribbles back, which no one had been able to decipher or determine if it was a written language or not. It certainly didn't look like anything any of the other species used. Without being allowed to interact with them for any length of time, they had no basis to even begin translating.

Could they be taught to use a tablet? Myra wondered, then shook her head. They weren't allowed to interact with them for more than five minutes at a time, and that wasn't nearly enough time to teach them.

Besides, there was no way the Council would authorize five hundred tablets, especially not after the bipeds had started destroying the toys they'd already been given. Every citizen was guaranteed a basic tablet, since it was used for education, voting, and communication, and could use their credits to upgrade it with the features needed for their craft, if not provided by the guild they were associated with, but there was no way the Council would authorize tablets for the bipeds until they were deemed sentient. They were just too expensive to produce, and the materials needed were too rare.

Her daughter had spent nearly a year saving up her credits to buy one that specialized in crafting and drawing, since she wasn't entitled to a better one through the Guild until she earned a Mentor.

Myra sighed and shook her head. They'd all been trying to figure out how to communicate with the bipeds, but everything depended on quarantine being lifted. She just prayed they'd live long enough for that before the species went mad.

If they haven't already, she thought bitterly.

Seven hours and five minutes later, Myra received a call from Jer. At exactly six hours after the start of the experiment, every councilor had left their chambers, recorded a vote of yes, and went home. Everyone that is, except for Councilor Surellis, Senior Councilor Tabor, and, of all people, Councilor Parner, who ultimately waited out the entire day before leaving their rooms to head to the council chamber and cast their vote. While the vote wasn't official until all members had voted and Tabor ratified it, it was clear they'd won.

Myra ran to find Brice, who hadn't picked up when she'd called. "We did it!" she exclaimed when she finally tracked her protege down. "We've got permission to do as we like within the Agency, which means we can start reintroduction and repopulation procedures."

Brice and the three other healers in the room cheered at the news. To Myra and Jer's utter astonishment, the final vote was unanimous. Even Councilor Paxton Parner had agreed.

14

JESSICA: VICTIM

Jessica wasn't sure how long she'd been held in her cell, but it felt like years. She'd lost count of the days, weeks, and months. Her once short hair had grown well past her shoulders and turned into a tangled and matted mess that she no longer bothered to even try to comb out with her fingers.

She still had no more of an idea of what they wanted from her than the day she'd first woken up in her cell, and she'd long since stopped caring. This was her new life, and it was as boring as Hell, but on the flip side, food and medical care were provided, and she hadn't had to take a single Spanish test.

After an eternity of the old pattern, the routine suddenly changed one day when Doc started up the short visits again. They brought the toys back with them, but didn't leave them behind when they left.

Still, she had never been so happy as she was the day that stupid, little, floating pyramid appeared and hovered above her as she lay on her bed, staring at the ceiling. She wasn't even sure she was really seeing it at first.

The short sessions quickly became the highlight of her day. After a few days of this, Doc left the pyramid in the room. She could have wept with happiness, and she played with the toy for hours after they left.

After a week of apparently good behavior on her part, Doc returned with one of the unbroken puzzle boxes. It took her days to figure out how to open it, but when she finally did, she found a stuffed, cat-shaped doll inside.

It didn't do anything particularly special. It was firm enough to be adjustable into different positions and had some weight to it, but was still soft and squishy. Its coat was mostly light gray, but darkened at the ears, feet, and tip of its tail, and it was the softest thing she'd ever felt.

The face had light blue eyes and a few tiny whiskers, and had the most dignified expression she'd ever seen on a stuffed animal. Most importantly, though, was the fact that it had just enough wear and tear to tell her this toy had once been well-loved by someone.

She fell in love with him instantly.

"Hello there. What's your name?" she asked the doll.

Why, I am none other than Sir Fuzzleton McFuzzface the Third, but you can call me Fuzzy, the doll replied with a bow and a thick English accent.

"It's nice to meet you, Sir Fuzzy. My name is Jessica. Tell me. What were you doing all cramped up in that tiny box?" she asked the doll back.

I was sent by a very special little cub who told me you badly needed a friend, and asked me if I could, pretty please, go live with you for a while to keep you company. That is, if you'd like my company, he replied with a voice that almost sounded like he was afraid she'd say no.

"I really need a friend. Please stay," she replied. "As you can see, there's plenty of room for you, but there's only one bed. I hope you don't mind sharing?"

Honestly, that would be perfect. I don't like to sleep alone, and the box was very lonely. Do you think maybe I could have a hug? I've been in that box for a while, and I could really use one.

Jessica hugged Fuzzy with everything she had. "Better?" she asked. "I'm really sorry it took me so long to get you out of there."

Much better. Thank you! Fuzzy replied.

She slept with Fuzzy, shared her meals with Fuzzy, and had long conversations with her new friend, telling him about everything that had happened. He listened patiently and then hugged her when she cried. He never criticized her when she forgot a word or forgot to speak mid-sentence. He asked her about her family, and she told him everything she could remember about them. They told each other stories that they made up, and he guarded her while she slept.

Part of her knew this wasn't normal, and that she'd probably gone mad, but as far as she was concerned, Fuzzy was as real and as alive as anyone she'd ever known. She was absolutely sure the toy responded to her questions, and at this point, she honestly didn't care if she had gone mad. A voice, even an imaginary one, was far better than the silence.

This routine continued without change for some time, until one day Doc woke her from a nap with a gentle tap on her shoulder.

Surprised, since she'd never once been woken, she sat up and rubbed at her eyes to make sure she wasn't dreaming.

Doc motioned for her to follow, and to her shock, there was an open door where Doc normally entered.

She quickly jumped up to follow. If nothing else, it looked like she was finally going to be able to leave her cell. She went to pick up Fuzzy for their new adventure, but Doc motioned for her to leave the doll. Frowning, she shook her head and held the doll tightly. There was no way she was leaving her only friend behind.

Doc sighed, twitched her whiskers forward, and motioned again for her to follow.

Exiting the room, she looked around to see the same tan walls from her one excursion. It had happened so long ago that she'd almost begun to believe she'd imagined it.

The second she was out, she bolted as fast as she could down the hallway in the other direction. She'd made it maybe twenty steps before Doc leapt over her and landed on all fours.

Sliding to a stop, she tried running in the other direction, but Doc's paws wrapped around her, forcing her to stop. She struggled and tried to get away, hissed, growled, clawed, and even managed to bite the giant paws trying to contain her, but Doc eventually managed to pin her arms down.

When she finally stopped struggling, Doc let her go and gave her a small shove in the other direction.

She turned and glared up at Doc, who looked far more sad than upset at her attempt to escape.

With an angry sigh, Jessica turned, picked up Fuzzy, whom she'd dropped in her attempt to get out of Doc's grip, and started storming off with Doc following close behind her.

Don't these people know how to decorate? she thought, as she was forced down the long tan hallway.

Stopping her, Doc placed a paw on the wall. A door opened, showing yet another tan, empty room—from what she could see anyway. Doc turned and motioned for her to enter.

Am I just being moved to another cell? she wondered with a sigh, but stepped through anyway, knowing if she didn't that Doc would probably just pick her up and carry her inside.

Once inside, however, she realized with growing excitement that she wasn't alone. There was someone sleeping in the corner.

Doc walked over and woke him up. His hair was long and unkempt, like hers, and he looked to be a few years older than her. Once he was awake, Doc stood and backed off over by the door, sitting down to observe.

She watched Doc for a second, then, turning back to the other person, she realized that he was trying to talk to her.

She tapped an ear. "I can't hear you. Something's wrong with my ears," she said.

He nodded his understanding, then walked over to her. When he was right in front of her, he hesitantly reached out and caressed the side of her face, almost as if he was afraid that she wasn't real.

To be fair, she wasn't really sure he was real either. She closed her eyes and leaned into the caress. It was the first time her face had been touched in what felt like years. The next thing she knew, they were holding each other in a tight hug. She felt something wet on her back and realized that he was crying. She was, too, in large hiccupping sobs.

After one of the longest hugs she'd ever experienced, they broke apart, and he motioned to his food, asking if she was hungry.

She shook her head no.

They just stood there staring at each other, far more hungry for the sight of another person. He was taller than her, by at least a foot or more, thin and wiry, like she was now, but strong. She'd felt the strength of his hug.

In that moment, she realized with a blush that he was most definitely male and fully naked. So was she, she remembered, and quickly crossed her arms over her chest. Somehow, in the months or years of solitude, she'd forgotten about her lack of clothing.

He seemed to realize at the same moment, but before either of them could do or say anything about it, Doc was there, tapping her on the shoulder and motioning for her to follow.

"Visitation time must be over," she said.

She reached out a hand to the man, but instead of shaking it, he pulled her in for another quick embrace.

When she felt Doc's paw on her shoulder, gently pulling her away, she turned and followed, afraid that if she didn't, she'd never get the opportunity for another visit.

That night, she could barely sleep, hoping that there would be another visit in the morning. The moment the lights came on, she wrapped her blanket around herself as best she could, hoping that she'd get to see him again.

When Doc entered and motioned for her to follow, she jumped up, this time leaving Fuzzy behind.

"I'll be right back, Fuzzy," she told her friend, "And I'll tell you all about it." From her past experience, she fully expected she'd only be given a few minutes of visitation with the other person. She wasn't wrong.

When she arrived at his room, he was awake and seemed just as excited to see her. Like her, he'd wrapped his blanket around his waist, and the moment she entered, they ran to each other and hugged each other tightly again.

After a time, he pulled away slightly and once again caressed her face.

She closed her eyes and nearly sobbed with happiness at the small gesture. When she opened her eyes again, she saw that his eyes were wet with tears, too.

"My name is Mitch," he said, and then, perhaps remembering that she couldn't hear, drew his name in the air.

"Jess," she replied, and he smiled.

"Hello, Jess! It's so wonderful to meet you!" he said, or at least that's what she thought he said by reading his lips, and then he gave an elaborate theatrical bow.

She laughed. "It's a pleasure, Mitch," she said with a huge grin, and did her best to curtsy. "Do you like my ball gown? I hear it's the latest fashion."

He laughed. "I love it! We must have the same tailor since our outfits match. Does my suit make me look dashing?" he said, posing for her.

"Absolutely debonair!" she replied, and then frowned as Doc tapped her on her shoulder. "Ahh, it must be midnight. My pumpkin awaits. Till the next ball?" she asked.

"It would be my greatest pleasure," he replied. They hugged each other briefly, but tightly, then Jess turned and followed Doc out.

After a week of short visits, their time was suddenly expanded to what she guessed was about three times what it had been before. They talked about what they thought was going on, but never talked about their past, and any time it started to come up, they both got awkward and quiet, lost in their own grief and trauma.

One day, she brought her flying pyramid with her, and they played a game of three-way toss with Doc.

Another day, he asked for a dance, and they slowly waltzed around the room. With his arms wrapped around her and her head resting on his chest, she could almost hear the beat of his heart. The sound of it was more amazing than the greatest orchestra she'd ever heard.

After the second week, Doc suddenly left them alone for nearly twice the length as before, leaving them both confused and wondering what was going on. Was she being moved to his room, or were they just being given some privacy? They talked a little about what they thought was going on, but he had no more of an idea than she did.

When Doc eventually returned for her, they at least knew the pattern of the week. The next day, she brought her puzzle box in for him to try, and he gave her one of his games. It turned out to be a kind of Simon-like toy where you had to follow the light pattern in the same sequence. After another week, their visits extended drastically, and she was left there until lunchtime, with breakfast left for both of them.

On the third day of this, though, her happy new world suddenly ended.

After Doc left, Mitch turned and motioned her over to his bed, sat down, and patted the spot next to him. There wasn't anywhere else to sit, so she did, just like she had many times before, and went to pick up one of his other strange toys to examine it.

She didn't think much of it when he took her other hand and squeezed it. She squeezed back, still enjoying the physical touch of another human being after so long in solitary confinement. But rather than letting go, he ran his thumb over her palm as if trying to remember what the touch of another person was like.

They sat there, side by side, for some time.

She wished she knew more than the absolute basics of sign language, or that she had something to write with. She wanted to ask him all sorts of questions, and while she was okay at reading lips, it was hard to do when you were sitting next to each other.

She was distracted by her own thoughts when he let go of her hand and instead reached out and put his hand on her exposed thigh. She froze, not understanding at first what he was doing as he rubbed his hand slowly up and down her leg.

It was doing odd things to her stomach that she'd never felt before. She turned her head to look at him in confusion, and he smiled at her.

Then, without warning, his hand slid under her blanket, and she understood.

She scrambled away, shaking her head no.

He motioned to the door and then to the two of them. "I think that's what they want," he said.

Horror filled her, and she backed away further, struggling to get to her feet. "No!" she said out loud, shaking her head again.

He stood up to follow her. His blanket slid off as he did, exposing for all the world what he wanted to do.

She turned and ran for the door, banging on it. "Help! Let me out!" she cried, but the door didn't open.

She felt his hands caress her backside, and she spun to face him. "No!" she yelled and tried to push his hands away.

"They aren't coming. They won't be back for a while," he said, and she realized he was right. They hadn't come.

"No," she whimpered.

"We don't have any choice. They'll keep doing this until they get what they want or decide we aren't worth the effort," he explained.

"No. Please. I don't want this," she begged, trying to push him away, but she couldn't budge him.

"It doesn't matter what we want. I'll make it good for you, I promise," he said, and caressed her face again.

This time, rather than feeling good, the touch made her want to throw up. She panicked and froze, unable to move or figure out what to do. She was trapped in his room with nowhere to run.

He let his hand travel down the side of her face and neck, running it slowly along her shoulders. Then, without warning, he yanked on her blanket, pulling it off of her before she could grab it.

She covered her breasts with her arms, feeling more exposed than she ever had before.

"No. Please stop," she begged.

But he didn't stop. Instead, he ran his fingers over her lips as if trying to shush her, and then slid them down her neck. When he moved his hand to caress the side of her breast, she slapped it away.

"No!" she yelled, but that only seemed to make him excited, and he grabbed her breasts, squeezing them painfully, pushing her against the door.

"I said no!" she yelled again.

The pain broke her free of her paralysis, and she started fighting back. She tried to get away and kicked at him, but he dodged out of the way. Then, before she could stop him, he picked her up and threw her over his back.

She screamed and hit him as hard as she could on his back. She thrashed, tried to kick him, then scratched at his back, but he didn't even seem to notice as he carried her over to the bed and tossed her on it.

She quickly tried to scramble away but he pinned her down before she could get up, and grabbed her arms and pinned them in place above her head with one of his much bigger hands, then started to force her legs apart with his knees while continuing to use his other hand to rub hard at her breasts.

When he reached down and grabbed her groin instead, she screamed and managed to get a hand free, then punched him as hard as she could in the nose.

This caused his head to snap back and blood to trickle out, but he didn't let go, and he retaliated by punching her in the head so hard her vision blurred. He grabbed her arm again, pinning it, then hit her several more times until she stopped struggling, half unconscious from the blows. Then he forced himself inside her.

She yelled and struggled to pull her hand free again, but he just grinned down at her and forced himself inside her again, hard, causing her to scream in pain. She managed to get her hand free once more, but he blocked her punch and hit her again in retaliation, this time knocking her out completely.

15

BRICE: FIGHT

Brice yawned as she climbed out of her tiny bed, exhausted from poor sleep the night before. Not only had Myra spent half the night snoring from her room next door, which the flimsy walls did nothing to keep out, but one of her patients kept triggering her alarms for the other half. Still, no matter how tired she was, her wards needed to be fed and cared for.

She now had sixteen patients. It had taken them several days to decide who would be paired up together based on approximate age and sex, and there hadn't been a good fit for everyone based on those in each pod.

They didn't want to move too many people around for fear the Council would shut them down again, but eventually, they'd transferred Nazari's young male cub to her care, so that she'd have an even number and could be paired up with one of the females in her care.

84 was not doing well with the transfer, completely ignored the female he'd been placed with, and had been up crying for hours every night since.

She was also worried about a few of the others in her care. They had all been doing better since reintroduction started, but several were still showing symptoms of isolation sickness. She hoped that the extended visits would help to further reduce their symptoms, as the supervised visits had taken up so much of her time.

She had wanted to put 1A1 in with one of the females like they were doing with the younger cubs, but the numbers didn't work out in her pod, so they'd put her in with the next youngest male. She'd been worried that the age difference would be too great, and they'd briefly considered putting 2A84 in with 1A1 as they were both cubs, but that would have required supervision, and they'd eventually decided that 84 needed a mother more. Thankfully, so far it had been working out between 1A1 and 2A326.

On her way to the common room for breakfast, she stopped to grab a stimulant and frowned at the empty box. Someone had taken the last one and hadn't let her know, so she could add it to the list of items to restock.

Maybe there's some in one of the other pods. She doubted it, though. They were all relying on the stimulants to stay focused. Months of being stuck in quarantine with their wards were taking a toll on everyone.

Shrugging, she added it to her list and continued on her way. The common room was packed with the other Healers in her pod, so she grabbed her breakfast and made her way outside to sit by the small pool around the bandala tree while she ate. She wasn't the least bit surprised to see dozens of other healers there as well. Work kept them cooped up inside for most of the day, and it was usually dark by the time she finished with the evening meal.

She ate slowly, enjoying the early morning coolness, which would quickly change to the baking heat of the summer sun.

Nazari sat down beside her a few minutes later. "How's 84 doing?"

"Honestly, not good. He was up half the night crying again, hard enough to set off my alarms, and he doesn't seem to pay any attention to the female we put him with. When he saw me, he cried even harder. I'm considering talking with Myra about making a change."

Nazari frowned and was silent for a while. "I didn't have problems with him like that before. I suppose it's possible he's become attached. Maybe they imprint as cubs like the akeer do."

Brice shrugged. "I suppose that's possible. I'll talk to Myra about it in our meeting this afternoon."

"If Myra doesn't want to swap him out, I'll be glad to monitor him for you. Maybe if I showed up, he'll settle down."

"If you want to take the night alerts, I wouldn't complain. I could use a good night's sleep," Brice replied. "I'd almost forgotten what it was like having young cubs."

Nazari chuckled. "That's evolution for you. If we didn't forget the painful stuff, we'd never have a second litter."

Brice's tail curled in amusement, but she shifted her focus to the conversation going on around her. With the bipeds interacting now, there was far more interesting behavior to observe, and several of the others were discussing it.

"Why do you think they wear the blankets wrapped around themselves? They don't appear to be cold," one of the healers asked.

"When we rescued them, they were all wrapped in various forms of material. Everyone wore something different, though. Perhaps it's a status symbol," another replied.

"Two of my wards appeared to be showing theirs off the second day," Brice said. "Maybe the garments represent affiliation with a guild, like our badges do."

"It does seem to be gender specific in how they wear it. Could it be a mating display?" another suggested.

"I suppose that's possible, but all but the youngest cubs do the same, and they're not big enough to mate," Brice replied.

"True, well, either way, I'm just glad they're starting to come out of their isolation sickness. One of mine kept hitting and kicking the door until he was bloody. I'm not even sure how he managed to do that with a static shield," another said.

"Agreed," Nazari replied. "I'm still worried about the cubs, though. From what I've been able to observe and what others have told me, they're progressing far slower than the rest. I just hope they haven't been in isolation too long."

"They've all been in isolation too long," another healer said.

"Isn't that the moons' forsaken truth?" Brice replied. "I'm just glad

Myra was finally able to convince the Council to relax the restrictions."

"Seven months too late, if you ask me," another healer muttered.

More murmurs of agreement went around the group.

"Well, enough gossip. Our wards are waiting for their breakfast too," Nazari said, then left. The others quickly finished their food and followed after her.

Now that they knew what their wards could eat, they each took turns preparing the meals to reduce the number of people in the kitchen at the same time. Today wasn't her day, so when Brice returned to the kitchen to drop off her breakfast dishes, her meals were already prepared.

She quickly located the first two trays and logged them before making her way down the habitats. She dropped the food off at 2A326 before leaving to retrieve 1A1. Thankfully, the cub had stopped running off after the first day.

She hadn't been the only one to try. More than half of the people they'd transported had tried to escape, either before or after their visit, and many still regularly tried. They'd never be able to get outside, but it was still depressing to witness.

1A1 was up and waiting the moment Brice opened the door and walked quickly to 326's habitat without any signs of trying to escape. After a brief check to make sure they were both good, Brice returned to gather her next set of meals.

When the last of the food had been delivered and her wards transferred to their cells, Brice made her way to her office. There was a mound of paperwork waiting for her from the other pods. She could have let someone else manage this, but she'd spent decades as a staffer in the Healer's Guild before deciding she wanted to become a healer instead, so she was familiar with everything that needed to be done, and she hoped that this would go a long way towards promoting her to Master.

She loved working in Myra's clinic and the relationships she'd made with the families that lived nearby, but it made for a very slow promotion track. There was little opportunity to show any sort of leadership skills when you only worked with two other healers on a daily basis.

As she often did, she placed feeds from her wards up on one of her monitors so she could check in on them and observe. They were baffling in their behavior, but far more interesting to watch now that they were interacting with each other.

After a quick scan of the feeds, she pulled up the first requisition form and began to work. Ten minutes later, though, her tablet blared with a low oxygen alert in her young cub.

A quick look up to the monitors revealed the old woman with the young cub waving frantically, trying to get her attention, grabbing her throat, and pointing to the cub. Unlike the night before when the alert had been triggered by crying too hard, this time it was obvious he was having difficulty breathing.

Brice clipped her tablet to her carry harness and bolted out of her office at a full run for the trauma bay. She grabbed the suction tool they used to unplug blocked airways and a hypo to treat an allergic reaction, not knowing which was the cause of his trouble breathing, then bolted back to the isolation unit.

By the time she arrived, the cub was lying down and struggling hard to take a breath, but based on the sound of his wheezing, the airway wasn't completely blocked.

She quickly scanned the cub and found a piece of fruit blocking the airway. She attached the suction tool. After several unsuccessful attempts, she grabbed the cub and bolted out of the room to the trauma bay, where she placed him on a bed. The monitors sprang to life, which she quickly scanned again.

Frowning at his oxygen level, she flipped out the anti-inflammatory medication in her hypo for a sedative and sedated the child so she could try to see if she could grab the food instead.

Once the cub was sedated, she placed an oxygen mask on him, hoping it would help, and ran to the equipment room to grab what she needed, but while she was doing that, her tablet blared with another alert.

She quickly scanned it and saw that 1A1 had an elevated heart rate. She dismissed that as not being critical, figuring they were likely just playing, as they had in the past, and returned to the cub.

His oxygen level was lower but not quite critical yet, at least for her own species. After several failed attempts, she placed an oxygen mask back on the cub and called Myra.

"Myra, I need your help. I have a choking cub, and I can't dislodge the obstruction," Brice explained in a rush.

"I'll be right there," Myra replied and hung up.

While she waited, Brice returned to the equipment room and grabbed a surgery kit and began prepping the cub for surgery, hoping she wouldn't need it.

Myra arrived a minute later, quickly examined the scans, and tried dislodging the obstruction as well. "We'll need to operate," Myra said. "I can't get a grip on it."

"Neither could I," Brice replied. "He's already prepped."

"Good. Begin," Myra ordered.

"Me?!" Brice asked, surprised, as she'd expected Myra to operate. Unless she was alone, covering the night shift at the clinic, she rarely took the lead on a surgery this critical.

Myra just raised a brow.

"Yes, ma'am," Brice said, took a deep breath, and grabbed the scalpel. Taking another deep breath to steady her paws, she began carefully cutting into the neck of the cub. It didn't take long to expose the obstruction, remove it, and repair the incision.

Myra watched the entire time but didn't comment until she was done. "Well done, Brice," Myra said with a grin, as the cub's oxygen levels returned to normal.

When the cub was awake and they'd determined that there were no side effects from his trauma, Brice carried him back to his room. The female was pacing anxiously in her cell and ran over the moment she entered, taking him back. The cub didn't want anything to do with the female and immediately wiggled to get down, running over to one of his toys instead, proving no lasting harm had been done.

The female shrugged and went back to eating. Brice chuckled and left, then started making her way back to her office when she remembered the high heart rate alert from 1A1. Deciding to check on them in person, since she was so close, she turned around and walked back to 326's room.

She hit the switch to open the door and blinked in shock at what she saw. The male was beating the unconscious cub with one of his toys.

"Stop!" Brice yelled, running over and physically pulling the male off the cub. When he struggled against her, she growled at him and bared her fangs.

He stopped struggling, his face quickly turning from anger to fear, or at least that's what she thought the expressions meant. She set him down, and he quickly backed out of the way the moment she let him go.

With a final warning growl at him, she turned her attention to the unconscious cub and winced at what she saw. She was covered in cuts and bruises. Scans revealed another concussion and two of the ribs that had been broken before had been broken again.

Unwilling to leave the cub in the room with the dangerous male, Brice carefully picked her up and turned around, instantly realizing her mistake. The door was wide open, and the male was missing.

With a frustrated growl, she set the cub down and walked out, locking the door behind her. She sniffed deeply and followed the male's scent down the hallway, where she found him trying to figure out how to get through the door to the trauma bay.

He spun, saw her, and tried running in the other direction, but she easily caught him and carried him back. She hit the switch that allowed her to pass through without opening the door and set him down, as far away from the cub as she could.

Ears pinned in warning for the male to stay back, she picked up the cub again and carried her down to the trauma bay. The higher quality scans in the trauma bay made her wince again.

The poor thing, Brice thought. Thankfully, none of these injuries were life-threatening and didn't require surgery to treat. She'd repaired more than her fair share of broken bones at the clinic, and as a Journeyman, she was certified to make those repairs on her own, without having to call in Myra to supervise.

Grabbing the bone knitter, she made quick work of the repairs to the rib, then treated the concussion. She was just starting to suture the worst of the cuts when the cub woke and started screaming as she tried to get away.

Brice tried to calm her down and restrain her, but the cub was in a full-blown panic, screaming and struggling hard against her. Both eyes were swollen shut from her injuries, and realizing that the cub probably thought she was still being attacked, Brice sedated her instead.

It took nearly an hour to suture all of the cuts and remove several small pieces of glass that she found. She ended up using an entire jar of nanos to treat all of the bruises on the poor thing. After another scan to make sure she hadn't missed anything, she carried the cub back into her room and placed her gently on her bed.

She watched her sleep for several moments, worried about how she'd react to the fight. The cub had been nearly critical with isolation sickness before, and Brice knew this would likely set her back.

With a heavy sigh, she returned to the male's room to treat his injuries. He had several bruises, scratches, and a broken nose. She motioned for him to follow, and he stood.

She half expected him to make a run for it again, and he didn't disappoint. She had no problem catching him before he even made it two steps, and rather than having him walk, she picked him up, arms pinned down to his side. She held him away from her body, knowing how much they liked to bite, and carried him to the trauma bay. She didn't take any further chances with him either and sedated him the moment she arrived. His wounds were quickly treated, and she carried him back to his room afterwards.

Letting out a frustrated sigh, she examined the room, trying to figure out what might have caused the fight. They'd been getting along well for the past few weeks, so a fight was completely unexpected after all this time.

Her eyes caught on the male's favorite toy, the one he'd been beating her with, and she realized it was cracked and broken. Picking it up, she examined it closely. Several pieces of glass were missing.

This must be where the glass came from. Did they fight over the toy, or was this just another escape attempt? she wondered.

Sighing, she stood and checked the area for signs of more broken glass. She found several pieces, picked those up, and carried the glass and the broken toy out to the recycler. She tossed the glass, but placed the toy in a box for broken electronics next to it.

When the quarantine was lifted, they'd be cleaned and repaired or stripped for parts if they couldn't be repaired.

What a shame. That was an expensive toy, too. There's no way the Council will pay to replace it. Oh well. Hopefully, quarantine will be lifted soon.

She returned to the trauma bay and cleaned up, then grabbed another jar of nano's and made her way back to the kitchen to grab food and water for 1A1 when she woke.

As expected, the cub was still sleeping when she arrived. Brice set the tray down and frowned at the poor cub for a moment before leaving to find Myra to let her know what had happened.

16

JESSICA: LIVESTOCK

Jessica bolted awake, scrambling to her feet, only to find she was alone once again and had been placed back in her cell. Food and water had been left behind, as well as the old container of bruise cream. Her head throbbed, making it hard to think, and she hurt in places she didn't even know she could hurt, places that told her what he'd done after she'd been knocked out.

But her injuries didn't matter. She hurt in the very depths of her soul, and no amount of pain cream could touch it. After all this time, she finally had an answer as to why she'd been kept alive. She was nothing more than breeding stock for her alien captors.

Grabbing Fuzzy and her flimsy blanket, she curled into a tight ball and cried for hours until she was out of tears.

Doc arrived some time later and scanned her before leaving briefly and returning with an older man she'd never met before.

Jessica screamed in absolute terror when she saw him and bolted for her puzzle box and threw it at him as hard as she could.

"GET OUT!" she yelled. "If you come anywhere near me, I'll kill you! I swear I will!"

Doc blocked the puzzle box from hitting the man and frowned at her reaction.

"What happened to you?" he asked, or at least that was what she thought he asked.

"What do you *think* happened?" she growled.

He looked at her in horror and then backed away, shaking his head, and yelled in anger at Doc.

That calmed her some.

Doc tried to push him forward, but he refused, then kicked Doc in the shin and bolted down the hall. A few minutes later, Doc returned without the male and just looked at her with a sigh before picking up the puzzle box and leaving again.

Jessica collapsed into a shaking heap in the corner. It was then that she made a decision. There was no way she was allowing a child to be born into captivity, into a life like this. Nor was she allowing anyone else a chance to rape her. She would rather die first.

But how, she wondered. There was nothing in the room she could use to make it happen.

Eventually, she remembered that it would only take three days to die of dehydration. She could do that.

Just three more days and this hell will finally be over.

When Doc entered sometime later and found the food and water untouched, they tried to get her out of bed, but Jessica just rolled over and ignored the cat.

When they tried to apply the pain cream and they touched her, she lost it.

Screaming, she grabbed the jar of goop from Doc's paws and threw it at them, then ran to the other side of the room.

Doc tried to follow, but Jessica growled and hissed and backed away.

"DON'T TOUCH ME!" she yelled, absolutely terrified that they were going to carry her back into someone else's room.

Doc sighed, set the cream down, and left the room.

The next morning, when her food and water still remained untouched, Doc brought the water over to her and shook her shoulder, trying to get her to respond, but she just lay there unmoving, staring at the wall, weak and already delirious from dehydration. She didn't even have the strength or energy to try running away.

They lifted her up into a sitting position and tried to force her to drink, like they did the first time, but she kept her mouth firmly shut and let the water pour down her.

They tried forcing her mouth open and eventually succeeded. Jessica took a sip to get them to stop, and when Doc backed off, she spit it back out at them.

They sighed and let her go, and she flopped back down on her bed and rolled over, facing away from them, and did her best to ignore them. A few minutes later, she felt something pressed into her arm, and then she felt nothing more as sweet darkness dragged her under.

17

JERAN: GUARDIANSHIP

Jeran sat in his office in Council City, reading through the latest reports from the Agency and Healer's Guild, and sighed with relief. The tests were finally complete, and they'd found nothing transmissible between the various species that they couldn't easily treat.

It was the scientists' belief that quarantine could now be lifted. He prayed the Council would agree. Paxton Parner had been a royal pain in his tail from the very first day of the Cataclysm. He'd resisted every measure to relax quarantine from day one, and he was sure today would be no different.

Still, he placed the reports on the docket for their next meeting, later that morning, with a grin. He missed Myra dearly and couldn't wait for her to come home, even if it was only for a short visit.

He grinned further when a call came in from her, expecting her to be excited about the reports as well, but frowned when he saw her expression.

"What is it?" he said, almost afraid to ask.

"We lost two of the red chested flyers today, and we're very close to losing 1A1," Myra replied.

"Oh no. What happened?"

"The environmental controls in pod six malfunctioned, and we believe it got too hot for the flyers. By the time their monitors alerted, it was too late. The rest of the creatures in that pod were fine, though. The flyers are in stasis now, and we'll be beginning the autopsy shortly to confirm. However, they are one of the shorter-lived species, so it could just be old age and a coincidence," Myra replied.

Jeran nodded his understanding. "So you don't think they were sick?"

"No. The scans showed nothing else wrong, just a highly elevated temperature before they died," Myra replied.

"Regrettable, but hopefully not a show-stopper for ending quarantine, although we might have to wait for the autopsy now," he said. "And the cub? You told me the other day she was doing much better."

Myra frowned. "She was until yesterday. She had a fight with the male we placed her with. He beat her until she was unconscious with one of his toys. She ended up with two broken ribs, a concussion, and multiple cuts and bruises everywhere. He had a broken nose and some minor cuts and bruises. Everything was easily treated, but the cub's isolation sickness has worsened significantly. Brice tried to bring another biped to her habitat, but she reacted violently, and the other biped refused to enter, then kicked Brice and tried to escape after 1A1 threw a toy at him. When Brice tried to treat the cub's injuries later, 1A1 threw the jar of nanos at her and refused treatment. Now she won't eat or drink. Brice has her sedated and on fluids for now."

Jeran sighed. "I thought you said the aggression had stopped."

"It had," Myra replied. "The others are all doing well, or better anyway. The worst of the symptoms has stopped, but they're all still showing the effects of their isolation. It'll take time for them to fully recover."

"Any idea how the fight started?" he asked.

She shrugged. "Neither of us has had a chance to watch the recordings yet, but Brice did say his toy was broken. It's possible that's what started it. We've seen territorial fights over toys with some of the other species, too. He also tried to escape. Brice accidentally left the door open when she saw him beating the cub and rushed to stop him.

While she was checking on the cub, he ran out and down the hall. He didn't get very far, though. He's not the only one. We're still seeing attempts to escape daily."

He frowned at both possible reasons. "That they're trying to escape doesn't surprise me, but if they're fighting amongst themselves or hurting someone else to get away, that's going to make it significantly harder to prove their sentience," he said.

"Well, no judgment on that should be taken until we can communicate with them, and they're out of quarantine. We have no idea if any of their behavior is normal or just a result of their isolation and captivity," Myra said. "How long do you think either of us would go before reacting in violence if we were held in similar conditions?"

Jeran nodded the point. "So what are your plans with the cub if she won't eat or drink? You can't just keep her sedated, although I suppose you could put her in stasis."

"I want to bring her home," Myra said.

"You want to do what?!" Jeran asked, thoroughly surprised, although he shouldn't have been. They'd fostered injured creatures at their compound before.

"She's not thriving here. She's been beaten by the first biped she's interacted with and held in isolation for months. Brice can't find anything else wrong with her. She's far less injured than she was when she arrived. Her behavior is consistent with a critical case of isolation sickness, and she was nearly there before. Several of the other Healers have offered to foster as well, including Brice, but frankly, I think she needs to form associations away from the Agency, with someone closer to her own age and who has more time to spend with her. What she really needs right now, more than anything, is a friend."

"Wait, you want *Marsee* to care for her?" Jeran asked, realizing what Myra was intending. "Today's her Name Day. She may want to move out, not stay home and foster a sick cub. She doesn't have any experience with that."

"Not true. She has more experience than most people her age, from helping with the creatures we've fostered in the past, and helping me at the clinic. Marsee's small enough to interact with her, better than we can, but since today is her Name Day, she's also old enough to be given the responsibility to care for her when we can't. Besides, she hasn't said she wants to move out. Not to me anyway. I'm hoping that if she does, she'd be willing to hold off for a week or two."

"I don't know, Myra," Jeran said, rubbing the back of his neck. "That's a lot of responsibility, and you and I are frankly buried in our work. And what if something happens to the cub or if Marsee hurts her?"

"Marsee won't hurt her. She's perfectly fine with Jenny's cubs and has helped me care for the wild animals we've treated in the past without issues. Plus, it's been almost a year since we had a report of a flare-up."

He frowned. That was true, but he didn't get to spend nearly enough time with her, and with her taking classes from home, she wasn't around people where it would be noticeable.

"Jer, 1A1 is going to die if she stays here. She's given up the will to live. Putting her in with one of the other bipeds won't solve that. And if she does die, I'd rather her last memory not be of captivity and being beaten by that male. A friend will be good for Marsee, too."

"What about putting her in stasis?" Jeran asked and raised his paw before she growled at him again. "I'm only asking because I know that question will come up in the Council meeting."

"Stasis won't treat the problem, only postpone it, and we still don't know if long-term stasis contributed to the death of that elderly male or if it was just a problem with the replacement heart. It's still an option, but I'd rather try fixing the problem first. If she still won't eat or drink, we can put her in stasis then, but that's a last resort."

Jeran nodded. "I'll talk to Marcus and see what he thinks. I sincerely doubt Paxton will allow this."

"Then her death will be on his paws," Myra stated, matter-of-factly. "As it is, I blame him for the cub being in this condition in the first place."

Jeran frowned, disliking where his thoughts and her accusations led him. On behalf of anyone else, he'd be legally bound to follow up on that complaint, but the cub wasn't a member of the Consortium yet or even recognized as sentient, which didn't give him a lot of leeway or her a lot of rights, even though he and Marcus were doing what they could to advocate for the species.

"I'll see what I can do," he said. "For now, make sure any interactions between the male and any of the others are supervised."

"Already done. I've got the healers observing all the other interactions remotely now. It's incredibly time-consuming, but they need social interaction, more than we need the rest," Myra replied.

Jeran nodded, hung up, and placed a call to his Mentor. Marcus's face made the same abrupt change he was sure his own had done, only a few minutes before.

"What's wrong now, cub?" Marcus asked with a heavy sigh.

"The Agency lost two of the flyers and 1A1 is refusing to eat or drink after being beaten by the male she was placed with," Jeran explained.

"Moons," Marcus muttered. "You always do call with the best news, little brother."

Jeran snorted. "Well, I wouldn't want to disappoint you," he replied, and filled him in on the details Myra had shared with him.

Marcus was silent for a long time, considering Myra's request and complaint.

"Paxton won't go for it, but getting 1A1 out of the agency is the right plan," Marcus eventually said. "Focus on the fact that your home is several leagues away from your nearest neighbor, which should help. Have you spoken to Marsee about it yet?"

"No, she's in class right now," Jeran replied. "And I wanted to talk to you first and get your...thoughts on it."

Marcus frowned at what he was implying. "Have you had any reports from the Guild recently?"

"Not in almost a year," he replied. "But then, for the last several months, she's taken most of her classes remotely. Her new teachers say she's excelling in her studies, with nearly perfect scores in her language classes, and they're thrilled to have someone with her artistic abilities to work on the restorations. She showed me one of the books she'd just finished the other day. I have to admit, I was pretty impressed."

"That kind of work takes a ridiculous amount of focus and patience," Marcus said. "If she's able to do that, then it's probably safe. Still, watch for issues when she first sees the cub. They're small and defenseless. If anything will trigger her instinct, that'll be when it happens. We'll need to know if that's a possibility, regardless. And, I suppose, if we have to lose one of the bipeds, it would be better if it's already dying."

Jer scowled at his brother.

"Don't look at me like that," Marcus said. "You know I'm right, and you know the rest of the Council will be thinking the same thing."

Jer didn't stop his scowl, but that was only to cover his fear.

"And who knows," Marcus continued, "perhaps having someone around all the time will be good for Marsee. It'll prove if she has gained control, and she could use a friend just as much as the cub. She's far too isolated in your compound."

Jeran nodded that point. "That's what Myra thought, too."

They spent the next hour planning for the council meeting and trying to figure out how to get around Paxton and his crew.

The council meeting was just as heated as they expected, but to his immense surprise, when the vote came in, they'd managed to convince far more than he'd expected, and it was a tie, which meant it was now entirely in Tabor's paws to decide.

"Councilor Chenzira," Tabor said, after chewing over the results for far longer than he expected. "I will release the cub to your care on the following conditions. First, neither you nor your family will go anywhere but your compound or the Agency, unless there's an emergency, until such time as the cub recovers, or is placed into stasis if she doesn't, and it is determined that there are no other medical reasons why she is not eating or drinking besides isolation sickness. And secondly, she will wear a harness and leash any time she's outside, or in a location where she might escape or hurt herself. And finally, I'll need you to take the oath of guardianship in the event that she is deemed sentient."

Jeran carefully considered her requirements. "I have no problem taking the oath of guardianship or remaining in quarantine, but as I stated when it was suggested earlier, I am concerned that a leash would send her the wrong message."

"Your concerns are valid, Councilor," Tabor stated. "But I am concerned that if she is trying to take her own life by refusing to eat or drink, that she will run off into the desert to do so, or find some other way to hurt herself the first chance she gets. As small and defenseless as she is, she wouldn't survive a day out there on her own. If she improves to the point where I believe she will no longer try to take her own life, then I will remove that restriction."

Jeran flicked his whiskers forward in agreement. "Then I accept."

Tabor administered the oath and then continued. "As far as quarantine goes at the Agency, I will allow the other Healers the same opportunity given to Myra Chenzira. They may return home, but with the same quarantine restrictions for their families, until the flyer's autopsy is complete and 1A1 shows signs of improving. While it would appear they are isolated incidents, I don't want to take any chances."

With that decision made, Tabor moved on to the next item on the docket.

Jeran absently paid attention as he fired off a message to Myra letting her know that Tabor had approved the cub's transfer to their home along with the restrictions, although he didn't mention the guardianship requirement. He knew if that was an option, Myra would want to do so as well, but if something did happen to the cub, he didn't want his partner held responsible.

She was understandably annoyed about the harness, but there was little either of them could do, and Tabor had a point. Myra said she would order the harness to the cub's size and asked him to pick it up on his way home, which he agreed to do.

The Guild attendant gave him a funny look when he picked up his package, along with Marsee's Name Day gift from grandparents, but Jeran said nothing, just nodded his thanks and left.

He had no interest in explaining the harness and leash, and was far more worried about how Marsee would handle their little surprise.

He spent the entirety of his long flight home from Council City praying that there wouldn't be any issues with Marsee's hunting instinct, knowing that if there was, he'd be trading his daughter's life for that of a cub that might die anyway, and he knew he wouldn't be strong enough to do what would need to be done if that happened.

CASTLE CHENZIRA

18

MARSEE: NAME DAY GIFT

arsee lay in a haphazard sprawl on her balcony, just under the east-facing archway of her tower room, whiskers deep in the book her uncle had sent her for her Name Day, a signed, first edition of the latest book from one of her favorite authors.

Her guild assignments completed earlier in the day, she'd been reading for hours and had eventually drifted out onto the balcony following the afternoon sun. It was the best location to catch the fading light of Surellis, her world's primary sun, and as far away from the annoying whine of the hydroponics units as she could get.

Octavius, their world's other sun, was too far away this time of year to be much more than a faint dot on the horizon. Its distant light was almost completely overshadowed by the brilliance and size of Surellis. The air rippled from the intense heat radiating from the sunbaked landscape, and while many might find this environment inhospitable, to Marsee, who had grown up here, it was perfect.

Her long fur and thick skin provided more than adequate protection from the heat, and there was nothing she enjoyed more than sprawling in a sunbeam, reading a good book.

That was part of the reason Marsee had claimed this ancient tower as her own. It had once been a lookout where her ancestors had watched for encroaching predators and the ever-present risk of wildfires and sandstorms during the dry season.

The large domed roof and massive archways provided a clear view in all directions while simultaneously providing shade and a breeze during the long, hot summers. When necessary, heavy wooden doors could be closed to provide shelter from the late summer sandstorms and the torrential rains that fell every spring.

"Marsee! Your Mother's Home!" her father called out from the base of the tower, but she didn't hear him, lost as she was in her book.

She could have claimed any of the empty rooms in the main compound, but she had fallen in love with the view from the old tower at a very young age. It reminded her of some of her ancient storybooks of life back before the Great Awakening, when the world was still full of magic and mystery, and when evil villains and epic heroes fought to control the destiny of their now long since destroyed home world — a world that they'd been forced to flee more than ten thousand years before.

She had played here on her own, long before she'd been able to persuade her parents to let her fix the tower and move up here. But perhaps the most important feature for her was its almost complete lack of modern electronics. Everything in the main compound seemed to let off a high-pitched whine that apparently only she could hear, and this was one of the few places she could escape it. She'd found a few lightbulbs that didn't bother her, and aside from her tablets, everything else was mechanical in nature, rather than electronic. It was pure bliss to her sensitive ears.

Marsee had been born the only cub in her parents' second litter, and rarely had anyone else to play with, as the nearest neighbor lived several leagues away. Being an only cub was exceptionally rare for her species, four or five cubs being the norm, and her parents worried about her desire to be by herself all the time. It just wasn't normal.

No matter where her parents dragged her, Marsee inevitably

found herself sneaking off to some quiet corner when no one was watching her. She absolutely loathed the sound of large crowds and found her age-mates to be baffling, immature, and far too often impossible to understand, and they clearly found her just as baffling.

Perhaps that had to do with being homeschooled through the distance learning program as a young cub. They lived too far away to make the regular flight into Sand Dune to take classes in person, and classes ended long before her father was done with his work with the Council.

She'd spent most of her early childhood with her mother at her small clinic, although occasionally she'd gone to Council City with her father and spent time there with the other cubs in the nursery, but she hadn't done that for years.

She had few friends, certainly none she considered close. It didn't really bother her, most days. Her books were her friends, and she had more than enough to do to keep her busy.

"Marsee! Dinner's ready!"

Eventually, she'd managed to make a bargain with her parents that she would not only do all of the work necessary to fix up the old tower, but also apprentice at the Guild to learn how to make all of the furniture she wanted to add.

Since she had a tendency to jump from one hobby or interest to another, never staying focused long enough to complete anything, they'd expected her to give up long before getting anywhere on the project, and had agreed.

Mostly, she suspected they were just glad it would mean she would interact more with people her own age. So, she'd switched to in-person classes for her primary education, and then spent the remainder of the day at the Guild until her father was done and could bring her home. That was until she'd graduated from primary school.

To her parents' shock and utter surprise, Marsee had attacked the problem with far more focus and determination than they'd ever seen from her.

The top two rooms of the tower had been badly neglected and

closed up for several generations. It had taken her nearly a month just to clean out the space, which had been turned into a storage room for old, broken items that hadn't been recycled and were being kept around solely for spare parts. A hole in the roof had gone unnoticed and had let the rain and sand in, leaving the top room full of broken and rotting items and nearly knee-high, hard-packed sand to clean out.

Once the space was clean and functional, if bare and empty, and the rotting junk tossed in the compost or shipped off to be recycled, she'd moved in with nothing but her favorite sleeping pillow and her tablet for company.

Her parents had objected, but she'd successfully argued that they'd never said she had to build any of the furniture before moving in, and a sleeping pillow on its own wasn't really furniture, and it had already been made.

Outmaneuvered, although secretly impressed and highly amused at their daughter's audacity, they'd given in. They were honestly more surprised that she had accomplished as much as she had. Much to their continued surprise, Marsee had honored their deal and had spent the next several years apprenticing at the Guild as a crafter.

Over the years, Marsee finished the furniture for her room, then started working on the rooms below. The second floor she turned into a library to store her overflow of books, and to keep them safer from the elements, as she preferred to keep the doors in her room wide open to let the breeze in. The bottom floor she'd turned into her workshop for her major crafting projects, building all of the work benches, and most of the tools there as well.

"Marsee! Don't make me walk all the way up there! Come on. It's time to eat!"

While she hated attending school in person and being stuck to the pace of her classmates and teachers, she found she enjoyed crafting so much that she'd petitioned her parents to let her switch over to the Guild full time, as long as she kept up her schoolwork.

They'd begrudgingly agreed, and she'd attacked her schoolwork with such focus that she'd graduated several years early, and managed to earn her Journeyman's rank in crafting after only a few years.

She'd then switched over to the Artist Guild for several more years, so she could learn how to decorate her creations, and had recently earned her Journeyman's rank there, too.

Then she'd met Darvo, an artist and poet from one of the other sentient worlds, and had fallen in love with the music that made up the Flyer's language, as well as the lost art of making and restoring books.

Few people owned actual books anymore, but she loved everything about them, the feel, smell, even the weight of them. Her Uncle Marcus had his own personal library, which she raided often.

At his encouragement, and with the tantalizing promise of being able to handle the ancient books he kept locked in his climate-controlled archives, if she earned her Journeyman's rank there, she'd switched to the Writers Guild and so far, she had become reasonably fluent in four of the five languages, and was thoroughly enjoying the delicate work of illustrating and restoring the old works. That she was able to read those old works while she restored them was an added bonus.

The tablet Marsee had silenced and left on her bed buzzed unnoticed several times before going silent again as she turned a page in her book.

If she'd been looking at the view from her balcony, she'd have seen the distant snow-capped mountains to the west lit up a vibrant golden red by the last rays of the setting suns, and the eastern sky turning glorious shades of pinks and purples. It was a sky that the ancient observers would have said warned of a storm in the near future.

However, Marsee was not paying attention to anything around her. She was, in fact, so completely engrossed in her book that the world around her had ceased to exist.

Curled in a loose ball with her head resting on her front paws, she held the book propped carefully in a crook of her tail. Its fur-covered white tip gently held the pages down as the evening breeze threatened to rustle and turn the page before she had a chance to finish reading.

"Marsee Bet Chenzira, put that book away and come eat! Your mother is home from the Agency, and she brought a surprise for your Name Day."

Marsee yelped at the tap on her shoulder, nearly flinging the book over the balcony in her surprise, but with a mad fumble, she managed to catch it a split second before it went flying over the edge.

Breathing hard from her fright, she clutched the book tight to her chest and turned to face her father.

His ears were twitching in the slightly bemused expression he often wore around his youngest child.

She knew from the curl of his tail and by the fact that he'd used her full name that it was likely he'd been calling her for some time now, but that once again, she'd not heard him. It was far too common of an occurrence with her.

"Hey, Papa," she replied sheepishly as she stretched, working the kink out of her tail, before standing up and walking over to him. "I didn't hear you come up." She wrapped her arms around his waist, and he returned the hug.

"Obviously," he teased. "I've only been calling you for the last half hour." Releasing from the hug, he placed a paw gently on the side of her face and sighed. "I can't believe how much you've grown. It seems like only yesterday you were a cub that could fit in my paws, and now look at you, twenty years old, and an adult."

This caused Marsee to roll her eyes, proving that she was still full of the attitude and mischief befitting a young cub, even if today *was* her Name Day.

"Before I know it, you'll be as big as your mother," he added.

"That's only if I decide to have cubs, and that's a *very* long time away," Marsee replied.

She might be an adult now, but she was still only about half the size of her mother, and would remain that way for the next twenty years or more before she entered the next stage of growth, and would need to decide if she wanted cubs or not.

In the old days, she would have had no choice but to become a mother and go into heat. Now, thanks to the wonders of modern science, she had full control over the entire process, which was a really good thing, especially for her species.

Far too often, second litters proved fatal, and third ones almost always were, even now. Her mother had nearly died trying for a second litter, against her healer's recommendation.

If she chose not to have cubs, she would remain the same size as her father, but if she decided to have cubs, then she would continue to grow and enter her first heat. A mother's larger size helped to offset the risk of having multiple cubs, and before the Great Awakening, gave her a better chance of being able to protect them until they reached maturity, or so she'd been told.

There was little actual history from that time left, at least none that she was authorized to see, so it was really anyone's guess what life was really like before then.

Still, today *was* her Name Day. She was now officially old enough to take the oath of adulthood, start making her own decisions, live on her own, if she wanted, and vote — not that her parents had ever curtailed any of her interests as long as she was safe.

Many in-betweeners moved out during this time to experience life on their own, often moving where they could best master their chosen craft or skill, but she was not ready to move out yet.

Maybe in a few years, she told herself. There was more than enough space for her here at the compound, and she had no desire to live in one of the cities. They were just too loud and overwhelming for her — good to visit, but she had no desire to stay.

She loved her tower, and if she was completely honest with herself, while she might be legally old enough to make her own decisions, she didn't really feel like an adult. Not only did she still struggle with controlling her hunting instinct, but she'd get so distracted working on a project, or even reading a book, that she'd forget everything else around her, sometimes even forgetting to eat or drink, and that worried her. How could she be an adult if she couldn't even remember to eat when she was hungry, or stop herself from pouncing on someone's tail?

The last time it had happened, she managed to hide it by

pretending that she'd caught a crawly and her guildmate had actually thanked her for looking out for her.

She was terrified of what would happen if someone found out. She'd probably have to move to a different planet — if she didn't die from embarrassment first. As it was, she'd been so upset about it that she'd stopped going to classes in person, and that conversation had been ugly when her parents had found out. They'd thankfully believed her misdirection. What she'd said had been the truth, but not the whole truth.

"...miss your Name Day meal, do you? And, since you probably didn't hear me the first six hundred and forty-three times I told you, your mother is home and she has a surprise for you," her father said, interrupting her drifting thoughts.

"She is? She does? What is it?" Marsee asked. Her tail spiraled in excitement as her focus shifted back to her father, and she caught the tail end of what he'd said.

"Now, if I told you, it wouldn't be a surprise, would it? Come on, your mother is waiting for us in the garden."

As they descended from the tower, Marsee saw that the massive shields that normally protected the outer compound during the intense midday suns had already been retracted for the evening and that the doors to the inner garden had been propped wide open to allow the last of the suns' rays to reach the plants inside.

This time of year, the suns were too strong for many of the exotic plants her mother liked to grow, but they still needed sunlight. It was a constant challenge to ensure they had enough light to grow without burning them to a crisp in the process, and one that her mother seemed to thrive on.

A small gust of wind ruffled Marsee's fur as they exited the ramp, causing a shiver to run down her spine. The breeze passed by her and into the courtyard, swirling the ever-present sand in its wake. The leaves of the great bandala tree that rose out of the center of the garden rustled slightly, and several of the wind chimes scattered about tinkled and chimed in a gentle harmony to the breeze.

One sound was decidedly not harmonious, though, and Marsee

flattened her ears to the side of her head as they passed by one of the many ancient hydroponics units that filled up the majority of the enormous outer courtyard. Like most electronics, the high-pitched whine of the units always made her brain itch if she stood too close, although no one but her ever seemed to notice or care. One in particular was especially annoying tonight.

"Hey, Papa?" she called out, stopping him. "We should probably get this unit looked at. It sounds funny." She gave it a light kick to see if it would stop.

"They always sound funny to you, kitten," her father teased, ruffling her ears. "And you really shouldn't kick the units."

"Well, they do. I can't help it if you can't hear them." She glared back, annoyed by his teasing, and lashed her tail slightly. "But this one sounds funny…er. It's making my ears itch."

"Alright, I'll have it checked out if it will make you feel better," he said, humoring her.

"Thank you, Papa. Although I'd be just as happy if you'd let me kick it again," she muttered, and rubbed at her ears to try and get the itch out. It never worked, but she tried anyway.

Her father's tail curled in amusement at the complaint. "If there is a problem with the unit, I don't think kicking it will help," he replied.

"Maybe not, but it would make me feel better, and it is my Name Day." She smiled up at him with an innocent expression. "One really good kick? Pretty please?" she asked sweetly, then grabbed her tail, trying to look as cute as possible.

"No. Council's orders. I'm pretty sure that would be illegal," he said, seriously, but was unable to hide his grin or the curl to his tail.

"Tell me where it says in the Charter that I can't kick it?" She glared back at him with a fake lash of her tail, but it quickly curled in amusement when he chuckled.

"If you really want to have article and section recited, ask your Uncle Marcus, but I'm pretty sure there's a section or two about destroying other people's property in there," he teased. "And I'm not sure you'd want to spend all of your Name Day credits on replacing an ancient hydroponics unit."

"That depends. How much would it cost to replace?" Marsee asked with an evil grin, honestly wondering if she could afford it. It might almost be worth it, especially if she could find one that didn't make her ears itch.

He laughed but didn't answer as he started walking again, tail curled tightly in humor behind him and clearly believing she was joking.

She rolled her eyes and followed after.

As they passed through the arches of the inner garden, Marsee felt herself immediately relax. The thick stone walls blocked the sounds from the outer courtyard. Where the outer courtyard had been methodical and mechanical, devoted to feeding the body, the inner garden was its complete opposite — a barely tamed riot of color dedicated to feeding the soul.

The great tree provided natural shade for the plants within, and the garden was always the coolest outdoor area in the entire compound. Luminescent moss-covered paths wound through the garden, the soft texture a welcome relief from the harsh sand and stone of the rest of the compound.

Small foot bridges arched over the tree's sprawling support roots and three small tributaries. The small brooks gurgled in a spiral pattern around the base of the tree and out through the compound, providing irrigation to the plants within and the hydroponics units in the courtyard, before being collected in underground storage tanks for use in the kitchen and outdoor watering stations.

In addition to the massive support roots, the bandala tree had much smaller feeder roots that extended all the way down into an aquifer below. During the dry season, animals could break off the roots to find water. This was where their water supply came from, but rather than breaking off the roots, small taps had been added that they moved every few weeks as the tree healed over them. The water that flowed from the taps was pure and safe to drink, filtered naturally by the tree.

To balance the impact they had on the surrounding wildlife by containing the tree behind stone walls, they pumped this water out to several distant watering stations, far enough to not invite animals into the compound, but close enough for easy maintenance.

The small variety of plants and fish that inhabited the pool that surrounded the tree provided most of the nutrients needed by the other plants in both gardens, but the water was filtered again before being stored in the tanks that the rest of the compound used.

Vibrant flowers of every color bloomed throughout the garden. Flowering vines hung from the massive twisting tree and swayed gently in the evening breeze, while dozens of small nocturnal winged creatures emerged as the suns set and began flitting from flower to flower, harvesting the sweet nectar.

When she was a cub, Marsee had loved seeing if she could get the tiny multi-colored creatures to land on her paw. She still tried on occasion, although she'd never been successful. Like the moss, they too glowed at night, providing a soft but flickering light. It made the garden feel like a magical place, especially this time of year when the rest of their part of the world was dry and dusty in the hot summer heat.

They paid as much attention to beauty as they did to practicality, for while almost everything in the compound was edible, or had some other medicinal or functional purpose, they believed that feeding the soul was just as important as feeding the body.

As her father had indicated, Marsee's mother was waiting for them, pruning away some of the dead blossoms. Gardening was her mother's favorite form of relaxation, as it provided a much-needed escape from what could often be difficult and heartbreaking days as a healer.

Her mother chose to maintain the inner courtyard by hand as her mother had before her. Marsee personally found gardening tedious, although she loved being in the garden. She was interested in the uses of the plants as it pertained to her crafts, but weeding and caring for the garden made her want to pull her fur out.

Since it made her mother happy when she joined her, she often did. She'd been trying to tend the garden in her mother's long absence, but her heart just hadn't been in it. Not only did it make her miss her mother even more, but she usually ended up distracted long before the work was done, and her neglect was really starting to show.

This was the first time her mother had returned home since the call had come in, and as far as Marsee was concerned, it was the best Name Day gift she could have ever been given.

"Mama! You're finally home!" she cried out, dropping down into a full run the moment she saw her mother.

By the droop of her mother's shoulders and tail, and the position of her ears, she could tell her mother was absolutely exhausted, but at the sound of their approach, her mother turned and brightened, her tail curling in happiness at the sight of her youngest cub.

"Marsee! Happy Name Day!" her mother exclaimed, as Marsee leapt into her waiting arms for a fierce and long overdue hug.

She wrapped her tail tightly around her mother and settled into her mother's arms, feeling safe and loved. She had missed her mother fiercely, and she'd asked regularly to be allowed to come help, but the Council was adamant. No one was allowed in or out, especially not a cub.

The best she'd been able to do to help was to send some of her old toys and craft some puzzle boxes to help keep some of the bipeds entertained during their long isolation. That, at least, had proven to be a challenging and interesting distraction.

"Thanks, Mama," she replied, and then motioned to the flowers. "Is something wrong, or did you just miss working in the garden?"

Her mother let out a heavy sigh. "I did miss the garden, but I missed you far more. Where have you been? I've been home for a while."

Her father came over and hugged them both. "I found her on her balcony, whiskers glued to a book."

Her mother smiled. "I see some things never change."

Marsee rolled her eyes at the teasing and jumped down, but still stayed close and leaned up against her mother's side. Her mother wrapped her tail around her and squeezed.

Marsee purred with contentment. "So, what was it like working with all the strange creatures and plants?" Marsee asked.

"Challenging, interesting, and sometimes very sad. You were right. Today was a bad day. We lost two of the red-chested flyers, and we're very concerned about one of the biped cubs. She's refusing to eat or drink."

"Aww Mama, I'm sorry. That's really rough." Marsee gave her mother a sympathetic squeeze with her tail. To make it all this time just to lose them when quarantine ended was awful. She was surprised they'd ended quarantine, though, if two of the creatures had died. "What happened? Were they sick?"

"No. We had a mechanical problem with the climate systems in the flyer's habitat, and we believe it just got too hot for them before we were able to fix it, although it's possible they died from old age. We won't be sure for a few days. As for the cub, she's been lethargic and losing weight and interest in the toys we've given her for months now. We believe it's caused by something called isolation sickness, and we'd hoped that contact with another of her species would perk her up. We introduced her to one of her kind several weeks ago, and it seemed to help at first, but they ended up fighting yesterday, and she was hurt pretty badly, so we had to separate them for their safety. We treated her injuries and can't find anything else wrong, but now, she's refusing to eat or drink at all." Her mother let out another heavy sigh, tail drooping again with her concern.

Marsee hugged her again in sympathy. Her mother rarely showed her emotions like this, even in the privacy of her own home, so Marsee knew just how upset she really was.

"The poor little thing. She must be so scared and lonely," Marsee said. "I like being by myself, but I can't even imagine what it would be like if I had to go through what they've been through. Losing your home and family in an instant, and then finding yourself held in isolation by some unknown giant predator for months on end, only to end up fighting with the first person you see..." She shook her head and gave her mother another tight squeeze with her tail. "It was hard enough without you here, and we got to talk all the time."

"The footage from the rescue indicates that they must have been a highly social species to have technology advanced enough to put objects in orbit around their planet, but it is strange that none of them have tried to communicate with us outside of some basic gestures," her father commented. "And you'd think they'd want to be reunited with each other, Myra, not fight."

Marsee's mother just shrugged. "Your guess is as good as mine, Jer. They do make noises on occasion that seem to have a purpose, but we've not been able to determine any meaning from them. The others are thriving again with the contact, so I don't know what happened with the cub. I've never known a species to stop eating or drinking if they weren't sick or injured, and the injuries she has now are minor compared to what she arrived with. It has to be isolation sickness. That's the only thing that makes sense."

"So, what's your plan with the cub?" Marsee asked. "If she won't interact with her own kind or care for herself at the Agency, maybe she needs a change of scenery. Anything would be better than those isolation chambers. Ugh. Seriously, I'd go mad if I had to stay in one of those for months on end."

Her parents gave each other a look, and then her father smiled.

"What?" Marsee asked with suspicion. She knew that look, and she didn't like it. It usually meant she would be stuck doing something she didn't want to do, like go into town, or clean the water filters on the hydroponics units, or worse, the compost bins.

"Happy Name Day, Marsee," her mother said instead and handed her a small box.

"What's this?" she asked, examining the tiny box cautiously, not following the sudden change in the conversation.

"It's your Name Day gift, silly," her mother teased. "Open it." She did, but she was just as mystified by what she found in the box.

"Thanks, but…I don't have a clue what this is," she said, holding it up and turning it over and around, unable to make heads or tails of what it might be. It looked kind of like a carry harness, but it was far too small to fit her. She didn't even think it would fit Maggie, the smallest of her younger nephlings.

"It's a harness and leash, designed to fit a biped," her father said. His tail curled in amusement at her confused look. "Your mother asked and was granted permission to bring the cub home with her today."

"What?! Really?!" Marsee's voice squeaked. "Here? Where is she?" Her tail corkscrewed so tightly in excitement that it hurt. She looked around, trying to spot the cub.

Her mother raised a paw and looked at her with a very serious expression. "I don't want you to get too excited. All of our treatments have failed, and there's still a very good chance we'll lose her," her mother softly cautioned. "Our healers came to the same conclusion you did, that her failure to thrive was from a combination of fear and isolation, not anything physically wrong. We've been giving her fluids to keep her alive, since she's refusing to eat or drink, but we can't keep doing that for long, and I'd rather not have to put a feeding tube in if we don't have to. I doubt she'd even stop from ripping it out if we did. So, I spoke to your father, and your father convinced the Council to let us remove her from the Agency and bring her home, so we could try to foster her here. That way, we can give her more undivided attention than we can at the Agency with so many others to care for."

Marsee's tail and ears drooped at her mother's words, but lifted in excitement again at the realization that *she* was going to be one of the first people to really interact with an entirely new species. Even the healers had been restricted from more than essential contact with any of the creatures for fear of contagion. Before she could say anything, though, her father spoke up in a tone that she rarely heard from him. It took her a moment to realize that he was speaking to her, not as her father, but as her councilor.

His face had shifted from the amusement of earlier to the calm, serious mask he wore as a councilor. "I know today is your name day, and usually new adults will move out, but you haven't said anything about doing so, and we could really use your help caring for her, at least for a little while. Your mother and I still have our normal responsibilities at the Agency and the Council, although we will both be working from here for at least the next week or two. We were hoping you might be willing to take responsibility for her and watch her during the day when we can't. We would also need a report of any observations you have at the end of each day. These reports will be shared with both the Agency and Council. Do you feel you're up to that?"

Marsee gulped at the level of responsibility being asked of her. Sure, she was now an adult, but she didn't know if she was ready to care for another creature when she could barely care for herself. Still, without hesitation, she straightened her shoulders back and arched her whiskers forward in a yes. As an adult, she would be expected to care for anyone in need, and this cub clearly needed a friend, and her parents would be there to help.

"We've successfully helped the injured animals we've found at the watering stations before, and I helped Mama for years at the clinic, so I'm sure we can help her, but what about my classes?" Marsee asked.

Her father smiled at her with pride, but it was her mother who answered. "We were hoping you'd be willing to take a break for a week or two, or continue to take classes remotely, just until she's doing better. Besides, I want to spend time with the two of you."

Marsee looked at her mother in surprise. Her mother was usually the one pushing her to go to class in person rather than staying home, but that worked for her. This was far more interesting anyway.

Those musty old books will still be there in a couple of weeks, she thought.

"Sure, I can do that," she said. "So where is she? Is she here, or do we need to go pick her up from the Agency?" Marsee's excitement overrode her concerns, and her tail spiraled again.

"She's here. I brought her home with me this evening," her mother replied, smiling at her daughter's enthusiasm.

"You'd have seen us unloading her from the shuttle if you hadn't had your nose stuck in that book of yours," her father teased, and then beckoned her to follow to the other side of the massive tree where a small crate had been hidden from view.

"She should be asleep for at least another couple of hours, maybe more," her mother said as they walked over. "She's so weak that it could take longer than we expect for her to wake from the sedative, but she needs the rest, too. She had a couple of broken bones from her fight, and the bone knitter always takes a lot of energy out of a person. She's lost more than a third of her weight since she was rescued, and we didn't want her to get hurt or to scare her even more with the move, so we decided to keep her sedated for transport. She'll probably be sick when she wakes up. The sedative tends to make them queasy, although we haven't figured out why."

Her mother carefully lifted the latch on the crate, and they all peered in to see a small creature curled in a tight ball on her side, limbs tucked in, and her head resting on one of her sand-colored paws. The biped appeared to be completely furless, except for a wild tuft of tangled and curly black fur on her head that faded to a light teal. A small blanket had been tucked in around her.

"Aww, she's adorable," Marsee crooned. "Look how tiny her paws are. I knew they were small, but I didn't realize how small. She's even smaller than Maggie. How old do you think she is, and is teal fur normal for their kind? They look so different without fur. How do they keep warm or cool without it?"

Her parents grinned at her string of excited and rambling questions, but it was her mother who attempted to answer them. "We don't know how old any of them are for sure, but she's the smallest female we rescued. The cubs that have been born since the Cataclysm have all been male, so we don't have a good understanding of the female growth cycle. Their cubs are only about the size of my paw when they're born. Honestly, you weren't much bigger, but then you were born prematurely. Based on the height and physical attributes of the other females, she's not fully grown, but it's hard to tell. There's such a small sample size to know what's normal for their species. She hasn't gained any height since she arrived, unlike the male cubs we rescued, but we think that may be because of the hormone blockers we put all the females on when the first one started showing signs of going into heat. We didn't want to risk them only having one or two heats like us and losing the chance to save the species. Sadly, two of the females miscarried due to their injuries, although thankfully, neither of the mothers died. We just hope they'll have another heat. We took all of the females off the blockers a few days ago, hoping that some of them would choose to mate with the males they were part-nered with, so if it was the blockers stopping her growth, we should hopefully start to see some changes there. Regardless, she's not showing the other signs of physical maturity that we've been able to identify, such as the development of breasts, at least not compared to the other females we rescued. Although it is possible that her breasts won't develop until she has her first cub."

"How will we know when she's in heat?" Marsee asked.

"Hormone and pheromone changes like us, and quite likely arousal by the males, if she's around them. I have the monitor checking for increases in specific hormones. The male she was with never showed signs of arousal when monitored by Brice. Many of the other males did around their females, which is also leading us to believe that she's not physically mature yet either."

"Do you know why they fought?" Marsee asked.

Her mother shrugged. "We have some ideas. Brice said that his favorite toy was broken, so we think that might have caused it. We've seen some of the other species fight over their toys and food when reintroduced. Almost all of the bipeds have shown some form of violence in the past few months due to their isolation sickness, although there had been no signs of violence prior to the two of them being left alone. Now, as for the color of her fur, we believe it has been artificially dyed. If you look at the base of her skull, you can see that her fur is almost black where it's growing in, not teal. Addition-ally, the color has lightened considerably since we rescued her. It was a dark blue then, almost purple."

Her mother demonstrated by gently pushing some of the tangled and matted fur aside. "We don't know if the color is simply for deco-ration, or if it has some cultural significance, as several of the others also had dyed fur. The males tend to have more fur covering their bodies, but nothing like ours. You'll have to be extra careful when handling her and watch your claws. Their skin is very delicate and easily scratched. It comes in a range of different shades and patterns, although most of the ones we rescued have similarly colored and striped skin. Like her fur, her skin has lightened by several shades since she arrived. We aren't sure if that's normal or if that's a sign of illness, although we can't find anything wrong. A few even appear to have drawn on their skin with some sort of permanent ink."

Marsee reached down and felt the small cub's fur, and then the back of the one paw that was slightly extended, tracing one of the sparkling patterns on her skin. "She's so soft, like the toe pads on a newborn cub, but all over!"

She carefully pulled the blanket away to get a better look at the cub. Her ears drooped at what she saw. While the cub appeared to be about the same length as her two-year-old niece, she was far less substantial and scrawny. She was so skinny, in fact, that Marsee could easily see the bones along her spine and rib cage, and her body was covered in fading bruises from the fight she'd had with the other biped.

"Most of the bruises should be gone by morning," her mother said, then gently covered the cub back up before moving Marsee's arm out of the way so that she could lower the lid to the crate and lock it back in place.

Marsee looked up to see both her parents grinning at her.

Her mother nodded towards the direction of the door. "Come on. Let's get her settled, then we can eat and have your Name Day celebration."

THE THREE MOONS had fully risen by the time Marsee and her parents had decided that the cub would stay with Marsee in her room rather than in the nursery with her mother.

Marsee argued that she'd be far less afraid of her than her mother. Her parents finally agreed, after Marsee agreed to put a small cooling unit in her room, so that the cub wouldn't overheat during the day.

She wasn't too particularly happy about having to listen to the whine of the unit, but the cub needed it, and she couldn't argue against it after her mother reminded her what happened to the tiny flyers in just the few minutes it took them to repair the environmental units in their habitat.

After dragging up and installing the ancient cooling unit from the storage room, her parents carefully carried the crate with the cub up to her room, then left to grab the additional supplies her mother had brought with her from the Agency. That done, she and her mother started unpacking, while her father left to gather their evening meal from the kitchen.

"What's all this?" Marsee asked as she opened a box and found a few of the puzzle boxes she'd made, along with other supplies.

"That box contains her sleeping pad and her favorite toys," her mother responded, peering into the box. "Where do you want to put it?" Her mother grabbed the roll, unhooked the strap that held it rolled up, and shook it out.

Marsee peered at the small, thin mat in her mother's hands and put her ears back in disgust. "She's been sleeping on that?!" she asked her mother, horrified.

"Yes. We couldn't risk cross-contamination by removing bedding all the time for cleaning," her mother explained. "These mats, like the walls of her isolation chambers, are hydrophobic, so we didn't have to worry about cleaning them all the time."

"Oh," Marsee said in response. "I guess that makes sense. We don't have to worry about that now, do we?"

"No, there's little point here," her mother replied.

"Good. Then we can do better than that awful thing for a bed. I don't think we should do anything to remind her of the room she's been stuck in for so long."

Her mother agreed. "Do you want me to drag the nest from the nursery up?"

"No. That's far too big for her." Marsee thought for a moment, then peered in the other crate again to look at the tiny, sleeping cub. "I'll be right back. You can put that awful mat away," she told her mother, and then ran down the spiraling ramp and into the courtyard where she met her father returning from the kitchen with their meal.

"Where are you going?" he asked her as she sprinted past on all fours, barely missing him and the large tray of food.

"To the shed," she replied in passing, not slowing down.

"What for?" he called after her retreating back.

"I'm not sure yet!" she hollered back, then disappeared from his view as she made her way around to the other side of the courtyard.

Jer just shrugged and continued on his way up to her room with the tray of food he was carrying. He'd given up trying to figure out his youngest cub a very long time ago. He was just thankful Marsee was so excited about the biped cub, and that there hadn't been the slightest hint of an issue when they'd introduced the two.

Marsee skidded to a stop and fiddled with the latch on the ancient door, which always stuck. With a hard yank, she pulled it open. The light in the shed flickered on when Marsee stepped inside. She stood in the middle of the room, looking around at the organized chaos where they kept all of the various gardening supplies and tools. She padded over to a haphazard pile of the crates they used for harvesting the produce, and rifled through them until she found one that was both wide and low, and seemed to be about the right length.

Running over to the sanitation room, she thoroughly cleaned the crate before running back up to her room. Halfway back, though, she stopped, turned around, and ducked into the storage bay, grabbing several more items before finally bolting back up to her room.

She was breathing hard from running up the steep ramp that circled the three-story tower and skidded to a stop in her doorway, nearly crashing into her father again as she did. Their species was designed to run on four feet, not two, and it tired her out quickly.

"Got it!" she wheezed as she lifted the crate of objects.

"Got what?" her father asked, peering into the crate.

"Stuff to make her a nest. One that should be far more comfortable than that thin old mat she had at the Agency," she explained, then stepped around him to set the bundle down on the floor.

After staring at the crate for a moment, she walked over to her own bed and tossed several pillows aside until she found the one that she was looking for, and brought it over.

She dumped everything out of the crate and placed the pillow inside it instead. Just as she thought, it fit perfectly, coming almost to the top. It should work nicely for a mattress.

She unwound the skein of long-haired chenzie fur and cut off a large swath. She tossed it over the top of the crate, furry side out, then tucked it in around the pillow and sides of the crate. When it was where she wanted it, she used the fastener tool to clip the fur to the sides of the crate to keep it in place, and gave the whole thing a test push for softness.

"There. That should work for now. It should be nice and soft, and the sides will keep her from rolling out as she sleeps. I'll build her something better later," Marsee declared. "Once I know what she likes."

Her mother walked over, having finished unpacking all of the cub's toys and arranging them neatly on her shortest table, and examined the nest she had made.

"That should do nicely," her mother said, then walked over to the cub's crate, reached in, and carefully lifted the small creature out. Slowly walking back over to the improvised nest, her mother gently laid the biped down on her back, proving that there was plenty of room for her.

Marsee cut off another piece of the chenzie wool and placed that on top of the creature, this time, furry side down. When she did, the tiny cub stretched, grabbed the improvised blanket, and rolled back over, pulling the fabric in close with a tiny high-pitched groan.

All three of them let out a quiet 'aww' and stood there watching her sleep for several long moments.

Her father wrapped his tail around her, and Marsee looked up into his twinkling blue eyes. "You were just as adorable when you were a cub, but a bit of warning. You didn't stay that way when you woke up."

Marsee glared at him, and he chuckled.

"Then you turned into a little whirlwind of mass destruction. I suggest moving some of your more delicate crafts higher up on your shelves," he explained. "Then again, that never stopped you either."

Marsee rolled her eyes at him, but she did take his warning seriously and moved a few of the items higher up, just in case.

It was a beautiful night, so they decided to eat out on the balcony. She grabbed several of the larger pillows in her room for them to sit on, rather than the hard stone floor.

Her father brought the tray of food out and set it between them, while her mother closed the lower half of the doors, so that the cub couldn't get out if she happened to wake while they ate, but she left the top open to allow the cool evening breeze and light of the three moons to enter.

They ate in companionable silence, looking out at the stars and moonlit horizon. Marsee purred with happiness as she leaned up against her mother's side. It had been a very long time since she'd had a meal with both her parents, and far too often she ended up eating alone when her father was stuck in council meetings well past meal times.

"I've sent you her medical records from the Agency, as well as a link to all of the footage we've kept," her mother said when they were done eating. "Brice was her primary caregiver, and I had her write up a summary. If you have any questions about the various medical terms, let me know, and we'll go over them.

Curious, Marsee jumped up and went back into her room to grab her tablet and stopped to briefly check on the cub, who was still sleeping soundly. With a happy sigh, she turned and went back outside. Flopping back down on her pillow, she flipped open her tablet to pull up the information, starting with Healer Brice's summary.

"What's wrong with her ears?" Marsee asked when she was part of the way through. "Is she deaf?"

"We're not entirely sure, but it would seem that way. We've tried playing sounds in her room to see if she would react to them, but she never seemed to," her mother replied. "We've done what we can to treat them, but as far as we can tell, she hasn't regained much, if any of her hearing. It's a pretty common injury among the survivors, which may account for most of our communication issues. I've requested specialized equipment to better test and treat their hearing, but it hasn't been approved yet."

"Why not?" Marsee asked, surprised to hear that it would be denied.

Her father frowned and looked over at her mother, seemingly just as surprised.

Her mother shrugged. "I'm honestly not sure. It's on my list of a million and one things to check up on. It's fairly expensive equipment, and not commonly made or requisitioned, so I'm guessing that's part of it. The Agency has already pulled significant resources away from other communities, both in healers and equipment. More than likely, it just hasn't made its way to the top of the list yet."

"Oh, I guess that makes sense. Does she talk at all?" Marsee asked next.

"She's vocalized a few times, but not nearly as much as the rest," her mother replied. "The males seem to be more vocal. Mostly, she makes a funny little squeak if someone surprises her, which apparently Brice does pretty regularly. Although there was this one time she actually swore at Brice, but we think she was just imitating her, not actually talking, since I'm guessing Brice has never said that particular phrase in front of her before."

Her father chuckled. "I don't know, Myra. Her body language said that was exactly what she was thinking. She was pretty angry at Brice that day."

"Well, that's the only time she's said anything even remotely close to being an actual word, but it could be like a cub learning to speak, making sounds and the inflection of speech, but not actually forming words. Although usually their first words are Mama and Papa, and not an insult. You will need to be careful, though, Marsee. She bites when she's scared, and according to Healer Brice, she's got very good aim with throwing small objects when she's angry. If she does bite you, come see me. The nanos will take care of it. It'll hurt, but shouldn't do much damage. Her teeth aren't very sharp, but they will leave a bruise."

Marsee flicked her whiskers to indicate her understanding and went back to reading the report.

"As I mentioned, I've given you access to all of the recordings, not just hers, but all of the bipeds we've rescued. Feel free to peruse them at your convenience, but I recommend that you review her first interactions with Healer Brice and the fight to start. Those have been tagged and added to your list of favorites, along with a few others. To be honest, we've only reviewed a fraction of the footage we've taken, since everything has been recorded, and there just aren't enough hours in the day to watch it all. Mostly, we just watch what the system has flagged for us to look at or pick random moments. If you find something of interest, flag it and let me know."

Marsee flicked her whiskers again, then set the tablet down beside her, deciding to review those later.

They spent another hour or so talking about Marsee's plans for the future and the projects she'd been working on at the Guild. She showed her mother the book she'd just finished restoring but hadn't had a chance to send back to her instructors, and they gave her her real Name Day gift, a brand new tablet that her grandparents had helped them pay for.

Marsee drooled over it as it was nearly twice the size of her old one and far nicer than she could have ever afforded on her own.

Then, under the light of the three moons and with her mother behind her, her father administered the oath of adulthood, and Marsee was officially registered as an adult, with all of the rights and responsibilities that went along with it.

With the weight of that responsibility settling heavily on her shoulders, her parents left to spend some time alone.

Marsee returned to her room, lowered her hanging bed down to the floor, and climbed in. She curled up to wait, trying to appear as tiny and harmless as possible, should the cub wake without her noticing.

She read through more of the information her mother had provided and watched the videos her mother had mentioned, along with others. Something about the fight bothered her, but she wasn't sure what. It was hard enough watching someone get beaten and not be able to do anything about it, but she felt like she was missing something important. It didn't help that the angle of the camera made it hard to see everything that was going on.

She decided to watch it again later when she knew more about the species. She was having a hard time reading their facial expressions and body language. Their faces seemed so static without whiskers and ears that moved. She set her tablet aside and waited for the little cub to wake.

And waited...

19

JESSICA: HOUSE PET

It was almost morning, the moons low on the western sky, when Jessica finally woke. Her eyes were heavy and refused to open as the grogginess of the sedative wore off. She eventually gave up trying to open them, sighed, and resigned herself to one more day in her tan hell.

When her brain cleared enough to notice she wasn't wracked with the horrible thirst she'd had the day before, she swore, realizing that her captors must have pumped her full of fluids, refusing to let her have the escape she so desperately wanted.

She was filled with so much loathing and hatred for them, for what they'd done to her, that she felt like she was going to explode. With a growl, she rolled over, tucked the soft blanket in tight, and willed herself to go back to sleep in the warm comfort of her bed. At least when she was asleep, she didn't have to face the reality of her situation. It was an escape of sorts, and the only one she was ever likely to get.

She hadn't quite drifted back to sleep when the softness of the bed and the texture of her blanket suddenly cut through the grogginess of the sedative, snapping her wide awake. It was not the thin pad and blanket she'd had for the months or years of her captivity. She tried to open her eyes again, but it was like they were glued shut. Rubbing at them, she peeled away thick gobs of caked-on muck and was finally able to get them to open. She blinked hard to clear her vision. Her eyes felt dry and gritty, like she hadn't opened them for days.

When she could finally see clearly, she sat up with a gasp. She was no longer in her tan cell, but in a massive room that wouldn't have looked out of place in a medieval castle. It would have easily fit her entire house inside with room to spare. A floor-to-ceiling bookcase lined the stone wall directly in front of her.

She struggled with the scale of it. It was the biggest bookcase she'd ever seen, and the proportions were all wrong. On either side, though, were arched doorways that reminded her of cathedral doors. More importantly, the top half was open to the night sky, and she could see stars in the distance, beautiful twinkling stars. She hadn't realized how much she'd missed them.

It took her several moments to pull her attention away from the glorious sight of the night sky to continue looking around the room. Turning to her left, she saw another massive bookcase and a table with what looked like all the toys she'd had in her cell arranged on top, including Fuzzy. However, rather than chairs, there was a massive pillow beside it, bigger than her parents' mattress.

"Where are we, Fuzzy?" she asked her friend, but oddly, Fuzzy didn't answer. He just stared behind her with a look of warning. Turning to follow his gaze, she found herself staring directly into the face of one of her alien captors, and jumped in surprise.

Or maybe not, she thought after her heart stopped racing.

The creature before her was like Doc, but half the size, closer to the size of a small horse than a mammoth. The cat was still massive but nowhere near as intimidating as it lay in a large round basket-like platform, with their feet tucked neatly underneath their body, and their large fluffy tail wrapped around the front of them.

This cat had a beautiful, long-haired calico coat, predominantly jet black but splattered with a delicate patchwork of white and gold that darkened to copper in places, and large emerald green eyes that sparkled with curiosity.

Jessica sat there staring back, mesmerized by those eyes. Giant alien aside, it was one of the most beautiful cats she'd ever seen, regal almost.

I wonder if this is one of their children, Jessica thought. *If it is, it's the biggest kitten I've ever seen.*

When Jessica didn't move, the kitten slowly sat up, revealing silky black arms that ended in what looked like a pair of mismatched white and tan gloves.

Jessica still didn't move. She watched as they reached over and opened a box sitting on the floor next to the odd bed and slowly pulled out one of the thermoses that she'd grown used to seeing, along with another of the odd food containers.

They set those down on the floor and gave both a little shove towards her. When Jessica just sat there unmoving, they gave the food and water another small shove. Then, after tilting their head in thought, they picked up a piece of the food and pretended to eat it, before putting it back in the container.

When she still didn't move, the kitten slowly backed off the bed towards the far side of the room, clearly thinking Jessica wasn't coming forward because she was afraid to get too close.

"As if, Kitten," Jessica muttered. "I've taken on bigger cats than you."

Jessica stared at the kitten for several moments, sighed in frustration, and then shrugged, realizing that if they weren't going to allow her to starve herself to death, she'd have to figure out another way to escape her captivity.

Might as well humor the kitten, at least until I can figure out what's going on. If nothing else, I'm finally out of that infernal cell.

She flipped the luxuriously soft, furry blanket off of her, noting briefly that she was still naked, and in her pique envisioned making a coat out of the kitten's furry hide.

The bed she was in had tall sides, nearly a half a foot above the mattress. She peered over and, after confirming that she wasn't too far off the floor, tucked her feet under her and stood. Wobbling slightly on the soft mattress, she stepped over the edge of the bed. Taking a closer look, she realized it looked like nothing more than a larger version of the wooden crate her grandfather's barn cat had slept in.

Who's the pet now? she wondered.

Jessica slowly made her way over to the water and gingerly squatted down. The room was spinning like she'd just been on the tilt-a-whirl at the fair. She felt lightheaded and weak, as if she hadn't eaten in weeks, not days, and she still hurt, although not as badly as before.

How long did I sleep? she wondered.

Once her head stopped spinning somewhat, she reached over and took a sip of the water. It was unexpectedly ice cold. Everything they'd ever given her had been room temperature. She drank deeply, savoring the coolness, but it hit her stomach hard, and it lurched in complaint. She set the cup down, closed her eyes, and took several large, slow breaths, trying to keep from throwing it back up.

When her stomach finally settled to an annoyed grumble, she opened her eyes again and looked to see if that was enough to make the kitten happy.

They looked at the food and then made a motion with their head, clearly indicating that she should eat something.

She took the smallest piece of food she could find and forced it down. Her stomach lurched again, and she blanched. She hated throwing up. Sweat formed on her brow as she sat, lowering her head to her knees, breathing shallow and fast.

At a gentle touch on her arm, Jessica opened her eyes and looked up into a concerned face. She gave a weak smile and a thumbs up to indicate she was okay, although she briefly considered throwing up all over them out of spite.

Whether some of her spite came across or not, the kitten arched its whiskers forward, took several steps back, and sat back down, giving her some space again.

She glared at the kitten for a moment, but then turned her attention back to the room, while still trying to keep her stomach from staging a coup, and wondered what they'd knocked her out with. She hadn't felt this sick since the start of her captivity.

The room was massive, and there was so much to see that she didn't know where to look first. After so long without anything to look at, she felt overwhelmed. Everything was so much bigger than she was used to, at least the objects that she could identify, and there was color everywhere, although thankfully not a spec of that horrible tan.

Based on the grain and rich stain, most of the furniture in the room appeared to be made of wood or something similar. The dark stain of the wood contrasted with the light gray stone walls beautifully, at least what she could see.

Artwork covered the walls, depicting strange landscapes and creatures. Sculptures were displayed on various shelves, half in shadow by the dim lighting in the room.

Shadows! She hadn't seen a real shadow in ages.

The arches of the doorways were painted a shade darker than the walls, and the lower half of the doors were intricately carved, although she couldn't make out the details from here. There weren't any chairs in the room, just low tables, surrounded by more of the massive cushions.

In the very center of the room was the kitten's bed. Up close, she could see that the base of it was a large round wooden ring with a wicker-basket base, all stained the same dark stain as the rest of the furniture. On it was a thick mattress that curled up slightly along the sides. Braided ropes were attached to the ring on four sides and hung slack.

She followed the ropes up towards the ceiling, where they came together in an intricate weave to form one thicker rope that continued all the way up to the very center of the domed roof, where the arches met. The rope passed through the wheel of a large wooden pulley down to another pulley and back up to the first before coming back down and wrapping around a large wooden cleat bolted to the wall.

I wonder why they're using pulleys instead of whatever anti-gravity tech they used with that floating pyramid toy, Jessica thought, thoroughly surprised to see such simple tech when more advanced options were clearly available.

The kitten, observing where Jessica was looking, stood up and slowly walked over to the rope, unwound it from the cleat on the wall, and slowly pulled on the rope until the bed lifted off the floor.

Beautifully colored drapes on the back side of the basket, that she hadn't seen at first, fluttered in the light breeze as the bed was lifted. When it was several feet up, the kitten tied the rope off again and leapt onto the platform, causing it to swing wildly from side to side. As it settled, the kitten shifted so that their front paws and head were leaning over, looking down at Jessica to see what she thought.

The motions and mannerisms were so childlike and innocent that Jessica momentarily forgot her fury and smiled. She personally thought the bed looked like a lot of fun, and far better than the mattress she'd been sleeping on for the past millennia, or the wooden box she'd woken up in. She was curious what it would be like to sleep on something that swayed beneath her.

Better wait until your stomach is being less of a grouch before you try it, though, she thought to herself, then unsteadily stood up, only to find herself at eye level with the platform and the kitten's giant paws.

Curiosity got the best of her, and she slowly reached out to touch one of the paws. Doc had touched and held her several times, but she'd never really had the opportunity to take a closer look.

Stopping just short of touching, Jessica looked into the glowing eyes of the kitten, looking for permission.

They arched their whiskers forward at her.

I'll take that as a yes, she thought, then slowly ran her hand over the back of their paw. The fur was incredibly soft and thick, far softer than Doc's had been.

They slowly turned their paw over so she could examine the underside and the thick, rough, multi-colored pads. Hidden in the fur were the tips of very sharp-looking claws.

Jessica touched the tip of one to see how sharp it was, and the kitten slowly flexed her paw, extending the claw so she could see how large it was, too. Fully extended, it was nearly as long as Jessica's hand.

She swallowed hard at the reminder of how easy it would be for them to hurt her without even trying. Somehow, she kept forgetting how ridiculously huge they were. She'd gotten used to Doc, and this kitten somehow had seemed both tiny and unthreatening in comparison.

As if sensing her unease, the kitten retracted the claw, then moved their paw so that they were just about touching Jessica's hand, as if to ask for the same permission.

Jessica looked into the kitten's eyes, and when she saw nothing but curiosity, she smiled and nodded her head, giving her permission.

Ever so gently, the kitten stroked the back of Jessica's hand and then turned it over to look at the underside. Following the same pattern, Jessica curled her hand into a fist, showing how her hands worked, then relaxed them. The kitten carefully felt the end of one of her fingernails.

"Not nearly as sharp as yours, eh?" Jessica said.

The kitten tilted their head sideways at this, their furry ears twitching, and opened their mouth.

Jessica realized that they were speaking back to her. Frowning, she tapped her ears to indicate she couldn't hear and shook her head.

The kitten's ears and shoulders drooped as they said something else.

Jessica shook her head again and, with a deep sigh, looked down and closed her eyes. Oh, how she wished she could hear right now.

I wonder what their name is, she thought, surprised at how sad she felt when she realized that she'd probably never know, and decided to call them Cali, short for calico.

Opening her eyes again, she found herself looking at a beautiful eight-pointed star-shaped mosaic that had been hidden under the sleeping platform. A rainbow of colors made an intricate pattern within the star. The colors were nearly blinding after months of only seeing tan and silver. She bent down to touch them, not really convinced the colors were real. They were just so vibrant.

Looking back up at the kitten, who was now leaning over the bed watching her, she smiled and looked around the room again. Her eyes first landed on the bookcase that took up the nearest wall. She looked back at the kitten, who motioned that she could go take a look, so she walked over and took one of the smaller books down off one of the lower shelves.

Small, though, was an understatement. The book was bigger than her textbooks and nearly twice as heavy. She awkwardly opened it. Sure enough, it was a book filled with beautiful, if unreadable, symbols like the ones on her bracelet. When she went to compare the bracelet to the writing in the book, she realized her bracelet had been removed.

I wonder what that means, she thought. *Does this mean I'm no longer a prisoner?*

Shrugging, as she had no way to ask, she flipped through a few pages of the book and examined the unusual texture of the paper before closing it and returning the book to its spot on the shelf.

She shifted over to the next section of shelves to examine a metallic-looking object on display. Not sure if it was a piece of artwork or if it served some other purpose, she reached out and gave it a tentative touch.

She felt the light thump of the kitten jumping down from their hanging perch and turned to see them padding across on all fours. When they arrived at her side, they sat and reached out, giving the base a slight twirl, which caused the rest to spin in a mesmerizing pattern.

She watched for a little bit as it spun and then slowed to a stop. She turned to the kitten and smiled, realizing that sitting like that, the kitten wasn't much taller than her, if you didn't count the several extra inches of height from her fur-tipped ears.

"It's very pretty. Did you make it?" she asked, pointing to the kitten and then the spinning model.

The kitten tilted its head and looked at her as if trying to figure out what she was asking, and then reached over and spun it again.

She smiled her appreciation, even though it wasn't what she'd asked. They were at least trying to understand her, which was more than Doc had done most of the time. Heck, most of the time it was as if Doc hadn't even heard her, but the kitten's ears twitched every time she spoke.

Jessica turned, trying to decide what she wanted to look at next, and spotted several strange objects on a nearby table.

Before she made it halfway there, light caught her attention from the open archway. She turned to gaze up into the night sky, then just stood there in shock. She rubbed her eyes again to make sure she was seeing clearly and not just still dizzy from whatever they'd knocked her out with. Her vision didn't change, and she had to accept that what she was seeing was real.

Three moons?!

Intellectually, she'd known she wasn't on earth anymore, giant alien cats in stone cathedrals being proof of that, but seeing three moons was a punch to her already queasy stomach.

Her legs buckled out from under her, and she collapsed into a heap on the stone floor. Hugging her knees tightly, she sat there and stared up at the alien night sky, and the three incredible moons it contained, all of which were far larger than the moon had been back on Earth.

After a minute or two, Cali slowly sat down beside her, then gently wrapped their tail around her waist, and looked up at the night sky with her.

Unable to look away from the beautiful but unearthly sight, she rocked as tears started quietly streaming down her face, as the realization that she was never going to see her home again sank in.

Who knows if there's even a home to go back to, she thought.

She was stuck on some distant alien planet, who knew how far from her home and family, and forced to breed by mammoth-sized cats, for what purpose she still had no idea.

Have I been on a spaceship this whole time? Is that why I wasn't let out? How long would it take to get to another planet, and what kind of technology do they have to be able to travel that far so quickly?

She was pretty sure that, with Earth's current technology, it would have taken thousands of years to reach the nearest solar system with a potentially inhabitable planet.

Cali applied a gentle squeeze with their tail and slowly pulled her in close.

Jessica gave in and sagged against their soft side, not doing anything to stop the tears. She kept staring at the sky, feeling hopelessly lost as she grieved for the home and people she knew she would probably never see again.

But unlike before when she'd grieved alone in her cell, there was now just the tiniest sliver of hope that maybe, just maybe, things might be a little better than they'd been before, because for the first time in months, maybe years for all she knew, she wasn't grieving alone.

2 0

MARSEE: THE UNIVERSE'S WORST CUB-SITTER

Marsee sat with the little cub, watching the moons until they faded under the slowly brightening light of Surellis and the approaching dawn. Her heart broke at the sadness radiating off of the small creature, and empathy for what the cub had clearly lost, wishing she could figure out how to communicate to her that she was safe, with friends, and that everything would be okay.

As the suns rose, Marsee shut the upper doors and turned on the portable cooling unit. Her ears flattened to block out some of the noise as it grumbled to life. She gave the old thing a thwap with the side of her paw, and it settled into a more agreeable hum, barely.

I really should just kick that pump. Maybe when Papa's not watching, Marsee thought absently. *I wonder how much a new cooling unit would cost, and if I could find one that isn't so noisy.*

She didn't have all that much credit to her name, but if the old unit suddenly stopped working, she imagined her parents would pay for a new one, if not the Council, since the cub's life depended on it.

Somehow, I doubt they'd believe me if I said it just accidentally fell off the balcony, Marsee mused with some humor. To be fair, she wasn't even sure she could move as it had taken both of her parents to lug it up here.

She hit it again to see if that helped further, which it didn't.

The cub came over to see what she was doing, and Marsee noticed that her eyes were red and puffy. She wasn't sure if they were irritated by something, or if it was a normal reaction to the tears she'd shed earlier.

When the cub stood in front of the cool air, Marsee confirmed her suspicions that the cub was hot. The reports indicated they had no idea what temperatures the creature could comfortably survive at, so Marsee took note of the current temperature in her room and that the cub's internal temperature had risen slightly.

After standing in front of the cooling unit for several minutes, the cub walked over and drank some more water. When this did not seem to upset her like it had the first time, she added it to her notes and texted her mother, pleased to report that the cub was awake and choosing to drink on her own.

Her mother responded almost immediately with a "Blessed moons! Well done, Marsee!"

The cub proceeded to investigate Marsee's room, looking at everything she could get her little paws on. If there was something up too high and the cub pointed to it, Marsee took it down for her and showed her what it was. She wasn't sure if the little creature understood, but she seemed to, and unlike the warning her father had given, she treated everything with care.

After another hour or two, the cub started squirming, then waved her arms and chittered, and then squirmed some more, clearly trying to communicate something, but Marsee couldn't figure out what she wanted.

Frowning, head tilted, the cub thought for a moment, then turned and walked over to the water and pretended to drink. Then, after setting the cup down, she drew a finger from her mouth down to her stomach and squirmed again.

You're a fur-brained bumble crawler, Marsee, she berated herself. *Of course! She needs to pee.*

Marsee quickly grabbed the harness her mother had given her and brought it over to the cub, but frowned. *How do I explain that she needs to wear this before going outside? I don't want to scare her by putting it on.*

She thought for a moment, then handed the harness to the cub, who took it and tried to figure out what it was, holding it up and turning it to hold the straps from different angles. The cub moved her shoulders up and down and handed it back.

Marsee curled her tail and snickered to herself, realizing that she'd looked almost exactly the same the night before. She unhooked the small buckles, then slowly and gently laid it over the cub's head and clipped it into place, making small adjustments so that it was snug but not too tight.

The cub felt the harness, then reached down and unclipped one of the buckles.

She's smart enough to get out of it. That could be a real problem if she refuses to wear it, Marsee thought, but then put a paw over the cub's to stop her before she undid another one. She shook her head using the motion she'd figured out meant 'no' to the little cub and hooked the first one back in place.

Everything was fine until she attached the leash to the ring on the back of the harness. The moment the cub realized what it was, she became visibly angry and spun around to face Marsee with what could only be described as a growl.

The cub quickly backed up, shaking her head hard no, and before Marsee could stop her, unclipped the harness and tossed the whole thing back at her. The cub continued to back up, growling her anger, until she bumped into one of the bookcases, where she stopped and closed her paws tight, as if she was struggling to control her emotions.

There's no doubt she understands what this is, and if she had a tail, it would be lashing furiously right now, Marsee thought.

Marsee pointed to the door, then to the harness, and back again to the door, trying to pantomime that she had to wear it to go outside. Even though she wasn't sure the cub understood, Marsee stepped towards the cub with the harness in hand, but the moment she did, the cub let out the cutest hiss Marsee had ever heard, bared her tiny little teeth, and flexed her paws as if she had claws.

It was adorable. Marsee's tail spiraled with amusement, but that only seemed to infuriate the tiny cub more.

She started screaming a whole litany of high-pitched chittering sounds that made Marsee's ears hurt worse than the hydroponics units did.

Pinning her ears back at the sound, Marsee thought for a bit, trying to figure out what to do.

If she won't wear the harness, maybe she'll let me carry her.

Marsee slowly set the harness down.

The cub stopped chittering and watched, tense with suspicion.

She waited for a moment or two for the cub to calm before taking a cautious step forward.

The cub screeched at her, grabbed a small sculpture off the shelf behind her, and threw it at her.

Marsee managed to catch it, stepped back, and sighed, scratching her ears as she tried to come up with something else. She set the sculpture down on a table and walked over to the hook where she'd hung her own carry harness and put it on, then walked over to the door, nodding her head 'yes'. She took the harness off and shook her head 'no'. Marsee tried to look as apologetic as she could.

With a glare, a heavy sigh, and several angry chitters that ended with another hiss, the cub squirmed again, clearly needing to pee, and nodded. She wasn't happy about it, but she understood. If she wanted to go outside, she had to have the harness and leash on.

Marsee sighed with relief. The leash was retractable, so once it was back on, she motioned for the cub to move towards the other side of the room so that she could get a sense of how long it was. Marsee then gave a little tug to indicate she should return, which the cub did, arms crossed and fuming mad.

She felt horrible for making the cub wear it, but the Senior Councilor herself had ordered that the cub was to remain leashed, for her own safety, any time she was outside. She'd tried running away once before, and running off here would likely mean her death. It would only be a question of whether the heat, lack of food and water, or a predator got her first.

Marsee was pretty sure the cub was smart enough to know running off wouldn't be a good idea, but that didn't mean she wouldn't try, or worse, try jumping off the balcony. Suicide in the face of tragedy was rare but not unheard of for her people, and this poor cub had been through more trauma and tragedy than anyone should ever have to go through.

It was nearly midday by the time Marsee unlocked and opened the door nearest the ramp.

Heat blasted the air-conditioned room, causing the cub to visibly flinch. When she tried to follow Marsee outside, she let out a painful-sounding squeak and hopped back in quickly, sitting down and rubbing at her foot, which had instantly turned a bright shade of red.

Oh no! Marsee's panicked thoughts raced as she examined the cub's foot. *It must be too hot for you to walk outside. Is your paw burned? It's all red.*

Marsee gently touched the foot, which felt warm to her touch, and the cub hissed.

What am I going to do? I could try carrying her again, if she'll let me. She's so mad already. What if she bites? If I don't, how will I get her to Mama to make sure she's okay or even to the waste room?

I guess I'll just have to risk it, she finally decided.

Marsee motioned for the cub to stand up, which she did, but she wasn't putting her weight on the injured foot. It was clearly causing her pain.

Marsee looked outside and then back at the limping cub and made up her mind. She slowly reached down and gently picked her up.

The cub stiffened but didn't fight her.

Thank the moons! she thought. *She understands!*

Then, it was Marsee's turn to stiffen as the small cub wrapped her arms around Marsee's neck.

Is she trying to hurt me? Marsee wondered, but when the cub only grabbed some of her fur without yanking on it, she realized the cub was just holding on.

It didn't take long to make it down the ramp and back inside the compound, but even in that short amount of time, liquid had started running down the cub's face, and she was breathing hard.

When Marsee set her down, the cub wiped the liquid that was now dripping into her eyes off with the back of her paw. While the cub didn't seem concerned about the strange liquid, Marsee was now on the verge of panic that the cub was sick or overheating.

She wished she'd thought to grab her tablet so she could check the cub's temperature, but she'd left it on her bed and didn't want to go back outside and expose the cub to even more heat.

She shouldn't be leaking fluids like that, should she?

She'd go right to her mother's office after the cub had a chance to pee, she decided.

Marsee showed the cub where the waste receptacle was and waited.

When the cub didn't go and just looked at the opening and then back at her, Marsee used the same pantomime the cub had used to indicate she needed to go, then pointed to the hole.

Healer Brice's report said the cub was trained to use the receptacle at the Agency, so why isn't she using it now? Marsee wondered.

When the cub pointed to herself, the receptacle, and then to Marsee and the door, she realized that the cub must want privacy to go.

How very odd, she thought, wondering why someone would need privacy for a completely natural body function, but Marsee nodded and stepped outside, figuring it must be a cultural difference. There was nowhere for the cub to go from the small room but out into the hallway anyway.

After a few minutes, the cub limped out of the room. Her face and neck were now starting to turn a bright shade of red as well, just like the burns on the bottom of her foot.

She must be overheating!

Marsee was really starting to panic now. She scooped up the cub and took off at a fast walk towards her mother's office. She wanted to run, but she didn't want to scare the cub, and it took everything she had to slow her pace.

When she arrived at her mother's office, she gently set the cub down and knocked on the door.

"Mama, it's me. Can I come in?"

She always knocked when the door was closed because she never knew when her mother was going to be in a meeting or talking with a patient. Her mother's office had the same busy light and privacy shield that her father's did, but her mother rarely used them unless she was seeing a patient in person.

"Come on in, sweetheart," her mother called.

Marsee opened the door and walked inside. She stopped when she saw her mother on a conference call.

"Oh, you're in a meeting. I'm sorry! I didn't mean to interrupt," Marsee said, unsure if she should leave or if the cub's injuries warranted interrupting.

"It's quite alright, I was just talking to Brice about the observations you sent this morning. We're very relieved to see she's drinking on her own again," her mother replied. "What brings you here? Is everything okay?"

"Good morning, Healer Morningstar," Marsee said formally, and then turned to her mother. "No, maybe? Oh, I don't know."

Flustered, not sure how to proceed now that she was here and Healer Brice was watching, she struggled to form her words. She'd been in charge of the cub for less than a day, and the poor thing was already burned and maybe sick and overheating, and Marsee felt positively awful.

Some adult I'm turning out to be.

"Are her eyes watering again?" her mother asked gently, used to dealing with Marsee in this state. It didn't take much to get her overwhelmed most days.

"No..." Marsee turned, and realized that the cub had not entered behind her, but was still out in the hall and shaking, her eyes locked unblinking on Healer Brice's image on the wall monitor, with the same look of rage she'd seen before, and perhaps something else she couldn't quite decipher on her tiny face.

Fear maybe?

Marsee wasn't sure why the cub would be afraid of Healer Brice, and decided the shaking must be from pain or overheating. Anger she could understand, but fear? She'd known her mother's protege for as long as she could remember, and Brice would never have hurt the cub. Mama would have flayed her protege alive if she had.

"It's okay. Come on," she motioned and then gave a little tug on the leash.

After a moment of hesitation, the cub limped towards Marsee, eyes firmly locked on Healer Brice the entire time.

Marsee's mother stood as the cub entered. This must have startled the poor thing, because she suddenly rushed in and hid behind Marsee.

"Mama, can you sit back down? I think you must have scared her."

Her mother's ears twitched back in surprise, but she did as she was asked.

The cub relaxed slightly, confirming her suspicions. Marsee reached down and picked her up, and the cub settled in close like she had before. Marsee used this as a distraction to take a calming breath to gather her thoughts.

"My word! She's actually letting you hold her?" Healer Brice exclaimed. "The last time I tried that, she bit me!"

"Yes. No, I mean…" Marsee paused and took another deep breath, rubbing the back of her neck with her free hand. "Yes, she's letting me hold her. No, her eyes haven't leaked again, although they still look irritated. I came here because when she told me she had to pee…"

"She spoke to you?" her mother interrupted.

"No. She didn't speak to me. She told me. She pretended to have something to drink and then drew a line through her body and out. She was squirming a lot, too."

Marsee demonstrated using her free hand.

"Anyway, I took her outside so we could go down to use the waste receptacle, and I think…well… It must have been too hot for her, and I think she burned her paw on the hot stone. She made a loud squeak and jumped back into the room, then started rubbing at her foot. When I looked, it had turned bright red, and she flinched and squeaked when I touched it. You could see she was still limping when she came in. So, I risked picking her up, and carried her down, but then by the time we made it back inside she was breathing hard, and water was dripping from her face and arms, and when she came out of the waste room her face and neck had also turned bright red, although it's not so much now. I'm worried she got too hot or maybe she's sick." Marsee blurted everything out in a panicked rush.

"Bring her over here and let's take a look," her mother said calmly, tapping on the edge of her desk.

Marsee walked over. The cub clutched her fur tighter as she approached her mother.

"Shhh. It's ok, little one. My mother's going to take a look and make sure you're okay. No one is going to hurt you."

She started purring to comfort the cub. Even though she knew the cub couldn't hear her, she hoped maybe she could feel the purr and the vibration of her talking. When the cub relaxed a little, she carefully pried the cub's paws from her fur and set her down on the edge of her mother's desk.

Her mother pulled up the cub's vitals on the screen next to the image of Healer Brice.

"Nothing appears out of normal ranges," her mother said. "Her temperature is slightly elevated but not really enough to be concerning."

Her mother turned back to the cub and slowly reached out and touched the side of the cub's face.

The cub flinched but didn't move away.

"There's still some moisture, but you said she was dripping. She doesn't appear to be doing so now."

"She wiped a lot of it away, but my fur is still wet where I was holding her," Marsee replied, and showed her mother, who reached out to confirm the damp fur.

"Perhaps it's a cooling mechanism, since she wouldn't have fur to help regulate her temperature like we do, as would breathing hard," Healer Brice suggested. "It could be their way of panting. We saw the same thing with her and the other bipeds who developed infections from their injuries."

"True. It could be an infection, but that wouldn't show on the monitor we implanted."

Her mother stood and walked over to her bag, which was sitting on a side table, and rummaged through it for a bit before returning with her scanner.

"I'm not seeing any signs of infection, but your idea that it's a cooling mechanism seems reasonable, and is certainly easy enough to test," her mother replied, after taking a more detailed scan. "We can try raising the temperature in one of the habitats and see if they have the same reaction. If they do, we'll know not to worry about it. We have the temperature Marsee noted this morning, as well as our current temperature for a guide."

"I'm worried that might put too much stress on them, especially after what happened with the flyers," Healer Brice stated.

"I am, too. But we really do need to know what temperatures are safe for them," her mother replied, turning to look at the other healer. "Let's try adjusting the temperature by a degree every half hour or so in six of the habitats. There might be differences based on sex. Pick three of each. Once you have a reaction for each direction, note it and return to the current temperature. Let's start by figuring out when they start to notice the change in temperature. If there's any change in their internal temperature, stop immediately. I'll set an alert to notify us if her internal temperature changes more than two degrees in either direction. Do the same with the others. There's no point in putting any of them at risk for now. I don't want a repeat of what happened to the flyers."

Turning back to Marsee and the cub, her mother stared at the cub for a moment. "Marsee, if the cub refuses to go outside or insists on going back in, honor her wishes, record the temperature, and let me know. Now, let's take a look at her eyes."

Her mother reached out to open the lids more, but this time the cub pulled her head away. Marsee pantomimed opening her own eyes wide with her fingers. When the cub copied her, her mother leaned in close to take a look but didn't touch.

"Her eyes do seem a little irritated," her mother said after a bit.

"They were really red and puffier earlier," Marsee explained.

"Redness seems to be pretty common when their eyes tear up, at least with the bipeds I cared for. As far as I know, we've only witnessed any significant crying from the bipeds, who seem to do so quite regularly, especially around moments of extreme emotion or pain, not just if there is something in their eyes. Their eyes all cleared up within a couple of hours at most. If something was irritating it, they'd be blinking a lot or the lid would be closed," Healer Brice commented.

Her mother grunted in agreement, then looked over at her. "Which paw was burned?" she asked, then gently picked up the indicated foot.

The cub watched but didn't pull her foot away.

Her mother picked up the other foot to compare the color. One foot was definitely redder than the other, but the cub didn't flinch when her mother touched either one.

"It's definitely hotter than the rest of her skin, but I don't think it's badly burned, as I'm not seeing any blisters." Still, she picked up her scanner and ran it over the foot. "Sensors confirm it, minor burns on the skin, but I'm not seeing any indication of subdermal burning."

Her mother let go of the foot and sat back, thinking for a moment. "Bring her into the kitchen and fill up the sink with cold water. Have her put her feet in it as long as she will allow it. If you start to see any blisters, or if her limping gets worse, bring her back immediately." Then her mother stood and walked back over to her medical bag and put her scanner away, but she returned with a small container, which she handed to her. "Put some of this on her foot after you've soaked it. This should repair the damage as well as numb the pain."

"Thank you, Mama. I will. I'm so sorry she got hurt. I promise I'll do better!"

Marsee still felt horrible and embarrassed that so much had happened in such a short amount of time.

I've got to be the worst cub-sub sitter in the universe, she thought.

"Don't be sorry," her mother said. "You did nothing wrong. We knew their skin was delicate, but we had no idea it would burn just from going outside."

"I agree. You've really done very well," Healer Brice added. "Not only does she seem to trust you already, but you've gotten her to eat and drink, which I've been unable to do, and I've been her healer for months. This is new territory for all of us. I've grown fond of this little one, and I was very worried about her when she stopped drinking."

Her mother indicated her agreement. "This must be why they wrapped themselves in fabric. We thought it was just for decoration since it was so varied, but it must have served a more practical purpose. We'll have to figure out something to replace it."

Marsee made a mental note to review the recordings from the rescue, thinking she might be able to craft something. Her report had stated that everything they'd worn had been disposed of due to radiation contamination.

Her mother gave Marsee an affectionate squeeze with her tail, then shooed her out so she could continue her discussions with Healer Brice.

21

JESSICA: LEASHED

Holy Hades in a handbasket! This planet is an inferno! Jessica thought as the kitten carried her down the hallway. She took several deep breaths as she tried to bring her panic back under control.

The last few minutes had been a roller coaster of emotions. She'd been consumed with fury when Cali had clipped the leash on her, like she was nothing more than an animal.

That had changed to resignation when she realized that the planet was so hot and bright that she'd literally cook if left outside for very long. Even the hallway, while cooler, was still too warm for her comfort, and she knew that without clothing and shoes, she'd never be able to escape, even if she was left alone and could find a way out of here.

Then she'd experienced nearly crippling embarrassment at having to use the heinously horrendous hole of horror with her hairbrained holder of the hated harness hovering outside in the hall. At least she'd been able to make Cali understand that she wanted privacy, although she'd been sure they were listening and had heard the whole thing.

But worst of all had been the full-blown panic she'd felt the moment she saw Doc on the monitor of the strange office belonging to the gold cat. For a moment, she'd hoped that she'd escaped her prison, but apparently not. This was just a change of location.

Possibly the home of the gold doctor, she thought.

She was pretty sure the giant gold cat was the same one that had treated her infected arm all those months or years ago, as they had similar facial markings.

Cali shared some of the same markings, too, which made Jessica suspect that they were related.

Am I being fostered out now that I've been bred? God, I hope I'm not pregnant.

She slammed that thought hard behind a door in the closet of her mind and locked it tightly. She had enough to try and figure out, and she didn't need a child on top of it.

Would they even let me keep my child?

She slammed that thought away, too, or tried to, but her emotions and thoughts kept sneaking through the cracks.

The sight of Doc had brought back memories that she'd been able to forget as she'd examined the strange room, and it had been everything she could do to contain the loathing and rage she felt as she followed Cali's command to enter the room.

When the gold cat had moved, it had startled her so much that she'd reacted without thinking, and hid behind the one source of protection she had. She had no idea if she could trust Cali, but so far, outside of the loathsome leash, they had shown her more care and compassion than Doc had in the months she'd been stuck in her cell.

She was pretty sure they didn't understand why she'd been sweating, as they'd felt the side of her face and examined the moisture on Cali's fur, and had a fairly long conversation about it.

Cali had looked downright panicky when she'd first wiped the sweat off her face. The poor cat's tail had poofed out more than double in size and clamped tightly between their legs, and their ears had drooped in what could only have been described as pathetic. Between that and the concern they'd shown over her burned foot, Jessica had the sense that Cali actually cared about her well-being.

The gold cat had eventually checked out her burned foot, but hadn't treated it. Although they had handed a jar of what she hoped was that miracle cream to Cali, as her foot still throbbed.

Like Cali's room, the gold cat's office also had several bookcases, although they were shorter and there were far fewer books, which were all fairly uniform in size, shape, and binding, reminding her of medical journals or some other form of reference book.

There was the massive desk she'd been sitting on, along with several relatively smaller tables, one of which was padded and looked like it folded out, which made the place feel like a doctor's office.

Two chairs sat in front of the desk, while another sat on the side against the wall, under the monitor. The chairs were oddly shaped, curved at the base with a large c-shaped hole in the back, which she supposed made sense if you needed to account for room for their tails.

Outside of the massive monitor, which took up almost half of the wall, there was little in the way of tech in the room, which, compared to the hospital room she'd witnessed, made the space feel almost antiquated. That they were clearly in a stone castle of some kind didn't lessen the impression either.

There had been a large window on the far wall, letting in light, but a shade built into the glass had been drawn, and she hadn't been able to see anything but sand in the few inches left open at the bottom.

One large picture looked like a family portrait containing eight individuals. She recognized Cali, who was being held in the gold cat's arms, confirming her suspicions that they were family, although Cali had been much younger in the picture.

Well, smaller anyway. Who knows how quickly they grow?

A few of the sculptures and paintings in the room reminded her of the ones in Cali's room, and she wondered if Cali had made those or if there was another artist in the family.

When she'd seen the paintings in Cali's room, she'd tried to get the kitten to give her something to paint with, but they hadn't understood and had just pulled the painting down off the wall for her to look at. It had been beautifully done, although the color choices had been odd. Purple leaves on the tree in the background, for instance.

Then again, maybe they have purple leaves.

Long before Jessica had calmed, Cali entered a new room that was only about half the width of the room they'd just been in. It was wedge-shaped and appeared to be mostly empty. From what she could see, there was a counter that ran along the entire length of one wall, about shoulder high on her kitten, and a wall of what she thought might be cupboards on the other. Light entered the room through a small window along the far wall, but this one was too high up for her to see anything but the sky.

Cali walked over and tapped a spot on the bottom of the counter with her foot, and a set of steps popped out in response. They climbed the steps and gently placed her and the leash on the counter next to what looked like a large bathtub or a small pool.

She sat there and watched as the kitten leaned over the tub, just barely able to touch a spot on the wall behind it. As soon as they did, a small section of the wall slid open, and water started filling the tub.

No, not bathtub, sink. You've got the scale all wrong. You're being cared for by one of their children, and everything here is built to accommodate the adults.

As the water filled the sink, Cali pointed to her and then to the counter.

That was an order to 'stay' if I've ever seen one, she thought.

Still, she was being trusted not to run off, so she might as well earn some brownie points by being a good little puppy, for the moment anyway. Maybe if she did, they'd take the leash off. As soon as she figured out how to safely get away, though, she was gone.

Ooohhh brownies. Don't think about brownies, Jessica, she chided herself, but it was no good. Her mouth watered, and her stomach rumbled. *Oh God, how I miss brownies, or chocolate anything, for that matter.*

Leaving Jessica sitting with her feet dangling off the edge of the counter, nearly eight feet off the floor, Cali went over to the opposite wall and opened a door, letting a blast of cold enter the room. Inside were various items on several shelves, and she recognized some of the foods she'd had before.

Oh! It's a refrigerator! This must be a kitchen, then. I wonder where their stove is. Is it hidden like the fridge? Do they even cook? Nothing they've ever given me was cooked, so maybe not.

Cali grabbed several items from the fridge, took a large platter out of another cabinet, and placed everything on the counter next to Jessica. Then they turned, walked down the counter a short distance, opened a drawer, pulled out what looked like a machete, and turned towards her.

Instantly panicking with the thought that *she* was going to be lunch, Jessica swore and bolted to her feet, looking frantically for a place to hide or run. Not finding anywhere to run, or anything to hide behind, she leapt off the counter, hissing with the pain of her foot as she landed hard on her hands and feet, and flew out the door as fast as she could run.

22

MARSEE: INSTINCT

arsee froze the moment she saw the cubs panic, then spun, trying to figure out what had set her off. She expected to see a creepy crawly but found nothing.

Thoroughly confused, she glanced down, then realized that *she* must have been the one to scare her with the knife.

Why would she be afraid of a knife? Marsee wondered, but quickly spun to put the knife back in the drawer, hoping the cub would realize she hadn't intended to hurt her. But it was too late.

By the time she turned back around, the cub had fled, and all she saw was the end of the leash going out the door.

Instinct kicked in harder than it ever had, matched as it was with her own desire to keep the cub from running off.

It's getting away! her instinct screamed, and she bolted out the door and pounced on the end of the leash before she even knew what she was doing.

Yes! Got it! She purred, thrilled at her successful pounce, but then the leash was nearly yanked out of her paws.

Mine! her instinct growled, and grabbed it tighter.

She looked up to see what was trying to pull it away, and caught sight of the trapped and squirming cub at the end of the leash, which she'd completely forgotten about.

Suddenly, everything changed.

Prey! Her instinct growled, low and quiet in her throat, excited by the prospect of a real hunt.

No! Marsee screamed in her brain to stop, horrified, but her body wouldn't listen. Her instinct had control.

Slowly, methodically, she crept forward, one paw placed on the thin rope of the leash at all times.

Her prey was terrified and let off the most *delectable* of fear-scents, then screamed as it turned and saw her.

You should fear me, little prey, for I am a mighty hunter and I am starving, her instinct mocked. ***Just a few more steps, and we will find out if you taste as good as you smell.***

Horrified by her thoughts, Marsee struggled to force her body to stop, but it kept moving forward. She was just about to reach out and grab her prey, her mouth watering in anticipation, when the cub pulled out of her harness and bolted.

Run, little cub! Marsee tried to scream, but the words wouldn't form.

Pounce! her instinct demanded as her muscles tensed to leap.

Marsee imagined her instinct as a separate beast, and pounced on it instead, slamming her instinct to the ground and pinning it there.

No! she growled at it, fighting hard against the instinct that urged her to chase after her prey as it disappeared around the corner.

Her body froze as she fought for control of it.

Our prey is getting away, you fool! Run! Her instinct growled and fought her harder for control.

NO! That's not prey! she screamed back, then shoved her hunting instinct down further. She imagined biting it with her teeth, which she clamped so tightly her jaws hurt, and pinning it to the floor with her claws, which she dug into the stone floor below her.

Ahead, she heard the sound of a door slamming shut.

Thank the moons, she thought. *Hide, little cub!*

Our prey is trapped and hiding. We should stalk it, her instinct insisted as it freed itself enough by her distraction to stand up and start walking forward again. *It will be fun to play with, and our prey will be so tasty, seasoned by its fear.*

I. SAID. NO! She growled and slammed it into the floor again, clawing at it and biting at it, until her instinct ran away, whimpering.

AND DON'T COME BACK! she yelled after it, then followed it up with a final swipe of her claws.

When she was sure it was gone, Marsee collapsed to the floor, panting hard.

What in the darkest night of a triple eclipse was that? she wondered, horrified and confused by what she'd almost done.

It had been nothing like her hunting instinct. That had always just been a single pounce and done, not this!

I could have killed her! Marsee gasped.

Hiccupping with horror, she stood and slowly padded after the terrified cub, following the nearly overpowering scent of the cub's fear and wondering why it was so strong, or how she knew it was a fear scent. She'd never smelled anything like it before.

She has every right to be terrified, Marsee thought. *I know I am.*

She followed the scent to her parents' bedroom, of all places, and slowly opened the door.

Yes! You've found her! Well done! Her instinct purred, walking up beside her again. *Doesn't her fear smell delicious? Just imagine how wonderful she will taste.*

SHUT UP! she growled, swiping at it again until it backed off.

After a few calming breaths, she carefully entered, looking around the room. There weren't very many places to hide, so she walked over and peered under the bed.

There in the far back corner, curled up in a tiny ball, was the cub, panting hard. Fear reeked from under the bed, and Marsee drooled, hating herself for how much she wanted to eat the cub.

You've got her cornered! Easy prey! Just sit here and wait for...

I. SAID. SHUT. UP! she snarled, and quickly backed out of the room, no longer trusting herself to stay in the same room with the cub. She shut the door firmly and then curled herself up into a tiny ball, tucking her claws under her securely and panting hard as she closed her eyes and hid under her tail.

What are you waiting for? her instinct asked. ***You have her trapped. Kill her!***

Marsee growled and turned to face her instinct and pounced, claws and teeth outstretched as she attacked.

YOU LEAVE HER ALONE! she screamed, and bit and clawed at her instinct until it ran away again.

Marsee opened her eyes, relieved to find that she was still in the hallway, door shut, and claws still safely tucked under her. She shuddered with fear, not understanding what was wrong with her.

Why am I doing this?

"Marsee! Where are you?" her mother called out from down the hall.

Marsee groaned. *Great, now Mama's going to know how badly I messed up.* She buried her head back under her tail and shook.

"Marsee, what's going on?" her mother asked when she came around the bend in the hall and saw her lying there. "Where's the cub? The monitors alerted. Her heart rate spiked like I've never seen in the species, and her temperature has shot up several degrees."

"In your room, hiding under the bed," Marsee mumbled, not looking up at her mother.

"*Why* is she hiding under my bed, and *why* is the leash in the hallway?" her mother pressed.

Marsee didn't answer or lift her head from under her tail. She couldn't. She was far too mortified by her own actions and terrified by the consequences.

Her mother sighed, then turned and left, returning a few minutes later with food and drink. She set them just inside the room for the cub and shut the door again.

Marsee heard her mother let out another heavy sigh before sitting down beside her. A moment later, her mother reached over and pulled her onto her lap.

"Tell me what happened," her mother said quietly as she began to purr.

Marsee buried her head in her mother's fur and continued to shake. After several hiccupping sobs and with her voice muffled by her mother's fur, she finally found the words to explain. "I set her on the counter and then started getting food for us to eat. I got some star fruit, like you said, as well as a banta melon for myself. When I grabbed a knife out of the drawer to cut it with, she started panicking. I spun around, thinking there was a crawly behind me, not realizing that it was me she was afraid of. By the time I realized it and spun back around, she'd jumped down off the counter and run out of the kitchen trailing the leash behind her…"

She couldn't continue. She was ashamed of what she'd done.

"Hunting instinct?" her mother asked. When she didn't answer, not really sure how to explain what had happened, her mother added softly, "Did you hurt her?"

"No, but I scared her pretty badly," Marsee mumbled. "I'm so sorry, Mama."

"Shhh, it's okay…" her mother said, and began rocking and purring louder.

"No, it's not!" Marsee wailed. "I could have killed her. I almost did!"

"But you didn't, and look, her heart rate and temperature are coming back down to normal. She's okay. Now, let's go through it step by step, and we'll work through the triggers, just like we did when you were a little cub."

Marsee cautiously peered out from her mother's fur to look at the scanner and confirm she hadn't hurt the cub, then explained step-by-step what had set her off.

Her mother helped her identify the initial triggers. She felt horrible, but this process had been so much a part of her routine as a small cub that it was comforting. But no matter how hard she tried, she couldn't bring herself to explain what had happened *after* she'd pounced on the leash and simply told her mother that the cub had unclipped the harness and run off.

As they talked, she heard the sounds of drawers opening and closing and furniture being moved about.

"What is she doing in there?" Marsee finally asked as her curiosity broke through her fear.

"Exploring and probably trying to find another way out. She won't be able to reach the window switch, so she can't go anywhere, but at least we know she's out from under the bed now. Are you feeling better?" her mother asked.

"Not really. I feel awful about it," she admitted.

"Ultimately, this is a good thing," her mother said after a long pause and another heavy sigh.

"How can this be a good thing?" Marsee asked incredulously.

"Because now we know for sure that their species *can* set off our hunting instinct. That's always been a risk we've been worried about when we saw how small and defenseless they were. It's something we can prepare for and train both our species to avoid issues in the future, and you know how we fix this, right?"

Marsee nodded. "Practice."

Her mother nodded. "Take it slow. Avoid running until you're sure you can see her as a friend and not prey. Take things at her speed. If she initiates play, join in, but only as hard as she does. If she yelps or stops, you stop. If your brain thinks 'food', immediately think of the most vile-tasting thing you can think of, and remember, their species is poisonous to us. If you eat her, you'll get horrible stomach cramps, all of your fur will fall out, and your skin will turn blue."

Marsee snorted at that. "Seriously? My fur will fall out and my skin will turn blue?"

"Well, it worked when you were little," her mother replied with a grin. "I doubt your fur will turn blue, but they could very well be poisonous. Now, are you ready to go in and make friends with her again?"

"Do I have to?" Marsee asked, terrified. "What if it happens again?"

"It won't," her mother said, giving her a hug.

"How can you be so sure?" Marsee asked, pushing away slightly and frowning up at her mother.

"Because I know you, and because the situation isn't the same. There's nothing for you to chase. You needed to catch her to keep her from running off, and you pounced on the leash, not her, which was a perfectly valid response for the situation. I probably would have done the same. Now go on," her mother said, giving her a little shove.

Marsee reluctantly crawled out of her mother's lap and opened the door a crack. She took a deep breath, making sure the scent didn't trigger her again, and, when her instinct, or whatever it was, remained silent and hidden, she peered in.

23

JESSICA: PREY

Jessica bolted out of the kitchen but only made it a short distance down the hall before she was brought up hard by the harness as Cali pounced on the end of the leash. She frantically fumbled with the strange buckles on the harness as she turned to look behind her.

The giant beast had landed on the ends of the leash and had its gaze fixed squarely on her. The expression on the cat was positively feral as it slowly stalked towards her. There was nothing cute or kitten-like about them now.

This was a predator, and she was being hunted.

She screamed with absolute terror as she finally unclipped the last buckle. The moment she was free, she ran faster than she'd ever run before, frantically looking for a place to hide, and fully expecting to be pounced on and eaten at any moment.

It was one thing to take your own life, but it was a completely different beast to face down becoming someone's lunch, and her instincts were screaming at her to flee and to find somewhere safe to hide.

Spotting an open door ahead, she bolted through it, slammed it shut behind her, and found herself in what looked like a bedroom.

Assessing her limited options, she dove under the massive bed against the far wall, crawling as far under it as possible.

Gasping and wheezing from a combination of her fear and running for the first time in forever, she spun around expecting to see a large paw full of razor-sharp claws swiping at her, but there was nothing.

Sweat poured off her, and her skin felt like it was on fire. She was weak, out of shape, burning up, and beyond terrified. When death didn't come immediately, her terror eased some, but then the door opened.

She froze, trying desperately to calm her ragged breathing so that it wasn't immediately obvious where she was. It didn't matter, though. Cali's feet approached the bed without hesitation, then her head appeared as she flattened to look under it.

Cali grinned at her, but all Jessica saw were the massive, razor-sharp teeth.

She whimpered and pushed herself tight against the wall, tucking her knees in closer. She lay there, frozen in fear, wondering what the giant predator would do next, but was entirely caught off guard when they suddenly left the room, shutting the door behind them.

She lay on the floor panting and trying to figure out what to do next. When her breathing finally came back down to normal, and she didn't feel like she was going to spontaneously combust from the heat, she crawled slowly towards the edge of the bed and peered out. As far as she could tell, she was alone in the room.

She'd nearly gathered the courage to crawl out when the door opened again. She quickly scampered back under and watched as a plate of food and a cup of water were shoved through the partially opened door, then the door was shut again.

Several minutes passed before Jessica mustered enough courage to climb out from under the bed and look around. The bed she had been hiding under was massive, at least twenty-five feet across and round like the kitten's bed had been, although it didn't have the same curved sides. There were a number of large pillows thrown randomly on the bed, but no blankets.

The thick mattress was covered in a beautiful floral print sheet. A wooden headboard of sorts was placed along the edge of the round bed that was pushed up against the corner, forming a sort of raised table that fit the odd shape of the room and bed perfectly. A number of framed portraits sat on top.

Two large padded chairs sat against one wall, with a table in between. On the other wall was a desk and chair similar to the ones in the other room. More artwork decorated the walls, but most were photographs. She recognized some of the cats from the other photograph she'd seen, but there were dozens of others she didn't know.

She walked over to the desk and climbed up onto the tall chair. A small book, several additional photographs in ornate wooden frames, and what looked like assorted knick-knacks covered the surface.

She opened the book to find what looked like handwriting, but didn't see anything to write with. She opened one of the drawers and found a large pile of randomly shaped pieces of paper or their equivalent, anyway. The texture was strange, smooth, more like plastic than paper. Some had writing on them, others crudely drawn pictures, as if done by a small child.

In another drawer, she found what looked like the kind of nail clippers you'd use for a dog, but far bigger, along with a massive brush and a rough file. All three had ornate carved handles. There were a number of other items in the drawers, but she had no idea what they might even be, and nothing that looked even remotely like a pen.

There was a large window above the bed on the far wall, but it was a good ten feet above her. She jumped down from the chair and climbed onto the bed. Walking awkwardly over to the window, she tried jumping up, but there wasn't anything she could use to pull herself up with. Large curtains covered the window, so she pulled on them to see how sturdy they were. When they didn't give under her test pull, she tried climbing them, but the moment she put her full weight on it, the whole thing came crashing down.

"Oops," she said, jumping out of the way, not in the least bit upset about destroying their items, but annoyed she couldn't look out the window.

She jumped down off the bed and walked over to one of the two other doors in the room. She peered up at the door handles that were far above her and considered her options. Then, she dragged the smallest of the chairs over and climbed on it. She could reach, just barely. The door unlatched and swung open slightly. She jumped down again and peered cautiously through the doorway, but was very disappointed.

"It's just a bathroom," she muttered to herself. The room looked nearly identical to the one Cali had brought her to earlier.

With some effort, she slid the chair over to the door on the other side of the room and found another room just as large but without any exits or windows.

There was another massive bed, similar in size to the one in the other room, but curved on the sides like Cali's and quite a bit lower, with the mattress practically on the ground. Low shelves surrounded the room, filled with what looked like small books and toys. Stuffed animals and pillows were scattered everywhere. She walked over and pulled out one of the books, finding pictures with just a few of the strange alien words underneath.

Nursery? Jessica wondered.

Not finding anywhere to hide or another exit, she made her way back into the other room and stared at the door, trying to decide what to do. Then, her eyes caught sight of the food and water left for her.

She was hot and thirsty after her frantic run, so she cautiously walked over, expecting the door to swing open at any moment and the cat to pounce, but it didn't.

She grabbed the drink and swallowed, not even looking at it to see what it was, as she remained focused on the door, ready to bolt for the bed if the door opened even the slightest. She was pleasantly surprised to find it wasn't water but some sort of sweet fruit juice, ice cold, and delicious.

She drank the entire thing in one long gulp, then grabbed the plate of food and carried it over to one of the padded chairs, which she climbed up into to eat and think.

After eating a few of her favorites, she stared at the plate and the neatly sliced pieces of fruit, then smacked herself in the forehead.

You idiot, Jessica. They weren't trying to eat you. They were getting you something to eat. It was just a cat-sized knife, not a machete. Scale. You've got to stop thinking in human sizes. If they wanted to eat you, they could just bite your head off. For that matter, why would they want to eat you? You're nothing but skin and bones right now, anyway.

With a sigh, she tossed another piece of fruit back and considered what to do next, but before she could decide, the door opened a crack and then enough that Cali's head could fit through.

They peered around the door and found her sitting on the edge of the chair, eating. Cali let out a heavy sigh, then slowly came into the room and curled up on the floor next to the empty cup, tucking their paws neatly under them and wrapping their tail around them to wait.

They stared at each other for a long time before Cali said something to her that she couldn't hear, but they looked absolutely pathetic.

"Are you trying to tell me you're sorry for scaring the non-existent pants off me?" she asked the kitten.

The kitten tilted her head in response, and if anything, looked more pathetic.

"*Fine.* I forgive you. Thanks for not using me for a chew toy," she said, then slid off the chair, wincing as her foot hit the floor. With the adrenaline worn off, the pain of her burned foot was back, and it was twice as bad as it had been before.

She was honestly surprised she hadn't hurt herself when she'd jumped off the counter. It had been a long way down. She limped over to the kitten, who proceeded to look even more pathetic, ears flat, and slinking down until her head was almost resting on the floor.

"I'm the one who's supposed to look pathetic. What are you complaining about?" Jessica muttered. She stopped a few feet away from the kitten, well within striking distance, and stared at them for a few moments. Then, letting out a sigh, she walked over, picked up the cup, and held it up, asking for more.

Cali brightened immediately, and their whiskers arched forward in their form of 'yes'. Then, as if remembering, they bobbed their head up and down several times. They slowly sat up, then stood when Jessica didn't run away.

After cautiously picking her up again, Cali carried her out of the room. The gold cat was sitting just outside, waiting for them, and Cali walked over.

Goldy ran the scanner over her and said something to Cali before standing and walking into the room they'd just left.

Probably to pick up the mess I left in there, Jessica thought.

Her fuzzy kitten carried her back to the kitchen and set her back up on the counter. Jessica frowned when she saw the hated leash and harness on the counter beside her.

Cali took both the plate of half-eaten fruit and the empty cup from her. They set the plate down on the counter beside her, then turned, and immediately filled the cup back up with more juice.

Jessica drank about half of it before setting it down as well and smiled at the kitten. "Thank you."

Cali responded with an enormous grin, and Jessica tried hard not to flinch at the large fangs that were exposed. They must have noticed, though, because the smile went away instantly, and they looked just as pathetic as they had before.

With a heavy sigh, the overgrown kitten made a few gestures, but Jessica didn't have a clue what they wanted.

Apparently, they recognized her confusion because they reached over and carefully picked up her feet, spun her around so she was facing the sink, and then slowly put her feet in the water.

She let out a sigh. It was cool and refreshing, and clearly not the boiling water she'd envisioned in her panic earlier, and it felt really good on her burned foot. She hadn't seen this much water in one place in forever, and she certainly hadn't had a bath in all the time she'd been locked up. Whatever it was they hosed her down with didn't count.

Am I being allowed to take a bath? she wondered, *or are they just treating the burns on my foot? It seems a shame to let all this water go to waste, though.*

She decided to see if her captor would let her go all the way in, and slowly slid down into the water. The water in the sink came almost all the way up to her chest, once again making her marvel at the size differences between their two species.

It was cool enough to make her gasp, but considering how hot she'd been moments before, it felt wonderful. When the kitten didn't stop her, just stood there watching her curiously, head tilted in confusion, she decided to dive all the way under.

The next thing she knew, a set of furry paws was scooping her out and lifting her back onto the counter. When she finished spluttering from the surprise and wiped the hair out of her eyes, she noticed that Cali's tail was sticking straight out and had poofed even more than earlier, as had the fur along her scruff and back.

If that were a normal house cat reaction, I just scared three of their nine lives out of them. Either they don't swim, or they thought I was trying to drown myself. I wonder how they bathe. Do they lick themselves like other cats, or do they have some other way of keeping clean? God, I hope it's not that stuff they sprayed me down with. I never want to see that ever again.

She hadn't seen Cali lick her fur yet, though.

With all that fur, that'd be quite the hairball to have to clean up, she thought, slightly horrified.

Jessica tried saying she was okay with a smile and a thumbs up, but she doubted they understood. Eventually, she just pushed the still-dripping paws away and slid back in. This time, not going all the way under, just up to her neck. Then, curious to see what her captor would do, she stretched herself out and floated.

The terrified kitten looked like they were going to have a fit, clearly not believing that Jessica *wanted* to be in the water, but she didn't care.

"Good. That's what you get for scaring me into thinking you're going to turn me into soup. Consider us even," she said, then closed her eyes and sighed, trying to allow herself to enjoy the feel of the cool water for however long she was allowed.

When nearly a minute passed without being frantically scooped up again, she opened her eyes and found the kitten staring at her, head tilted in confusion.

With an evil glare, Jessica stood back up and splashed Cali squarely in the face.

The kitten spluttered and jumped back off the steps in surprise, tail back to full poof. After shaking their head, they wiped their face with their paws to get the remaining water off.

"How do you like being doused? Not so fun, is it?" she taunted the cat.

When they approached again, she splashed them a second time, laughed, and then dove to the other side of the sink-pool.

Coming up, she saw Cali had approached the sink, cautiously this time. Then their whiskers twitched, their ears went back, and their eyes squinted with a look of pure mischief. They slowly stuck a paw in the water and carefully splashed her back.

Mayhem ensued and only ended when Jessica started coughing as water went up her nose. She raised her hands up in defeat, half choking, half laughing.

Cali stopped immediately, fur dripping with water, and took several steps back, as if to show her she understood the play was over.

Jessica snorted and decided that since she was already wet, she might as well try to take a bath. For lack of anything better to use, she just started rubbing at her exposed skin and the months of caked-on dirt that no amount of spit baths or whatever it was they sprayed her down with had been able to get rid of. She wished she had some soap and a wash cloth, but this was better than nothing.

Cali stood there and watched her, head tilted again, trying to figure out what she was doing now and not paying any attention to the water that dripped from her fur onto the floor.

Jessica's attention was on a particularly stubborn spot of dirt when the kitten tapped her on her shoulder.

Looking up, Cali handed her what looked like a brick.

She took it, surprised to find it was light and squishy, and wondered if it was a sponge. When she didn't do anything with it, Cali took it back, dipped it in the water, and then squeezed. As they did, a foamy substance appeared. Then they reached over and started wiping it gently on her arm.

It must be soap and a sponge, she realized. *That's convenient.*

She took the soap sponge back and scrubbed hard at her arms and face, scraping layers of dead skin and dirt off with every swipe, then attacked her hair with a vengeance. When she'd rinsed her matted hair out as best she could, she climbed back up on the edge of the counter and started scrubbing at her body and legs until they were practically raw.

Cali took the sponge from her when she couldn't get a spot in the middle of her back and gently scrubbed. She leaned into it, so Cali increased pressure, rubbing where Jessica indicated by shifting her back. Nothing had ever felt so good.

She jumped back in the sink for a final rinse and wash of her more private areas, which made her wince and begin to shake again, as the reminder of what had happened caused her hate and fury to return. She tried hard to control her reaction, not to show what she was really feeling, because she wanted the kitten to know she was very grateful for the bath, in the hopes that it wouldn't be her last.

The water that had been clean a few minutes before was now black and grimy, with thick clumps of dead and matted hair floating on top. Plastering a fake smile on her face, she leaned over and grabbed a piece of fruit and popped it in her mouth, which caused her kitten's tail to curl.

Not only had she not been chopped up and turned into soup, she was finally clean, and they were happy she was eating. So overall, she'd consider it a win.

She still wanted to rip them all apart, limb from limb, for what they'd done, but maybe she might spare her kitten. If they were truly the child they appeared to be, then they wouldn't have been responsible for what happened to her, and they'd been kind to her so far. That kindness was starting to crack her intense hatred of them, just the tiniest bit.

24

MARSEE: DRONE RACING

The kitchen was a mess. There was water *everywhere*. Her fur was soaked, and though she usually loathed being wet, she couldn't remember a time when she'd had more fun, especially after how horrible she'd felt only a few minutes before.

Who knew playing with water could be so much fun, she thought.

Still, if her mother saw the mess, she'd be in a lot of trouble for wasting so much water, even if it had been her mother's instructions to soak the cub's foot.

Look how happy the cub looks now, Marsee thought. *I need to make sure to tell Mama that they like playing in water and use it to clean themselves. That might help perk the others up.*

She grabbed a small towel and tossed it at the cub who climbed out of the sink and started drying herself off. She grabbed a second, larger one for herself, drying her own fur as best she could, then wiped the counters down.

When she finished, she looked up to see that the cub had wrapped the towel around herself and tucked the ends in, somehow securing it in place, and then, without prompting, had put the harness back on over the towel and was adjusting the straps.

How odd. I wonder why she's doing that, Marsee thought, and then shrugged and tossed her own towel in the hamper, deciding to let the cub keep hers. *Maybe the straps on the harness are uncomfortable. I'll check for signs of rubbing later, and if it makes her happy, she can keep the towel. At least I won't have to fight with her to put the harness back on. I'm honestly surprised she did after everything that happened. I know I wouldn't have.*

While the cub ate, Marsee slathered a thick gob of the cream her mother had given her on the cub's burned foot and rubbed gently until it was fully absorbed. When the cub let out a sigh, she knew the pain reliever had started to kick in, and she sighed with her own relief, still mortified by what she'd nearly done and the added pain and fear she'd caused the cub.

She set the cream and the leash on the tray with the remaining fruit, then went back to the cooler and grabbed the half empty container of fruit juice that the cub seemed to like so much, the bowl of chopped banta melon that her mother had chopped up for her, and a cup for herself. She placed everything on the tray and picked it up. Balancing the tray on one paw, she motioned for the cub to stand up, picked her up in her other arm, and brought everything down to the family room so they could finish eating in comfort.

This was where they usually ate meals or gathered in the evening to work on projects in the companionship of others. Sometimes they watched her older siblings' concerts on the big screen or played games.

One wall had built-in shelving where a large selection of games were stored, but those she rarely played unless her nephlings were visiting. From her perspective, the best feature of the room was a massive window that took up most of the south-facing wall. A large padded bench stretched the entire length of the window, with padded and angled sides on either end, that she could lean comfortably up against.

It was one of her favorite reading places, especially when the weather was bad. She loved watching the storms howl and rage out the window while she was safely tucked inside. The rest of the room consisted of several dozen pillows of various sizes haphazardly strewn around a collection of low tables.

It was one of the few rooms in which she'd spent her own credit to replace the lighting and fixtures so it didn't buzz annoyingly, although she doubted her parents even noticed.

To her parents' annoyance, she'd also replaced all of the fabric on all of the pillows and benches in the room, after her parents had just replaced them. Something about the fabric her parents had chosen made her skin crawl.

They'd spent a year in a silent battle over it. Marsee would go through and change them out every time her parents put the new coverings back on. When she couldn't swap them out, she'd been less than gentle with them, an 'accidental' claw here, or a clumsy spilling of her drink there.

Eventually, they'd stopped fighting her, but it had taken learning to weave and sew to accomplish it. There was little they could say when she'd gone to the effort to learn, and made them herself, as a gift to replace the 'damage' she'd done to the other ones.

Over time, she'd become fairly good at it, although it was nothing like what her neighbors could do. She didn't have the patience for that. Her fabrics were all fairly utilitarian, with a simple pattern, but they were made from materials that made her purr and want to roll on, not run for the Wilds screaming.

The cub pointed to the window, so Marsee gently set her and the tray down on the bench.

The cub stood there, one paw on the window, staring outside.

Marsee took a sip of her drink and peered out the window with her, wondering what she thought of her new world. In the spring when the rains came, everything grew and bloomed in a riot of colors, but right now it was nearing the end of high summer, and everything was dry and brown.

Several bandala trees were visible in the distance, and a plume of dust showed where some animal was likely traveling, but it was too far away for her to make out what it was.

The sky is a glorious blue today, though, she thought. *It must look so desolate to her. I wonder what her world looked like before the Cataclysm.*

Was it like ours? Seeing a mournful expression on the cub's face, she sighed. *I really hope she'll be able to find some happiness here with us.*

After a few minutes, the cub sat down and leaned up against the side of the bench.

Marsee refilled her drink and handed it to her. She drank for a long time before setting it down.

She must really like it, Marsee thought, *or she's really thirsty.*

The cub absently grabbed for another piece of fruit without taking her eyes off the window, but after a while, she must have grown bored with the view, because she turned her attention back to the room and Marsee.

Now what? I'd take her for a tour of the compound, but it's too hot outside, and she really should stay cool and stay off that foot for a while, Marsee thought. Then her eyes caught on the wall of games. *Maybe I can teach her a game, but which one? It's got to be simple since I won't be able to tell her the rules very easily.*

Setting her drink on the table, she walked over to take a look at the games. Many she hadn't played with in years. Then her eyes caught sight of the drone racers.

Yes!

It was her favorite game, but one she could rarely get her parents to join in on.

Grabbing two racers and their controllers, Marsee handed a set to the cub. She tossed her drone into the air, which caused it to turn on and hover.

The cub did the same.

Marsee picked up her controller and showed the cub how to make the drone move. Where she could use her thumbs to shift the controllers, the cub had to use her whole paw.

The cub attempted to copy her and promptly ran hers into the wall. Then, cringing, she looked up at Marsee with another hint of that fear scent and visibly shrank herself down to appear smaller.

Thankfully, her instinct didn't respond to the scent this time. Remembering what had happened to the poor cub the last time a toy had been damaged, Marsee started purring, smiled, and curled her tail in response.

Then, she ran her own drone into the wall to show that it was okay, and that she wouldn't damage it by accidentally bumping it into a wall. That was half the fun. Then she took her drone and rammed into the side of the cub's, causing the cub's drone to flash blue and start spinning for a few seconds.

The cub chittered something at her, and Marsee motioned for her to try again.

The cub relaxed and seemed to understand that she wasn't in trouble, and carefully made another attempt. This time, she was able to move the drone around without running into anything.

After a couple of tries, she even managed to bump her drone into Marsee's, which lit up blue and started spinning. She again looked up at her to make sure it was okay.

Marsee nodded her approval and smiled.

The cub's face lit up, and the last of the fear scent vanished.

She motioned for the cub to keep practicing, while she grabbed half a dozen different colored rings and tossed them up into the air randomly about the room, where they hovered too.

Let's start off easy, she thought, only grabbing a few of the rings.

When the last one was in the air, she hit a button on her controller, and they all started blinking. A moment later, all but one dimmed to indicate the starting ring.

Marsee maneuvered her drone through the ring, and as soon as she did, the second one lit up, and so on, until she went through all six. Once she'd gone through the last ring, all six rings started flashing again, and her drone spun and flashed red to indicate she'd won. After a few seconds, the rings all stopped flashing except for one, a different one this time.

Marsee motioned for the cub to give it a try, and watched as she maneuvered through the first ring, only taking two tries, then the second. By the time she'd made it through the sixth, the cub was comfortable enough with the controls that she decided it was time to race.

When the rings flashed ready for the next round, Marsee motioned for the cub to try again, giving her a head start. She waited until the cub was through the first ring before starting, then bumped the cub's drone on the way to the second.

The cub growled as her drone started spinning, and Marsee chuckled and let her tail curl, as she ducked through the second ring and flew on to the third.

By that point, the cub's drone had stopped spinning, and she promptly followed chase, knocking into Marsee's drone before swinging back to go through the second.

Marsee had purposely not moved her drone out of the way to see what the cub would do.

And then the race was on!

Marsee won, of course, but the cub wasn't far behind.

She learns very quickly! Marsee thought.

They played for about an hour, adding the rest of the rings to make things more interesting, until the drones flashed green and lowered to the ground, their batteries drained.

They must not have been fully charged, she thought as she picked them up and carefully put everything back on the charger so they could play again later.

Marsee yawned and realized just how exhausted she was. She normally napped during the worst of the afternoon heat, and she hadn't slept a wink the night before.

Unfortunately, the cub did not look the least bit tired.

She checked on the cub's burned foot, and it looked like the cold water and cream had worked because her feet didn't look any different now, and when the cub climbed down off the bench she no longer limped.

Oh good! Marsee thought. *Maybe if I take her for a walk the long way around the compound, it'll tire her out and she'll want to take a nap when we get back to our room.*

Marsee grabbed the leash and went to hook it up to the cub's harness, hating to have to do so. She was not the least bit surprised when the cub shook her head no and backed away, growling and hissing at her again.

She sighed. She'd been afraid of that, but she had hoped that since the cub had put the harness back on without prompting, that she understood she had to wear it.

Marsee nodded yes.

The cub shook her head no again. But then, thoroughly confusing Marsee, she walked up to her other side, the one currently not holding the leash, and turned to face the same way as Marsee, pointing to herself and then the floor. She chittered something and made several hand motions, then ran a little ways away, shook her head no, and ran back to Marsee's side.

Is she trying to tell me she won't run off again? Marsee wondered. *I wish I could explain that it's not my rule that she has to wear it.* She sighed and shook her head no again, holding up the leash and frowning sadly.

The cub grumbled something that Marsee was sure was not meant to be said in polite company, but then turned and stood with her arms crossed and back to Marsee, looking thoroughly peeved.

Marsee shrugged. She may be an adult now, but there was no way she was going to disobey the Council over a direct order, much less the Senior Councilor. They might be elected officials, but once they voted on an issue, it was the law. They didn't make decisions lightly, and the consequences for disobeying were far too high for her to consider challenging, even if one of those councilors happened to be her father.

They'd spent the better part of another two hours wandering and exploring the common areas inside the compound. Marsee was fascinated by what the cub focused on, seeing everything in a new light, and wondering if they'd had something similar in their world, or if the cub had any idea what any of it was.

Sometimes Marsee was just as fascinated when the cub ignored something that she was sure she would check out. Eventually, they made it back to her room.

Marsee lowered her bed back down, then sprawled on her bed to text her mother an update.

The cub followed and sat next to her, legs crossed in a position that made Marsee flinch, fiddling with a puzzle box Marsee had given her. It was one she'd just finished but hadn't had a chance to send to the Agency yet.

> Hey Mama, I'm back in my room. Her foot seems better. What time are we having supper?

> Good. I'm not sure. Your father ended up having to go to Council City for an unexpected meeting. I'll call you when he gets home. How are you doing?

> Ok, I Guess. No further incidents, and not the slightest peep out of my hunting instinct. I'm going to take a nap or try to anyway. The cub seems to be wide awake.

> If you have any issues with your instinct again, or you need to talk about it more, come find me. As for the cub, she sounds just like you when you were a cub. You never wanted to take a nap either.

> So helpful...

> You're welcome! Consider it practice for when you have your own cubs. Good luck!

Marsee rolled her eyes and tossed her tablet on the bed.

Cubs? I can barely keep one biped alive for a single day. How could I possibly manage a litter of cubs?

She let out a heavy sigh, which morphed into a huge yawn, then kneaded the bed a bit and placed her head on her paws.

The cub looked up at the motion, seemed to realize that she was tired, set the puzzle down, and laid down, too.

Oh good, Marsee thought, and closed her eyes. Thoroughly exhausted, she was asleep in seconds, but her sleep was haunted by the memory of her hunt.

2 5

JESSICA: PLAYMATE

essica lay on the bed watching the kitten fall asleep, and tried to make sense of the day she'd had so far, and everything she'd seen and learned, but the pieces just didn't add up.

Every new piece of information just made her more confused. She had no idea where she was or why, although she now knew she was stuck in the middle of nowhere, surrounded by desert, in what appeared to be a giant stone castle, complete with a tower.

There was enough space to house hundreds of people, but she'd only seen Cali and the gold cat. They had advanced technology, yet rarely used it, and the way they treated her left her more unsettled than anything. They made her wear the leash but didn't restrict where she went.

She couldn't tell if she was a prisoner or a pet. She was leaning towards pet, since they seemed to go out of their way to make sure she was unhurt. Cali had checked her burned foot multiple times.

After the water fight and bath, she'd been carried into another room, filled with tables, cushions, and a monitor on one wall, almost but not quite as big as the one in the gold cat's office.

What had really captured her attention was the wall-length

window to the outside. It was the first time she'd had a good look at her new world. She'd expected to see nothing but sand dunes from the heat she'd experienced, but what she saw took her breath away.

Massive twisting trees with lavender colored leaves towered far above anything she'd ever seen before.

I bet they're taller than the redwoods.

She wasn't sure, since she'd never seen one in person, but she knew they used to grow big enough to drive vehicles through them. It was hard to tell exactly how big they were, since they were so far away, but these were at least as tall and many times wider.

Rock sculptures dotted the landscape in rainbow-hued formations, softened by the drifting sand. In the distance, she could see matching rainbow-striped hills that led to jagged snow-capped mountains.

Closer by, dust billowed as some sort of six-legged creature ambled towards one of the massive trees. She watched as a bird almost as tall as her, with four iridescent purple wings, flew down, grabbed a two-foot-long green centipede-like insect with its massive talons, and flew off again.

Everything is just enormous here! I'll be picked off like that bug the moment I step outside if I'm not careful, she thought to herself.

It was a beautiful, if harsh and alien landscape, and nearly impossible to look away from, but as far as she could tell, there wasn't another building in sight.

The living room had been big enough to seat several dozen of the giant cats, with tables and cushions scattered everywhere, but she hadn't seen anyone.

Had they all grown up and moved out, or were they away working? For that matter, where was I before, and where are the rest of my people?

She tried not to think about her family, although in her heart, she knew they were probably dead. The questions she really needed answers to remained unanswered, and she had more questions now than when she'd first arrived.

The lack of other people made her wonder if she'd been purchased as a playmate or companion for the kitten when they'd spent a good portion of the day in play.

They'd raced drones for several hours, and based on the curled tail and body language, Cali had been having as much fun as she'd had. She'd been worried at first when she'd crashed the drone into the wall, but that had clearly been part of the game, and she'd even come close to winning a few times before they'd apparently run out of power, and Cali had put everything away.

She'd had so much fun that she'd completely forgotten about the loathsome leash until Cali tried to put it back on, and the reminder made her want to cry. Crossing her arms and shaking her head 'no', she'd pressed her luck at refusing again.

Surprisingly, though, all the kitten did was nod their head 'yes' and continue to hold out the leash.

She'd tried to explain with pantomime that she wouldn't run away. Cali seemed to understand but still shook their head 'no'.

There was no anger or malice. If anything, they'd looked apologetic, as if they didn't want to have to have her put the leash on.

If they don't want to, why are they? Is someone making them, and if so, why? she wondered.

She'd begrudgingly turned her back so the leash could be clipped on, doing her best to make it known she was not happy about being leashed like an animal again.

Once the evil thing was clipped on, Cali had brought the remains of their meal back to the kitchen, with Jessica following behind like a petulant puppy, staying as far back as the leash allowed without being pulled.

She'd been half tempted to flop on her side and have them drag her, but figured they'd just pick her up and carry her if she wouldn't walk. Thankfully, though, they'd kept to her pace, and she hadn't had to run to keep up. She'd watched as they washed the dishes by hand and put them on a rack that popped out of the counter to dry, surprised to see such a normal activity.

They'd spent the next several hours exploring one room after another, and she still hadn't seen everything. Cali let her look in many of the rooms, but not all of them. They'd passed the door Jessica recognized as the one belonging to the gold cat, and nearly a dozen other doors before starting up again. She wondered what was in those rooms. *Off limits anyway,* but of course, that just made her even more curious.

There had been windows periodically along the inside wall at regular intervals that had let in light, but were too high up for her to look out of, as well as four enormous sets of arched split-level double doors, like the ones in Cali's room and just as intricately carved.

They all had a matching set of doors on the other side of the hall, inset enough on the end of short, arched hallways to clearly be the exits, not that she had any way of opening them. The wheeled locks were a good ten feet up. She'd tried to ask to go out anyway, but Cali had shaken her head and pointed to her burned foot.

She'd understood. It was too hot for her to go outside, or at least that was the excuse Cali was using.

What she'd seen amazed and baffled her at the same time. Some things she had no idea what their use was for until Cali demonstrated, but at the same time, there was so much that was oddly familiar, if strangely proportioned.

There was such a strange dichotomy of advanced and ancient tech that just didn't make sense either. It was almost like they had the tech but chose not to use it, if there was a simpler option, like her kitten's bed. They clearly had tech that would allow toys to hover, yet Cali's bed was nothing more than a giant basket attached to a pulley.

Her cell had walls that you could walk through instead of doors, but here they had normal wooden doors, if you could call doors that were six feet wide and twenty feet tall normal.

They washed their dishes by hand, but apparently had machines that could clean and sanitize things too, if she'd understood that machine's purpose, when Cali had demonstrated.

They had a cream that could heal cuts, bruises, and burns, and completely numbed pain, but had also soaked her foot in cold water, and with all of the technology needed to travel between worlds, her kitten lived in a stone tower with almost nothing in the way of electronics, just the air conditioner, a few lights, and her tablet, surrounded by hundreds, if not thousands of books.

Everything she saw, though, was well-maintained and of the highest caliber.

Eventually, they'd made it back to the decidedly disgusting drain of dung, where, after they'd both made use of the facilities, Cali had picked her up and carried her outside and back up the ramp. It had been just as hot and bright, if not more so, but her towel had kept her cool enough until they'd made it back to Cali's room.

She'd tried squinting through the light to see more of the world around her, but it was so bright it made her eyes sting and water, so she'd kept them closed and her face buried into Cali's fur until they were back inside.

The cool air of the room was a welcome relief from the outside and the rest of the compound. Cali hadn't stopped her when she had unclipped the leash the moment she was set down and walked over to the air conditioner, enjoying the breeze. Instead, the furry feline had lowered the bed back down on the floor and flopped on it before picking up her tablet and unfolding it.

From what she could tell, they appeared to be texting someone, as more of the strange writing appeared on the screen in an interface that didn't look all that different from what she was used to, outside of the fact that there were far more symbols on the screen. Fully open, the tablet was at least twice the size of an iPad, but still looked tiny in the kitten's massive paws. And from what Jessica could tell, it could fold in half to become a keyboard and screen, fully extend to be one big display without any sign of a seam, or collapse down into a small and convenient size to carry, not much bigger than Jessica's hand.

She'd grabbed the puzzle they'd given her earlier, flopped down on the bed beside the overgrown kitten, and went back to trying to figure it out.

I wonder if Cali made the puzzle boxes that I had in my cell, or if this was a common toy among their kind.

If Cali had made them, she felt bad about having destroyed them in her fit of rage, although it had felt so good at the time to do so. That realization surprised her. She glanced at the sleeping cat, wondering once again what their intentions were with her. If she had been captured as a playmate, would that be her kitten's fault, and if so, could they even be friends?

I suppose it could be worse. She does at least seem to care for me, and I did have a lot of fun today. The others, though...

Her feelings towards the adults were still ones of rage, and she wrapped herself around that feeling. Somehow, someway, they would pay for what they'd done to her and her people.

When she was sure Cali was really sleeping, their whiskers, paws, and tail twitching with some dream, she carefully stood and walked over to one of the doors, and scowled up at the latch. It was far too high for her to reach, and moving anything over to it would surely wake the sleeping furball, not that she'd get very far in the heat anyway.

Still, if they left her alone and she could move one of the tables, she might be able to reach it. The tables were significantly lower than the back of the chair she'd climbed earlier, but maybe if she stacked a pile of books on it, she'd be able to reach.

Sighing, she walked over and grabbed the furry blanket she'd been covered in earlier and dragged it back over to the bigger bed. She was actually feeling a little chilly in the air-conditioned room now. She curled up under the soft blanket and continued to think about everything that had happened that day.

She was too wired to sleep, or so she thought, but she was more exhausted than she realized, and was sound asleep in a matter of minutes.

Hours later, she was jarred awake by the feel of something buzzing and the bed shifting as Cali lunged for the source of the vibration. When Cali picked up her tablet and hit a few buttons, Jessica realized it must have been an alarm of some sort, or maybe someone had texted her.

She watched as they stood up on all fours, yawned and stretched just like her grandfather's cat would have, and then padded over to the door and opened it. Outside, the sky had darkened. The sun had apparently set while they slept, and with it, brought cooler temperatures.

She felt like she'd slept for days, and was feeling stiff and sore from all the activity earlier. She stretched, too, as Cali turned off the air conditioner and opened the other doors, letting in a warm but gentle breeze that smelled of sand, salt, and the slightest hint of flowers.

Is there an ocean nearby? Jessica wondered when she smelled the salt air. She peered out one of the doors, seeing lights far off in the distance, but didn't step outside, figuring that was probably against the rules since she didn't have the blasted leash on.

Not surprisingly, Cali soon made her way over to her with it.

Jessica adjusted the towel that had shifted in her sleep and turned her back to allow Cali to clip it on.

While she'd had the leash on earlier, Cali had let her go wherever her interests had taken her, so she didn't feel quite so trapped with it on. She still despised it with every fiber of her being, but she would tolerate it for now. She needed to figure out who was in charge and why they wanted her leashed.

Maybe they do think I'm nothing more than a pampered house pet that needs to be leashed when going out for a walk. I am tiny compared to them. So, how do I go about showing them that I'm not?

Once leashed, Cali led her out onto the balcony and let her have a good look around, although they kept the leash short, not letting her go anywhere close to the edge.

She didn't push it, figuring the more she at least pretended to behave, the more likely they'd let her free later. She peered around at her surroundings and the building she was in, and was amazed at what she could see in the dimmer light.

One of the massive trees she'd seen in the distance earlier was actually in the center of the compound, surrounded by a large octagonal stone wall. Outside of that wall was an even bigger courtyard that was now lit up by colored lights that left an intricate pattern on the ground below. Evenly spaced rows of something filled the courtyard, but she couldn't make out what they were from up here.

Surrounding that courtyard was the main part of the castle that they'd explored earlier. One giant octagonal ring, like she'd thought. However, she could now see that two smaller wings jutted off on either side of the compound. She couldn't see past the tree, but she thought there might be one on the other side as well, based on the light pattern that lit up the outside of the building.

Several sets of lights led away from one of the wings. While ridiculously large, the whole place was small enough that she concluded that she'd been moved from wherever she'd been held. That and the fact that nothing she'd seen here looked remotely like that place.

They stood there and watched as a triangular-shaped craft flew down, circled around the tree, and flew straight into the lit-up wing, leaving a plume of sand in its wake.

It's an aircraft hangar! I wonder who just arrived. Is it someone new, or did the gold cat leave and come back?

Cali gave her a tap on her shoulder and motioned for her to follow her down the ramp.

After another quick stop at that particularly putrid portal of poop, they exited back out of the building, and into the inner compound. As they approached one of the long rectangular objects, she could finally see that it was a raised garden, although she couldn't make out what kind of plants they were.

Are those leaves purple too? She couldn't quite tell in the dimming light, but she thought they might be.

Cali wound her way around the raised beds, heading towards an open door in the inner wall.

Jessica rubbed her ear as one of the phantom tones she heard occasionally started ringing in her head, but she quickly forgot about it as they passed through the doorway and found herself dumbstruck by the sight in front of her.

Somehow, in crossing through that archway, she'd gone from the desert landscapes of Dune to the glowing jungles of Avatar. Flowers, creatures flitting through the air, even the very ground glowed with vibrant luminescent colors. Scents she couldn't even begin to describe filled the air, and she could even see light refracting off a small trickling stream beside her.

Cali led her down a winding moss-covered path that eventually brought them to the base of the tree, which was completely surrounded by an equally massive pool of water.

This has to be the source of the stream, but where are they getting the water from, and how are they keeping it from evaporating during the heat of the day? she wondered.

The gold cat she'd seen earlier in the day was already there, pruning flowers with a large pair of scissors.

Again, the use of such familiar technology surprised her, especially when compared to the large floating cart that hovered beside the gold cat. Goldy placed some of the pruned flowers in a vase on top, but those that were past their prime were tossed in a large bucket on the shelf below.

The two cats greeted each other with a hug, wrapping their tails around each other. Goldy then turned to her and gently stroked the top of her head.

That's a really odd feeling, she thought. *Nice, but odd.* Although it did add significantly to the impression that she was a pet.

Goldy handed her the enormous glowing lily-shaped flower she had in her paws, rather than placing it in the vase. It had to be at least as big as Jessica's head, and she marveled at its exotic beauty before taking a deep sniff.

It smells like chocolate! she thought, completely amazed. *I wonder if it's edible.* She didn't try tasting it, though, as she had no idea if it was poisonous.

Cali motioned her over to look at the pool, where several strange creatures were swimming towards them.

The dog-sized fish were like a cross between a manta ray and an octopus, and they glowed too.

Cali took the flower from her and gently placed it on the water. One of the octorays reached out and batted at it with one of its tentacles, and it floated over to one of the others, who batted it back.

They're playing catch with the flower! Jessica thought, amazed.

Then one of the others dashed in, grabbed the flower by the stem, and took off with the others swarming after.

Cali's tail curled at the creature's antics, but then they suddenly turned to look behind them.

Jessica followed their gaze and realized a third cat had entered the garden.

Cali dropped the leash and ran over to give this one a hug, too, and was clearly telling them something.

Probably about everything that happened during the day.

When they made a splashing motion, it confirmed her suspicions. While they talked, Jessica observed the newcomer. This cat was several feet shorter than the gold cat, and nowhere near as bulky, almost halfway between the size of the other two cats, but moved with innate grace and authority.

She didn't know why, but her gut said this person was in charge.

They listened with their full attention to whatever Cali was telling them, even when hugging Goldy. She couldn't quite make out the color of their coat in the dim lighting, but it shimmered in the light of the moons. After a while, Jessica decided that the two big cats must be a couple, Cali's parents most likely, based on how they all interacted. The new cat looked at Goldy as if completely starved for the sight of them, and remained with paws and tails entwined as Cali started pouring something to drink.

She still hadn't found anything that might indicate sex or gender, and she had no idea if they even reproduced like Earth cats did. For all she knew, they could be completely asexual, have ten different sexes, or could metamorphosize into a giant six-winged butterfly. Just because they looked like cats didn't mean they were anything like them, and she wasn't going to just walk up and lift their furry tails to try and find out.

If they were anything like the felines of Earth, then they'd all be female, at least based on what she'd seen when Cali had used the hole of muck. Cali hadn't let her leave the room while she'd gone, clearly afraid she'd run off. It had been entirely too embarrassing, even if she had the impression that Cali didn't care that she was watching. The only difference she'd seen was size, and that could mean nothing more than age.

When they left her alone, although they were clearly still watching her, Jessica shrugged and went back to observing the octorays, who were still chasing each other around after the flower, all except for one smaller ray that had remained behind.

"They won't let you play with them?" she asked it, then placed her hand in the water, hoping it wasn't dangerous.

She figured Cali wouldn't have dragged her over to see them if they were. The baby octoray cautiously swam over and looked at her finger, before reaching out and touching it with the tip of one of its tentacles.

"Boop!" she said as it did.

As soon as it touched her, it swam away to hide, then peered at her from behind a clover-shaped lily pad.

I know exactly how you feel, little one.

She looked up as Cali came back over and handed her a tray of food.

"I hope there's more of that fruit juice," she said, while placing the oversized tray on her lap. She took a tentative sip of the drink and smiled. "Oh, good, it is. Thank you!"

She smiled in appreciation and took a long drink before really looking at the rest of the items on her tray. On it were all of her favorite foods—every last one of them.

Why are they being so nice to me? she wondered. *It doesn't make sense. Do they feel guilty for what happened, or are they just trying to be nice to their new pet?*

When she was done eating, she stood, causing Cali to grab the leash.

Jessica ignored her and brought the tray over and set it on one of the empty shelves of the floating cart, where Cali had set hers when she'd finished eating. She couldn't reach the top shelf, though. Then, grabbing her cup, she raised it up, asking the new cat for more to drink, curious to see if they would or not.

Seemingly surprised by her actions, they nonetheless obliged.

Cup in hand, Jessica wandered around as far as the stupid leash would go, checking out the other plants. She looked up when Cali joined her and motioned for her to continue, so she did.

They spent at least an hour wandering the garden, looking at whatever fancied her. Cali didn't stop her or indicate boredom, just followed wherever she went, and pointed out items of interest.

Sometime later, they'd made it back to the entrance of the garden when Jessica's ear started ringing again. She rubbed at her ear, but the noise didn't stop.

Cali looked at her questioningly, but Jessica just shrugged, not having any way to explain phantom noises or the pain in her ear.

It's been hurting ever since...

"No, don't think about that," she muttered to herself.

As she walked away from the door to check out a sculpture, the ringing suddenly stopped. She froze.

Nah, it's just my imagination, she thought, shaking her head. Still, she stepped back into the doorway, and the ringing started up again. She stepped away, and it stopped.

Excited but trying hard not to get her hopes up, she stepped back into the archway, and the ringing started again.

She looked up at Cali with barely controlled excitement.

Cali just stood there watching her with an utterly perplexed expression on their face, trying to figure out what she was doing.

She exited the garden and tried to figure out where the noise was coming from. It wasn't until she walked past one of the raised beds and the sound shifted behind her that she found the source, then fell to her knees crying.

26

MARSEE: A JOYFUL NOISE

"Mama! Papa! Get out here quick!" Marsee yelled in excitement when she realized what was going on with the cub.

Moments later, her parents came at a full run on all fours.

"What's wrong?" her mother asked as her longer legs brought her there first, although her father was right behind.

"Nothing. Look! She can hear! Papa, it's the hydroponics unit I told you was making funny noises yesterday. She can hear it, too!" Marsee exclaimed.

"What noise?" her mother asked. "I don't hear anything."

"It's there, I'm telling you," Marsee insisted with a hint of frustration. "It's a high-pitched whine. All the units make it. I've been saying so for years, but this one is off somehow, more grating."

Her father walked around to the other side. "Well, this is the one she kicked yesterday, Myra. You can still see her footprint on the side," Her father pointed to the smudge she'd left.

"What makes you think she can hear it? She's crying again. Are you sure she's not hurt?" her mother asked, squatting down low to examine the cub.

The tiny cub looked up at her, tears streaming down her face, then tapped her ear before putting her paw on the casing that covered the water pump.

"See! She can hear it!" Marsee whooped in joy, picked up the cub, and spun her around, both of them laughing with glee.

"Marsee!" her father yelled, "Stop that at once! You're hurting her!"

"It's ok, Papa! That's the sound she makes when she's happy!" Marsee replied, but put the cub down anyway.

She wobbled unsteadily for a moment, wiped the tears from her eyes, and then walked back over and touched the pump again, almost reverently.

"Well, come on then," her mother said, standing up and walking away.

"Where are we going?" Marsee asked.

"To my office to check her ears. *Obviously,*" her mother replied, her tone dripping with sarcasm, although her tail curled in humor.

"Go on. I'll clean up the dishes, and meet you in your mother's office when I'm done," her father told her, picking up the cup the cub had dropped on the ground when Marsee had spun her around.

"Love you, dear!" Marsee's mother called back from across the courtyard.

Marsee smiled at her father, picked up the cub again, and took off after her mother. The cub held on and made funny squeaking noises as she ran, but Marsee didn't stop until she caught up with her mother.

The lights flickered on and buzzed as they entered her mother's office. Marsee pinned her ears back in annoyance.

I should replace these lights, too, she thought absently.

"Set her down on the desk again," her mother ordered as she pulled the scanner out of her medical bag.

Marsee did, and her mother first ran the scanner over the ear the cub had indicated, studied the results for a bit, then ran it over the cub's other ear to compare.

With a scowl, her mother sat down at her desk and transferred the images from the scanner to her tablet to take a better look.

"What is it?" Marsee asked. "Did you find something?"

Her mother didn't answer right away.

"To be perfectly honest, I'm not really sure," she admitted, setting the tablet on the desk and looking up at Marsee and the cub, who were both watching her intently.

Marsee frowned, surprised that her mother didn't know.

"Good news. There are clearly improvements from the original scan, taken just after she arrived, to now. Bad news. I have no idea why she can't hear. Her other ear looks far better to me than the one she indicated, so I would expect her to be able to hear just fine out of that ear. That she can't and that she's hearing out of the one far more damaged is baffling. But I'll be honest, this is pretty far outside my scope of expertise. I've never had to deal with hearing loss, all that much."

"So, what do you need to find out?" her father asked.

Marsee and her mother both turned to look at her father, who had just entered the office.

"What I *need*...is someone who specializes in hearing loss, and far better equipment than I have here or at the Agency." Her mother held up her scanner for reference.

"I thought the Council shipped you all new medical equipment," her father said, confused. "I don't understand why you need more?"

"They did, but that was all trauma gear specialized to treat major injuries, like broken bones and burns, and the genetic equipment we needed, to figure out what was safe for them to eat or whether or not we were going to wipe each other out with a cold. Like I said last night, it's not the kind of medical equipment we need to figure out what is going on and repair her hearing, if that's even possible, and that equipment hasn't been approved yet."

"Do you think her hearing can be repaired, Mama?" Marsee asked.

"Well, if she's regained any hearing, then it's a possibility. How much remains to be seen," her mother replied.

"So, get me a list of what you need and who you need, and I'll get the Council's authorization to have them sent to the Agency, unless you'd rather they came here, that is," her father said.

"That's the problem, Jer. There are only a handful of specialists who deal with hearing loss. It's just not common enough for our species to have to treat on a regular basis. The equipment is one thing, but the person we really need is my mentor. Ammond's semi-retired now, and he's turned into a bit of a curmudgeon in his old age. To be fair, he was always a bit of a curmudgeon, but he's the best there is. Getting him to fly here is going to be a challenge, though. You know I've tried to get him and his partner to come for a visit for decades. He hates to travel for any length of time. Sitting still makes his old bones hurt, and really, we need to take the cub there. It would be risky to move all of his specialized equipment."

"Why is that a problem?" Marsee asked. "Why can't we just fly to him? I thought quarantine was lifted."

"It is and it isn't," her mother answered with a sigh. "They've relaxed restrictions to allow the healers and other volunteers to return home for a visit, but not more than that. They aren't allowing the creatures at the agency to leave just yet. Getting the Council to authorize the trip will be a challenge. They've only authorized the cub's travel to our home because we're so isolated, and she's not allowed to go anywhere outside of the compound, as they're concerned her illness isn't isolation sickness. We're restricted in our travel as well. I didn't mention it because you never like to leave the compound, so I figured it wouldn't come up."

"But you went in for a Council meeting today," she said to her father, confused.

Her father nodded the point, but tried to explain. "I needed to pick up several items for the cases I'm working on, so I can set up here for the duration."

"Well, if they can make an exception for you, they can make one for her," Marsee growled.

"I wish it were that easy," her father replied. "There's a fairly substantial faction in the Council that isn't convinced it's safe yet for the quarantine to be lifted, and they fought hard to keep it in place. The measure to bring the cub here only just passed, and only because we were at risk of losing her. As I'd only had minimal contact with her last night, my travel was approved, but I never left my shuttle. Sam brought what I needed over to me, and we both wore shields the entire time."

"What?! You mean to tell me they'd actually let her remain deaf, rather than let her get the medical care she needs?" Marsee exclaimed, horrified.

"Fear can be a powerful motivator," her mother replied. "And they were understandably concerned about the risk to others. As hard to understand as it might be, even the death of a person can sometimes be an acceptable sacrifice, if it means protecting others."

"Well, that's just stupid, short-sighted, and...and...self-centered!" Marsee spluttered in indignation. "What makes our species more valuable than theirs? There are millions of us and only a few hundred of them. Every one of their lives is *far* more valuable, because the loss of even one of their lives could mean the extinction of an entire species!"

She was completely at a loss to understand why the Council would stand in the way of someone getting the care recommended by their healer, or, for that matter, why they would even have a say in it. She understood quarantine, but not denying care.

Her father snorted in response and put a paw over his mouth to keep himself from laughing.

"It's not funny!" Marsee fumed, ears back and tail lashing in fury at her father for laughing about it. "What right does the Council have to deny someone medical care, or to even have a say in what treatment they receive? They aren't Healers. They don't have the training or the certification to make those kinds of decisions."

"No, you're right. It's not funny," her father said, after taking a deep breath, bringing his emotions back under control, and placing them neatly behind his councilor's mask. "Forgive my laughter. I wasn't laughing at you or the situation, only that I've just wanted to call Councilor Parner stupid, short-sighted, and self-centered to his face, at least twice a day since the day I met him."

"Well, maybe you should. Sounds like he needs it," Marsee muttered, although her tail calmed some when she realized her father hadn't been laughing at her, and was taking her concerns seriously, not as her father but as her councilor.

His eyes glittered with his evident amusement at her comment, but he otherwise remained serious.

She'd never understood how either of her parents was able to keep from letting their emotions show, but the calm focus he presented reassured her more than his apology.

"To answer your question, though, several on the Council, Parner included, believe that we did *not* rescue a sentient species. Our lack of ability to communicate with any of them, being their primary argument, and they feel that risking a known sentient species, for what might be nothing more than an 'alien chenzie' is 'too high of a risk, no matter how cute they are,'" her father continued. The barest hint of frustration escaped with his response.

"But of course she's sentient! The fact that *you* haven't been able to communicate with her doesn't mean she can't communicate. She has her own spoken language and is clearly able to communicate her needs. *You* just haven't been paying attention!" Marsee spat, her tail lashing again. "Besides, when's the last time you heard of a chenzie flying a drone?"

"Smart does not mean sentient," her mother replied.

"Well, apparently for some of our Councilors, sentient doesn't mean smart, either," Marsee countered, tail thwapping hard against the side of her mother's desk.

Her father burst out laughing, and the complete lack of control startled her.

"Oh, kitten. Please don't ever change!" His tail spiraled in humor before he reached over to pull her in for a hug to comfort her. "You are absolutely right. We haven't been paying attention, and it's a good thing she has you to advocate for her. Myra, send me that information, and I'll see what I can do to...*un-stupefy* the Council, *again*. In the meantime, contact your curmudgeonly old Mentor, and see if he might be persuaded to make a house call."

27

MARSEE: COUNCIL REPORT

*L*ater that evening, Marsee lay on her bed trying to write up her report for the day. She'd written it three times already and had just deleted her third attempt in disgust.

So much had happened in just one day that she struggled to figure out how to condense it into a report that she knew both the Healer's Guild and the Council would read. She knew, even though it hadn't been mentioned, that her interactions with the cub would become part of history, and likely something children would be taught in school. Her report *had* to be perfect both for the cub's well-being and the long-term survival of her species.

She wanted to show the Council how intelligent and clearly sentient the cub was, but so much of the day's activities revolved around play and the cub getting hurt and scared. She didn't know how to show the Council the individual she was starting to know, and there was no way she was going to let the Council know she'd hunted and nearly killed the poor thing.

She wasn't entirely sure, but she had a feeling that if the Council knew what she'd done, she'd be in a world of hurt, if not executed outright for her actions. She thanked whatever ancient gods were out there that she'd been able to stop her instinct from taking control, but she was terrified it might happen again.

She was also furious to find out that the Council would refuse the cub, or anyone for that matter, the medical care that they needed. She understood the need for quarantine and the restrictions that had been in place for the last several months, but the care of the survivors had to be a top priority.

Eventually, she gave up with a frustrated growl and sent a message to her father.

Papa, I'm having a hard time writing the report for the Council. Any suggestions?

What part are you having trouble with?

All of it! I want to make the Council see her as an individual so they'll let her get the care she needs, but so much has happened that I don't know where to even start.

Why don't you start by keeping a journal of everything that happened, including your thoughts and impressions? That will give you something to reference and ensure that nothing gets lost, even if it doesn't go in your report.

All of it?

Marsee shuddered at the idea of having what she'd done written down where someone might read it. She figured her mother had told her father what had happened, but her father hadn't said anything, and while she wanted to protect the cub and her species from the possibility of being hurt by someone losing control of their hunting instinct, there was no way she was telling the Council that she'd nearly killed the cub on her first day as an adult.

As much as possible. Then go back through and pick out the five most important things that you think the Council should know about. List those out as your summary. Below that, write a brief description about how you came to those conclusions. If anyone in the Council wants more than that, I'll have them send me a list of questions, and we can answer those together.

How do I pick just five, though? So much happened today.

It doesn't have to be exactly five. That's just a guide. Start by making a list of everything you learned. Then try to rank those items from the cub's perspective. Until we learn to communicate, you're going to have to speak for her. What do you think she'd want us to know? What is most important for ensuring her species' survival or happiness?

Okay. I'll give that a try. Thanks, Papa.

Of course, kitten. When you have a draft ready, send it to me. I'll look it over and suggest edits, if necessary, before sending it along. Try not to stay up too late working on it, either.

Yes, Papa.

Marsee set the tablet down, rolling her eyes, and sighed.

"Easier said than done," she muttered, then watched the cub drag her nest into the moonbeam, crawl inside, and lie on her back with her tiny paws laced behind her head to look up at the moons in comfort.

What would you have me tell the Council, little one?

She wrote for a good hour about most everything that had happened that day, skipping over the part where she'd almost eaten the cub. Then she went back through and tried to pick the five impor-tant points. It took her another two hours to decide and finally finish writing something she thought sounded reasonably okay.

Biped Observations by Marsee Bet Chenzira 10165.11.5

- Bipeds are highly sensitive to the heat of our world, and burn easily during a normal mid-summer day.
- She's angry about being forced to wear the leash, but seems to understand that it's required.
- They use water to clean themselves, as part of their play and relaxation, and can swim.
- The cub has expressed a wide range of emotions and cried when experiencing both grief and joy.
- She is highly intelligent and capable of learning complex tasks, like flying a drone, and effectively communicates her needs and desires without being able to speak our language.

The cub's foot burned when she first stepped outside. I carried her to avoid burning her feet further on the hot stone, but liquid formed on her skin, and she started breathing hard after only a minute in direct sunlight.

Healer Morningstar said she believes this may be a cooling mechanism. The cub also shielded her eyes from the bright-ness. It's my belief that the items they were wearing when rescued were for protection from the elements, likely needed due to sensitive skin and lack of protective fur, scales, or feathers.

She has taken to wrapping a towel around her body and holding it in place with the harness. I am unsure if this is for protection or if the harness is uncomfortable, but she gets very angry every time the leash is attached.

The first time I put the harness on, she wasn't sure what it was until I hooked the leash to the back. As soon as I did, her entire body language changed, and she went from curious about everything to looking like she wanted to attack.

She hissed and growled, and immediately removed the harness and threw it back at me. Her shoulders and facial features all hardened, and she closed her paws tightly, perhaps to restrain herself from trying to claw me.

She eventually let me put it back on, but it is clear to me that she could take it off at any time, and is simply choosing not to, perhaps out of fear of repercussions.

The second time I attached the leash, I believe she tried to tell me she wouldn't run off. I don't believe she understands why the leash is required, but I've tried to restrict her motion as little as possible. Since she is capable of removing it, I see no point in its continued use and recommend we stop using it.

After the cub's foot was burned, my mother instructed me to soak the cub's foot in cold water. I expected to have difficulty making the cub put her feet in the water, but instead, she chose to go all the way in, even going completely under.

They use water for play by splashing each other and for relaxation by floating on top. They also use water for cleaning themselves. When a soap sponge was provided, she understood its use immediately and used it to clean herself thoroughly, although interestingly, there was a spot in the middle of her back that she couldn't reach. She allowed me to help and seemed to enjoy the attention.

They appear to express emotions in much the same way we do. However, without tails, whiskers, and ears that move, they use their mouth, eyelids, and hands for emphasis. Over the course of the day, I have witnessed curiosity, caution, grief, shock, competitiveness, fairness, fear, anger, resignation, and happiness.

She seems to enjoy exploring and learning about her new surroundings and examining everything. I don't know if she understands the purpose of everything she's been shown, but she waits to be shown how things work and checks for permission before touching.

While she does appear to understand our yes and no, I've also determined that a nod of the head up and down means yes, and side to side means no.

She has communicated her need to use the waste room through pantomime, and effectively communicated when she wanted more to eat or drink. She follows basic gestures easily, such as come and stay, and she has expressed that her hearing is important to her, by leading me to a hydroponics unit that was making a high-pitched grating noise, touching her ear, and then the pump. She was both crying and smiling at this time, too.

Her first sight of the moons also caused her to cry. She clearly recognizes that she is on a different planet and not just on some part of her own that she's not familiar with.

She cried and she made a high-pitched keening noise while rocking back and forth, hugging her knees. I believe this motion is equivalent to the wringing of our tails. She shook and grieved for a good hour before calming and returning to exploring the rest of my room.

She expressed fear when I grabbed a knife to prepare breakfast. I believe she misunderstood my intentions and thought I was going to use the knife on her as she ran and hid under my parents' bed. I am unsure why she thought I was going to use the knife on her, but her body was shaking and curled into a tiny ball, and she let off a very strong scent. I'm unsure if the smell was a defensive mechanism or simply the result of her fear and the liquid covering her skin from the heat and her run. My mother says her heart rate and temperature spiked.

She appears to be quite intelligent. She learned how to use our drone racers quickly and has a strong desire to win, but stays within the rules that I have been able to communicate to her. Although she did express worry and visibly shrank when she accidentally crashed the drone into the wall the first time she tried to use it, perhaps because of her fight at the agency.

She's reasonably good at racing the drones after only a few hours of play. She even came close to winning a few times. During play, she's made a high-pitched chittering noise on a number of occasions. I believe this is their form of laughter.

Overall, she has made significant progress. She's eating and drinking on her own and engaging in play. Her burned foot no longer appears to bother her. However, I believe that there are places from her fight that are still hurting, as she flinched when cleaning several areas, and she made liberal use of the nano cream on her bruises this evening without prompting.

Marsee struggled for a long time about whether to include the fact that she'd scared the cub at all, but decided it was important for them to know, and figured they would understand the possible ramifications. Her mother knew what had happened, and she would make sure the right people were notified on how best to handle it.

After completing her report and sending it along to her parents for review, Marsee checked on the cub and saw that she'd fallen asleep. She yawned and turned off the lights so the cub could sleep, then opened up the recordings her mother had sent her of the actual rescue attempt.

She'd only seen what little footage had been released to the public, so she was completely horrified and unprepared by the scenes of destruction of the cub's world and the injuries of those rescued.

"Moons protect us!" she whispered. "How did anything survive at all?"

After some digging, she was able to backtrack from when the cub was tagged after being brought on board the ship, to the body camera of her rescuer, to find the video of the cub's actual rescue.

She blanched when she saw the full extent of the cub's original injuries. Blood was running from the side of her head, and it was clear her arm was badly broken, yet she was still picking her way through the rubble of her home, trying to find safety.

To be that injured and still move forward!

Marsee was amazed at the little cub's resilience. When she realized her hunting instinct hadn't responded at all to the sight of all the blood or the cub's weakened state, she finally relaxed. She'd been horrified, not tempted. The cub was a person, not prey, and Marsee's maternal instincts now screamed that she needed to be protected, like the small cub she was, not hunted, and she prayed that she'd defeated the beast inside her.

After watching the rescue and the cub's initial triage, she went back and pulled up the video of first contact, as that had a clearer image of the cub and the clothing she was wearing, then tried hard to make sense of it. There were so many pieces and such intricate detail that she knew she'd never be able to reproduce them, not quickly anyway. She pulled up recordings from other bipeds to compare what they were wearing, and found a few that looked simple enough to reproduce, and still give the full body protection that the cub would need.

She was saving stills to her tablet when the cub started screaming.

Marsee's tail stuck straight out in fear and surprise, and she scrambled to turn the lights back on, afraid some creepy crawly had snuck in and attacked in the night.

With the lights on, she found the cub sitting up in her bed, breathing hard.

Marsee ran over to the cub and frantically checked for creepy crawlies or anything else that might have climbed into her nest. As the cub's breathing calmed, and she saw nothing physically wrong, her own panic started to lessen.

The cub demonstrated pretending to sleep and jerking awake, and Marsee realized it had only been a night terror.

No wonder she's having night terrors, Marsee thought, thinking back to everything that had happened today, and the horror she'd just watched. *I'll probably have some just from watching the recordings.*

That made her remember having night terrors as a cub when she first moved out of the nursery and the stuffy her mother had given her to keep her company and protect her at night.

Marsee went back to her bed and grabbed the cub's furry blanket and the stuffed toy that had come with her from the Agency.

The cub took the tiny stuffy from her and hugged it tightly.

Marsee smiled and covered the cub with the blanket, tucking her and the stuffy back in, then patted the little cub on the head before trotting back to bed and turning the lights off again, but it was a long time before the fur on her tail relaxed.

JESSICA: MEERKAT

The next morning, Jessica woke long before Cali. She stared up at the stone ceiling above her, thinking about everything that had happened the day before. She was finally free of that thrice-forsaken cell, she'd had a real bath, and she'd actually heard something!

She wondered if they would be able to do anything to fix her hearing or if that was as good as it was going to get. She was concerned about whatever they had been arguing about the night before. Whatever it was, it had made Cali furious at the copper-colored cat. She wondered if that had anything to do with her hearing or if something else was going on.

She wandered around for a while, checking things out, then fiddled with the puzzle box some more, but eventually, she started to feel very uncomfortable. As the sun rose, the temperature in the room increased to the point where she was starting to find it hard to breathe.

The upper portions of the doors were still open, and Cali had turned the air conditioner off. She also really needed to use the Hole of Muck, but Cali was still sleeping, and she was more than a little afraid to wake them, especially after her panic the day before.

Her father had been in the military when he was younger, and she'd learned at a very young age never to wake her father up. If Cali reacted before they fully woke up, there was no way she'd be able to get out of the way of those sharp teeth and claws in time.

She tried turning on the air conditioner and pushed the various buttons, but nothing happened, and the doors opened outward, so there was little she could do there to shut it while she was stuck inside. Even if she did manage to open the lower door, she wouldn't be able to walk outside to shut either of them.

She put her harness on and hooked on the loathsome leash so she'd be ready to leave right away, tucking it inside the harness so she wouldn't have to carry it, then considered how to wake her sleeping lion.

Grinning as the old tune popped in her head, she walked over to one of the bookcases and grabbed a book off the shelf, humming to herself.

She dropped the heavy book as hard as she could, hoping it would wake the cat while she was a nice safe distance away.

Cali didn't so much as twitch a whisker.

"Drats!" she muttered. Frowning, she picked the book up and dropped it again, harder this time. Nothing. "Double drats!" She put the book back and considered her other options.

Her humming turned to singing as she walked over to the bed. She carefully tapped Cali on her nose, then backed quickly away.

Cali's giant paw came up and rubbed at her nose. Then she rolled over on her back and stretched, claws flexing, but she was still not awake, or if she was, she wasn't letting on about it, as her eyes remained closed.

She walked around to the other side of the bed and sang, feeling a bit like Timon from The Lion King. Getting into the song now, she started dancing and singing at the top of her lungs, which didn't get her any more than a twitch from the big cat.

So, gathering her courage, she yanked on a section of fur on her lion's tail and scurried back as fast as she could.

Cali leapt straight up in the air and flipped, landing on all fours facing her, teeth bared, claws out, and growling.

Jessica stopped backing up, put her sweetest expression on, crossed her legs, so she didn't pee herself from fright and an overly full bladder, and held up the leash up trying not to let on just how scared she really was. "I wee mo that-a-way?" she asked, tilting her head in the direction of the door.

Cali blinked several times, closed their mouth, relaxed their claws, and then flipped their tail around to make sure it was still attached, before looking back at her.

Jessica smiled as innocently as she could, raised the leash up a bit higher, and pointed to the door.

Cali blinked at her several more times before nodding, then let out a massive yawn and stretched again, before padding over to the door and opening it.

She wasn't sure if that yawn was a warning about how sharp and pointy her teeth were or not, but she followed anyway. She really had to pee.

29

MARSEE: LITTLE FLOWER

*M*arsee padded over to the door and looked out. She'd slept in later than she'd planned, and it was already nearing noon.

No wonder the cub woke me, she chided herself. *I need to remember to set an alarm tonight.* She picked up the squirming cub and quickly carried her down the ramp.

As she waited outside the waste room for the cub to finish, she checked the tip of her tail again. It still stung a bit where the cub had bitten her, but she didn't see any blood or teeth marks, so she dropped it.

It's my own fault for sleeping in so late, she thought, with another yawn, trying to wake up. *If it still hurts after breakfast, I'll have Mama look at it. She's pretty brave, though. I clearly scared her again, but she didn't run and hide.*

Needs met, they made their way to the kitchen for breakfast, or more realistically, lunch, since she had slept in so late. She stared at the selections in the fridge, unsure of what she wanted. Nothing seemed to fit her mood.

The little cub walked up and pointed at the pitcher of juice, making Marsee smile.

She sure seems to like the star fruit juice.

Marsee grabbed it and the fruit that the cub pointed out next, then quickly chopped it up.

While she did, the cub opened and shut every cabinet door in the room she could reach, checking everything out.

She hadn't bothered exploring this room the day before, figuring the cub wouldn't be interested. It mostly held the equipment they used for preserving the food they grew, stored on the bottom shelves, along with a supply of empty jars, and some of the larger pots and strainers they occasionally used, and Marsee knew it would be difficult explaining their purpose without actually showing her.

Food prepared, she followed the end of the leash to a cabinet door, where she found the cub had climbed inside an empty one, and was peering down the open interior.

Looking for a place to hide, little one? Marsee wondered. *I wouldn't blame you after yesterday. Maybe I can make her some sort of safe room, but what would be strong enough to be safe from me?* She mulled over the problem as she watched the cub explore.

Eventually, the cub turned around, saw Marsee there, and grinned, jumping up to show she couldn't even reach the top.

Oh, is everything just really big for you? I guess it would be. Marsee remembered when she was a much smaller cub and how much difficulty she had doing everything.

She'd actually completely refurbished the kitchen a few years back, for her parents, to work out all of the claw marks she'd left as a cub scrabbling up onto the counters, and added the steps to make it easier for her and her nephlings when they visited. She'd needed a project for her guild classes at the time, and that had worked.

Her parents had actually paid her for it, one of her first commissions, and it had allowed her to finally purchase the drawing tablet she'd been drooling over for months, although the new tablet she had now, far exceeded her old drawing tablet's capability, at least according to the specs. She hadn't actually tried drawing anything on it yet.

Marsee motioned for the cub to follow her, and she did so without hesitation. She grabbed the platter of food on the way out, and they slowly made their way down to the family room at the cub's pace.

The little cub scrabbled up onto the window seat, and Marsee marveled at how she climbed.

I suppose that would make sense without claws to hold on with, she decided, and set the tray down on the seat between them. They ate in companionable silence as the cub sat transfixed on the view outside.

Her father stopped in briefly while they were eating, to let her know he thought her report was perfectly fine, and had sent it along to the Council. That thought made her tail twitch with nerves when she realized the Council was now reading *her* report, and she wondered what they thought.

He also let her know they would be meeting in the afternoon to discuss lifting the quarantine so that they could travel to Mama's Mentor, and that he agreed with her about ditching the harness.

"I'll let you know this evening how the meeting goes," he told her. "So, what are your plans for today?"

"I want to try making something to cover her skin so she can be more comfortable, and hopefully find a way to protect her feet, so she can at least walk outside without getting burned," she told him.

"Do you have any ideas on what to make?" he asked her.

"The glass blowers and metal crafters use gear to protect their paws and fur from the intense heat of the fires," she told him. "I figure if it can protect our hands from being burned, then the same material should work to protect her feet from the stone. I'm pretty sure I still have my gloves in storage from when I spent time there as an apprentice."

"That's not a bad idea," her father said.

"She seems fairly comfortable with the material used in the towel, so I figure regular fabric will be good enough for the rest of her body, at least to start. Maybe something white or light colored to reflect the sun. I examined the items they were wearing when they were rescued, so I have a general idea of what to make. The one thing I'm not sure about is how to protect her head and eyes. The sunlight seems far too strong for her at midday. She keeps hiding her face in my fur when we go outside."

"She doesn't seem to have any problems looking out the window," her father said, nodding in the direction of the cub, who was leaning up against the window seat, and watching a large bumble crawler amble its way across the yard.

"You're right!" Marsee said. "She loves looking out this window. They're tinted to block the sun to help keep the room cooler. If only we could make mini windows for her eyes."

"Maybe you can. Why don't you talk to those glassblower friends of yours, and see if they can make something," her father suggested. "As for protecting her head, maybe you can make something out of the material we use for the sun shades in the courtyard. I think we have extra material in the storage room. If not, let me know and I'll order some. We should have a roll around anyway, just in case."

"A portable sun shade?" Marsee asked.

"Well, why not? She seems to be about as delicate as your mother's flowers, just more mobile than a plant. What works for them should work for her, too," he said with a shrug.

"True..." Marsee replied, lost in thought as ideas swirled in her head. "Well, come on then, Little Flower, let's go see what we can do to protect you from the sun."

"I like it," her father said with a grin.

"Like what?" Marsee asked.

"Little Flower. It's a good name for her," her father replied. "Much better than 1A1."

Marsee shrugged, then picked up the now-empty platter and the end of the leash, which was still attached to the harness, and motioned again for the cub to follow.

Little Flower frowned at the leash, then at her father, before sliding down and walking straight over to him.

They both watched her with curiosity as she stopped in front of him, reached behind her, unhooked the leash, and let it go deliberately as she glared up at him, daring him to say no.

He sighed and shook his head no, holding out his paw for the leash. Marsee walked over and handed it to him.

Little Flower crossed her arms, looking very annoyed.

"Papa, she's not going to run off. Why does she still have to wear the leash? If you agree, why can't she take it off?"

"I'm sorry, kitten. I would in a heartbeat, but those are Senior Councilor Tabor's specific orders, and she's the only one that can change them," he replied, "not without convincing the majority of the Council anyway."

"It's not right. She's not a prisoner, and she's clearly smart enough to take it off, so what's the point?" Marsee asked.

Her father sighed but didn't answer.

The cub stared up at him, clearly aware they were discussing it, and waited.

"I'm sorry, Little Flower. Until Tabor changes her mind, I can't do anything about it. You'll have to wear the leash," her father said eventually, then shook his head again and held it out to her.

Little Flower chittered something and then made a gesture that Marsee was sure was not polite, before taking the leash back.

Her father must have thought so too, as he let out a snort. "I don't blame you one bit for being mad at us," he said with an apologetic expression.

Little Flower glared at him, but clipped it back on and handed the end back to Marsee, never once taking her glare off her father.

Marsee reluctantly took it back.

Little Flower gave another huff of annoyance and stormed out of the room, with Marsee following obediently behind, wondering just who was wearing the leash.

30

JESSICA: DOLL

essica fumed as she stomped her way out of the living room towards the kitchen, so Cali could wash the dishes. The dynamic between Cali and the copper cat, that she'd decided to call Fox, as they had much the same coloring, clearly showed Fox was in control, as she'd assumed from prior encounters.

Yet they seemed just as apologetic about the leash, although they surprisingly hadn't forced it back on her. That had helped calm her anger slightly.

If Fox isn't in control, who is, and why do they want me leashed? Jessica wondered.

When Cali was done with the dishes, they led her to a room that they hadn't explored the day before. This room was some sort of massive warehouse. Row upon row of shelves were stacked full of items on display. There was far more than the three people she'd seen could ever use.

As they wound deep into the room around various stacks, she realized they must be in one of the wings. They made their way past what looked like nothing more than stacks of giant canning jars full of different foods, past boxes, wooden crates, and shelves of unknown items, until they came to a shelf full of colorful fabrics, including more of the same fur that made up her bed and blanket.

Cali pawed through the collection and pulled out three reams of fabric, holding them out to her.

"Are you going to make clothes for me?" Jessica asked, fervently hoping so. She pointed to her favorite, a light blue fabric decorated with multi-colored flowers shaped like the chocolate-smelling lily from the night before. She then picked up her foot and pointed to it, hoping for some shoes.

Cali nodded and continued looking through the pile, paused, then moved on to another shelf, looking through a box there before pulling out what looked like a giant pair of oven mitts.

After rifling through several more boxes and grabbing a collection of other items, most of which Jessica didn't recognize, they motioned for her to follow them back up to their room.

Somehow, Cali managed to carry all of the various items and Jessica up the ramp without dropping anything, but when they set Jessica down, the smaller objects spilled everywhere.

She helped pick everything up and carried it over to one of the tables in the room. Then Cali closed up the room and turned on the air conditioner. She watched closely to see what buttons they pressed, but apparently, it was temperamental, as Cali hit it several times before walking away.

Apparently, some things are constant in the universe. I wonder if they have duct tape and bailing twine, too.

As the room began to cool, Cali returned to the table and stood there for some time, looking back and forth between Jessica and the items now scattered across the table.

She wasn't sure if the kitten was expecting her to make the clothes or was trying to figure out how to do so herself. She had no idea how to make clothing or shoes or use any of the strange implements on the table, so she just shrugged.

I suppose maybe I could figure out how to make a dress. Worst case, I could cut a hole in the middle and tie it closed. It would still be better than a towel, she thought, looking at the pile on the table. *I'd hate to ruin that beautiful fabric, though.*

Her furry feline must have had the same idea, as they unrolled and cut off a section of fabric about twice Jessica's height, folded it in half and used some device, that looked nothing like scissors, to cut a hole out of the center, then stuck the whole thing over Jessica's head.

The fabric practically swallowed her, but thankfully, Cali wasn't done. They had Jessica stick her arms out to the side, which didn't even come to either side of the wide swath of fabric. Pressing the pieces together, Cali used the same device she had a moment before to cut the fabric, but this time the strange device sewed the fabric together, and cut it at the same time.

Cali did the same on the other side, and suddenly Jessica had sleeves, very long sleeves, but sleeves. She tried moving her arms to check the fit and found there was plenty of room to cross her arms.

With pantomime, Cali asked her where she wanted the sleeves cut, and then trimmed off the excess length. She examined the edges of the sleeves and noticed that a hem had also been cut, folded over, and neatly stitched.

That certainly saves time, Jessica thought.

When Jessica was done examining the sleeves, Cali had her stand with her feet wide apart, then continued to sew the fabric down her sides and outside of her legs, leaving a loose but overly long dress.

Jessica showed where she wanted the hem cut, and before long, she had a crude but passable dress. She moved around a bit, testing it out, then had Cali cut a little more off the bottom, so she wouldn't step on the hem. It certainly wasn't the fanciest dress she'd ever owned, but it was far better than the towel she'd been wearing, and she absolutely loved it.

There was only one thing missing. *Pockets!*

Jessica thought for several moments about how to explain pockets when miming putting her hands in them failed to make sense to the kitten.

As Cali sat there, head tilted in confusion, Jessica grabbed a piece of the discarded fabric and did her best to mime what she wanted.

Cali followed her instructions until Jessica had what looked like a simple cloth envelope—basically, a pocket with a flap. Her thoroughly confused kitten examined the pocket, trying to figure out its purpose, then gave her an overly exaggerated human shrug.

Jessica took the pocket back from Cali, picked up one of her small toys that had been shoved aside to make room, then pressed the pocket against her dress, holding it in place with one hand. Then awkwardly, with her other hand, she placed the toy in the pocket and closed the flap.

Cali's ears went back, and her eyes widened with shock and immediate understanding before nodding their agreement.

Jessica showed where she wanted the pockets.

Cali nodded again, took the pocket back, and examined it before suddenly turning it over and watching the toy fall out.

Have they never seen a pocket before? Jessica wondered. *Goldy had a bag she kept all her medical stuff in, so they must be used to carrying things. How do I explain buttons?*

Cali figured out the problem, though, before she could even try. They walked over and pawed through a drawer before returning with something. Cali attached whatever it was to the edges of the flap, closed it, pressed down for a moment, then opened it back up and put the toy back in the pocket. They put the flap down and turned the pocket upside down. This time the toy didn't fall out.

The kitten flashed an enormous grin and handed the pocket back to Jessica to look at.

She examined the flap and the two thin strips that had been added. *Magnetic or something similar,* she decided.

She smiled at Cali, whose tail curled as she grabbed another piece of fabric and made a duplicate of the first. But this time, they cut the fabric so that the entirety of a flower was on the front, even when the pocket was closed.

Cali carefully pinned both pockets with another odd tool where Jessica wanted them to go, then motioned for her to take the dress off, which she did.

A few minutes later, the pockets were attached, and the dress was handed back to her. Once back on, she flipped open both pockets, stuck her hands in them, and twirled around, smiling and laughing.

Cali's tail practically corkscrewed in response.

Once the dress was complete, Cali grabbed the other fabrics and cut off a small section of each. They also took the giant oven mitt and cut it open before walking over to the door, motioning for Jessica to follow.

Surprised, as they hadn't had her put her harness and leash back on, Jessica joined her at the door, staying in the shade to avoid the hot sun that blasted the room the moment Cali opened the door.

Cali set the various objects on the ground just outside the doorway on the stone balcony, and then demonstrated stepping on them.

Oh! They want to know what material will protect my feet, she realized, then cautiously stepped out onto the first fabric, shielding her eyes and squinting as she stepped outside, barely able to see where she was stepping.

The first two were too thin. The heat radiated up through, although not bad enough to burn her feet like before, at least not right away, but the thick oven mitt seemed to do the trick.

Jessica pointed to that one and then ran back inside to get away from the glare of the sun.

Cali grabbed the materials, shut the door, and returned to the table. They discarded the rejected materials, then tapped the top of the table, motioning for Jessica to have a seat, so she hopped up, letting her legs dangle over the edge.

Cali took the oven mitt and wrapped the fabric around her foot, trying to get a sense for how it might go together. After a lot of trial and error, and an awful lot of laughter, when Cali figured out that Jessica's feet were ticklish, she had herself a pair of moccasin-like slippers.

Cali opened the door again, and Jessica stepped out. She stood there for as long as she could take the heat, but it worked. Her feet remained cool and blissfully unburnt.

When she couldn't take the heat anymore, she ran over to the air conditioner to cool down and wiped off some of the sweat that had formed on her brow.

The dress had done a reasonably good job of protecting her body, but her head was still exposed. What she needed now was a hat and sunglasses, but she was far better clothed now than she'd been that morning.

Her kitten came over and frowned at the sweat on her forehead, wiping some of it off and sniffing at it.

Jessica gave them a thumbs-up to say she was fine, but Cali didn't look convinced. They slid her sleeves up, checked her arm, then placed her on the table and took her shoes off to confirm her feet were unscathed.

She smiled up at the concerned cat, then wiggled her toes to show that her little piggies hadn't been carted off to market and turned into a side of bacon.

MARSEE: THE SENIOR GUILD MASTER

After completing the garment and footwear for Little Flower, Marsee sat stumped, trying to figure out how to make a miniature sunshield and eye protection for the little cub.

She hadn't found any of the sun shield fabric in storage, or anything that could be used to protect the cub's eyes. Some of the crafters used a visor to protect their eyes, but she didn't have any of that material handy either, not that it would have blocked the UV light, and the fabric she had was all too flimsy.

She was contemplating whether she could weave a basket and cover it with fabric, but she wasn't sure how big it would need to be. None of the bipeds rescued had been wearing anything like what she was envisioning, at least not the ones she'd looked at yet.

She was about to head back to the storage room to grab more supplies when Little Flower dragged her over to a painting she'd done when she was younger and pointed to it, chittering something while making motions with her paws. The cub had examined this painting before, so she was confused as to what Little wanted, then she realized what the motions meant.

"Do you want to learn to paint, Little Flower?" Marsee asked, making the same motions.

The cub grinned and nodded her head vigorously, so Marsee went over to her crafting desk and flipped open the lid, showing all of her favorite art supplies, including several canvases, paper of various sizes and colors, and her collection of paints, pencils, and other drawing implements. When the cub squeaked in evident excitement, Marsee grabbed a few pieces of paper and a charcoal writing stick and set them on the table.

Marsee sat down on the cushion next to the table and waited with curiosity to see what the little cub would do.

Does she really understand what they are?

It didn't take her long to find out. She watched in amazement as the cub drew a quick sketch of a head covering and eye protection, both as stand-alone drawings and on a drawing of a likeness of herself. The cub continued by drawing additional garments that she wanted, and adding those to the likeness as well.

When Little Flower was done, Marsee picked up the paper and examined the drawings closely, shocked at how detailed they were. She thought she could make some of them, but she wasn't sure about others. She decided to post the drawings on the guild board to see if anyone was interested in trying to craft the items shown.

She doubted it, since it was such a small project, but who knew? Maybe another Apprentice or Journeyman would be interested in trying something different. It was worth a try anyway.

She really didn't expect much of a response, so she was shocked when not one, but three master crafters responded within moments of posting, and a dozen more not long after, all freely gifting their assistance, not just in outfitting Little Flower, but all the other bipeds at the Agency.

Marsee had just finished forwarding that bit of surprising information to her mother, to get the dimensions of the other bipeds for the crafters, when her tablet rang with an actual call from the Senior Guild Master herself.

Marsee blinked in shock when the name came up on the screen. This wasn't just any Guild Master, but *The* Guild Master, as in the person in charge of the entire Guild on all five planets, and they were calling her!

It was a good thing she was already sitting down, or she might have fallen over. Her paws shook as she answered the call, wondering if she was in trouble.

Had her guildmate reported her for pouncing on her tail? She couldn't figure out any other reason why the Guild Master would be calling her, certainly not for those tiny little projects, even if the other masters were gifting their time.

Maybe that's it. Maybe she's mad that I took their time? Master craftsmanship was a valuable commodity after all, and one rarely gifted.

"Senior Guild Master? This is an honor!" Marsee stammered out, barely able to breathe.

"Nonsense, nonsense, Journeyman Chenzira. The honor is all mine. It's not every day that the Guild has the opportunity to be involved in a project of such magnitude as this!"

Marsee just blinked, not even sure how to respond. That hadn't been what she'd expected to hear at all.

Magnitude? How could a couple of small items be of magnitude?

Little Flower took that moment to lean over Marsee's shoulder and peer at the screen.

"Three moons! Is that her?" the Senior Guild Master asked.

"Uhh...Yes, Senior Guild Master. This is Little Flower." Marsee shook herself out of her surprise and turned the tablet slightly so that the Guild Master could get a better look.

Little Flower waved.

"Oh my! She is just as adorable as I've heard! Tell me, what is it that she's wearing? Is that something you've made for her already?"

"Yes, Senior Guild Master." Marsee motioned for Little Flower to back up and then flipped the camera around so the Guild Master could see the whole outfit.

"Have Little Flower turn around," the Guild Master ordered.

Marsee made a circular motion with one claw, and the cub thankfully understood and did as requested.

"We just finished it. It's my first attempt. I wasn't sure what would work. So, I just kind of made it up as I went along. She seems quite happy with it, though," Marsee explained, suddenly very aware of all the mistakes and flaws in the garment. She never expected the Senior Guild Master herself to be examining her work. If she had, she would have taken more time with it.

No, be real Marsee. If you'd known she was going to be looking at it, you'd have probably been too paralyzed with fear to even start.

"But of course," the Guild Master responded. "For something as new as this, a prototype is completely expected, and the proper approach to take. It's not like you had anything to base it on."

"Well, I did, somewhat," Marsee deflected. "My mother gave me access to the rescue footage, so I was able to see what they were wearing when we rescued them. This garment seemed the easiest to attempt."

"Ahh... That does help. Still, it looks like you did a fine job, especially for a prototype. It seems to fit her reasonably well. You should be quite proud of yourself. Wait, is there something on the front?"

"Yes, Senior Guild Master. I'm not really sure what to call them. Little Flower asked me to make them. I guess you could say they're miniature carry sacks. She puts small items in them." Marsee motioned for the cub to come closer, and she showed how they worked.

"Ingenious! I could see adding those to our carry harnesses...hmm...perhaps in a stiffer material... But, I digress. Sadly, I don't have the opportunity to craft as much as I'd like these days, and it's far too easy to get lost in project ideas. Anyway, speaking of materials, how did you decide on which ones to use?"

Marsee's eyes bugged out when she realized *the* Senior Guild Master got lost working on projects, too! It wasn't just her!

Marsee shook herself out of her surprise again, praying there hadn't been too long of a delay in answering. "Well, for the garment, I just showed her a few of the lighter colored fabrics we had enough material of, and let her pick the one she liked best. I think it suits her. As for the foot coverings, I set several samples outside, and had her stand on each, and tell me which one worked best to protect her feet from the heat of the stone. It ended up being my old pair of glass-blowing gloves. Since I had so little material to work with, I used scraps from the dress to figure out a pattern before cutting the footwear."

"Oh, excellent! Do you still have the pattern?" the Guild Master asked.

"I do, Senior Guild Master," Marsee replied.

"Good. Scan that in, and send it to me, along with the images you used for reference, and please, enough with the 'Senior Guild Master' bit. I hear far too much of that all day, every day, and I have a feeling we're going to be working together quite a bit in the near future, so I would really appreciate it if you would *please* call me Ellie."

"Yes, Sen...uh...Ellie... Please call me Marsee then, too."

Marsee's tail practically tied itself in a knot at the honor of being allowed to call the Senior Guild Master by her first name, but then Marsee frowned. "I can send you a picture of the garments and the pattern we made, only the pictures from the rescue..." She hesitated, not sure how to explain.

"What is it, Marsee? If you're concerned about access permissions, I can assure you I already have clearance, but I can confirm that with your parents if that would help ease your concerns."

"No. It's not that at all. It's the pictures themselves... I had no idea...well..." Marsee struggled to get her thoughts out. "I had no idea how badly injured they were until I saw the rescue footage. The injuries to the survivors were...well... Horrific just isn't a strong enough word to describe it. I thought you should be warned, and... I think maybe they shouldn't be shared with everyone, especially the younger guild members. There's a lot of blood..."

Marsee's tail sagged as she looked at Little Flower, who was just watching her with curiosity. The thought of the injuries she'd been through made her heart ache in both sympathy and remorse at nearly adding to them.

"I understand, child," Ellie said softly. "I've seen some of that footage myself. It was very kind of you to look through all of that to find a way to help her, and thank you for warning me. I know a lot of people who would have done as I asked, even if they knew it was the wrong thing. Now, in your post, you sent along several sketches of what you were looking for. Those were well done, by the way…"

"I didn't draw those, Little Flower did," Marsee interrupted.

"Little Flower drew them?!" Ellie exclaimed and then glared at her. "You're not pulling my tail, are you?"

"No. I mean. Yes…Oh…" Marsee stammered, flustered again, and pulled at the fur on the back of her neck. *Focus brain!* "Yes, Little Flower drew them, and no, I would never ever pull your tail! I promise! I can have her draw something if you'd like."

"Yes, please!" Ellie responded excitedly.

Marsee scrambled to her feet, pulled another piece of paper out of her supply, and motioned the cub over to the table, handing the cub the pencil. The cub looked at her in curiosity, wondering what she wanted.

"What would you like her to draw?" Marsee asked.

Ellie thought for a bit. "I don't have any preference. Have her draw whatever she wants, but give her that pack of colored pencils I saw. I'm curious to see how she does with color."

Marsee hastily opened her desk again, grabbed the box of colored pencils, and set them down on the table as ordered. Then, she did her best to try to tell the little cub to draw something, *anything*.

Little Flower seemed to understand, as she started drawing with the large pencil gripped awkwardly in her tiny paws.

Marsee held the tablet up so that the Guild Master could watch. Partway through, though, Marsee started recording.

When Little Flower was done drawing, she set down her pencil and walked away without looking at either of them.

They watched as she crawled into her nest to hide under her blanket. Marsee and Ellie sat there for a long time in equally stunned silence.

"She really thinks we destroyed her world. Doesn't she?" Marsee asked in a quiet voice.

"It would appear so, child," Ellie replied, just as softly.

On the paper in front of them, was what Marsee was sure was a master level sketch, that went from an idyllic scene of a strange alien world, with trees that had green leaves instead of purple, oddly proportioned buildings and ground crawlers, with cubs playing out front, drawn in bright vibrant colors, to seamlessly transition into a scene of destruction done entirely in black, white, and red, of those same buildings crumbled and burning, dead cubs, and one of their kind, angry and menacing, shooting a bleeding and clearly injured Little Flower in the back, as she tried to run away.

"Marsee, this is very important. After we finish here, you need to show this drawing to your parents and then have them call me as soon as possible. Send me a copy of that drawing, and the recording I saw you take as well. I promise you this, though: the entire Guild is at your disposal. Whatever she or the rest of her kind need to make this world habitable, you let me know, and I will personally make sure that it's given top priority. I mean that. You are to contact me at any time for anything you need for her. Do you understand?"

"Yes, Senior Guild Master. Thank you," Marsee said, absolutely stunned by the offer.

"Ellie, *please*," the Senior Guild Master sighed. "Now, let's talk about what else you know she needs..."

JERAN: DISEASED CREATURE

"Council is now in session. Please be seated. First order of business is a status update from the Agency. Councilor Chenzira, you have the floor."

"Thank you, Senior Councilor. I'm going to start today's update with good news. As of this morning, the Agency has announced the healthy arrival of not one, but two of the long-legged grazers, both male. The mother was pregnant at the time of the rescue, although due to the severity of the injuries that the mother sustained, she was kept in stasis for several months until the healers were sure they could treat her injuries and save her children. Thankfully, the mother and both of her children appear to be doing well."

Jeran paused to share a video of the newest arrivals. "As there were no fertile males rescued for this particular species, the arrival of two healthy males means we now have a better chance of saving them."

He watched with the others as the two creatures took their first wobbling steps and began nursing. When the video finished, Jeran continued. "On a less happy note, the Agency has confirmed that the cause of death for the two red-chested flyers we lost the other day was from their environment overheating. Additionally, the biped cub my family is fostering has shown an intolerance for the intense midday suns in our district. She suffered minor burns on her paws during her first foray outside. As such, the Agency has begun carefully controlled experiments to determine the safe temperature range for each of the species in our care. I've sent detailed descriptions of the experiments and safeguards to each of you. Healer Chenzira has indicated that those experiments should be concluded by the end of the week. My daughter intends to work with the Guild to design protective garments for Little Flower so that she may walk outside without burning her feet again."

A light appeared on the screen indicating one of the councilors had a question. Jeran indicated that they could speak.

"Little Flower?" Councilor Griffith asked.

"Yes. That is the name my daughter has given the cub," Jeran explained.

Griffith tilted his head in acknowledgement and released the floor.

"Do we have an update on the health of Little Flower? The last we've heard, she was quite sick," the Senior Councilor asked.

"Yes. Outside of the burns I mentioned before, she is actually significantly better. She's eating and drinking again, and most of her injuries from her fight appear to have healed, with only a few small bruises remaining today. She also appears to be forming a friendship with my daughter, as we had hoped, and has engaged in play with her."

Jeran paused again to bring up the video he took of Marsee and Little Flower drone racing the night before. This caused several of the councilors to gasp in astonishment.

"Are you telling me this creature has learned how to pilot a drone racer in *one* day?" This, not surprisingly, came from Councilor Parner.

Jeran flicked his whiskers forward in a yes. "My daughter informed me that she had the basics of the game down in half an hour. I watched for some time and even participated in a game myself. She came close to beating me, and I have no doubt she fully understands the rules. She is proving to be quite intelligent and inquisitive, but cautious at the same time. She's shown me that she's capable of removing the harness and leash if she chooses, and has asked both me and my daughter to stop wearing it, although she seems to understand it's required. I agree with my daughter's assessment that we should remove the leash requirement, as it serves no purpose but to tell her she is a prisoner at this point. Additionally, it would appear that she may have regained some of her hearing. As I've mentioned before, most of the bipeds and many of the other creatures experienced damage to their ears during the Cataclysm. My partner examined Little Flower's ears last night and has indicated that there have been some improvements. She recommends that a specialist see Little Flower, as she is not an expert in hearing loss, nor are any of the healers at the Agency, as it is apparently quite rare for our species. She has submitted a request for additional specialized hearing equipment to test and treat the bipeds, but is still waiting for approval, and is asking the Council for that funding and for permission to take Little Flower to see an expert in hearing loss, specifically, her mentor, Healer Ammond Greyfoot, who runs a hearing clinic in the Jandolf Square district."

"You want to let a sick and diseased creature wander loose in *my* district?" Parner asked incredulously.

"Little Flower has shown no signs of any physical illness. Her rapid change upon leaving the Agency significantly supports the diagnosis that she was suffering from isolation sickness, not anything communicable."

"But you don't know that for sure," Parner replied.

"Nothing in this world is for sure, Councilor Parner, but I trust my partner. If she says the cub is free of transmissible illnesses and safe to travel, then she is. Nor would she be running loose. She would still be supervised. She has shown her ability to follow basic instructions, and I do not believe she will run off. Additionally, restoration of her hearing may help treat the others, and allow us to establish communication with them," he retorted.

"Order! Councilors, please take your seats," The Senior Councilor bellowed, when the conversation following Jeran's comments turned into yelling and tail lashing, with people clearly passionate about the issue on both sides. "We will start with an initial vote to see how the Council stands."

When the vote ended with a majority still undecided, Jer sighed, disappointed by his peers, as the Council began deliberation proceedings on each request.

MYRA: OLD FRIENDS AND NEW CHALLENGES

Myra sat at her desk, absently eating a late lunch as she read through the latest report from the Agency.

"Mama? Can we talk?" Marsee asked from outside her office.

"Of course! Come on in," she said. "Just give me a second." She typed up a quick response to Brice, then set her tablet down and looked up.

Marsee was still standing in the doorway, holding her tablet and a piece of paper, looking confused and sad.

"Where's the cub?" Myra asked, starting to worry, and reached for her tablet when she realized the cub was missing. "Did something happen to her?"

"She's fine," Marsee said, so Myra set the tablet down. "She's in my room taking a nap. She wouldn't come with me, so I locked her in," Marsee explained, finally walking into the office and sitting down in a chair by the desk with a sigh deep enough to hold the moons in it.

"Why not? Is she feeling sick again?" Myra reached for her tablet again to check on the cub's stats, but Marsee stopped her.

"No... It's not that. The cub is fine. Well, physically healthy anyway, but something happened this afternoon." Marsee paused to collect her thoughts and took a deep breath. "I received a call from the Senior Guild Master."

"You did?! That is a surprise," Myra said, leaning back in her chair. "What did she want?"

"She called to promise the Guild's help in outfitting Little Flower, and all of her kind, with whatever they needed to protect them, and wanted additional information about what they needed," Marsee replied.

"That's fantastic news, and it does make sense after all the responses that you had earlier that she would reach out to you," Myra said, and then paused, taking a really good look at her daughter. "I would expect you to be wiggling with excitement right now, but you're not. What did she say that upset you so much?"

"*She* didn't say anything. She was really kind and even asked me to call her by her first name. It's just that..." Marsee let out another heavy sigh before continuing. "When I sent the initial request to the Guild, I sent them a picture of what Little Flower drew of the things she wanted. When I told Ellie that Little Flower drew them, not me, she had me have the cub draw something else for her, and, well... This is what she drew."

Marsee gently placed the drawing on the desk.

"Oh..." Myra said, carefully picking up the drawing and examining it closely, absolutely horrified at what she saw, although she was careful not to let it show.

"Yeah... Ellie said I should show you and Papa, and she asked that you call her as soon as possible."

"Have you shown this to your father yet?" Myra asked.

"No. He's already in the Council meeting. I swung by his office first, but the door was shut and his busy light was on, so I came here. I didn't know if I should interrupt a Council meeting about this or not."

Myra nodded and set the drawing back down on her desk. "You made the right choice. Your father will need time to process this before speaking to the Council, but they will need to be informed. Did you try explaining to her that it wasn't true?"

"No. She crawled into her nest after and wouldn't look at me. I don't even know how to explain something like that," Marsee replied with a half-strangled sob.

Myra held her arms out, and her daughter came around the desk and climbed onto her lap. They sat there for some time, taking comfort from each other.

"Don't worry about it. I'll talk to your father and we'll figure out what to do," Myra said as she hugged her daughter, then with considerably more enthusiasm added, "Now, tell me more about your meeting with the Senior Guild Master."

When Marsee left to return to her room, Myra left a message for Jer asking him to come to her office once he was done with his meeting. Then, with a heavy sigh, she placed a call to her old friend.

Ellie answered immediately. "Myra! Thank you for calling me back. How are you? The last time we spoke, we didn't exactly have time to chat. I can't believe how big your daughter is. She's practically all grown up!"

"It has been far too long since I've seen you and had a chance to really talk. I've missed you, and I'm sorry if I was a little harsh with that call. Things were just a tad busy that day. I'm doing quite well, and Marsee is all grown up. She just had her adulthood ceremony two days ago."

Ellie snorted at her ridiculous understatement of the mass chaos that had been the first few days of the rescue mission. "*Already?* The last time I saw her, she was still in the nursery. How time flies when you're buried under paperwork."

"Tell me about it! I went from running a small clinic that saw maybe ten patients a day, on a busy day, to running the entire Agency overnight. Remind me again why I agreed to go along with Jer's furbrained scheme?"

"Ha! Probably for the same reason I thought it was a good idea to combine several of the guilds together. Big ideas and very little sense of self-preservation, and probably a severe case of chronic sleep deprivation."

"Sleep? What's that?" Myra asked.

"Not sure, I haven't had any in about a hundred years, or so. So, I take it Marsee told you what happened?"

Myra sighed and held up the drawing. "She did."

"It doesn't surprise me at all that's what she thinks happened. They would have had very little warning or time to let their people know, if they even saw it coming at all. And spending months in quarantine gives a person a lot of time to think and come to the wrong conclusions."

"That was always a known risk," Myra replied.

"And the right one to take at the time, too," Ellie agreed. "So, what do you plan to do about it?"

"I honestly don't know yet. I haven't had a chance to talk with Jer. At this point, without being able to talk to them, the best we could do is show them the rescue footage and hope they understand what happened."

"Still no luck in communicating with them?" Ellie asked.

"Words no, but Marsee seems to be doing fairly well with basic gestures. She's even taught her how to race drones. Unfortunately, Little Flower has pretty substantial damage to her ears from the Cataclysm, as did many of the others. Their little ears just couldn't handle the immensity of the explosion. We've tried to treat them as best we could, but I don't think it helped much."

"I've seen the footage, and Marsee shared some stills she captured for research on what they were wearing. I'm surprised anyone survived, to be honest," Ellie said sadly.

She nodded her agreement. "You and me both, and I've treated some pretty horrific injuries in my day. I want to thank you for reaching out to Marsee about this project and for your offer of assistance. It was very generous. Are you sure? The Council has been less than forthcoming with funds for them."

"The Council can stuff it. I'm still livid about that session. I meant what I told her. If they need anything, you let me know, and I'll put my best crafters on it. *Anything*. Half the Master Crafters have already reached out to me letting me know they want to help in any way they can, and are gifting their time, and the rest likely just haven't seen the notice yet, heads still down lost in some project I'm sure, and will reach out once they surface. If they can't survive without these items on our planet, then the Council has no argument. This...clothing should be listed as medically necessary for them, and if they don't, I intend to make a big stink about it."

"Thank you, Ellie, and please give my thanks to everyone who volunteers. I already have one of my staff working to gather the information requested by the masters who reached out initially. Let me send you her contact information. If you need anything else, send it directly to her. I'll make sure she knows to expect to hear from you, and that you have clearance for anything you need."

"What would really help would be to have Little Flower here in person so that we can make adjustments," Ellie stated. "Think you could fly her over to the Guild for a visit?"

"I'll see what I can do, but I can't guarantee anything. Jer is currently fighting with the Council now to get her restrictions lifted so we can go and see Ammond about her hearing loss."

"That fur-brained Council, your partner not included, of course. I'm assuming it's the current band of troublemakers, Parner and his crew, objecting?"

Myra flicked her whiskers forward in a yes.

"You tell Jer to send me a list of anyone who objects, and I'll give them...incentive...to change their vote. Heck, if I have to, I'll come there myself and quarantine for a month. I could use a vacation. Got a spare pillow for an old friend?"

"For you, always! I might even be able to scrounge up two, and thank you. I'll let him know, and I appreciate it. Is there anything I can do for you in return?" Myra asked with a grin.

"Are you kidding? This project is the most fun I've had in months. We've taken the cub's drawings and already put together several prototypes. I'll have a delivery for you tomorrow morning. Say around ten?" Ellie asked.

"And just who is going to be making that delivery?" Myra chuckled, already knowing the answer.

"What the Council doesn't know won't hurt them," Ellie replied with mock innocence.

"They're going to throw you in a cell one of these days for insubordination, I just know it," Myra said, shaking her head at her friend's audacity.

Then again, Ellie was probably one of the few people who could take on the Senior Council and win. She had almost as much authority in her own way as they did, and Ellie had always been a force to reckon with.

"I'd like to see them try," Ellie growled, causing them both to laugh.

They talked for a few minutes longer, catching up on the years it had been since they'd last really spoken, before Ellie hung up to get back to the 'hard work' of ordering Guild Masters around and making sure they did everything to her satisfaction. Myra knew she just wanted to get her hands dirty and craft with the others. She might run the Guild now, but Ellie would always be a crafter at heart.

It was well after the evening meal when Jer leaned up against her open door with a frown.

"They said no, didn't they?" Myra asked when she saw his expression.

"No, but they didn't say yes either. Over half of the Council is *still* undecided, so the motion was tabled for the next session," Jer answered. "I saw your message. What's up?"

Myra pushed the drawing towards him. She'd flipped it over some time earlier, unable to look at it any longer.

Jer pushed off the door frame and walked over. "What's this?" he asked as he approached, then flipped it over. "Oh…"

"Oh, indeed," Myra replied.

"Little Flower drew this?" Jer asked for confirmation.

"She did. She drew some sketches of the clothing she wanted as well. Marsee sent those to the Guild for assistance and got a call back from Ellie. On that call, Marsee told Ellie that Little Flower had been the one to draw the sketches, so Ellie asked to have Little Flower draw something else. *This* is what she drew."

Jer absently took the seat Marsee had vacated earlier in the day, as he continued to stare at the drawing. With a heavy sigh, nearly matching the one Marsee had given earlier, he set the drawing gently back down on the desk.

"Ellie has offered the assistance of the Guild for whatever we need for Little Flower and the rest. The first delivery will be here tomorrow at ten," Myra continued.

"I take it Ellie will be delivering it herself?" Jer asked with a snort.

"Would you expect anything less from her?" Myra asked with a raised brow.

"Not really," he chuckled. Honestly, I'm surprised she's not already here. I'd report her for breaking quarantine, but honestly, I'm a little afraid of her, and I personally think the quarantine is pointless. Besides, no one said there couldn't be visitors, just that we couldn't leave."

Myra snorted, thoroughly surprised at her partner for bending the rules so much. "If I know her, she'll have the entire Guild working through the night. She also wants to know who you need her to 'incentivise' in the Council, to drop the travel restrictions."

This caused her partner to snort and flip his ears back with matching surprise. "Sadly, that would be illegal, but remind me to never piss off the Senior Guild Master. She could destroy this district's economy with a single command."

"If you can't remember that, then you should probably step down from the Council," Myra teased, and then sobered. "So, what do you think we should do about the drawing?" she asked.

"*That* I don't know. I wish we could talk to her, but this drawing will go a long way towards convincing the Council of her sentience and the need to remove the harness. Where are Marsee and Little Flower, anyway?"

Myra looked at the time. "Probably in bed by now. Marsee brought food up to her room tonight. Little Flower refused to come down for dinner, and Marsee said she didn't eat very much. She gave Little

Flower a sketch book and some colored pencils, and apparently, she's been drawing for most of the evening, but she won't let Marsee see what she's drawing."

Jer nodded. "Well, if we're having company tomorrow, we should probably go to bed soon, too, but I need something to eat first. Care to join me for a midnight snack and a moonlit walk around the garden?"

Myra stood and walked over to wrap her tail around his. "I thought you'd never ask!"

34

JESSICA:ARTIST

*J*essica's stomach ached, and the food tasted off. She just wasn't hungry. After months of day after day, after day, of nothing, the last few days felt like a lifetime. She was emotionally and physically exhausted long before it got dark, even with a nap in the middle of the day.

She was thrilled about her new clothes. The dress fit reasonably well, and while not the fanciest thing she'd ever owned, the fabric was soft and pretty, and it had the largest pockets she'd ever had in a dress, or in any clothing for that matter. The shoes were more like slippers, but she could at least go outside without having to be carried everywhere, so that was nice, but they didn't fit quite right, and were rubbing a little without socks or padding. All of the callouses she'd used to have had worn off from months stuck in that cell.

But the most important improvement was that she finally had drawing supplies again. Oh, how she had missed being able to draw. Her fingers twitched with the need to get the images out of her brain and onto paper. She hoped that once she did, her brain would stop playing the scenes over and over, and over again in her head whenever she tried to sleep or had a moment to think.

She wondered who the cat was that had called Cali. It was

someone she'd not met before, a beautiful cat with shiny black fur, except for white whiskers, a small heart-shaped white spot on her chest, and the most piercing yellow eyes she'd ever seen.

They seemed interested in the clothing, so she wondered if they were going to make more for her. She hoped so. It looked like Cali had taken pictures of her sketches and sent them off somewhere, so maybe this was the person, but she wasn't sure. The dynamic between the two was *very* interesting.

Cali had seemed shocked to get the call. Her tail had poofed straight out and practically vibrated, and even through the tablet, everything about that cat screamed of power and confidence, making her wonder if this was who was in charge.

It was almost as if I'd gotten a call from the President. Who knows, maybe it was. I suppose it's not every day you kidnap an alien species and invent clothing for them.

She was convinced they had no concept of clothing, except in rare instances, like the mittens or that odd harness they wore to carry things. So, when Cali asked her to draw something for the black cat, she decided to take a chance that they were, in fact, someone important, and let them know what she thought they'd done, or at least part of it. More than anything, she needed answers.

She was honestly really proud of her drawing when it was done. It was by far one of her best pieces, especially considering how quickly she'd finished it, but it had been emotionally exhausting at the same time. So, when she'd finished it, she'd just walked away and crawled into her bed to think.

Cali had tried to make her leave the room with her, but she just shook her head no, and to her surprise, they'd gone without her, locking her in the room. It was the first time they'd really left her alone since taking her out of the cell, but she didn't even bother trying to see if she could open the massive door.

Partly it was because she knew there was nowhere for her to run, even if she could find a way out, but also because she was starting to develop a friendship with Cali, and she knew that her situation could be significantly worse than it was now. At the moment, they were feeding her, clothing her, and caring for her injuries, and not asking anything of her except to stay put and wear that stupid leash.

Instead, she took out the sketchbook Cali had given her and drew long after the kitten went to bed. Thankfully, they left a light on for her so she could keep drawing.

She drew until her hand cramped and her eyes grew heavy. She drew pictures of her friends and family that were already starting to fade in her memory. She drew pictures of her home, her grandfather's farm, and the animals there. She drew pictures of animals that she knew probably didn't exist anymore, capturing their image for posterity — perhaps the only legacy they would ever have.

She wrote their names and random facts, afraid she'd forget what and who they were. Then she drew pictures from the attack, of the destruction she'd witnessed, and of Susie's mangled body — the pages smudged and wet with her tears. She drew pictures from her captivity, of her injuries, of Doc and the flying pyramid, of her rape, of her anger, grief, fear, and demons, and more until she passed out from exhaustion in the early hours of the morning, the sketchbook nearly full.

Out of self-preservation, she subconsciously knew that to survive and gain her freedom, she needed to find a way to make this new world her home, and she knew she couldn't do that if she was still locked in the trauma of her past.

So, as she drew, she tried to pretend the drawings were images of something that had happened to someone else, not to her. With each drawing, she imagined locking those events away in a closet where they couldn't hurt her anymore, and prayed that the bulging door would hold.

35

MARSEE: SPECIAL DELIVERY

Biped Observations by Marsee Bet Chenzira 10165.11.6

- The same material used for protecting us during glass-blowing and other high-temperature crafting is adequate to protect the biped's paws from burns.
- The Guild has offered its support in creating protective eyewear and additional garments.
- Little Flower believes that we were responsible for the destruction of their world, and that she is a captive. Again, I recommend ending the use of the leash, as it reinforces that belief.

I crafted a garment made of light-colored fabric made from chenzie wool to protect the cub's body, and gloves for her feet, using material cut from an old pair of glass-blowing gloves. A lengthy test after the garments were made proved effective to keep her feet and covered areas from burning, but she still produced that same liquid on her exposed forehead, and ran inside to the cooling unit after a few minutes.

I don't have the materials on hand to produce proper eye

protection or some sort of sun shield for her head, but we've determined that she is perfectly capable of looking out a UV-protected window. I reached out to the Guild, and the Senior Guild Master personally indicated that the Guild would assist in making those items, as well as attempt to make other protective garments based on the designs seen in the rescue footage.

Little Flower is a very skilled artist, and she assisted in designing some of the protective gear she wanted, as well as a detailed drawing of what she believes happened during the Cataclysm.

I have attached both drawings to this report, as well as a video of her drawing her take on the rescue. It's very clear to me from this sketch that she believes we attacked her world and have taken her captive.

Continuing to require the harness just reinforces the idea that she is not free. I have no doubt that she is sentient, so further restraining her seems both cruel and sets the wrong impression.

I am not sure how to communicate what happened to her and her world, but I believe this should be of the utmost priority. I also recommend that the other bipeds be given drawing supplies as an enrichment activity, as Little Flower has spent most of this afternoon and evening drawing.

*O*nce Marsee finished her report for the night, she set her alarm and checked it three times before dimming the lights, leaving the one nearest Little Flower on so she could continue sketching.

She wondered what the little cub was drawing so frantically, but honored her request for privacy and gave her the space she so clearly wanted. From her own experiences, Marsee knew how cathartic drawing could be.

Her mother had informed her of Ellie's expected arrival in the morning, and seeing how much the cub liked to draw, Marsee had sent a request to Ellie, asking that she bring a few small drawing pads and supplies with her that might better fit the cub's paws, if she had any available.

A reply came moments later with only one word. "Gladly."

She could barely believe that the Senior Guild Master *herself* had called her, and was coming to her home in the morning, and that *she* was allowed to call one of the six most powerful people in the universe by her first name!

Marsee was an emotional wreck bouncing between excitement at meeting her and terror at what she'd think when she saw the garments she'd made in person. It had been all Marsee could do to keep herself from ripping the clothing off of Little Flower, and trying to fix all the mistakes she'd seen. The cub hadn't taken them off, though, so Marsee just prayed she didn't end up being demoted by the end of the day, for her sloppy work.

She woke briefly in the middle of the night, saw that the cub was still drawing, and went back to sleep. When her alarm went off the next morning, she woke to find Little Flower had finally fallen asleep, the drawing pad clutched tightly in her arms, and pencils scattered everywhere in her little nest.

She decided to let the cub sleep in and quietly exited the room to prepare breakfast for the two of them. The exhausted cub still hadn't woken up several hours later when Ellie's shuttle arrived, so Marsee decided to let her continue sleeping and made her way down to greet the Senior Guild Master.

Her mother was already there helping to unload the Guild Master's ship.

Marsee drooled over the personal ship, capable of jumping between the planets. Very few people ranked high enough to have their own ship, usually just the seniors of the various guilds and the Senior Council.

She had always wanted to learn how to fly, but she hadn't been an adult, and didn't have a high enough rank yet to qualify for the classes, although she had put her name on a list on the off chance there was an opening.

Her father had shown her how his shuttle worked, in the event of an emergency, and let her fly a few times, even if that was completely illegal. They lived out in the middle of nowhere, so there was little risk but to themselves. But his shuttle was only good for local travel. This one could fly between the stars. Her father still had to take the big Council transport ships for the meetings on the other planets, just like the rest of the Council.

Marsee ran her paw along the side of the spotless ship and stepped up into the cargo bay. "It's nice to meet you in person, Ellie," Marsee said when she found the Guild Master. "You have a beautiful ship."

She still felt horribly uncomfortable about calling the Senior Guild Master by her first name. It just seemed wrong and highly disrespectful, even if she'd been requested to do so.

"Thanks. It's nice to see you, too. Although you know, this is not the first time we've met," Ellie said, looking over at her with a grin.

"It's not?" Marsee asked, sure she'd remember meeting the Senior Guild Master in person. It wasn't exactly something that happened every day, even when you were in the Guild.

"The last time Ellie was here, you were only about a year old," her mother replied with a chuckle at her confused expression, then looked at Ellie. "I still can't believe it's been that long since I've seen you in person. Let's not make that a habit again, shall we?"

"You're going to be so sick of seeing me that you're going to lock the doors and turn out the lights when I show up," Ellie replied with a grin. At Marsee's further surprise and confusion, Ellie continued. "Your mother and I were roommates during her in-between years. She was an Apprentice attending the Healer's Guild, and I was failing to earn my master's.

"Oh, please, you weren't failing at anything," her mother scoffed.

"Don't you remember that chair I built? I almost lost my tail!" Ellie exclaimed.

"Moons! I'd almost forgotten about that. Marsee, I wish you could have seen this monstrosity of a chair. Instead of legs, it had a curved base that rocked back and forth. While testing it out, Ellie ran it over her tail. With the yelp and swears she let out, I thought for sure her tail had been amputated."

Ellie grabbed her tail and held it up, with the end dramatically flopped over. "I'm surprised it wasn't. It's honestly never been the same since. In my panic, I shot straight up out of that seat, only to end up going straight over backwards when I landed. The whole thing splintered into about a hundred different pieces in the process. Months of painstaking work lost in an instant." Ellie shook her head with a defeated and exaggerated sigh.

"Whatever you do, Marsee, never, *ever*, sit in a chair made by the Senior Guild Master," her mother teased.

"Hey! I got better at them!" Ellie scowled indignantly at her mother, and then grinned at Marsee, who stood there with her mouth ajar in surprise. "What? Did you think Senior Guild Masters were born good at everything all the time? Not only do we make mistakes... when we do, they are usually epic failures. How else do you think we learn?"

Marsee continued to stand there in shock, unable to make anything come out of her mouth in reply. She wasn't sure what surprised her more, that her mother was actually *friends* with the Senior Guild Master, or that Ellie admitted to making mistakes.

"Come on, Marsee. Help me bring all of this stuff inside," her mother ordered, giving her a playful shove and breaking her out of her shock. When the last of the boxes had been lugged into the family room, Ellie finally asked her where Little Flower was.

"In my room," Marsee replied. "She was still sleeping when I left. She was up most of the night drawing. I don't think she fell asleep until just before sunrise."

"What was she drawing?" Ellie asked, curious.

"I have no idea," she replied. "She wouldn't let me see, and I didn't push it. She deserves some privacy after everything she's been through."

"Drawing can be very therapeutic for working through traumatic experiences that you might not otherwise be able to talk about," her mother said. "It's something we often recommend for our patients. Now that we know for sure that they *can* draw, I'll make sure supplies are available in each of the habitats. That was a good suggestion you made in your report, Marsee. I should have thought of that myself."

"You've had more important things to worry about, like keeping them alive," Ellie said. "Anyway, your daughter was already one step ahead of you. Those three boxes over there are full of the drawing kits we make for small cubs. Marsee requested supplies better suited for her tiny paws, and I figured the others might want them too. I only had about a hundred or so on hand, but I already have several apprentices, under the direction of their instructors, working on making enough for the rest, and will have those shipped directly to the Agency."

"You're the best. You know that, don't you?" her mother said with a grin.

"Of course. I am the Senior Guild Master after all. But it's always good to hear it from a friend, and much easier to take than a reprimand, no matter how well deserved," Ellie replied.

Marsee looked at her mother in surprise. Had she really reprimanded the Senior Guild Master and actually come away unscathed? Her mother just winked at her. That was apparently not a story she was going to hear, but oh, did she want to!

"Now, these boxes hold the items Little Flower requested. While your mother and I unpack them, why don't you go wake up our little sleeping flower, and bring her down, so we can have her try everything on."

Marsee took off at a run down the long hall and up the winding ramp to the tower to wake up the cub. Thankfully, when she arrived, Little Flower was already awake and eating breakfast. She noticed that the sketch book was nowhere to be found and wondered where the cub had hidden it. Shrugging, she motioned for the cub to put on her harness, which Little Flower did without hesitation, thankfully picking up on her urgency. After a quick stop so Little Flower could use the waste room, they made their way back to the family room.

"Ah, there she is," Ellie cooed, squatting down to get a better look at the small cub. "She's even more adorable in person!"

When Marsee felt resistance on the leash, she turned to look back at Little Flower, who was standing in the doorway with an expression of shock on her face. Little Flower shook her head. At first, Marsee thought it was a refusal, but Little Flower walked slowly over to the first table, felt the clothing that had been laid out there, then walked over to another table that was full of art supplies. The look on her face was the same expression she'd made when she'd first seen the moons, and she looked like she was going to cry.

"What's with the leash?" Ellie asked her mother with a frown.

"Tabor's orders…," her mother replied. "Marsee's living in the Tower, and she ordered that Little Flower wear the harness and leash anytime she goes outside. We're trying to get that order lifted, but the Council is currently 'undecided', and Tabor refused to change her mind, still worried that she'll run off."

The disgust in her mother's voice surprised Marsee, and when she looked over at her, her tail was twitching. Her mother rarely lost control of her tail. That was part of her medical training.

She must be just as upset as I am, Marsee thought.

"Those fur-brained, moons-forsaken, self-centered, excuses for…Parner again?"

When her mother nodded, Ellie let out a string of the most colorful swears that Marsee had ever heard. She made a mental note to remember them for later use.

"I promise the Council will hear about this, and I will make their lives uncomfortable, until they change their minds," Ellie said with a growl, then turned and snapped at Marsee, "Well, she's not outside now, is she? Take it off."

Marsee gladly jumped to do as ordered, although absolutely terrified by the growl of displeasure in the Senior Guild Master's voice. She thanked every ancient god in the universe that it wasn't directed at her.

As soon as she did, Little Flower walked over to Ellie and pointed to the Guild Master, and then to all of the items, as if to ask if she'd brought them.

Ellie responded with the typical whiskers forward, yes.

Little Flower turned to Marsee for confirmation.

Marsee nodded. "They nod their heads up and down for yes, and side to side for no, since they don't have whiskers," Marsee told the Guild Master.

Ellie nodded her head up and down.

Then, to everyone's surprise, Little Flower hugged the Senior Guild Master.

Ears back in surprise, Ellie lifted one of her arms to get a better look, then gently wrapped her tail around the small cub and gave her a careful squeeze.

When Little Flower pulled away, there were tears in her eyes.

"Three moons! Did I hurt her?" Ellie cried, her own tail now fully poofed with fear.

"No, I don't think so," Marsee said. "She's tougher than she looks, even if she does burn easily. They cry when experiencing strong emotions. I think she's just really happy about everything you brought."

They watched as the cub walked back to one of the tables with a strange wicker contraption on it, picked it up, put it on her head, and turned back to them, smiling.

"Oh, good!" Ellie exclaimed, her tail now curling in happiness. "The sun shield fits!"

They spent the better part of the next two hours trying everything on, making adjustments where they could, and sending revisions to the other masters back at the Guild.

Little Flower communicated her requests by paw waving, pointing, and lots of sketching.

Around noon, they dressed her up in all of her protective gear and brought her outside to see how well it worked at keeping her safe.

Ellie thwapped her tail against the floor as the cub put the harness back on when Marsee handed it to her, but said nothing, and surprisingly neither did Little Flower. If anything, the cub seemed pleased that Ellie was clearly upset.

I wonder how long it will take for the Council to change their minds once Ellie sinks her claws into them? Marsee thought as she clipped on the leash.

The Senior Council might have a reputation for stoic control, but the Senior Guild Master did not, and she wondered who would win.

They made their way to the nearest exit at the cub's slower pace. Her mother swung the large wheel that pinned the mechanical lock in place on the ancient door and shoved hard when the powered switch did nothing.

They almost always left through the shuttle bay, but that was on the far side of the compound. Rarely used, the door was stiff, and sand had drifted against the door on the other side, leaving a deep gouge as her mother shoved the door open enough for them to step outside.

Little Flower cautiously followed them out, and they had to tap her on the shoulder to remind her that they were still there, as she'd gotten completely lost in looking around.

"I think it must be working, if she's not noticing the effects of the sun or the heat of the sand," Myra stated.

"Is this her first view of the outside?" Ellie asked as they watched the tiny cub explore.

"From this side of the compound, anyway. She's only gone out at night or seen the view through the family room," Marsee answered. "Anytime we've had to go outside during the day, she's hidden her face in my fur to get away from the sun."

"Shall we go for a walk then?" Ellie suggested. "Give her a little tour of the outside of the compound? It'll be a good test to see how well her protective gear holds up, and if she starts having issues, we can duck back inside right away."

So, they did, stopping whenever the cub wanted to check something out. An hour later, they were back in the family room and eating an impromptu celebratory lunch.

A quick examination of Little Flower's feet showed no burns, just some minor rubbing from the foot protection. Ellie made a note and sent everything along to the crafters waiting impatiently back at the Guild. While they talked and ate, Little Flower grabbed one of the drawing kits and climbed up on the window seat.

"So, where's this partner of yours?" Ellie asked after watching the cub climb up on the seat.

"Probably still stuck in the resource allocation meeting. They always run long," her mother said, popping a piece of fruit in her mouth.

"Ah, that they do. I probably should have been in that meeting, but it's good for my second to have the practice. Poor Nardal probably has his tail twisted in a knot by now, if he hasn't completely rolled up in his shell. So, what are your plans with the refugees, now that they've been cleared from quarantine?"

"Honestly, I don't know," her mother said. "I've been so busy keeping them alive that I've only partially followed what's been going on in the Council. We started reintroductions within the species, but after Little Flower's ended so badly, we've had to slow that down substantially. All visits are being monitored again, which is really hard on my healers. It just takes up so much time."

"Pah! If I know that useless bunch of stink worms, they haven't even thought about what to do next," Ellie said between bites of her fruit. "If you leave it up to them, they'll be left stuck at the Agency in their cells for the rest of their lives."

"So, what do you suggest?" her mother asked.

"Honestly, more of what you are doing right now with Little Flower. I've had no less than fifty calls asking if fostering was an option. The people at the Guild are completely enamored with Little Flower and her plight. They want to help, so you need to act quickly before they forget or lose interest. It's not very often I have Masters offering their services for free, although thankfully, much of what we're doing here qualifies as research, so I have some discretionary budget there to use to help pay for materials, if the Council doesn't eventually pay for it."

"I don't know about fostering. I mean, it's working well for Little Flower. She's improved so much in just the few days she's been here, but if we scatter everyone across the planet, we're going to have a hard time repopulating the species, and we can't afford for any of them to get injured or sick. We've only had a couple of births since the rescue, but those were all mothers who were pregnant before the Cataclysm."

"That does make things difficult," Ellie replied. "Although, as far as mating goes, shouldn't it be up to each individual who they pick for a mate?"

"I wish it could be, but there just aren't enough members of each species to allow that. At least not for a few generations anyway. Social pairings, sure, but each birth for the next several generations should really be from different parents, to ensure the greatest genetic diversity," her mother explained.

"So, bring them back together when it's time for them to mate," Ellie suggested.

"We're not even sure *when* it's time for each of the species to mate yet. This is all new science. Out of caution, we paused the hormonal cycles in the females while they were in isolation, only recently restarting them when we started pairing them up. We were worried they'd only get a few mating cycles like us, and we didn't want to lose that opportunity."

"What if we did the fostering at the Agency?" Marsee chimed in, then swallowed hard when they both turned to look at her. "We… could…put together a…program where people could donate the supplies and skills needed to build permanent habitats and homes for them, in exchange for being able to come to the Agency and interact with them in person. If the Council won't allow that, we could at least put together a guild board just for the refugees, with their picture, likes, and what they need. We could even have a contest where people could enter ideas for names for them. At least until we figure out a way for them to tell us what their names are."

Ellie and her mother stared at her, unblinking, for several long moments.

"When did your daughter get so smart?" Ellie asked.

"When I wasn't looking, apparently. That's a monumental amount of work to manage, though," her mother said.

"Oh, I think Marsee and I can handle it," Ellie said with a wicked smile.

"What? Me?!" Marsee squeaked. "I'm not a tech."

"Well, it was your idea," Ellie chuckled, "but don't worry, I have people who can handle the technical aspects of setting that all up. What we really need, though, is what only you and Little Flower can provide."

"What's that?" Marsee asked with a confused frown.

"To be the face and representative of the program. They need to see what you're doing here for Little Flower—see what she's capable of, and see her drawings if she'll share. It would be best if you gave an interview or three to the Press, but even just sharing recordings of the two of you playing, or her exploring the world for the first time, will be a big help."

"How will that help?" Marsee asked, not sure she wanted everyone to see videos of her playing, and the thought of giving an interview for the press was downright terrifying.

"By turning Little Flower into a real person, not just some exotic wild animal kept in a cage. People are more willing to help those they care about and those they feel like they know. The more people who know Little Flower and the rest as individuals, the more sway we'll have with the Council. They wouldn't dare restrict her travel or medical care if their constituents were calling them night and day, insisting she had the help she needed. Additionally, they're going to be living with us for a very long time. Maybe someday they'll be able to repopulate a planet of their own, but for now, they need us, and we need to be willing to support them and share our world with them, until they're back on their feet and capable of supporting themselves."

Marsee walked over to the window and stared out, thinking hard. "I can take videos of her if you think that will help, but I don't know if I can do more than that. I...I have a really hard time talking to people I don't know. I just about twisted my tail off showing you what I made for Little Flower yesterday. I'm not sure I can handle having the entire world watching me," she explained. Although what she really feared was losing control again while everyone was watching.

"Not just this world, child. All of them." Ellie said.

Marsee turned back around, with a look of horror on her face.

"I guarantee you, by tomorrow, every member of the Guild is going to know your name and Little Flower's, not just here, but on all five worlds," Ellie said softly. "That's why I called you, and it's why I personally came here today. Whether you like it or not, you are now a part of our worlds' history. I want to help you through the process. I *want* to help you help Little Flower."

Marsee crumpled onto the window seat, head buried in her paws, shaking with the very idea.

Her mother started to climb off her pillow to comfort her, but stopped as Little Flower crawled into Marsee's lap and gave her a hug. Marsee, surprised by the action, melted and wrapped her arms around the small cub.

When Marsee pulled back from the hug, Little Flower leaned over, grabbed her sketchbook, and handed it to her.

Marsee took it, opened the cover, and gasped.

Little Flower indicated she should turn the page, so she did, and again, and again. When she was done, she handed the book to Ellie, who was sitting closest to her, waiting impatiently to see what was in the book. Her mother walked over to stand beside Ellie and look over her shoulder.

The first page was a drawing of Little Flower and Marsee leaning together, Marsee's tail wrapped around the cub as they looked out at the three moons from Marsee's balcony, the barest hints of bandala trees and the mountains in the distance. On the second page was a picture of the two of them racing drones and laughing.

The third page had a drawing of the garden as they watched the fish chase after each other for the flower. The next held two drawings, one of Marsee washing Little Flower's back in the kitchen, and another of Little Flower splashing her with the water.

Marsee's shocked expression and her fur dripping with water made both Ellie and her mother burst out laughing.

"So that's why everything was wet," her mother teased.

"I tried cleaning it up!" Marsee whined, full of embarrassment.

There was a page with Marsee making clothing for Little Flower, her arms wide as Marsee trimmed the fabric, and a sketch of Little Flower hiding in Marsee's arms from the suns.

The next page had a scene with all four of them in the family room today, and all the things Ellie had brought with her, while Ellie adjusted Little Flower's foot protection. Then, finally, one with all four of them exploring the compound and stopping to look at a bumble crawler basking in the sun, a herd of chenzies in the background.

"How?" Myra finally whispered. "How did she draw so much in such a short amount of time?"

"This is mastery-level work," Ellie said. "They may just be sketches, but the level of detail and emotions in each of these drawings is incredible. The colors are all wrong, but… Did you see a herd of chenzies on our walk? I didn't."

"There was a cloud of dust in the distance, but I couldn't make out what it was," Marsee replied.

"Well, there's no way she could have drawn a chenzie so accurately, not without having seen one," her mother stated, then considered the rest of Ellie's comments. "I imagine being so vulnerable without sharp teeth or claws, being able to see long distances would be an evolutionary advantage worth giving up depth of color. I can have someone look into it."

"This is exactly what I'm talking about," Ellie said, tapping the sketch book. "The world needs to see through her eyes the friendship you're forming. They need to see these drawings, both the good and the bad."

Marsee looked down at the cub still sitting on her lap and sighed. "What do you think, Little Flower? Do we show the universe what you can do?"

Little Flower leaned in and gave her another hug.

"I guess that's a yes, then," Marsee whispered, absolutely terrified of what she'd just agreed to do.

MARSEE: PICT-IONARY

The four of them spent the next several hours working out the details of Marsee's fostering idea before her mother called a break.

"You were up all night, weren't you?" Myra asked, when Ellie let out a massive yawn. "Be honest with me."

"I'll sleep when I'm dead. Still, I should probably check to make sure there aren't any holes in my eyelids from the sticks propping them open," Ellie admitted.

"That's what I thought. Come on, I'll show you to our guest suite. Marsee, why don't you and Little Flower take the items we're keeping back up to your room, and take a nap as well. We'll deal with packing up the rest later."

Back in her room, Marsee set the large crate of items down next to Little Flower's nest and made a mental note to figure out something to put it all in later. For now, though, the crate would have to do. She was barely holding it together. Her anxiety and panic were on the verge of completely overwhelming her, and she could feel the beast inside her pacing and looking for cracks in her defenses while she was weak and distracted. Only her intense desire not to lose it completely in front of the Senior Guild Master had kept her from running away screaming.

The motion of her hanging bed always helped to calm her down, so she quickly raised it up off the floor and jumped in, closing the curtains behind her to make a warm and dark cocoon that blocked out some of the noise from the cooling unit.

Grabbing a pillow, she curled herself into a tight ball around it, trying to focus on nothing but timing her breathing to the rhythm of the swaying bed.

Three moons! What have I gotten myself into? she thought, *giving interviews to the press, ugh! I can't believe I said yes.*

She screamed into her pillow, letting her fear and panic out, but it was a long time before her heart stopped racing and her breathing slowed.

When her mother called her down for the evening meal, she'd almost managed to pull herself together. Hopping down from her bed, she found Little Flower propped up in her nest, drawing.

Little Flower looked up at her, giving her a quizzical expression, and climbed out of her own nest. After tucking the pencils into the pouches in her new garments, she waved Marsee over to look at her sketchbook.

Curious, Marsee stretched, her back and tail snapping and popping with the motion, and padded over to look, but she wasn't sure what to make of the drawings when she saw them or why Little Flower seemed so excited about them.

The first page had drawings of people: Little Flower, Marsee, her parents, the Guild Master, and Healer Brice. They were good, but nowhere near the quality of the drawings from earlier.

Little Flower turned the page over to reveal little sketches of the various rooms in the compound and one that looked like her habitat at the Agency. The next page had food, drink, and a dozen other items, while the last page was entirely full of Little Flower's face, with all sorts of different expressions. Some even had the color changed. One was red and another green, while others had arrows pointing up and down, and side to side.

Marsee shook her head and made the shrugging motion the cub used to express that she didn't know what Little Flower was trying to show her.

Little Flower turned back to the first page and pointed.

That's me, Marsee thought, and pointed to herself for confirmation.

Little Flower nodded, then pointed to the picture of Little Flower's face with what looked like tears running from her eyes.

Sad? Are you asking if I'm sad? Wait? Is this a picture dictionary?! Marsee wondered excitedly. She shook her head and scanned the images to find the one that looked like Little Flower when she thought Marsee was going to eat her.

"I'm scared."

Little Flower frowned at her reply and pointed to the curious-looking face.

Why? Oh, gods, how do I explain that? Marsee flipped the pages and pointed to the Guild Master.

Little Flower pointed to the Guild Master, then to the red, angry-looking face, and then back to the picture of Marsee.

Is the Guild Master angry with me? She shook her head no.

Little Flower frowned and did the same, but with her picture instead of Marsee's.

Is the Guild Master mad at you? Marsee shook her head no again.

Then Little Flower pointed to a picture of a knife and back to Little Flower.

Knife? Little Flower? What the heck does that mean? Oh! Are you asking if you're in danger? Marsee shook her head no again, harder this time, and then shrugged. *Sorry, Little Flower, I don't know how to tell you why I'm scared.*

Little Flower seemed to understand that there weren't enough words to explain it, but then pointed to the picture of the waste room.

"Do you need to use the waste room?" Marsee asked, even though she knew the cub couldn't hear her, but nodded her understanding anyway, and then, for good measure, pointed to the pictures of the waste room, the garden, fruit, and a drink. It was time for supper.

Little Flower nodded and put her harness on.

When they entered the garden, her parents and the Guild Master were already there, sprawled out by the pool and laughing. It was good to hear her mother laughing again, even if she herself still wanted to scream.

"Do you think Ammond ever forgave me?" Ellie asked.

Her mother chuckled. "I doubt it. It must have taken months for that green dye to wash out of his fur." Her mother turned to them as they approached. "Did you have a good nap?"

"Not really," Marsee admitted. "Too much to think about." Her mother nodded her understanding. "But Little Flower was busy," Marsee added. "She's drawn a dictionary."

"She drew what?!" Ellie asked, sitting up with her ears forward in excitement.

Marsee motioned to Little Flower and pointed to her sketchbook.

Little Flower handed it to her.

"She drew a lot of pictures to help us talk to her," Marsee explained. "People, foods, rooms, that kind of thing. I'm going to ask her to give a piece of fruit to Mama, or at least I'm going to try to."

Marsee pointed to Little Flower, a fruit, and her mother.

Without hesitation, Little Flower walked over to the cart with a tray of food on top and cautiously placed a foot on the bottom shelf to see if it would take her weight, which Marsee knew it could. When it proved to be stable, Little Flower climbed up to look at the items on the tray and picked up a piece of star fruit before jumping down and bringing it over to her mother.

"Fantastic! Let me see that!" Ellie said and held her hand out for the book. Her parents climbed to their feet and walked over to check out the book, too.

"This is wonderful!" Ellie said after flipping through a few pages. "What an incredible idea! Although I'm not sure about all these facial expressions. They're so hard to make out without ear and whisker positions. What do they all mean?"

"I'm not really sure about all of them, but I've figured out a few," Marsee said, and pointed. "This is happy, sad, scared, and angry. This one is curious or confused, or maybe just asking why. I think this one might be sick. That's kind of how she looked when she woke up the first day. I'm not really sure about the rest. She used the knife to represent danger or harm. She was scared I was going to eat her the first day when I went to cut up some fruit."

Little Flower wiggled her way in between all of them and reached for the book.

Ellie handed it back to her, and Little Flower began flipping through the pages and pointing.

Marsee spoke her translation. "Mama - Juice - Little Flower - Little Flower - Happy."

"I think she wants the star fruit juice, Mama. She seems to really like it," Marsee said after trying to figure out what the juice drawing indicated.

Her mother nodded and poured Little Flower something to drink.

"Little Flower - Happy - Juice - Mama," the cub pointed.

"That sounds like a thank you if I've ever heard one," Ellie said.

Her mother took the book and flipped through it herself. "Myra - Happy - Little Flower - Happy."

Little Flower smiled at her mother, took her book back, and carried both the book and her drink over by the pool. Once there, she set her drink on the stone, sat down, unhooked the leash, sending it flying back to Marsee, with a look that dared them all to say something, then with a chitter that Marsee was sure was another insult, the cub flipped open the book and started drawing again.

Ellie snorted at the cub's audacity and her father's expression. Marsee expected him to say something or put the leash back on himself, but he said and did nothing.

After a moment, Marsee walked over to the cart, put together a plate of fruit for the cub, and brought it over to her. She set the leash and plate down next to Little Flower but didn't hook the leash back on. If her father wasn't going to order the leash back on, Marsee certainly wasn't going to make her, and with everyone there, it wasn't likely the cub was going to run off, anyway.

After grabbing a plate for herself, she found an empty spot next to her father to sit. No one said anything.

Her mother was the first to break the silence. "Marsee, as soon as you figure out what each drawing represents, write what it means underneath. Try to work with her on that tomorrow as much as possible. Once we have the drawings identified, I'll have copies made and given to each of the healers to use with their charges. This should help a great deal."

"Be prepared for them to ask questions you won't be able to answer, though," Marsee warned, popping a piece of fruit in her mouth. "Little Flower already has."

"Oh?" her mother said. "Do you mean the drawing she did this afternoon?"

"No, this evening she asked if I was sad. I told her I was scared, but when I tried to explain why, the best I could do was tell her that she wasn't in danger. At least I think she understood."

"We really need to figure out a way to tell them what happened to their planet and that we are only trying to help," her mother said with a sigh in the cub's direction.

"Agreed. Have you given any thought as to how?" Ellie asked.

"I have," her mother replied. "And, I started working on it this afternoon while you were busy checking for holes in your eyelids. I asked Sampson for the bridge footage from the rescue so we could try to show her what happened. He said he would have that for me tomorrow. I'm not the best at editing videos, so that it might take a while, but I should be able to splice something together to show her what happened. We probably should wait until we have more words in that dictionary, though. She's going to have a lot of questions, and 'juice' isn't going to be one of the answers."

"Send the footage to me," Ellie ordered. "I'll put my best tech and writer on it. Between the two of them, we should be able to craft a video that explains what happened."

"Thanks, Ellie," her mother said. "That would be very helpful."

"So, Marsee. Your mother tells me you're famous now," her father said, changing the subject.

"Ugh, don't remind me." Marsee groaned and collapsed back

against the tree root behind her, rubbing her face with her paws. "I'd forgotten about it for three whole seconds."

"Try not to worry about it too much, everyone is going to be far more interested in Little Flower than you," her father said. "Think of yourself as her translator. Several of the councilors have personal translators on staff as they're not fluent or capable of speaking in all five of the languages."

She mulled that idea over. "Huh. I guess that might work. I'm really worried I'll freeze, though, especially if I have to answer questions in front of a lot of people. You know how I am around crowds and public speaking."

"That probably won't happen for a while, so we have time to practice," Ellie said. "You're not the first person to have problems with public speaking. At the first council meeting I had to speak at, as Senior Guild Master, I thought for sure I was going to pass out. It gets easier with practice, but we can control the format of any interviews to make you and Little Flower more comfortable. Think about what would help you, and we'll make it happen."

"Okay," Marsee said with a frown. "I'll try."

"Just be yourself and you'll be fine," Ellie said. Taking pressure off of Marsee, Ellie turned to her mother. "Have you heard anything from that old coot of a Mentor of yours, about Little Flower's ears yet?"

"Who are you calling an old coot?" boomed a loud voice from behind them.

MYRA: HOUSE CALL

*A*mmond! What are you doing here?" Myra exclaimed as they all turned in the direction of the gruff voice.

"What do you *think* I'm doing here? I'm making a house call, like you asked. Now get over here and give your 'old coot of a Mentor' a hug already. I haven't seen you in forever."

Myra scrambled to do as requested, then made a round of introductions. "Healer Ammond, I'm sure you remember Senior Guild Master Khihar."

"Do you honestly think I'd forget someone who dyed my fur green, even if they weren't the *Senior* Guild Master?" Ammond replied with mock indignation, but gave Ellie a hug anyway. "Looks like you turned out okay, though. Running the Guild now, eh? Bet you wish you were still making those rocking chairs. How's your tail by the way?"

"It's never been the same, but I'll survive," Ellie replied. "Do you forgive me for the paint job?"

"Forgive you? Ha! It's one of my favorite stories to tell! 'Let me tell you of the time the Senior Guild Master dyed my fur green!' Sadly, no one ever believes me. If only I'd taken a picture," Ammond pouted.

"I'd be glad to whip you up another batch of that stain any time you want. Just say the word," Ellie teased.

Ammond glared at her, but couldn't maintain it for more than a second before his tail curled. "And who is this young lady? This can't be Marsee? Why, she's all grown up!"

"Yes, this is my daughter, Marsee. She just had her adulthood ceremony a few days ago."

"*Already?!* Three moons. I am getting old," Ammond muttered.

"Nonsense, you don't look a day over nine hundred and twelve," Myra teased, and continued with the introductions, after receiving a mock growl and tail lashing from her mentor that made everyone laugh. "And you remember my partner, Jer?"

"Of course," Ammond said, nodding in respect to Jer. "Councilor, it's been a long time. I've seen the good work you've been doing for your district and for the refugees."

"Thank you. Myra speaks highly of you as well," Jer said.

"Sure, she does. I bet she has lots of wonderful things to say about the old coot," Ammond said with a wink. "So, where's this patient that only I could help?"

"She's over by the pond," Marsee said, pointing.

Little Flower was lying on the stones around the pool, looking down at the fish and sketching, completely oblivious to the new arrival.

"I'll get her," Marsee said and took off.

"What is she doing?" Ammond asked.

"She's drawing a picture dictionary," Ellie replied. "The cub's a talented artist."

"Really? I'm intrigued. I want to see this pictionary," Ammond said, as they watched Marsee get the cub's attention, and then ask her to follow.

"This is Little Flower," Myra said. "Marsee, Ammond would like to see the dictionary."

Marsee asked for the book from Little Flower and handed it over to Ammond, who flipped through the pages.

"I see what you mean. These drawings are simple, but they convey real meaning. Tell me. What are the squiggles below each picture?"

"What squiggles?" everyone asked at the same time, and then they all peered over at the book. Under each picture was a set of symbols that hadn't been there before.

"Bright Moons!" Ellie exclaimed. "That must be her word for each drawing! They have a written language! Of course, they have a written language. Why wouldn't they have one?"

Little Flower held her hand out for the book, which they gave her, and they all watched as she drew a quick sketch of Ammond.

"Little Flower - confused - Ammond," Marsee translated. "I think she wants to know who you are or why you're here."

"Little Flower - sick," Marsee responded, and then tapped Little Flower's ear. "Ammond - ear..." and then paused. "I'm not sure how to say healer," but then she tapped Healer Brice's image, figuring that could stand in for 'healer', and hoping the cub would understand.

"Little Flower - sad - ear - sick," the cub replied, which Marsee had no problems translating, and then Little Flower sketched a drawing of herself sitting on the ground rubbing her foot, which she drew in red.

"Little Flower...Ear...Rubbing Foot?" Marsee said, trying to understand. "Oh! That means hurt or in pain!" Marsee exclaimed. "Her ear is hurting her!"

"Can you tell her I'm going to try to help stop her ear from hurting?" Ammond asked.

Marsee nodded and tried to explain. "Ammond - Little Flower - ear - no - hurt."

Apparently, that worked, because Little Flower grinned up at them.

"Do you want to examine her now, or wait until morning?" Myra asked.

"I didn't come halfway around the planet, dragging all of my equipment with me, to *wait* until morning," he said, rolling his eyes and glaring back at her. "Although something to drink and a trip to the facilities first would be welcome."

"I think we can manage that," Myra said with a laugh. She had missed his glares. It had been far too long since she had seen him in person. "Drink first or facilities?"

"Facilities. Please!" Ammond replied, with a hint of desperation in his scratchy old voice.

Marsee let Little Flower know what was going on. After Ammond had a chance to freshen up a bit from his long trip, Marsee, Little Flower, and Jer left to prepare one of the guest rooms for Ammond to use, while Myra left with Ammond to help him unload his shuttle.

Ellie begged off to answer an urgent call from Nardal and promised to meet them as soon as she was done.

"Thank you for coming, Ammond. I wasn't even sure if you saw my message," Myra said, when they were alone.

"Of course, I came! They need my help, and you should know me by now. I was so intrigued by the scans you sent me that I completely forgot to send a reply. I was packed and almost here before I remembered I hadn't. Besides, I figured that fur-brained Council wouldn't approve her travel, so I came here instead. No one said I couldn't. What are they going to do about it anyway, throw me in quarantine? I'm going to be spending the next several months at the Agency anyway, so that's an empty threat."

Myra hugged her old mentor again. "You are? Thank you!"

Ammond huffed, but looked pleased. "If they are all as bad as she is, it's going to take a long time to help everyone. And besides, it would be impractical to ship them all to my clinic. Far easier to ship one old coot to them instead. Theresa will be following once she has everything packed up."

"What about your clinic?" Myra asked.

"Ahh, well...I...uh...I sort of retired about six months ago," Ammond said a bit sheepishly.

"What do you mean, *sort* of retired?" Myra asked.

"I handed the clinic over to a couple of young cubs right out of training. I've been mentoring them for a few years now. They're smart cubs with far more energy than I have. The last month or so, I've let them take charge and have only been assisting with consultations as needed."

"I didn't know," Myra said. "I'm sorry to have dragged you out of retirement."

"Oh, don't be. You had far more important things to worry about than me, and it was fine for all of about three days. My partner is already sick of me following her around our compound all day, trying to find something to do. Honestly, I've been bored silly, and haven't been this excited about a case in years."

Myra opened the back of his shuttle and found it so packed that there was barely room for Ammond to pilot the thing. "Did you leave any equipment at the clinic?" she asked.

"Ha!" he snorted. "Yes, the clinic is fine. We had backups of all of our equipment in storage, just in case something broke. I didn't know what I would need, so I brought everything. I know how long it takes for this equipment to get approved and built, so I figured you hadn't received anything yet, and we don't have time to wait. We only need to bring in this case and...this one, right now," Ammond said, pointing to a couple of black cases near the door. "The rest can wait until I know exactly what I'll need to treat her, assuming I can."

Myra grabbed the indicated cases, and Ammond shut the shuttle door again.

A few minutes later, they were all huddled in Ammond's guest suite, watching as he examined Little Flower. After performing a visual examination of her ears, he ran his scanners over her, then pulled some sort of odd-looking contraption out of one of the cases they'd brought in, and set it down gently on the desk Little Flower was currently sitting on.

He frowned for a moment and called Myra over to help. He had her hold the strange contraption while he spent the next several minutes hooking it up, until a massive collection of wires ran from the contraption to a box that was in the second case.

"Marsee, I'm going to run a specialized hearing test," Ammond said. "Can you tell Little Flower to raise her paw if she hears a sound?"

Marsee did her best to explain the instructions to the cub. "I think she understands," Marsee said finally, and sat on a nearby cushion.

Ammond placed something in each of Little Flower's ears before taking the large bowl-shaped contraption from Myra's paws, and placed it over the cub's head. He then made several adjustments to fit the shape and size of her head.

"How did you have equipment small enough to fit her?" Marsee asked the question Myra'd been wondering, but she'd learned not to interrupt her Mentor, knowing he would explain when he was ready.

To her surprise, he didn't grumble over the interruption like he usually did and answered Marsee's question.

"There are three main causes of hearing loss: birth defect, injury, and old age. A large percentage of my patients are young cubs, who are brought to me because their parents suspect something is wrong. It's not a perfect fit, since their heads are shaped differently, but it'll do for now. This device scans her brain to look for reactions to sounds since a young cub wouldn't be able to communicate as well as she can. I can compare the scans to what she says she can hear to get a better understanding of what's really going on. Now, I'll need everyone to be quiet until I'm done."

The tip of Myra's tail curled when the expected grumpiness returned at the command. *Some things never change,* she thought.

They sat there in silence for a good ten minutes as Ammond did something on his tablet. Little Flower never raised her paw, and as time went on, looked more and more dejected.

"I thought you said she heard something," Ammond said eventually.

"She did," Marsee insisted. "The motor on one of the hydroponics units is acting up. I know she heard it. She practically dragged me out of the garden and went straight to it. I heard it too."

"Technically, Marsee's the *only* one that heard it," Myra countered. "Neither Jeran nor I could hear anything."

Ammond twitched a whisker at that announcement. "Interesting. What did you hear, Marsee? What did it sound like?"

"It was a really high-pitched whine. Kind of like the chirps the flicker flyers make, but louder and more grating. Most of the electronics make a steady whine that I can usually tune out, but this had a sort of irregular cadence to it, like something was rubbing. I don't know how to explain it other than it made my brain itch."

"Flicker flyers don't chirp, Marsee," Jer said.

"Yes, they do," Marsee said, lashing her tail at her father. "I am sick to death of you telling me I can't hear the things I know I can hear. Please believe me, Papa. I heard the motor. I can hear the lights in this room, and I've heard the flicker flyers. They have several different chirps, one that they use for a greeting, one that means danger, and another that I think means hungry, that only the babies make."

Jer frowned, but didn't reply.

Marsee lashed her tail at him, then huffed and turned back to Ammond.

Ammond's whisker twitched again, but he didn't comment, either.

All of a sudden, Little Flower's hand shot straight up, and a smile lit up her face. Little Flower put her hand down after a moment, then raised it again and again. The fourth time, she hesitantly raised it, as if not sure she was hearing anything. That was the last time she raised her paw. Myra knew that didn't bode well, but the smile never left the cub's face.

Ammond took the contraption off of Little Flower's head and set it gently back in the case, then popped out the items he'd placed in her ears. "Marsee, if you don't mind, I'd like to test your hearing, too."

"Why?" Marsee asked, looking both concerned and annoyed. "I assure you, I can hear just fine."

"I believe you. I want to see just *how* well you can hear," Ammond explained.

Marsee calmed immediately, uncurled from her cushion, and walked over to the desk.

"We won't need the brain scanner for this, just the earpieces," Ammond said. "Same drill as before. Raise your hand when you hear a sound. Ammond placed a different set of earpieces gently in Marsee's ears and began the test.

When the test was done, Ammond took the earpieces back and put them away.

"Well?" Jer asked.

"I'll need a little time to review the result," Ammond replied. "Is there a bigger monitor I can hook up to? I brought one, but it's buried in my shuttle."

"You can use the monitor in my office. It's old, but still rated for medical use," Myra offered.

So they all followed her down the hall to her office, where everyone found a spot to sit or stand facing the monitor. Little Flower climbed up onto her chair and then onto the desk and sat with her feet dangling off the edge. Marsee sat on the floor next to her.

They waited without speaking as Ammond reviewed the test results, sometimes looking at his tablet and other times throwing images up on the monitor to examine something closer.

Myra flicked her ears back in surprise and stared at her daughter when Ammond brought up the results of Marsee's hearing test on the monitor and turned to the group.

"Okay, Marsee, let's start with you first, since your situation is the simplest. It will also give everyone else a basis for the discussion on Little Flower's issues. Before I begin, though, I want to confirm that you are okay discussing this with everyone in the room. If you want, I can ask everyone besides your mother to leave. She already knows, or should, if she hasn't forgotten *everything* I've taught her. As an adult, you now get to make medical decisions on your own behalf. That includes who you share this information with, including your parents and members of the Council."

"They can all hear. Please continue," Marsee said, giving her consent.

Ammond threw a different chart up on the monitor. "This chart shows the range of frequencies that our species can hear. This line, here, represents the normal range for an adult, and this one is the normal range for a child. As we age, we sometimes lose our hearing on the outer edges. For most people, this is not a problem, and we often don't even notice it. Injury is a different story, and can sometimes cause gaps to occur, as well as a reduction in the boundaries that you can hear. These points here and here are the outer ranges we've ever recorded of someone of our species being able to hear."

Ammond changed the graph and added two lines to the chart. "This is the result of your hearing test, Marsee. Your hearing is slightly better in your left ear. Modern electronics tend to emit frequencies in this range," he said, pointing to the screen. "As you can see, that overlaps with your upper range of hearing. It's no wonder that your brain itches around electronics. Mine would, too."

"You mean I haven't been imagining it? It's not all *just* in my head? I really *can* hear the lights and the pumps?" Marsee asked, her annoyance coming through her question.

"Marsee. Not only are you hearing those sounds. Your range of hearing far exceeds that of anyone ever recorded. Until today, I don't think anyone knew flicker fliers even made a noise. The biologists are going to have a field day with that information."

"Three moons!" Marsee exclaimed.

"Sounds like you no longer have an excuse to say you didn't hear me," her father teased.

"What one chooses to hear, or what they can process, is completely different from what they *can* hear," Ammond said with a wink towards Marsee, who had frowned and lashed her tail at her father's joke. "And while I can't do anything to fix that, I might be able to help you with your brain itch."

"You can?!" Marsee asked, her anger switching to excitement in an instant. "Really? How?"

"I've recently developed a special type of hearing aid that is designed to reduce certain frequencies commonly associated with background noises rather than amplify all sound. This makes it easier for some of my patients to hear in noisy places, like a crowded room. The volume of the room decreases, allowing other sounds, like people's speech, to come through more clearly. I see no reason why they shouldn't work on those higher frequencies as well."

"Really? That would be amazing! I hate crowds, especially when we're indoors. I get so overwhelmed with all the noise when everyone's talking. It gives me a headache trying to hear individual conversations. The voices all just jumble together. Sometimes it even makes me dizzy," Marsee said.

"I would imagine so," Ammond replied. "I'll get a pair out of my shuttle when we're done here, and you can try them out."

"Thank you!" Marsee said, and then gave her father an 'I told you so' look.

Myra frowned. She'd ignored Marsee's complaints for years, thinking she was just trying to get out of doing whatever she'd been asked to do, like tend the garden or go with them into town, not realizing that there was an actual physical complaint. She'd been so worried about her daughter's desire to be by herself that she hadn't taken Marsee seriously.

I should have brought her to have her hearing tested when she first said she could hear the lights.

Before she could apologize, Little Flower tugged on Marsee's fur, looking at her questioningly.

Marsee grabbed the notebook to try to explain and, as she'd done before, spoke aloud the symbols she was using for their benefit.

Marsee pointed to the normal line. "Mama - Jer - Ammond - Ellie - Ear." She then pointed to her own range. "Marsee - Ear." After pointing to the upper range, she added "Marsee - Head - Hurt. Ammond - Marsee - Head - No - Hurt."

Little Flower frowned, trying to puzzle it out. Then, to everyone's surprise, Little Flower pointed to Marsee, scratched her stubby claws along the desk, making a sharp noise, then covered her ears, making an expression of pain.

"I think she understands," Myra said, as Marsee nodded to Little Flower.

"Little Flower - Ear?" Little Flower asked.

Ammond displayed another line on the chart, with four tiny blue dots and maybe a dozen green ones. They all overlaid the upper part of Marsee's range.

Little Flower's shoulders slumped. "Little Flower - Ear - Sick - Sick," Little Flower said sadly.

Ammond nodded sadly in response.

"Ammond - Little Flower - Ear - No - Sick? No - Hurt?" Little Flower asked, looking hopeful.

Ammond didn't answer right away, which made Little Flower positively wilt. He sighed with a frown, then slowly knelt down so he could be face to face with her. He carefully lifted her chin to make her look him in the eyes.

Tears were streaming down her tiny face, which she wiped away with the back of her paw.

Ammond gently took the book out of her other paw, flipping through the pages, looking for a way to explain.

"Yes," he finally said. "Ammond - Little Flower - Ear - No - Hurt." He waited for her to nod, then continued. "Ammond - Little Flower - Ear - Yes - No - Sick."

Little Flower sniffed and wiped more tears off her face, but nodded her understanding.

To the rest, he said, "The good news is that I should be able to make her ear stop hurting tonight, but I'm not sure about restoring her hearing."

He handed the book to Marsee and climbed slowly back to his feet. Myra frowned at the signs of advanced age in her mentor, knowing she only had a few more years with him, if she were lucky.

"Let's start with her right ear. This is the one that showed the most signs of damage, both from the original scans after her rescue and the ones I took today."

Ammond looked to her to provide additional details about her injuries.

Myra pulled up a recording of Little Flower lying on an examination table. "This was taken during the initial triage during the rescue operation."

Little Flower pulled her knees up on the table and hugged them tight. Marsee put a comforting arm around the cub, and Little Flower leaned in.

"Oh, the poor cub," Ellie said, grabbing her own tail in sympathy.

The video showed the healers cutting away Little Flower's tattered clothing, careful of the severely broken arm. Her fur was matted with blood and debris, and her entire body looked to be one giant mass of cuts and bruises. As Myra detailed the extent of Little Flower's injuries, Marsee looked sick, and even Ammond, who had seen more than his fair share of traumatic injuries in his day, seemed affected.

"How did she even survive?" Ellie asked.

"Pure stubbornness, I think," Myra said. "She was up and walking around moments after her sedative wore off, although she was unsteady and needed the wall for support."

Ammond nodded. "So, you treated her ears for the cuts but did little else for her hearing loss?"

"That's correct. We did dose her with a round of nanos when she complained about her ears after waking, but that's all. She hasn't indicated to us that her ears were hurting her since that first day," Myra said. "But she was beaten fairly severely the other day by one of the males of her species. It's possible we missed an injury."

Ammond closed the video Myra had shown and fiddled with his tablet. A moment later, he opened another application. "I took the scans Myra sent me and put together a rough model of how I believe their hearing works. I'll be able to confirm this once I scan the others."

Marsee tried explaining to the small cub what Ammond was going to show.

When she was done, Ammond continued. "Sound enters the ear canal and makes this membrane vibrate. It's kind of like a tiny drum. This causes these three tiny bones to vibrate. That amplifies the sound by beating on this other membrane and causes the liquid in this spiral section to slosh. Kind of like if you tapped the side of a cup of water, you'd see ripples in the liquid on the surface."

Ammond zoomed in further. "The wave motion of the liquid then stimulates all of these tiny fur-like structures or hairs, which are actually nerve endings that are each tuned to a specific frequency. The ones on top trigger with lower frequencies, while the ones on the bottom trigger when there is a higher frequency. It's likely that this liquid is also involved in her sense of balance, as well as hearing. At least it is for us. Anyway, when one of these nerve endings is triggered, it sends an electrical impulse to this nerve and travels to this part of their brain for processing."

"Cool! Are our ears like that?" Marsee asked.

"Similar concept, but completely different structure, and thankfully one far less fragile, although I imagine we would have had fairly substantial hearing loss too if we'd been hit by that shockwave. I honestly can't even imagine what it must have been like on the surface." Ammond paused and shook his head. "Anyway, this is the scan taken shortly after Little Flower arrived at the agency."

"Little Flower - Ear - Agency," Marsee touched as she listened, and tapped the cub's right ear.

"Starting with the ear canal, you can see that the canal is completely closed off due to swelling and inflammation from the cuts she had. Sound wouldn't have been able to enter the ear at all."

He shifted the image. "Right here is where that first membrane should be, but it's completely missing. Most likely, the blast shredded it. As we continue, the swelling in the ear has completely pushed those three bones out of alignment, and if we zoom in close, this one here actually has a tiny fracture in it. Moving along to the spiral section..."

Ammond zoomed in again to show the fine hairs. "This is the worst of the damage. A large percentage of the hairs have been bent, broken, or completely sheared off."

He flipped to another scan, this one in far greater detail. "This is the scan I just took."

"Little Flower - Ear - Mama's Office."

"Starting with the ear canal, the swelling has gone away, except for one spot here, which I believe is the cause of her pain." Ammond pointed to the screen.

"Is that a scab peeling off?" Marsee asked.

"Good guess, and you're partially right. It *is* a scab, but it's what's *under* the scab that's probably causing her pain." Ammond tweaked the image slightly, and the scab started to glow."

"Why is it glowing?" Marsee asked.

"It's not. It's actually reflecting light. I believe it's a tiny piece of glass, or something similar. As her body tried to force it out, it would have swollen around it. My guess is that when she was hit in the head again this past week, she was hit with enough force to shift the shard enough to break through and let some of the pus and inflammation escape, which is why she was able to start hearing something again. It's been a fairly long time since the Cataclysm, though, so I'm not sure. It is possible that there just wasn't anything for her to hear at the Agency."

"The male who beat her, hit her repeatedly with one of his toys hard enough to shatter it," Myra said, "It's possible something broke off."

Ammond nodded. "That would make far more sense. Either way, I can take that shard out quite easily, and with another dose of nanos, she should be free of pain."

Marsee thought for a bit, trying to figure out how to translate, finally settling on "Little Flower - Knife - Ear," then tapped on the window behind her.

Little Flower nodded her understanding, so Ammond continued, although Myra wondered if the cub truly understood.

"This is where that first membrane should be. There's been some regrowth, but not much. All this white stuff is scar tissue. On the other side, those three bones have shifted back into position now that the swelling is gone. However, this one here that had the fracture has overgrown and attached itself to the bone next to it, which means it can't move as freely as it should. Both of these should be easily repairable with surgery, but I won't be able to do that here, as we'll need to regrow the membrane first. The real problem, though, is here."

He switched to the spiral structure and zoomed in. "She's lost most of the hairs, and what few remain are damaged, and unlike when we experience damage here, there's been no sign of regrowth since the first scan."

"So, what does that mean?" Ellie asked.

"It means that while the eardrum and bones can be fixed, she's never going to regain her full hearing in that ear," Ammond said, "But we might be able to make it a little better than it is now."

Little Flower tugged on Marsee's fur again, but Marsee didn't know how to explain. They just didn't have the words for it yet.

Finally, she tapped. "Ammond - knife - Little Flower - ear - Agency. Little Flower - ear - yes - no - sick."

Little Flower frowned but then tapped her other ear.

"What about her other ear?" Marsee asked, although they all understood the question.

"*That* ear is a completely different story." Ammond changed the image again. "This is from the original scan. There are only a couple of superficial cuts, and look at that membrane."

"It looks like it's got a tear in it," Marsee said.

"Correct. A fairly small tear at that. And, if you look at the scan I took today, you can see that it's actually all healed up."

"This is what I didn't understand, and why I contacted you," Myra said. "If her ear is all healed up, why can't she hear? Are the hairs damaged, too? My hand scanner isn't that precise."

"No, not particularly," Ammond replied. "There's some damage, but most of them are fine. She can't hear because she's never been able to hear in that ear. It's possible she never even knew it. The brain can compensate in amazing ways."

Ammond zoomed in. "The problem with this ear is that the nerve that is supposed to take the sound from her ear to her brain for processing never fully formed."

Marsee took the book and tapped. "Little Flower - Ear - No - Sick. Little Flower - No - Ear."

The cub frowned as she examined the screen again, then frowned at the sketchbook before pulling out her pencil and starting to sketch.

"What's this?" Marsee asked when Little Flower was done.

Myra leaned over to see a funny-looking creature that looked kind of like Little Flower but with different proportions. "That looks like one of their newborn cubs."

"Little Flower - Cub - No - Ear?" Little Flower asked.

Myra nodded, understanding immediately. "That's right! You couldn't hear as a cub."

Little Flower drew two other bipeds that looked like her, but with anatomical differences.

"That would be the male and female of the species," Myra said, tapping each.

"Little Flower - Male - No - Ear," Marsee spoke aloud, not really sure what that meant.

"Her father couldn't hear either?" Jer offered a possible translation.

"That would make sense," Ammond replied. "A defect like this could very well be hereditary."

"So can you fix her hearing?" Marsee once again asked the question they all wanted to know.

Ammond sighed. "Maybe." He paused to organize his thoughts. "For her right ear, we can remove the shard and treat her with another dose of nanos tonight. That will stop the pain she's experiencing, although I doubt it will do much else. The eardrum and fused bones will require surgery, but I'm not comfortable doing that until I've examined the others. What I can't fix are the broken and missing hairs in the spiral structure. It's possible that an injection of nanos directly into that section might repair them, but it might just make things worse. So basically, with surgery, we might be able to return some of her hearing, but probably not much. There were only the four tones she heard at normal volumes, but there were quite a few more that triggered the scan. Likely, she can hear those too, but they'd have to be really loud, someone yelling at the top of their lungs, a close thunder clap, that kind of thing. I might be able to develop a hearing aid that could boost those sounds that would fit the shape of her ear, but I'd be worried about further damaging the remaining hairs with a volume that loud."

"And the other ear?" Myra asked.

Ammond shrugged. "Maybe in the future we can develop some way to connect that nerve, but repairing that would require brain surgery and significant risk to Little Flower, which I can't recommend at this time."

Myra nodded, expecting that response, hoping perhaps her Mentor had other ideas.

"But that's not the biggest problem we face," Ammond continued.

"What else is there?" Myra asked, surprised, as she'd not been aware of any other medical issues. It was bad enough that she'd missed the shard and the nerve. She should have caught that even with her hand scanner.

In response, Ammond brought up the original chart with Marsee's hearing test, and overlaid it with the cubs. "If I'm correct, the sounds she heard were towards the lower end of her range of hearing, which means even if her hearing is fully restored, she wouldn't be able to hear us speak. Our natural speaking voices are in this range here, far lower than what she would be able to register. She should be able to hear Marsee or young cubs, but not the adults unless they talk in a really high voice. As you know, our voices deepen significantly as we transition into our fertility stage. Additionally, Marsee is likely the only person on this planet, if not all five, who is able to fully hear her when she speaks."

The room sat in stunned silence at Ammond's announcement.

Marsee was the first to speak up. "Are you saying that if I want to continue hearing her, I can't use the hearing aids you mentioned for me earlier?"

Marsee looked crushed.

Ammond hemmed. "For now, yes. It's possible we could build devices to shift our voices into the range the others could hear. But if the other biped's hearing loss is as bad as hers, and I imagine it will be, birth defect aside, there might not be a point until the next generation is born."

"So, what do you suggest?" Ellie asked. "This is going to make communicating with them very challenging, if not impossible."

"Two things," Ammond replied. "One, continue building out that pictionary. The more words and concepts we have, the better. Secondly, sign language."

"What language?" Jer asked.

"It's a language made up of hand and body motions that some of my deaf patients have started using so they don't have to write everything to communicate with each other. It's an extension of the movements we already use, but with more purpose. It would have to be modified to account for the way her body moves. Our sign language heavily depends on ear, whisker, and tail position for emphasis, as well as complex finger and claw motions. I'll send you Sina's contact information. She's the one who came up with the idea. If we can match up Little Flower's drawings and written language with our written language and Sina's sign language, I think we can come up with a way for us all to communicate."

Ammond set his tablet down on the desk.

"I'm going to grab the items I need to remove that glass shard. Marsee, do you still want the hearing aids?"

"I don't know," Marsee replied with a sigh. "I don't want to give up being able to hear Little Flower, but there are times when I would really like some peace and quiet."

Ammond nodded his understanding. "I'll bring them, and you can try them out. You'll be able to turn them off whenever you want, and I'll show you how to adjust which frequencies are filtered out so you can figure out what works best for you."

Marsee nodded, and Ammond left the room.

Her daughter let out a heavy sigh, then told Little Flower that Ammond was going to remove the glass shard, and tried to answer some of her questions while they waited.

Ammond returned with a case. He set it down on the desk and pulled out several items, which he placed on a tray beside Little Flower.

At Ammond's request, Myra grabbed the small container of nano wash she'd brought with her from the Agency. Their regular nano wash worked to an extent, but this had been adjusted specifically to work with the bipeds' anatomy.

Carefully tilting Little Flower's head to the side, he placed several drops of numbing agent in her ear. "This will numb the ear so she doesn't feel anything," he explained to the rest of the room.

The cub shivered as the liquid entered her ear, but otherwise she didn't move, as Ammond stood there and counted to thirty, before letting her tilt her head back up. Some liquid ran out of the ear, which he wiped away with an absorbent pad.

"Myra, I need you to hold her head perfectly still," Ammond ordered.

She walked over and gently took the cub's head in her paws, taking extra care to ensure she wasn't covering her nose and mouth, as her paws practically engulfed the tiny cub's head.

Little Flower didn't move a muscle or appear to be scared, impressing Myra with her bravery, trust, and understanding that they were trying to help.

She was just as brave after her rescue, Myra remembered, but knew that if she'd tried this with her or any of the bipeds even a few days earlier, she'd have been bitten. They'd long since used up any trust the bipeds might have had for them, and she'd seen just how strongly Little Flower had reacted to Brice.

I'd probably hate her, too, if I'd been held as long as her without knowing why. Honestly, if it hadn't been for the progress her daughter had made with communicating with the little cub, they'd probably have had to sedate her to ensure she didn't move. I wonder if she remembers me from her infected arm?

While Myra's thoughts were distracted, her hands remained steady as Ammond grabbed the scope and turned it on. The monitor on the wall switched to a fuzzy image.

She refocused her thoughts as Ammond adjusted the cub's head slightly and inserted the scope into her ear. On the screen, they could now see the inside of Little Flower's ear blown up huge. Once the scab was located, Ammond grabbed a pair of tweezers and they all watched as he gently pulled the scab off, causing all sorts of pus and gunk to ooze out of the wound.

"Ewww…" Marsee said quietly, causing the others in the room to chuckle, all except for Ammond and Myra, who remained still and quiet. Although if you'd looked closely, Ammond's whiskers twitched slightly in restrained humor.

After flushing out the ear with some of the nano wash and clearing away some of the pus so he could better see the shard, he carefully grabbed hold of it and slowly pulled it out. As he did, significantly more pus and blood ran out of the wound.

"Ugh. Moons. I think I'm going to be sick," Marsee said, and bolted out of the room.

Ammond held the tiny glass shard up so Little Flower could see it, then placed it on another piece of gauze. Setting the tweezers down, he grabbed the nano wash again and flushed it out, clearing out more of the puss and gunk. He checked on it again, pressing lightly against the sides of the wound to push out more, and continued to repeat the process several more times until it stopped oozing.

When he was done, he dripped several more drops of the nano wash into her ear and waited for several minutes before tipping her head back up. Unlike before, nothing dripped out this time.

"Thank you, Myra. That should do it," he said, and she let go of Little Flower's head.

Little Flower went to rub her ear, but Ammond stopped her and shook his head. She nodded her understanding and put her paw down.

"Is it over?" Marsee asked from the hall, and everyone burst out laughing. Surgery complete, Myra allowed her tail to curl in amusement.

Even her grumpy old Mentor chuckled. "Yes, you can come back in. The gross stuff is over," he called out.

"Did it work?" Marsee asked, peering around the corner, to confirm before stepping back inside.

"The shard is out and we'll check in the morning to see how well the nanos do to clear up the remaining infection," Ammond said, then picked up Little Flower's book. "Little Flower - Ear - Hurt?" he asked.

She shook her head no.

He grinned. "Little Flower - Ear - Hurt - See - Ammond," he instructed, pointing to his eyes for 'see' "Marsee, if you see her rubbing at her ear, let me or your mother know immediately."

"Yes, sir," Marsee responded, and nodded her head in under-standing.

That head motion for yes and no is being picked up quickly, Myra thought, as she took the used gauze and piece of glass and tossed them in the recycler next to her desk. She wiped down the devices

Ammond had used in his surgery before putting them back in their protective cases, where they would be fully sanitized for the next use.

Ammond squinted at her, watching as if to make sure she was doing it right. Her tail curled, amused by his act, which hadn't changed since she was an Apprentice. After a moment, he snorted at some internal thought and unclipped a small black case from his carry harness.

"Now for you, Marsee," Ammond said, holding up the case and flipping it open to reveal two devices similar to the ones he'd used to run the hearing test. "Let's see how these fit."

He proceeded to show her how they went in, checked the fit, popped them back out again, placed a silicone sleeve around them, and tried again.

"There, that should fit comfortably. I'll leave you with additional sleeves so you can try different thicknesses if your ears start to hurt or they don't stay in place. "Now, let's turn them on and see how they do."

Marsee gasped. "Oh, it's so quiet!" she whispered, then frowned. "My voice sounds funny. La la la la."

"You'll get used to that," Ammond said with a chuckle. "How do I sound?"

Marsee tilted her head. "You sound the same," she said after considering.

"Good. Now, to control it, you'll want to pair the devices with your tablet just like you would a set of speakers. I've sent an app to your mother, which she can pass along to you."

He flung the app up on the monitor. "They should last at least a month with continuous use before you need to recharge them. This setting allows you to control which frequencies you want to filter out." Ammond demonstrated by adjusting the sliders. "Or you can have complete noise canceling, if you want, just by clicking here. The best part, in my opinion, is that you can use them like miniature speakers, but if you click here, you can change between whether you want to allow outside sounds to come through or not, and you can control the volume of the outside noises with whatever you are listening to on your device. You can save your settings so you don't have to configure them every time. When you take them out of your ear, they will automatically go into standby until you put them back in or turn them off."

"Oh, that is so cool!" Marsee said. "Thank you!"

"Cool indeed," Ellie said. "I want a pair! Just think about it, Jer. Pop those in during a resource allocation meeting, and tune everyone out...ahh...such blissful silence!"

Everyone laughed but Jer.

He just sat there, brow raised and staring at Ellie, then finally shook his head. "In theory, it sounds like a wonderful idea, but I have a hard enough time staying awake in those meetings as it is. *You* might be able to nap and get away with it, but if *I* fell asleep, I would never hear the end of it from my brother." Jer let out a full-body shudder and poofed his fur dramatically.

The entire room burst out laughing again, but none so hard as Ellie, who couldn't stop laughing for several minutes.

JESSICA: HEARING IMPAIRED

After the piece of glass had been removed from her ear, Jessica sat there, arms wrapped around her knees, trying to come to grips with the reality of her hearing loss, while she absently watched the doctor treat Marsee.

When they all burst out laughing, it just highlighted the fact that she couldn't hear or understand them. She wasn't sure of all of the details, but her high school biology class had left her with enough understanding of what was being shown to know that her hearing loss was bad, really, really bad.

You were stupid to get your hopes up, she told herself.

Oddly enough, though, she was far more surprised to find out she'd been deaf in one ear since she was born than the extent of the damage from the attack.

I wonder if my parents ever knew? They must have, what with Dad's hearing loss. They must have checked my hearing, but why didn't they ever tell me?

Cali's sudden departure from the room, a few minutes later, surprised her out of her thoughts.

Where is she going? Jessica wondered, surprised to be left alone with the adults who were still talking about something. The hearing chart briefly returned to the screen before the monitor was turned off entirely. Still talking, the ear doctor did a quick scan of her ear and finished packing up.

The next thing she knew, the large, gold-colored cat scooped her up and carried her down the hall after the others. She was used to Cali carrying her now, but she felt positively tiny in this cat's giant paws. They stopped briefly at the room where the tests had been done so the ear doctor could put the medical equipment away, and then she was carried back out to the garden.

To her surprise, once inside, they shut the door and removed her harness before setting her down. She stood there watching as they all grabbed more refreshments and found places to lounge and talk, completely ignoring her.

She looked up at the moons, nearly full in their splendor, and so bright that she had no problem seeing. Needing privacy to think, she wandered off into the garden until she found a secluded location away from everyone and sat down, enjoying even the slightest semblance of freedom.

Leaning against one of the massive roots from the giant twisting tree in the center of the garden, she let out a long, slow breath, letting the peacefulness of the garden calm her, as she watched the strange flickering creatures dance from one exotic glowing flower to the next.

As she sat there, her mind racing with thoughts too fast to latch onto, one of the creatures flew down and hovered in front of her. Then, to her surprise, landed on her outstretched foot, letting out the tiniest of woofs.

She jumped slightly, far more shocked to have actually heard the creature.

It fluttered its wings and hovered, startled by her motion, but a moment later, it settled back on her foot. It was about the size of a robin but looked more like a puppy crossed with a dragonfly. Four iridescent wings flashed at her in a multitude of rainbow colors, as the creature tilted its head to look at her. Its body was covered in what looked like brown fur, and it had large floppy ears and two beautiful dark eyes. Between the ears, tiny antennae twitched in her direction. It was the most adorable creature she'd ever seen.

"Hello there," she said quietly, "Aren't you the cutest little thing!"

The tiny creature puffed out its chest almost as if it knew she was an admirer.

Slowly opening her sketchbook, she started drawing the tiny creature. It sat there and watched her as she drew, fluttering its flickering wings occasionally. She'd nearly finished the sketch when it hopped down onto her leg and walked up to look down at the paper.

"That's you," she said softly and slowly turned the book around, trying not to scare it. The puppy-fly…

No, it's far too majestic a creature to be called a bug, she thought. *Fairy dog? That'll work.*

The fairy dog tilted its head adorably, wagged its tiny tail, woofed, and then hopped up and down a couple of times before suddenly flying away.

"I don't know if that means you liked it or not," she chuckled after it.

Shrugging, she pulled out the colored pencils and started adding details to the sketch, hoping the act of drawing would calm her racing thoughts. She didn't look up until she felt something touch her foot.

"Woof woof!"

Her little friend was back, and there were several more with him.

"You brought your friends to see?" she asked, then held up the drawing so the others could look.

Lights flickered back and forth between them.

They must be talking to each other, she thought. *How much do they understand?*

The first one poofed out his fur and looked for all the world as if he were admiring himself, his little tail wagging for all its worth.

"Yes. You're very handsome," she told him.

One of the others flitted up to land on the back side of her other foot. Its tiny front paws held on to her shoe as it peered out from behind her foot. Clearly shyer than the first one, this one had blue fur and a narrower body.

"Hello there. Would you like your picture drawn, too?" she asked.

The creature let out a swirl of colors in response.

"I'll take that as a yes," she said, and started drawing.

She kept drawing as the others gained the confidence that she wasn't going to harm them and landed on her shoulders and hair to watch. When she was done, she turned the drawing to show the second creature, who hopped down on Jessica's leg to examine it closely, then hopped up and down like the first had, colors swirling.

"Woof! Woof! Woof!" the first one said, and suddenly they all took off.

She looked around to see what had startled them, but couldn't see anything, so she shrugged and flipped back through the drawings she'd done earlier in the day, and thought about everything that had happened.

The morning had been absolutely amazing. All of the clothing the black one had brought: strangely shaped sunglasses, floppy wicker-like hats, different shoes, and all the time they'd taken to make sure it all fit comfortably. It was like her fairy godmother had shown up with clothes for the ball.

Then they actually went outside, like *really* outside, not just in the garden. It had been a short walk, just around the perimeter of the complex, but she'd been exhausted by the time they went back inside. It was hard walking in the loose sand that surrounded the complex, but the clothing and protective gear had worked.

The sunglasses were bulkier than she was used to, wrapping around the side of her face, but she supposed that was a good thing, considering how bright this world was.

Everything was so different, even the rocks. That thought reminded her, and she felt in her pocket for one of the rocks she'd picked up. It was a smooth, heart-shaped rock that had a rainbow of colors swirling through it, like the mountains in the distance. In the moonlight, it sparkled.

It wasn't just the rocks. Every plant and creature she'd looked at had been so far outside of what she was used to that she didn't know what to make of half of it. A few, they'd warned her not to get too close to, and she'd examined them carefully for future reference. Off in the distance, there had been a herd of massive six-legged mammoth-like creatures with giant curving tusks and pink fur.

Pink?! What kind of evolutionary advantage does that give? she wondered.

Sadly, her euphoria had faded shortly after they returned to the living room. Something the black one had said or wanted had upset and scared her kitten badly, and that positively terrified her. She was pretty sure that they were talking about her since they kept looking in her direction.

She'd been drawing all of the good things that had happened, in an attempt to counteract her own fears and the darkness and horror that she'd drawn the night before. She also wanted to show how much she appreciated what they were now doing for her, in the hopes it would continue.

They seemed to be impressed with her drawings.

No, not impressed, shocked, she decided, as if they didn't expect her to be able to draw. *I suppose I'd be just as surprised if my grandfather's old barn cat suddenly started drawing.*

She still didn't have a clue what they wanted with her, but she prayed that if they were actually taking the time and effort to protect her and make her happy, that she wasn't actually a prisoner or their future lunch, and was leaning heavily towards the pampered pet theory.

It helped that she'd not seen them eat anything but the same foods they gave her, all of which appeared to be raw fruits and vegetables. She hadn't seen any indication that they ate meat or cooked their food, although she still wasn't sure what many of the foods were.

Her thoughts drifted back to Cali, who had remained tense the rest of the afternoon, especially when around the black cat. The moment they'd left the others, Cali's tail had poofed out so thick that it must have hurt. When they'd returned to the bedroom, Cali had sealed herself in her swinging bed and roared so loudly that she'd actually heard it.

On the edge of panic herself, she'd scrambled to figure out a way to find out what was wrong.

If it scared one of them, it had to be bad, she thought.

She'd finally had the idea of expanding on the drawings she'd used during the tailoring session to build a lexicon of words, remembering the sound board one of her classmates had used to talk. The idea had been an instant success, and she was finally able to communicate with them, albeit haltingly. It was far better than what she'd had before, and something she could expand on.

Cali had quickly assured her that she wasn't in danger, but she hadn't been able to explain what was wrong or why she was scared.

But out of everything that had happened, the best part of her day had been the change in how everyone was interacting with her.

Her fairy godmother had seemed livid at the fact that she was being forced to wear a leash. The speed at which Cali had taken it off had been impressive, but then they'd made her put it back on to go outside.

She'd pushed her luck by unhooking the leash earlier, but they hadn't said anything, and they'd all turned to look at Foxy for his reaction. The look the copper cat had given her had been calm but highly calculated. Foxy's only reaction had been a slight snort as if she'd surprised them by her disobedience. She was quite sure now that Foxy was in charge, at least out of this group, even though Foxy had waited on the others, preparing food for them and fixing up a room for the grey cat.

She glanced down at where the harness had been. Even though the gold cat had taken it off, she could still feel its weight and knew she wasn't really free. Still, she was pretty sure that the people here didn't want her to have to wear it. She really wanted to know who did, and why. She just didn't have the words to ask.

Her thoughts and gaze drifted over to her dictionary. Over the course of the day, they'd slowly shifted from treating her like a pet or animal to finally seeming to see her as an intelligent and talented creature, but it had been the dictionary that had changed everything. She'd clearly shocked everyone by adding words below each drawing, but from that moment, their entire demeanor had changed. That was the moment they'd finally seen her as a person.

The ear doctor was a bit of an enigma, though. She couldn't figure out where he fit into their hierarchy. She had the sense of really old age with him, somehow reminding her of her grandfather Ben, gruff and grumbly on the exterior, but with a kind heart.

She also wasn't sure why, but she had a sense of male about him, although there wasn't anything remotely different about him than any of the others, outside of the color of his coat and size. He was about the same size as Foxy, and wondered if that had anything to do with age or sex.

I wonder if the males are smaller than the females? she thought, *although I could be completely wrong about the ear doctor. It could be the other way around.* She made a mental note to try to figure out a way to ask that later.

The gray cat had moved slower than the others, not much, but enough that she could tell he was in some pain, and there was a smattering of white around his nose and ears that reminded her of her grandfather's old dog. What was interesting was the way Goldy and her fairy godmother seemed to respect him, much like Cali did with her fairy godmother, although he didn't have the same sense of authority that the copper and black cats did. His kindness and empathy were unmistakable, though.

As she thought, Jessica drew a quick sketch of Goldy and Gray hugging in the garden. She'd had the impression that it had been a long time since they'd seen each other, and that they cared deeply about each other.

Cali's grandfather? she wondered. *Nah, Cali hadn't known him.* One of *Goldy's instructors, perhaps? They are both doctors.* That seemed the most likely.

She sighed at the reminder of her damaged hearing. When Cali had said Grey was there to treat her ears, hope had bloomed so fiercely in her heart that it had hurt, but then the hearing test had gone on forever before she finally heard anything. She sketched the scene of them in the examination room, the odd helmet on her head, and everyone watching.

When she'd finally heard the tones, though, it was like fireworks going off. She was so happy! But then, seeing the recording of her injuries after the attack brought a flood of memories that she didn't want to think about. She'd been filled with fear and anxiety and close to panic again. *Why are they even bothering to fix me up after they'd hurt me so badly in the first place?*

She'd been shocked at the extent of her injuries, not realizing just how badly she'd been hurt, outside of the broken arm. Then, as Gray went over the results of the examination and she could see how badly her ears were injured, she just knew that she was never going to hear again.

At least my ear has stopped hurting, she thought. That was something, and there wasn't much to be done if she'd inherited her father's hearing loss. He'd been to multiple specialists over the years with no success.

She drew a sketch of her damaged ear and then paused as the image of the hearing chart kept flashing in her brain. There was something she was missing. She drew what she could remember of the chart and the different lines that had been on it, then stared at it.

What am I missing? she asked herself, as she tapped her pencil on the paper, trying to puzzle it out.

Okay. Take it one step at a time. This line represents their normal hearing range. This one was Cali's, and this one was mine. So, what does this tell you? We know Cali hears better than average, and that it was bothering her like nails on a chalkboard.

"Oh crap!" she said, suddenly putting the pieces together.

Even if I could hear, I wouldn't be able to hear them, and they can't hear me! Our charts don't overlap. Well, Cali's does, but the others don't. Is that why Doc never responded when I spoke?

She sat and thought about what this would mean for her future and the complications it would cause, and then another thought occurred to her, suddenly pivoting the past week in a new light.

All of the kindness she'd been shown these past few days grated harshly against the hate that she had for all their kind because of what Doc had either done to her or allowed to happen.

Was it possible they never heard me call for help? Would they have come if they had?

Jessica scooped up her pencils, which were spread out around her, and bolted back to the clearing. She had to know for sure.

When she ran into the clearing, they all turned to look at her, and she could see the alarm on their faces at her appearance at a run, but she didn't care, although she noticed that Marsee had joined them again.

She skidded to a stop next to Gray and pointed frantically to the graph. She then tapped out her question as best she could. "If my ear wasn't injured, would I be able to hear you, or would you be able to hear me?" she asked.

Gray shook his head sadly and then tapped out. "You can hear Cali but not the rest of us, and she can hear you, but we can't." It was far rougher than that, but he got the point across.

Jessica nodded her understanding. Her emotions were in a whirl. She just didn't know what to think or what to even say.

Does this change anything? Did they really want what had happened, or was that entirely his idea and doing? If not, why did they put us together? Why did they capture us in the first place? Ugh.

She pulled at her hair, trying to form a coherent question when all of them wanted to be answered at once, and she didn't have the words to ask any of them.

"Are you okay?" he asked.

"No. I'm not okay. I'm sad, angry, confused, and hurt," she told him in a rush. Then, unable to articulate further, she let out a scream of frustration, threw her sketchbook to the ground, and took off at a full run, trying to escape her emotions. When she found herself back in her secluded spot, she threw herself down on the ground, burying her head in her arms, and started to cry.

Goldy apparently followed her, because a few moments later the big cat sat down beside her, and gently stroked the back of her head.

When Jessica looked up, Goldy opened their arms, offering a hug.

What she needed in that moment, more than anything, was her mother, but her mother wasn't there and was probably dead in the attack. She didn't know what to feel, or think, or even who she could trust, but Goldy had been kind to her and had treated her injuries.

More than anything, she needed a hug and to feel safe, and she needed to know she wasn't alone anymore. So, with a hiccupping sob, she climbed onto the big cat's lap, leaned up against their soft fur, and allowed herself to be comforted, to be held, and to be soothed by the gentle vibration of their purr, not sure if she could trust them, but taking the solace they offered anyway.

They stayed that way for a long time, until Jessica, emotionally and physically worn out, fell asleep.

39

MARSEE: STAR FRUIT AND SIGN LANGUAGE

The next morning, Marsee woke early, long before Little Flower, with the first of the two suns just barely starting to peak above the horizon. The night before, her mother had carried the exhausted cub back up to Marsee's room, unwilling to transfer her over to Marsee's arms, saying that she didn't want to risk waking her in the transfer, but Marsee knew that look.

It was the same one her mother had when she'd held Marsee's younger nephlings when they were tiny cubs. Her mother wanted, needed cubs, *lots* of cubs, and when she'd only had one cub with her second litter, she transferred all of that need onto her grand cubs and the cubs of the surrounding community.

And, well, it was hard not to be thoroughly enamored by Little Flower. She was adorable when she slept, a whirlwind of barely controlled curiosity when she was awake, and somehow managing far better with her situation than she had any right to. That she managed to keep it together as well as she had for so long was a testament to her tenacity.

Marsee couldn't even imagine going through everything that poor cub had gone through: losing her family, her home, her very planet, and then finding out she'd also lost her hearing, and even if she hadn't wouldn't ever be able to hear those around her talk, or ever be heard again.

The poor cub, Marsee thought, with a heavy sigh.

She decided then and there that she was going to do everything she could to become fluent in this language of body motions that Healer Ammond had mentioned. That way, Little Flower would have at least one person she could talk to, and if that meant she would have to be Little Flower's translator in front of a large crowd of people, then so be it. As much as that thought terrified her, her friend deserved and needed a voice.

After her mother had tucked Little Flower into her nest with her favorite stuffy, she and her mother had sat out on the balcony and talked about everything that had happened that day.

Her mother had apologized for not taking her hearing issues seriously, and Marsee had taken the opportunity to talk frankly about some of the other issues she had, although not all of them. She still couldn't bring herself to talk about what had happened with her instinct. She'd tried, but the words wouldn't form, almost as if her instinct was stopping her.

But her mother had listened patiently to the things she had been able to say: how her body felt like it was going to vibrate itself apart if she didn't move, how her heart raced any time she had to be around crowds until she felt dizzy and like she couldn't breathe, how the electronics hurt until she couldn't stand it and had to leave the room, and, while her mother indicated she wasn't sure how to help her, she had promised that she would look into it. She knew her mother well enough to know that she wouldn't stop until she found a cure.

Marsee had taken notes of the day's events before bed, but her mother said she would handle the council's report for her and that she should try to get some sleep instead. Even still, it had taken Marsee hours to fall asleep, and that sleep had been far from restful.

She'd been plagued by night terrors, where she'd been trying to warn her friend that she was being hunted, but Little Flower hadn't heard. She'd woken just as the amorphous shape of her hunting instinct had leapt to pounce.

"Not on my watch," she growled, and lay there watching Little Flower sleep for a long time.

Eventually, she popped her new hearing aids in and fiddled with the programming, adjusting them until the cooling unit's grating whine disappeared. The quiet was so profound that she nearly wept.

Glancing over at Little Flower sleeping peacefully, she sighed and stored them back in their case.

I could really use one of Little Flower's carry sacks. Maybe I can figure out a way to clip them onto my fur so I wouldn't have to wear my carry harness all the time, Marsee thought, examining the case. *Nah, that would just pull on my fur. Oh well,* she thought, and tossed the case on her bed. *I'm hungry. Time for breakfast.*

There's a lovely snack right in front of you, her instinct suggested.

She growled and swiped at her instinct. *She's not food. Leave her alone!*

It backed off, but Marsee lay on the bed, shaking with fear.

What is wrong with me? Why do I keep having these thoughts?

There is nothing wrong with you. You are a fierce predator, and she's yummy smelling prey, it answered. **It is only natural for you to have these thoughts.**

She's my friend and I don't eat my friends. So just stop! she replied with another low growl. It didn't answer, and she felt it back off.

It was a long time before she felt safe to move and had nearly drifted off to sleep again before her need to pee became too painful to ignore. With a massive yawn, she jumped down off her bed, stretched, and padded over to Little Flower on all fours. She carefully nudged the cub awake, after double-checking that all of her claws were still sheathed.

Little Flower opened her eyes and looked around, seemingly surprised to find herself back in her nest.

With a shrug, the little cub climbed out of her nest, stretched, and changed into a different outfit. Two separate pieces this time, one for her legs and another for her body and arms, along with the tiny undergarment that went on beneath the leg protection.

They'd had a long discussion about the purpose of the smaller garments, as they'd all been surprised when she'd put both sets on. But it had been Marsee, who had first understood. When the tiny cub had rejected several, she'd examined the fabrics of the various pieces and realized they were necessary to keep the rougher materials from rubbing against her more sensitive areas.

She'd noticed the cub wincing when applying more of the pain cream to those areas, so she imagined they were still bruised from her beating. Ellie had accepted her reasoning without question and sent instructions back to remove the seams from between the legs and to use softer material.

When they'd found the chafing from her foot protection, it had confirmed her suspicions. Her skin was far more delicate than any of them had realized.

Marsee waited as the cub put on her footwear, shoved her sketchbooks and pencils into the carry sacks, clipped on her harness, and put on her eye and head protection, before finally giving Marsee that strange thumbs-up hand position to indicate she was ready.

How exhausting it must be to have to go through all that effort, just to go outside, Marsee thought. But with the cub safely outfitted, Marsee clipped the leash on and they made their way down for breakfast, where they found Ammond and both her parents in the family room.

"Morning. Where's Ellie?" Marsee asked her mother through another yawn.

"She left early this morning to deal with an issue at the Guild. She'll be back in a few days with more supplies for Little Flower and the others," her mother replied.

"Oh," Marsee said, surprised to find out she'd already left, and sad to have missed saying goodbye. "Mama said you were leaving today, too," she asked Ammond, while she poured Little Flower a glass of her favorite fruit juice.

"I am. After I finish my breakfast and check on Little Flower, your mother and I are heading to the Agency."

Marsee looked at her mother, concerned. "What if something happens to Little Flower?" she asked.

What if I hurt her? Marsee thought, but didn't say that out loud.

"I'll be back this evening, and your father will still be here. If there's an emergency, your father can fly you over to the Agency. Otherwise, I can make it back in half an hour or so with the ground crawler."

"I only have a few committee meetings today, but nothing super important," her father added. "If anything happens, feel free to interrupt."

"Okay," she said, as she grabbed her own breakfast off the trays and sat next to Little Flower, who had climbed onto her favorite place by the window, but Marsee's thoughts were in a whirlwind of panic.

"Do you have any plans for today?" her mother asked, and when Marsee didn't reply, called out her name. "Marsee?"

"Huh?" Marsee asked, not having processed what her mother had asked.

"Do you have any plans for today?" her mother repeated.

"Oh, yeah. I want to contact Sina about the sign language course and see if we can start learning some of it. Then maybe play some games or go for a walk around the compound again, if Little Flower wants to."

Her mother nodded. "Sounds like a plan. However, I could use your help in the garden, too. It looks like the star fruit is ready to start picking."

Marsee groaned and slumped back against the window. "Not the star fruit…"

"Little Flower is going to be very disappointed if we run out of her favorite fruit juice," her father teased.

"Fine…" Marsee muttered, with a heavy sigh. "I'll do that first, before it gets too hot out for her." She loathed picking star fruit. They were just so tiny, and the branches had evil little thorns that always got stuck in her fur.

"Think of it this way, you'll get to test out your new hearing aids," her father said. "Where are they, by the way?" he asked, seeing that she wasn't wearing them.

"In my room. I'm still not sure how I feel about not being able to hear Little Flower, and I didn't feel like putting on my carry harness this morning. I wish I had one of Little Flower's carry pouches so I didn't have to wear the harness just to hold the case," Marsee explained.

"Well, maybe the two of you can figure something out," her father said, then squinted his eyes at her. "*After* you're done picking the star fruit. I know you. If you start a project like that, you'd end up working on it for hours."

Marsee just rolled her eyes at his teasing. He wasn't wrong, though.

Ammond chuckled at the exchange. "Well, I think I'm going to pack up before I get roped into picking fruit too. My partner is the gardener. I keep people alive, plants, not so much. Marsee, when you and Little Flower are done eating, come find me so I can take a look at that ear."

Marsee nodded, and Ammond groaned his way up off the cushion he was sitting on. She noticed her mother frown, and wondered what she was worried about, but didn't ask.

Her parents left a few minutes later to prepare for their day as well. When Little Flower was done eating, Marsee picked up the remains of the breakfast and carried it all into the kitchen, with Little Flower following obediently behind.

Once the breakfast dishes were cleaned and put away, Marsee led Little Flower to Ammond's room, but found the guest room empty. She checked her mother's office next and found both of them there. Her mother motioned them in at her knock, and Marsee picked up Little Flower and held her while Ammond examined her ear.

"The wound from the glass shard has healed up quite nicely, but I'm not seeing much, if any, change to the rest of the ear, which is as I expected," Ammond said when he was done. "Frankly, that was always a long shot. The nanos don't really work that way. They repair damage to what's there, but don't typically regrow what isn't. At least not for our species. I had no idea what they would do with hers."

"Typically?" Marsee asked. "Is there a time it does?"

"Rowena's seen a few instances where it has with certain types of cells, but those are the kind of cells that are designed to regrow or regenerate. The behavior hasn't been consistent enough to offer treatment for anything, but it's an area that she's still studying."

"Who's Rowena?"

"A good friend of mine," Ammond replied, to which her mother snorted. He glared back at her.

"I'm pretty sure that's the first time I've ever heard you call Rowena a friend," her mother replied. "The two of you have been growling at each other the entire time I've known you."

Ammond shook his head and growled. "I would think you would know by now that I growl at everyone, even those I happen to like."

"Are you implying that you like me?" her mother asked.

"Impudent Apprentice," Ammond snorted and turned back to Marsee. "And your mother wonders why I moved to the other side of the planet. Anyway, to answer your question, Rowena is the one who invented nanos, and, if I'm not mistaken, worked on adapting them for the biped's unique anatomy."

Her mother nodded.

"Now go on," Ammond ordered. "Your mother and I have work to do."

Marsee left after wishing them both a safe trip and thanking Healer Ammond again for the hearing aids. They trudged back up to her room so she could grab her hearing aids and put them on. She was curious if they would block out the sounds of the hydroponics units.

With a heavy sigh, she threw on her carry harness and clipped the case on for later, as well as her tablet. She shifted and tried to get the harness to settle right. It always made her fur bunch and her skin itch, and she'd always found it stiff and uncomfortable to wear. She frowned when she realized how childish she sounded to herself. She at least had the option to wear it. Little Flower did not. She stopped fiddling with the harness and motioned for Little Flower to follow.

After making their way back down, Marsee crossed through the courtyard on the way to the storage shed, marveling at how quiet it was in the yard. The ever-present buzzing was gone, letting the gentle music of the wind chimes through. Marsee smiled. She'd never really been able to enjoy them before.

Opening the old shed door, which took several hard yanks and a well-practiced kick to open, she looked around, trying to decide what she wanted to use to harvest the fruit. Normally, she used the smaller hand cart just to avoid listening to the whine of the motor in the large powered flatbed, but deciding to test out the hearing aids further, she hit the switch on the cart to power it on and heard nothing. She had to double-check that it was actually running since she couldn't hear the motor's normal whine.

Sweet! she thought, then proceeded to stack the long flat boxes that they used to harvest the star fruit. Once the crates were stacked, she picked up Little Flower and told the cart to follow.

Marsee walked around the compound to the star fruit beds on the other side of the garden and groaned. There were thousands upon thousands of the small berries ready to be picked.

It will take hours, she thought miserably.

With a weary sigh, she walked up to the first bed, picked a berry, and handed it to Little Flower, then took one for herself and popped it in her mouth.

At least it's a good batch, she thought, savoring the kick of the tiny berry. With another sigh, she sat Little Flower down on the edge of the raised garden and carefully started picking.

A few minutes later, she hissed as one of the sharp thorns pricked the back of her paw, and she growled as she struggled to take it out. The evil little things were so tiny it was hard to get ahold of them, but if she didn't, they'd lodge themselves deep into her skin and would be even more painful to pull out later.

Little Flower tugged on her arm.

She glanced over at the tiny cub. Not sure what the cub wanted, she lowered her paw and was surprised when Little Flower carefully pushed the fur aside and pulled out the small thorn, holding it up with a smile.

Those little paws of hers are useful! Marsee thought, then watched in surprise as Little Flower leaned over and started picking. She had no problem avoiding the sharp thorns, and instead of catching on the cub's garments, the thorns just slid along them.

Ideas flashed through her mind, and she absently made motions for Little Flower to stay.

Little Flower nodded, and Marsee bolted back up to her room at a run on all fours. Once there, she pulled out the extra fabric that Ellie had left them, cut off a section, quickly fashioned herself a pair of crude gloves, and raced back down, praying that Little Flower had actually stayed put like she'd told her to do.

If her parents found out Little Flower had been left unattended outside, she would be in *big* trouble, but she hadn't wanted to take the time to lug the cub all the way back up to her room. She could run so much faster on all fours.

As she rounded the corner and Little Flower came into view, she breathed a sigh of relief, then gasped in shock. In the few minutes she'd been gone, Little Flower had filled up the first box and had almost filled a second.

Little Flower looked up at her as she came into her line of vision and smiled.

Marsee held up her makeshift gloves and wiggled her paws at Little Flower, to show what she'd been doing, then reached deep into the briar patch, purposely aiming for a berry that she'd normally avoid, and grabbed it.

The gloves worked! Marsee popped the berry in her mouth and then did a little dance of joy. *Yes! No more thorns!*

When she was done celebrating, she flipped the trays around so an empty one was on top and joined Little Flower in picking. They finished gathering the berries in the first bed, then moved on to the second, and the third in record time. Little Flower's tiny paws were able to pick three times the number of berries that Marsee could do in the same time.

She had just finished putting her tray on top of the stack when she looked over at Little Flower and saw her wipe more of that strange liquid off her face. Marsee looked up at the sun, just barely visible through the shields, realizing it must be near noon.

She must be hot, but she didn't complain, so maybe she's not that bad. The new clothing must be working. Still, if that liquid is forming, I'd better make sure she cools down and has something to drink.

Helping Little Flower down off the raised beds, Marsee guided the cart to the large walk-in cooler to unload the full crates. A blast of cold air hit them as she opened the door and brought the cart inside.

Quickly unloading the fruit and placing the trays on empty shelves, she told the cart to return to its charging dock and slammed the heavy cooler door shut with them inside. She'd worry about shutting the shed door later.

I should really fix it anyway. She snorted at the thought. The whole shed needed to be torn down and rebuilt, as it now had a fairly significant lean to it.

Somewhat lost in thought about ideas on how she could improve the old shed, she led Little Flower through the cooler to the side door that led directly into the kitchen, pulling off her gloves in the process.

Once in the kitchen, she started the water running in the sink before pouring a large glass of juice for both of them. After they both had a long drink, she helped Little Flower up onto the counter, handed her the soap sponge, shut off the water, and went off in search of something for lunch, something other than star fruit.

She growled at her instinct to keep quiet, and thankfully, she didn't hear a single peep from it.

Grabbing a banta melon and some sweet reed, deciding she wanted something crunchy, she shut the door of the fridge with her shoulder and carried her food across the room to the counter.

Little Flower had stripped out of her clothing and was floating on top of the water in the sink, her hands tucked behind her head, eyes closed, and feet crossed.

How is she doing that? Marsee wondered, then flicked some water at her to get her attention.

The cub opened her eyes, scowled at her, and then deliberately closed them again.

Laughing and tail curled, Marsee set to work preparing their lunch. By the time she was done, Little Flower had hopped back up onto the counter and started scrubbing.

A quick rinse later, Marsee handed her a towel to dry off with and popped a piece of sweet reed in her mouth with a satisfying crunch as she waited for the cub to dry off and get dressed again, then watched as Little Flower ran her fingers through her long fur and pulled at the tangled mat with a frown.

Her own fur was short in comparison and didn't get tangled, but they did have brushes they used when they shed out their thick protective undercoat in the spring. She wasn't sure it would work with Little Flower's matted fur, though.

Marsee made motions to mimic what Little Flower was doing, then watched as the cub drew a few objects in her sketch pad. Marsee nodded her understanding, as the implements honestly weren't all that much different from what she used. She took a picture of the drawings and sent them to Ellie, asking her to bring a set that would better fit the cub's paws.

Once that was done, she had Little Flower spin around, and she began carefully picking the tangles out with her claws. Little Flower seemed to enjoy the attention because she let out a sigh and her entire body relaxed.

When she was done, there was a large clump of tangled fur that had been pulled out. One clump was so bad that she'd been forced to cut it out, although she tried hard not to take too much. She didn't know how Little Flower felt about her fur, but Marsee hated how she looked in the late spring, when her undercoat shed out all splotchy and uneven.

By the time she'd finished, Little Flower's fur was dry and now had a curlier look to it and was nearly twice the length, coming halfway down her back, even though she'd carefully cut some of the ends off to make it look a little less ragged.

Little Flower seemed just as surprised by the length. Only the very end had the teal color now, as most of that had come off with the dead fur that Marsee had removed.

I hope she's not too upset about that. I suppose I could try to dye it. I wonder why they have so much fur on their heads but not much anywhere else. What she does have doesn't make sense. Why would she have fur under her arms and between her legs but not anywhere else? There's certainly not enough there to provide any sort of protection.

It was completely different from her own species, which had less fur in those areas than anywhere else.

Scent collectors, perhaps? She does smell stronger there. She made a note to ask her mother about it, to see if she had any ideas.

Marsee, once again distracted by her thoughts, walked over and tossed the clump of fur into the recycler but turned back in time to see Little Flower pick up her shirt, sniff at it, and scowl.

The sleeves and front were stained with juice just like Marsee's gloves and smelled like the cub, which didn't bother Marsee. She personally liked the smell, but apparently it must have bothered the cub based on the face she'd made.

It's surprising that she doesn't like her own smell. Marsee thought. *Still, the garments are stained with juice. Might as well clean them.*

Marsee held up the towel and motioned for the cub to wrap herself in it.

Little Flower did as suggested and put the harness on over it before picking up the discarded items.

Marsee helped her down off the counter, picked up their lunch tray and her gloves, and motioned for the cub to follow her.

Once in the family room, she set the lunch down on the window seat, but stopped Little Flower from climbing up, and held out her paws to the cub for the other items.

Marsee placed the head and eye protection on a nearby table before carefully taking the prized items out of Little Flower's carry sacks and setting them down next to the other items.

She was surprised to find two small rocks in there as well.

Why did she pick these up? Marsee wondered, checking them out. They were pretty and unusually shaped, but they meant nothing to her. Marsee shrugged and set them down with the rest of her stuff and motioned for the cub to follow her again.

She led the cub back down the hall to the sanitation room where she tossed the stained and stinky items into the cleaning unit, and started it. Then, deciding she could use a cleaning as well, she stored her hearing aids, removed her harness, and tossed it on a hook before stepping into the sonic shower.

The little cub giggled as the shower caused Marsee's fur to poof out, before the finishing setting smoothed it back down.

That's such a cute sound, Marsee thought, and then frowned afterwards, as she put her harness back on. Deciding she'd rather hear Little Flower, she left the hearing aids in their case.

By the time she was back in her harness and her fur comfortably settled, the cleaning unit dinged to indicate the cleaning cycle was done. She reached in and pulled out the clean and stain-free items, then handed them to Little Flower, who quickly donned them in place of the towel.

Fully garbed again, they returned to the family room to eat and relax. She left her gloves to pick up later as she intended to make some minor adjustments to make them fit better.

As always, Little Flower climbed up onto the window seat to eat and draw, so Marsee decided to take the opportunity to contact Sina about the sign language course Ammond had mentioned, hoping Sina was still awake, as it was late in Sina's part of the world.

It took Marsee three tries to write something that didn't sound as awkward as she felt. She loathed reaching out to people she didn't know.

> Good evening. Healer Ammond Greyfoot told me you had a course on sign language. I was hoping you might be willing to teach me.

A reply arrived almost immediately.

> Of course! It's nice to meet you. My grandfather let me know you would be reaching out and filled me in on the situation. He said you've already built a dictionary of words?

Marsee's ears went back in surprise. She hadn't realized that Sina was Ammond's granddaughter, although she supposed she should have, since they had the same family name.

Yes. The cub is a very talented artist. She's drawn pictures that have allowed us to communicate basic ideas. It looks like they have a written language too.

That's perfect. It will give us something to start with. Here, let me send you a reference guide with the signs we've come up with. We're constantly adding to it, so don't worry if something isn't there.

A link popped up, and Marsee opened it to see an indexed site containing words and a video next to each that could be played. Marsee clicked on one and watched as Sina demonstrated the word. It seemed easy enough to remember. Explaining to Little Flower would be the hard part.

Would you like to start now?

If it's not too late, that would be wonderful!

A call from Sina arrived a moment later. Marsee answered it and placed it on the big screen.

Little Flower looked up from her drawing as the screen turned on.

"Hello, Marsee. Hello, Little Flower. I'm Sina," Sina said in a voice that was off and clipped somehow. As she did, she made motions with her hands.

Little Flower sat straight up, gasped, and then jumped down off her seat, scribbling furiously. By the time she'd walked over to Marsee, several new drawings had been added to the cub's dictionary.

"Sina - No - Hear. Sina - Talk - Hands?" the cub asked.

Marsee's ears flicked back in surprise.

Is the cub right? Is Sina deaf? she wondered. *That would certainly explain why Mama would have a mentor who specialized in something she didn't know much about. He must have switched to help his granddaughter. I'll have to ask Mama about it later.*

"She asked if you're deaf, and if you're talking with your hands," Marsee told Sina.

"Yes, I was born deaf and talk with my hands. I have also learned to read lips and to speak, although I cannot hear myself speak," Sina said, and signed at the same time.

"Sina - Little Flower - Talk - Hands?" Little Flower asked, which Marsee translated.

Sina flicked her whiskers forward and said, "Yes."

Little Flower looked to Marsee for confirmation, and then she whooped and did a little happy dance, much like Marsee had done earlier in the courtyard.

"I think she's happy!" Marsee laughed at her antics and then asked. "Little Flower - Happy - Talk - Hands?"

In response, Little Flower nodded her head up and down enthusi-astically.

"They nod their head for yes and shake it for no," Marsee told Sina.

"Excellent! Let's start with basic needs," Sina said. "This is the sign for 'food'."

Marsee pointed to the drawing of food, and they both watched and carefully copied the motion. Sina made a correction, and they tried again.

This time, Sina seemed happy with their attempt. "Much better. This means 'I'm hungry.'" Sina pointed to herself and made a slight modification to the word food.

Little Flower copied the motion and then tapped the pictures for clarification. Marsee nodded yes, surprised that the cub had already picked up the meaning without being informed.

"Now, this is how you ask, 'Are you hungry?'" Sina said, and made a slightly different motion.

Marsee tapped 'Little Flower—Food—Curious' and followed up with the signs Sina had used.

Little Flower nodded yes, reached over and grabbed a piece of fruit off of Marsee's plate and popped it in her mouth with a grin, then, still chewing, made the same motion back at Marsee.

Marsee shook her head, picked up a piece of fruit, and dropped it for confirmation.

They did the same for 'drink' and 'thirsty' and then went over signs for different foods and drinks, as well as how to ask to go to the waste room, but when it came time to teach emotions, they were all stumped. Little Flower didn't have ears, whiskers, claws, or a tail to use, and they were heavily used in those signs.

"She uses her eyes, mouth, shoulders, and hands for expressing moods from what I've seen," Marsee told Sina.

Eventually, they just showed Little Flower their sign, and had her come up with as close of an equivalent as she could. She used her paws to make the ear motions, but when she wiggled her butt to try and mimic a lashing tail, it was too much, and both Sina and Marsee burst out laughing.

"That does not look angry in the least," Sina said.

"No. No, it doesn't," Marsee agreed, trying hard to stop laughing and failing miserably.

"How do they normally show anger?" Sina asked, so Marsee demonstrated, crossing her arms and scowling, or her best approximation of Little Flower scowling.

This apparently also failed, because Little Flower started laughing as hard as they'd been a moment before, and Sina struggled hard to keep her composure.

"You look like a stinger flew up your nose!" Sina said, and Marsee couldn't help but laugh too. "What if we combine the two, like this?"

Sina used her hands to demonstrate the ear position and made Little Flower's scowling expression.

"Can we do that?" Marsee asked.

"I don't see why not? We made everything else up, and we're adding words all the time. Still, it will be something that we'll have to adjust for. She'll have to know our signs, and we'll have to know hers. Let's record a video of her making the sign, and we can add it to the reference document. Hold on, let me give you access to edit."

Sina fiddled with her tablet, and a notification of access appeared on Marsee's screen a moment later.

"You said they have a written language, too?" Sina asked.

"I think so. She's added little symbols under each of the drawings." Marsee held it up so Sina could see.

"That certainly looks like a written language to me. I'm going to add several columns: one for video for signs that differ, and another two for her drawings and their written language. That way we'll have a reference for both species as we get further along."

"Could we use this for other species, too?" Marsee asked. "The Ice Giants and Water Sprites don't have tails either, and none of the other species have whiskers, but they could do the rest. Could this be a universal language for all of us? Then we wouldn't have to learn five languages to communicate, only one."

"You don't know how long I've wanted someone else to come to that same conclusion," Sina replied. "I've been trying for years to get my sign program in the schools, or even looked at by the Council. Councilor Parner said he didn't think there was much point when only a few people needed it."

"Of course he did," Marsee muttered. "He's the most short-sighted, stubborn, and fur-brained councilor there is."

Sina chuckled. "That he is. I've tried multiple times telling him that this language will only really work if everyone learns it, not just the deaf."

"Well, if the Senior Guild Master is right, you might have your chance now," Marsee said. "She says everything I do, and now I'm guessing, you do, for Little Flower and her species will become part of the history books. I'll talk to Papa about it. He's on the Council."

"In that case, I'm adding columns for the other species as well," Sina said.

"I'll help fill in the written language. I'm fairly fluent in all but Water Sprite, but I know enough to cover the basics, and if not, I need to learn it anyway," Marsee offered.

"That would be a wonderful help! Thank you!" Sina said with a grin.

Marsee recorded Little Flower demonstrating 'angry' and uploaded it, then scanned both the image for angry and the little word and uploaded those as well.

One down, eight million three hundred and sixty-four thousand to go, she thought, briefly wondering just how many words there were in a language.

They ran through a few more of the other emotions: happy, sad, scared, confused, and curious, before Sina called an end to the session. "Practice those, and we can meet again tomorrow if you want. Any more and you'll start to forget."

Before Marsee could answer, though, Little Flower flipped the book over and pointed to Marsee, then herself, then her parents.

"I think she wants to know how to sign our names," Marsee told Sina.

"Names are special," Sina replied. "There is a sign for each letter, which you can use to spell out your name, but that's slow. So, we have a custom of giving others a special sign, which can be based on your written name, or a characteristic about yourself that the other person likes. You can choose to use it or not. I can show you the name signs I use for myself, and the ones I used for you at the beginning of the call, if you like?"

Marsee nodded her head, using the cub's sign for yes, which made Sina smile.

"My name is…" Sina signed, then paused slightly, "Sina."

Marsee pointed to Sina's picture, and they both repeated the name sign.

"Marsee, your sign is…" Sina demonstrated another motion, then explained. "It's a combination of the words 'harm' and 'see'. We don't have a sign for 'mar' yet. 'damage' is probably a closer synonym, but I liked the way the two signs flowed together better."

Marsee repeated the sign, then the whole phrase. "My name is Marsee."

Little Flower repeated her name sign, then signed, "Curious Marsee."

Marsee thought for a second. She sighed the word mar, then picked up a piece of fruit and squeezed it, leaving a damaged spot. She then pointed to her eyes before staring closely at the damaged spot. After which, she signed the word "See."

Little Flower nodded her understanding and pointed to the picture of herself.

"She wants to know her name sign," Marsee told Sina.

They both watched closely.

"Curious Little Flower," the cub signed.

To answer, Marsee drew a flower and signed the second half of her name. Then, she drew a really big flower next to the first one, pointed to the little one, and signed 'little' again.

What's the sign for big?" Marsee asked Sina and then pointed to the big flower, signing 'big' and back to the little one, signing 'little' again, before putting the two words together. "Little Flower."

The cub frowned for a moment, as if considering the meaning, then looked up at her. "My name is Little Flower," the cub signed, and smiled.

40

JESSICA: THORN

Well, I suppose it could be far worse, like 'hairless rat', or 'stinky monkey butt', Jessica thought when the meaning of the name the cats had given her, was first revealed.

Then she remembered the beautiful glowing flower that smelled like chocolate that the golden cat had given her that first night, and decided she kind of liked the name.

This is so much easier than pointing to drawings all the time, she thought, ecstatic that someone had finally thought to teach her their sign language.

Maybe they just realized you were deaf, she chided herself.

Still, it was a massive improvement, and they were thankfully adapting it to her...physical limitations. She'd felt ridiculous trying to pretend to lash a non-existent tail, and based on their laughter, she'd looked it, too.

Sina signed off at that point, dragging Jessica's attention away from her thoughts.

Marsee looked at her, head tilted. "Curious. Little Flower name?" Marsee touched her mouth, and Jessica realized that they wanted to know what her spoken name was.

"Jess," she replied, deciding to keep it simple.

"Curious," Marsee replied.

Jessica drew a quick picture of a falcon on an outstretched arm and the jesses used to keep the falcon from flying off, then pointed to the straps. There were other religious meanings for Jessica, but she had no idea how to explain them, and trapped and forced to wear a leash, she no longer felt like her birth name really fit her anymore. It was almost as if Jessica O'Neil had died in the attack and only Jess had crawled out of the rubble.

Marsee frowned at the drawing, clearly not liking the meaning any more than she did.

Jessica shrugged. It didn't really matter. She would never hear her name again anyway, not with her hearing loss. It was unlikely that she'd ever find her way home or her family, and she had to find a way to survive and make a life for herself here. For better or worse, she was Little Flower now, whatever that meant.

"My name is Little Flower," she signed, and in an effort to diffuse the tension, she pointed to her empty glass. "Little Flower thirsty," she said, and pretended to wilt, causing Marsee to laugh.

Marsee picked up the remains of their lunch and motioned for her to follow to the kitchen. After Marsee set everything but her empty glass in the sink to clean, they walked over to the fridge to get some more juice, but frowned and held up the nearly empty pitcher.

They put what little remained in Jessica's glass and handed it back before ducking into the massive walk-in cooler where they'd left the berries. She drank, enjoying the cold air that blasted her, and watched as Marsee grabbed one of the large trays and brought it back into the kitchen.

Picking the berries had been surprisingly fun. It had reminded her of picking blackberries on her grandfather's farm, only these were bigger, about the size of a medium-sized strawberry, bright blue, and shaped like five-pointed stars.

Thankfully, she'd been able to avoid most of the thorns and only had a few small scratches on her hands. The fabric of her clothing seemed to protect the rest of her, although they seemed to like finding their way into Marsee's fur.

I guess being big and covered in fur has its disadvantages, too, she thought, and then a wicked thought crossed her mind. *I hope they realize this Little Flower has thorns, too.*

She'd been worried at first as they made their way out to the garden, wondering if she'd been captured just to work on their farm, but when Marsee had started working without any indication she was expected to help, she'd relaxed.

She'd been shocked when Marsee had left her alone, and had briefly considered running away, but she'd agreed to 'stay' and figured if they learned they could trust her not to run off, then they'd stop making her wear the harness and leash all the time.

Realistically, though, there just wasn't anywhere for her to run off to. The trip around the compound had proven that. They were miles from the nearest home, and she was surrounded by desert. She'd be dead in a day if she left the safety of the compound, and they seemed to want to take care of her and make her happy.

The new clothing and art supplies couldn't have been cheap either. She knew quality when she saw it. She'd have been perfectly happy with the clothing the black cat had brought with them. It had fit better than anything she'd ever been given from her cousins, but they weren't letting her have it until it fit perfectly. She'd never been to a tailor before, and wondered if that was a normal experience for the rich and famous.

The art supplies, though, had made her positively drool, and were finer than anything she'd ever used before. The colors were so vibrant and intense, and the variety of art supplies staggered her. She'd been in art stores that had been far less equipped, and it had all been for her. Marsee had her own supplies, but everything her fairy godmother had brought had been sized to fit her hands.

She had no idea why they were treating her so nicely, but she wasn't going to complain. She did wonder what it said about her that she could be bought so easily by a few pieces of nice clothing and some colored pencils, even if they were *really* nice clothes and colored pencils.

Again, there was no expectation that she needed to help, so Jessica just watched.

Marsee dumped the berries into something that looked like a kitchen strainer, only about three times bigger than what she was used to, and rinsed them in the sink.

I was right, it is a strainer. Are such devices constant throughout the universe? she wondered, and her thoughts drifted to consider what impact her own species' evolution had on technology.

The tech in the garden was much the same, yet they hadn't invented clothing, since they had no real need for it, outside of the gloves and harness they used in place of pockets. They'd both developed a written language and books, which made sense if you needed to communicate with people across distances and store knowledge, and much of their tech was similar if more advanced, yet their ability to travel between worlds was vastly different, and she wondered what need had caused that advancement.

That thought reminded her of the ship that had been parked outside the castle that she'd seen on their walk the day before. It had been massive compared to the tiny shuttle she'd seen that first night. It had gleamed in the sunlight, yet had felt so out of place, parked as it was next to a stone castle in the middle of a desert.

From what Marsee had tried to explain, it seemed like the ship belonged to her fairy godmother and that it was capable of traveling between the worlds. She'd wanted to explore the ship in the worst way, but that had been one thing they hadn't let her explore, although they'd had a fairly lengthy conversation about it. Eventually, the gold cat had shaken her head, and they'd moved on.

Jessica shrugged at her thoughts, figuring that she'd eventually learn their history and the reason why she hadn't been allowed on the ship once she could sign better.

She refocused her attention back on what Marsee was doing as Marsee rolled a contraption nearly as tall as Jessica out from under the counter and placed one of the large juice containers under what looked like a spigot. As soon as they did that, Jessica realized that it must be some kind of juicer.

Sure enough, moments later, Marsee started dumping the berries into the wide opening at the top, and after pushing a button, juice started dripping, and then gushing out. They repeated the process with four more juice containers until the berries in the strainer were all juiced. When Marsee was done, they pulled out a drawer full of the leftover fruit pulp, dumped that in the compost, rinsed the tray out, placed it back in the machine, and ran water through until it came out clean out of the spigot. Juicer cleaned, they put it away, and then placed the newly squeezed juice into the fridge to cool for later.

Well, at least all my hard work is going to good use, she thought. *That juice is amazing!*

That done, Marsee asked her if she wanted to go for a walk or play a game, using her book, but also looked up the signs. She chose to play a game, deciding she'd had enough of the hot sun for the day, so they returned to the living room and spent the afternoon playing one game after another, laughing and signing insults at each other. Granted, the insults weren't very inventive, with what few words they knew, but that somehow made them even funnier.

"Marsee is a sad fruit," Little Flower said, trying to distract Marsee as they made their next move.

"Yeah, well, Little Flower is an angry hole of muck," Marsee replied, with a mock snarl.

When words failed them, Jessica drew, and Marsee looked up the sign, or Marsee looked up the sign and used pantomime and her own drawings to explain.

Marsee was contemplating their next move on an intricate Jenga-like game when Goldy showed up and stood in the doorway watching them play. An expression flickered on Goldy's face that she couldn't quite place: a mix of exhaustion, sadness, and longing, and maybe something else, grief?

Before Jessica could figure it out, their expression changed to one of pure mischievousness, and they announced their presence loudly, startling Marsee and causing the wobbling structure to collapse.

"You lose!" Jessica signed.

In response, Marsee fell over backwards onto her cushion with such an exaggerated air of defeat that Jessica started laughing.

This caused Marsee's tail to curl, and then they started laughing, which caused Goldy to start laughing as well. Marsee looked back at Goldy. They spoke briefly, and Marsee sighed.

"Curious," she signed and nodded her head in the direction of the door, wanting to know what was being said.

"Little sleep," Marsee signed in response.

"Not tired," Jessica replied, not wanting to take a nap. She was having too much fun.

Marsee just pointed in the direction of Goldy's retreating back, shrugged, and rolled her eyes, which caused both of them to start snickering again. They ignored orders and played one more game, which Marsee won, putting her back in the lead.

She tried to convince Marsee to play another game, but Marsee shook her head, grinned wickedly, and picked everything up. Laughing, Jessica clipped on the leash and followed Marsee back out.

When they made it back to Marsee's tower bedroom, she asked Marsee if she could sleep in the swinging bed with her, curious to see what it felt like. Marsee agreed and helped her up onto the bed, then leapt in after, causing the bed to swing wildly. Jessica screeched with laughter.

Neither of them was in the least bit tired. So, once the bed had settled into a gentle sway, Marsee pulled out her tablet and brought up the language guide, then started scanning in her drawings and uploading them.

As they did, Marsee carefully wrote their own words underneath Jessica's drawings, so that anyone using the physical copy would know what they meant as well.

Jessica examined the odd script, determined to ask Marsee about it later. She needed to learn to read and write as well as sign.

One thing at a time, she thought.

As they worked through the sketchbook, they looked up the signs they didn't know and practiced those as well. By the time they'd worked through the book, they had everything but the names for the others figured out. They could communicate as well now by sign as they could using the book, if not better, since it was so much faster to sign, and there were quite a few words they'd added that they didn't have drawings for yet.

They floundered on the names, though. Marsee looked up how to spell the names, but that proved tedious and challenging to remember. It turned out they had fifty-three letters in their alphabet, and they were both struggling to remember all the signs.

Marsee eventually reached out to Sina to see if they already had a name sign for Healer Ammond. It turned out that they did, and it was a combination of the signs for 'healer' and 'ear'. So, they decided that Doc would be a combination of the words 'healer', 'morning', and 'star', the words that apparently made up her last name. The sign for healer was also a combination of signs that literally meant 'person who heals'.

For her fairy godmother, Marsee looked up several signs and spent the better part of an hour trying to explain what they meant. One of the words meant the place where the clothing had been made. That had been fairly straightforward, but the others seemed to involve some sort of complex hierarchy, where Marsee was only at the second level, and her fairy godmother was all the way at the top. The way Marsee was trying to describe it, it seemed like more than just the boss of a department store.

"Guild big?" she asked.

"Yes. Guild big big big," Marsee signed back, then thought for a moment and opened up her tablet to show her a picture of a planet from space, then looked up the sign for 'world' or 'planet'.

"Senior Guild Master five world," Marsee signed.

Holy hand grenades, Batman! Her fairy godmother was the CEO of the intergalactic version of Amazon. No wonder they could afford their own spaceship, and why Marsee was so nervous around them. The rest seemed super comfortable around this Senior Guild Master, though. Does that mean they're just as powerful, or is there some other connection? Friends, family? Is that why they're out in the middle of nowhere in a giant castle by themselves, for privacy? Because they're loaded, or royalty? So why are they picking their own food? I guess gardening could be a hobby.

Jessica's mind was spinning with the implications, so she just gulped and nodded. That just left the other two.

"Myra is my mother. Jeran is my father," Marsee signed after several minutes of trying to explain their names and failing.

Jessica nodded. She could work with and remember that, and so the two became Marsee's Mother and Marsee's Father.

"Is your mother a doctor?" she asked for confirmation. What she signed was more 'Curious - Marsee's Mother - Person who Heals', but Marsee seemed to understand.

Marsee nodded. "Senior Healer Agency."

Jessica blinked in shock. *Are they really saying that her mother was in charge of wherever I was held for so long, or just in charge of the doctors? Curse my limited vocabulary.* "Senior Agency or Senior Healer?" she asked, hoping her meaning came across.

"Senior Agency," Marsee signed and pointed to the org chart they'd used to describe the guild her fairy godmother ran. "Healer Guild."

They next pointed to one of the circled sections representing one part of the Guild. Jessica thought that meant a department or section within the Guild. "Agency."

Marsee then pointed to what had been a guild master for an individual department, "Mother."

Under her mother, they pointed and said, "Healer Morningstar," and then to the row under that, "No healer, No healer, No healer."

Jessica nodded. Marsee's mother was in charge of both healers and non-healers at the Agency, including Healer Morningstar. *If they're both doctors, does that mean the Agency is a hospital? If so, why was I held so long after my injuries were healed?*

She didn't really want to think about what had happened to her at the Agency, and she was struggling to keep the memories from overwhelming her. The mental door she had locked them behind was starting to bend and crack, and tiny thorned vines were starting to work their way through the cracks and around the edges, so she changed the subject.

"Ammond?" she asked.

Marsee pursed their lips, trying to figure out how to explain, and then looked up a new sign. "Ammond mentor Mother."

After some explanation, Jessica realized it meant teacher, just like she'd guessed, although it seemed like more than that, almost family, as while they had many teachers, they usually only had one mentor, or at least that's what she thought Marsee had indicated.

"Is your father a healer?" she asked next.

"No." Marsee looked up the word but then frowned. "No sign."

This was how they indicated they didn't know how to explain, but in this case, it appeared like there wasn't actually a sign for it yet, either.

"Father mouth yes no big choose my world," Marsee said, and then made up a sign for the missing word.

It took her a moment to figure out what Marsee was saying.

Her father makes the big decisions for her world. So, is he a king, elected official, or judge? she wondered.

Jessica leaned towards 'king', since Marsee lived in her own tower in what clearly looked like a stone castle. She pointed to the top of the hierarchy and signed. "Father Senior Marsee's world?"

Marsee started laughing, and her tail spiraled tightly. "No Tabor Senior Marsee's World."

Marsee used the same drawing, pointed to the top, and spelled out a word: "Tabor." She then opened her tablet and brought up a picture of Tabor. This cat had a spotted coat that made them look much like a snow leopard, but the fierceness of the expression on the cat's face made Jessica frown.

This was someone not to be trifled with, she thought. *Especially if Marsee's father was afraid of them or the consequences of disobeying.*

After showing her the picture, Marsee set the tablet aside and pointed to the department or division part of the diagram and signed, "Father."

"Tabor Marsee's father's father?" Jessica asked, trying to find out if this meant her father was a prince or something.

Marsee shook her head, picked up her tablet again, and brought up a map this time. She pointed to one section near the equator of one of their land masses. Unlike Earth, this planet was apparently mostly land with a few smaller oceans.

"Father," Marsee signed and tapped again, zooming the map in until she could see the outline of the compound. Then, she shifted over a short distance and pointed to a significantly larger collection of buildings. "Agency."

Jessica frowned, realizing that the Agency was fairly close by, and confirmed it was a hospital of some sort, not a spaceship as she'd been beginning to think.

If we were that close, why wasn't I brought here sooner? she wondered.

The closet door in her mind bulged again, the vines growing and starting to make their way up the side. She mentally kicked hard at them until they backed off some.

Marsee, perhaps sensing her mood, quickly zoomed back out to show the world map again. She tapped the neighboring country and spelled out another name, "Marcus," then added "Marcus mentor Father." Finally, she tapped a third country. "Tabor."

Okay, Jessica thought, still fighting hard to control the emotions triggered by the sight of the Agency. *They have leaders for various countries or territories, and Marsee's father is the leader of this one, which also contains the Agency.*

Since Marsee indicated that her father and Tabor were not related, she wondered if the position was elected. "You choose Father?" she asked.

Marsee smiled and nodded. "Father, Marcus, Tabor…" They tapped several of the other clearly demarcated areas. "Choose Tabor." Marsee put her paws over the whole map. "Tabor Senior World." Then they made a modification of the word they'd used to describe her father to represent the organization they belonged to, and pointed to the org chart again.

So, he's a part of their United Nations or something similar, that they elect, and then that congress elects a senior or president. Still, this is one heck of a powerful family you landed in, Jessica told herself.

The territory Marsee's father ruled had to be at least as big as

Texas, if this planet was around the same size as her own. Interestingly, they all appeared to be about the same size, with some minor variation to account for natural geographical boundaries.

So, if this is some form of democracy, did they collectively decide to invade her world and take her captive?

Her mental door bulged hard, with the thorny vines growing again. This time, cracking the wood. She mentally slammed her body against the door, leaned against it, and asked a different question.

"I'm female. You?" She expected Marsee to pick one or the other, since she seemed to understand male and female and used them to represent her mother and father.

Instead, Marsee signed, "I female no female."

"I'm confused," Jessica signed back.

In response, Marsee said, "Mother is female. Ellie is female. Father is male. Ammond is male. Marsee is female no female. Sina is female no female."

"I'm confused. Female no female?" Jessica signed.

Marsee thought for a while and drew two stick figures, complete with pointed ears and a tail, a big one and a small one. "Cub," she signed, pointing to the smaller one, and "No Cub. Big," pointing to the bigger one, and then looked up a word and signed that.

Does she mean 'adult'? Jessica wondered. "Marsee Mother, father, adult?" she asked.

Marsee nodded. "Marsee no cub. No adult. Marsee little adult," she signed and drew a middle-sized stick figure between the two, then looked up and made a different sign.

I'm guessing that sign means she's a teenager, but what does that have to do with whether she's male or female? Jessica wondered. *Is she just saying she hasn't hit puberty yet?*

At Jessica's confused expression, Marsee continued. "Marsee cub female. Teenager female. Adult choose male female."

Jessica was completely baffled by this.

Is she trying to say she's female now but could choose to be male or female when she's an adult? Is she talking about gender reassignment, or is this a normal part of their biology? she wondered, but of course, she had no way to ask that.

"Marsee choose female?" she asked instead.

Marsee shrugged. "I no male. I choose female. I no choose cub. I scared."

So, you feel like a female, but you don't want cubs. That's fair. But why is this a hard choice? Can you not be female and not have babies? That's some sexist bullcrap if that's the case.

"Choose female. No choose cub," she signed.

Marsee shook her head and drew another stick figure, bigger than the others. "Cub - Teenager - Male - Female," she signed, pointing to each, confirming Jessica's suspicions that the males were smaller than the females.

"Male little, female big?" Jessica asked for confirmation.

Marsee nodded. "I choose female, I big. I five cub. I choose male, I little. I no cub." Jessica nodded her understanding, so Marsee continued. "I choose female. I scared five cub. I no mother."

Oh! she realized. *She wants cubs but is afraid of having cubs. How do you even take care of that many children?"* Jessica wondered.

"Marsee's mother five cub?" she asked, wondering if Marsee had any siblings, not sure if she got the meaning across.

Marsee nodded and drew two cats, then a cluster of five little ones underneath, which she circled, and then a single little one, which she circled as well. Then she drew lines from the big ones down to each circle. "Mother. Father. Five cub. Marsee," she said, as she pointed out each.

So, your mom had a litter of five and then had you in a separate litter? It would certainly make sense why females would be bigger. I wonder if there are other societal differences between the two sexes, and where's the rest of the family?

"Curious," she signed. Pointing to the litter of five.

In answer, Marsee flipped open her tablet and scrolled through a bunch of pictures until she stopped at one showing a family portrait. It was the same one that was in her mother's office. She pointed out her siblings, who were all clearly older than she was by what had to be quite a few years, since Marsee looked tiny while the others looked fully grown. Based on sizes, it looked like two sisters and three brothers. Marsee looked up the signs for 'sibling', 'litter-mate', 'sister', and 'brother', explaining each.

"Little Flower sibling?" Marsee asked.

She shook her head. "No. Mother, father, me." She closed her eyes and took a deep breath, trying to keep from crying.

When she opened her eyes, Marsee looked at her with understanding and deep sorrow, which didn't help her contain her emotions at all.

Her mental door bulged hard again. The vines, now thick and sharp with massive thorns, wrapped around her painfully, digging in with her grief.

Three more deep breaths later, she'd almost succeeded in slamming the door shut and detangling herself from the vines, when Marsee asked, "Little Flower choose cub?"

The door burst open, and all the rage, hate, and fear she'd been trying to keep locked up exploded and trampled over her with pent-up fury, shredding all control to pieces and leaving her feeling bloody, raw, and beaten.

"NO! Marsee Mother choose. Healer Morningstar choose. Council choose. Marsee Mother hurt me. Healer Morningstar hurt me. Council hurt me. MALE HURT ME!" Jessica signed, with barely controlled fury, trying hard to make her point with the limited vocabulary she had available, and her arms shaking with emotion.

Marsee pulled back, looking horror-struck as she pieced together Jessica's meaning and shook her head hard. "Council no hurt you. Mother no hurt you. You hurt. Mother, Healer Morningstar heal you," Marsee tried to explain.

"No," Jessica signed again. "No heal. Hurt!"

"Curious hurt," Marsee signed, clearly trying to understand.

Jessica took a deep breath. It was obvious from Marsee's confusion that she didn't know what had happened, so she tried to explain. "Little Flower sign help Agency. Healer Morningstar no help. Marsee's Mother no help. Male hurt me. Why Council choose hurt me, mother, father, world? Why Agency? Why choose male? Why choose Little Flower cub? Why?"

When Marsee just sat there without answering, Jessica growled in frustration, wondering if Marsee didn't want to answer, didn't understand, or if she simply didn't know what had happened to her.

She jumped down from the bed, causing it to swing wildly, and stormed over to the bookcase closest to her bed. She pulled out the sketchbook she'd hidden there and hugged it close to herself for several long moments, not really sure if she was ready to share what was contained within.

Taking a deep, shuddering breath, she marched back over to the bed and threw the book at Marsee, hitting her square in the face with it.

"WHY?" she screamed and signed at the same time.

"Little Flower, no...I..."

She didn't wait to see what Marsee had to say. Instead, she spun around and ran back to her bed, dove in, and buried her head under the blanket as she curled around Fuzzy.

She wanted to run, but there was nowhere she could run to, and nowhere else in this gilded castle prison she could hide. She was so consumed with hate and fury that she just shook, consumed with pain and grief, completely unable to cry.

It was all she could do to contain her rage and keep from finding something sharper to attack Marsee with because she wanted to kill each and every last one of them for what they'd done to her and her planet.

41

MARSEE: THE HORRIBLE TRUTH

arsee sat stunned as she watched the cub climb into her nest and bury herself under her blanket.. The sketch book hadn't really hurt her, but it was the level of fury and hate, and the accusations that had Marsee at a loss for words. She'd seen the cub angry, upset, and cry before, but this was a whole new level, and it had come out of nowhere.

Her accusations didn't make any sense either.

Mama would never have done anything to hurt Little Flower, and neither would Brice.

Or had they?

She'd seen the way Little Flower had looked at Brice on the monitor that first day, and the way Little Flower had looked at her just now was as if Marsee was the most vile and disgusting thing she'd ever seen.

Is this just anger at being stuck in quarantine for so long, and for being beaten by that male, or did something else happen? Did Brice hurt her?

Marsee had just asked a logical follow-up question to the conversation they'd been having, and she felt horrible not having the words to explain what had happened to her parents or her planet. Although as angry and upset as Little Flower was right now, she doubted the cub would even wait for her to try to explain.

After a moment or two, she rubbed at her sore nose, opened the sketch book, and started flipping through the pages, trying to figure out what Little Flower wanted her to see. At first, they were normal, of people and strange creatures, but after a dozen or so pages, it changed, and she grew increasingly horrified with each page.

There were scenes of the death and destruction the cub had seen and endured after the asteroid had hit. One page even had water stains that Marsee guessed were from tears, and she wondered who the person was who had been so badly injured.

One page was nothing more than a black amorphous shape vaguely reminiscent of the cub's face. She had never seen a more stunning representation of the grief and rage the cub felt.

Later, though, the book changed to scenes of her time at the Agency. From the drawings, it was clear that Little Flower thought she was a prisoner. There were several drawings of her fight, but they left her confused, as one series of scenes showed her giving birth and her cub being taken away.

Is this what she thinks we're going to do with her? Marsee wondered. *Why would she think that?*

After looking through the entire sketch book and still no closer to understanding, she tried figuring out what had set Little Flower off.

Why did asking her if she wanted cubs cause her such rage, and what does she mean by 'Marsee Mother choose'? What did Mama choose, and what does this have to do with cubs?

Flipping back through the drawings, she sat and stared at them for a long time, then opened her tablet and pulled up the fight, which centered heavily in Little Flower's drawings, and was also the only one that had a drawing of a cub in it, as a horrible idea crossed her mind.

"No. It can't be. They wouldn't. Would they?"

This time, rather than starting where Healer Morningstar had marked the video, she scrolled back in time to watch the entire visit. She watched it three times before she was sure, then jumped down off her bed to find her parents. This was far more than she knew how to handle on her own. This might even require the Council's involvement, if what she was starting to believe had happened was true.

Marsee took one last look at the shaking lump buried under the blanket before she left the room. Her heart broke for the poor cub and everything she'd endured. She didn't want to believe it, but she knew in the very depths of her soul that if Little Flower was this upset, it must be true.

Oh, Little Flower, she thought. *I'm so sorry.*

ABOUT THE PAWTHOR

Laura Napoli was born and raised in northern Vermont and continues to make the area her home. When not spending her time on the warm clicky box (computer) working on the next book in the series, she is the caregiver to her heating cats who provide her with heat, massage, acu-paw-ture, and purr-therapy in exchange for pets and catnip treaties.

For more information, visit https://heatingcats.com

PAW-BLICATIONS:

- The Tails of Little Flower

NEXT IN THE SERIES:

- The Pride of Little Flower
- The Whiskers of Hope
- The Paws of Hope